Millennial Hospitality II

The World We Knew

By

Charles James Hall

This book is a work of fiction. Places, events, and situations in this story are purely fictional. Any resemblance to actual persons, living or dead, is coincidental.

ISBN: 1-4033-9203-X (e-book)
ISBN: 1-4033-9204-8 (Paperback)
ISBN: 1-4107-0508-0 (Dustjacket)

Library of Congress Control Number: 2002096332

This book is printed on acid free paper.

Printed in the United States of America
Bloomington, IN

1stBooks - rev. 12/26/02

This book is dedicated to the greater honor and glory of
God
Who created us all, aliens included.

Acknowledgements

Millennial Hospitality II is in print only because of my wife's support and encouragement. She is also responsible for the books title and the design for the cover. She was also my chief editor. I am also grateful to the young men whom it was my privilege to serve with during the Vietnam War years.

CONTENTS

The World We Knew

... For nightmares come with many cares ...
... Ecclesiastes 5:2

It was a hot summer night in the mid 1960's. I was 20, and I was practicing the game of pool at the Mojave Wells airman's club. I was alone at the club's only decent table. Suddenly the front door to the club opened and in walked airman Bridges with three of his close friends. They swept into the club, approached my table and cornered me. "Airman Baker," the tall heavyset airman named Oscar said sternly, "We need the table to help Bridges practice for the coming international pool tournament up in Las Vegas. He came in seventh best in the world last year. Now he's even better. We believe he can take it all."

Smiling, I said, "Why yes. Of course, you know the club rules. First Bridges has to play me a game of pool and win. Then you guys can have the table for the rest of the evening."

"Come on Baker," responded Oscar angrily, "Don't go getting cute with us. You know Bridges is a way better pool player than you could ever dream of becoming. If he has to challenge you to a game to get the table, he'll get to go first and you'll never even get a chance to shoot."

"Let's see if that's true," I grinned. Then, I took a $10 dollar bill from my wallet and placed it on the bar in front of the bartender. "Why don't we all put up $10 dollars for the bartender to hold? One game, Bridges starts, winner take all."

"Bridges is going to win this game so fast that you are never going to get a turn," laughed Oscar as he, Bridges, and the other two friends all anteed up $10 dollars each.

We set up the pool table and racked the balls for 8 ball, western rules. Bridges was naturally very quiet and still hadn't said anything. I understood his reasoning. The game of pool is a straightforward showdown in self-confidence. He believed that if he never said anything when he was playing pool, the competing player couldn't shake his self-confidence.

I understood Bridges. He was shorter and thinner than the average man. In fact, if he had been one quarter of an inch shorter, he wouldn't have been able to enlist in the US Air Force. He spent the night before he enlisted eating bananas and milk in order to gain an extra two pounds of weight. Otherwise he would have weighed too little to pass the Air Force physical. He had just returned from a two week leave that he spent in Chicago, his hometown.

After setting up the balls, he made the opening shot, knocking one of the solid balls into a pocket. Then he began running the table, knocking a ball into a pocket with every shot. As Bridges was knocking his fifth ball into a corner pocket, Oscar was laughing sarcastically, "You see, Airman Charlie Baker! I told you so! Bridges never misses. We're going to take your money and you'll never once get to touch a cue stick."

Bridges was standing holding his cue stick, studying the table intensely. He had two easy shots to make and then one easy shot on the eight ball to win. I decided that it was time to make my move. He was standing near me with his hands resting on the top of the vertical cue stick as the bottom of the cue stick rested on the floor. His elbows were straight out, leaving his thin frame exposed. Without warning, I reached my right hand over to him and gently touched the bony rib on his left side, just below his heart. As I did so, I said in a brotherly manner, "You look thin, Bridges. Have you been losing weight? You did get enough to eat back in Chicago, didn't you?"

Poor Bridges. He reacted as if I'd just hit him with a steel pipe. The rest of the game all he could think of was covering his ribs with his elbows as he was trying desperately to make even one more pool shot. I had all the time I needed to knock all of my striped balls into the pockets, sink the eight ball and collect the $50 dollars in the kitty. The fact that I needed three separate turns and 15 minutes to do so was not the slightest problem at all. Even though Bridges was a world-class player, it was the last pool game he was ever willing to play me.

The next game the heavyset Oscar beat me in record time. Of course, I was only willing to bet 25 cents when I was playing him. Oscar wasn't as tall, big boned, and heavyset as I was, but he did have too much muscle covering his ribs to fall victim to the same trick. I was bent over laughing as I was stuffing the $50 dollars in my wallet and handing him his quarter. After sinking the eight ball, Oscar proudly stood screaming at me, "Go ahead! Touch MY ribs! Nobody cares if I lose weight!"

As I was relinquishing the table to Bridges and his friends, Bridges shook my hand and said, "Thanks, Charlie. I never realized that I had that weakness. I better work on that before the tournament. You sure can observe details." We all parted the best of friends.

A few days later during Monday breakfast, I was sitting alone at a table in the chow hall when Oscar politely approached my table. He seemed shaken and nervous. "Is it alright if I join you, Charlie," he asked?

"Why sure, Oscar," I replied. "How are things with you these days?"

"Well, I'm not feeling well," he responded, "Something happened over the weekend that I wanted to talk over with you."

"Of course, go right ahead," I said. Bridges, Oscar, and their two friends were electricians who also maintained the base heating and ventilation systems. Mojave Wells was so small that it wasn't a full time year around task. Like me, they were permanently stationed down at the Desert Center air base just north of Palm Meadows. Periodically, they would be temporarily stationed up here at Mojave Wells for short periods of time, perhaps a month or two, and return to Desert Center when their tasks were completed. Unlike them, my temporary duty assignment at Mojave Wells was as permanent as I wished to make it.

"Charlie, you're the duty weather observer out there on the ranges and you spend every working day just sitting out there at Range Three looking at the winds, the sands, the clouds and everything. If there was anything unusual out there, you would have already seen it, wouldn't you," asked Oscar carefully?

"Yes," I said. "Of course, from time to time Desert Center asks for the wind and weather reports from Range One instead of Range Three. Every once in a while they ask for the reports from Ranges Two and Four as well. The upper level wind measurement requires that I fill a balloon with helium and release it into the sky. Then I track it using a theodolite. At night I attach a battery powered light so I can see the balloon. I take those measurements 5 or 6 times a day. The first release is at 4:30 in the morning. I return to the Wells for my meals and in the afternoon when my workday is done. I get to do most anything I want when I'm out there. The only rule is that whatever I do, I have to do it alone. It gets lonely out there but it's a beautiful desert and I've learned to enjoy it."

"When you are out there alone on the gunnery ranges, do you ever see anything unusual," Oscar asked defensively? "Do you ever see any … things?"

"Well, sometimes," I responded. "Sometimes my eyes play tricks on me or I get confused by the daytime heat waves and mirages. At night there's always the lights up the valley. Sometimes I dream that unusual things are happening. When it gets really hot, once in a while I even see things that my mind just refuses to process or let me believe in."

"Things like people," he asked quickly. "They're white and thin and tall with children, right?"

"Well, yes," I answered slowly. "How do you know what they look like?"

"Steve told me," he said.

"How's that," I asked.

"As you know, Steve was stationed up here straight out of boot camp. He said that a couple of weeks after he arrived, he was walking around in that hilly area up by Range Four out on the air-to-air ranges. He was looking for targets that had been dropped by the airplanes. He said that when he came over one of the low hills he was surprised to see a woman and three children hiding in a small sand-filled depression on the other side. They had apparently been playing in the sand, drawing hieroglyphs and making castles and things. They were knelling down looking at him as he came over the hill. Steve said as soon as he saw them he stopped and stood frozen in fear. Then the woman stood up slowly and motioned to the children to stand up slowly.

"He said the woman was about your height, just under 6 feet tall and that she was very thin. She had chalk white skin, large blue eyes that stretched part way around the sides of her head, and nearly transparent blonde hair. He said they were all wearing white aluminum jump suits with white nylon boots.

"Steve claimed that the woman made several sounds like that of a meadowlark. Then the children one by one, took off running over the hill behind her while she stood waiting between the children and him. He said that once the children had gone, the woman backed away from him, then quickly turned and took off running over the low hills as well. He said he just stood there watching until they finally disappeared over one of the ridges up to the northwest, several miles in the distance."

"I don't understand," I responded. "Why was Steve frozen in fear? Why was he afraid of a woman and children playing in the sand?"

"Steve said it was because as soon as he saw them, he realized they were perfectly real and they weren't human," replied Oscar.

"But I still don't understand," I stammered. "Something can't be right. The air-to-air ranges are more than 45 miles up the valley from here. They're over the hottest part of the ranges. On many summer days the rocks and sand down in those depressions up there get hotter then 150 degrees. Why would any woman with three children be playing out there in that kind of heat?"

"I don't know," said Oscar, "But I know Steve's story is true."

"Steve and I are good friends. Why hasn't he ever mentioned this story to me," I asked?

"He said its because he doesn't want to scare you," said Oscar. "He said that you're out there alone all of the time, and whatever is out there treats you differently than it treats the rest of us."

"I'm really confused now," I said. "Are you saying that when you were out there where Steve had been, that you saw this white woman with three children?"

"Not exactly," said Oscar, "but I did see the three children."

"How's that," I asked?

"Last Saturday I took the electrical detachment truck up the valley towards Range Four," he responded. "As you know, Bridges and I enlisted together and we will both be finishing our terms of enlistment at the end of summer. I wanted to get one of those parachute targets as a souvenir. They were being dropped out on the air-to-air ranges last Friday. After telling Smokey where I was going, I put lots of water in the truck and set out up the valley.

"When I got to the buildings of Range Four, I did not continue out onto the dry lakebed. Instead I did as Steve and the range maintenance men, the range rats do. I turned to the west just before the buildings and followed along that hard smooth area to that gravel side road. Then I followed that gravel side road for several miles over those low rolling hills down into the valley, until I got to the air-to-air ranges. It sure was hot down in there.

"Once I got down in there among those low hills, I parked my truck at a nice place in the road. I got out and walked around until I found a suitable parachute target lying out in the desert. I picked it up and carried it back to my truck. I became really nervous doing it. My nerves got really jangled because it seemed like every move I made was being watched. I got back into my truck and began driving back out of there. I was so nervous that I wasn't driving very well. I had just barely gotten my truck turned around on that narrow road when I strayed off the gravel road. I ran over some cactus along the side of the road and the back tire on the driver's side went flat. I was in a level area down in one of those depressions.

"I stopped the truck, turned off the engine, and set the parking brake. I got out to change the tire when I discovered the bad news. I had a fine spare tire and a good tire iron. I had a good scissors jack but I had lost the handle. I was really upset because it was in the truck when I checked everything before leaving base. I took out the spare tire and my tools and laid them on the ground. Then I tried for at least 20 minutes to jack up the truck but there simply wasn't any way to do it without the handle. Finally, with the heat getting to me, I gave up trying. I decided I was going to have to wait until nightfall when the range rats would come looking for me.

"Since I couldn't go anywhere, I decided to just relax in the shade of the truck and kill time for the rest of the day. I began, just for fun, by trying to get an echo off the distant mountains to the west. Two or three times I cupped my hands together and shouted 'Help' in that direction. After just a couple of minutes, I was shocked beyond belief when a tall white man with three children following behind him walked up over the top of the next hill in the road. He was about the same height as you, but he was very thin. He wasn't muscular with a heavy build like you have. He had large blue eyes that stretched around the sides of his head, and almost transparent blonde hair. He and the children were wearing white aluminum jump suits with white nylon boots. He stopped on the top of the hill, perhaps 50 feet from me and asked me in English, 'Do you need help with your truck?'

"'Who are you,' I blurted out in shock.

"'I'm Range Four Harry.' He replied. 'Do you need help with that flat tire?'

"'Yes, I have lost the handle to my jack so I can't jack up my truck,' I stammered. 'Where did you come from?'

"'Just over the hill,' he replied. Then he laughed at my confusion for a minute or so. Then he said, 'Do not worry. We're only here to help you. The boy left the handle to your jack on the road just over the hill behind you.'

"I stood up and walked up the road to the top of the hill. Lying there in the dirt was the handle to my jack. I grabbed my jack handle and hurried back to my truck shouting, 'Thanks, Harry!' As I was positioning my jack and beginning to jack up my truck, the man asked, 'is it OK if the children watch while you change your tire? They won't hurt anything.'

"'They sure can,' I told him. 'I'm so happy to have a working jack they can do anything they want.' But I tell you, Charlie, it must have taken me an hour to change that tire. Those three children were curious about everything, way more curious than any child I ever saw. I was trying to take off one of the lug nuts and the one fat little boy would get right up between the tire and me so I couldn't do anything. Then he would study everything, the threads, the bolts, rust flakes, everything. I had to just stand back on the road and wait for the longest time until all three of those children, both boys and the girl, had satisfied their curiosity.

"Finally I got my tire changed and got everything back in my truck. I turned around to thank the man again, but he and the children had just walked back over the hill and disappeared into the sagebrush without even saying goodbye. I started up my truck and drove out of there as carefully as I knew how."

Then Oscar paused and started breathing easier. He slapped me on the back and said, "Thanks Charlie, for letting me get that off my chest. I really appreciate it. I feel a lot better now. I still don't know why you're not afraid when you're out there alone. Man, by the time I got back in to the Wells, I was scared out of my skin. I'm never going out there alone again. I see it's late, I better get to work. See you."

With that, Oscar jumped up from his chair, picked up his tray and dishes and left. For my part, I sat there more bemused than anything. It certainly was odd that my pink elephants, Steve's pink elephants, and Oscar's pink elephants all looked the same.

A couple weeks passed. Late one Monday afternoon I was walking up to the chow hall for the evening meal when I passed Bridges, Oscar, Doug, and Bryan standing outside the day room laughing. As soon as I got close, they greeted me and all swarmed around me like little children. Bridges was laughing so hard he could hardly talk. "Charlie," he began, "Did you hear the news? This year I came in third in the international pool tournament!"

"Yes," I answered. "I was extremely impressed. I just came to congratulate you. That's an incredible accomplishment."

"But here's the best part," Bridges continued. "Once in the final rounds a player tried that trick of tickling me, but this time I was ready for it. If you hadn't done it previously, I might have gotten flustered and not finished any better than number 30."

"I'm truly happy for you Bridges," I answered. "You worked hard and you deserve every good thing that you've accomplished."

The next weekend there was a large forest fire in the mountains east of San Bernardino. Everyone except Bridges and I were sent to help fight it. To feed ourselves, we were given a copy of the key to the chow hall.

I was in my barracks listening to the radio. Both Bridges and I were preparing to take the bus into town that Saturday afternoon. The Mojave Wells base was deserted except for the two of us. Our barracks sat on a north-south line, with his barracks sitting next door just south of mine. Suddenly through the hot afternoon air, I heard Bridges screaming in terror. He was screaming, "Who are you? What are you doing in my barracks? Get back from me!" Then he broke down and began screaming incoherently in panic and abject terror.

Both of our barracks were single story wooden barracks of World War II vintage. They were long and thin and had been built with their floors perhaps 4 feet above the desert. Their only doors were on the ends, with wide wooden steps leading up to them. The showers and bathrooms were in the middle. When full, each barracks could sleep perhaps 16 men. Both of our barracks, however, sat more than two thirds empty.

As soon as I heard Bridges begin screaming, I immediately began hurrying down the aisle of my barracks to the door on the south. When I opened the door to the outside, I was quite surprised by the sight before me. Standing on the platform on top of the wooden steps that lead into Bridges' barracks next door stood one of the chalk white guards. The guard was taller than most, standing perhaps seven feet tall. When he saw me, he stood up straight, and smoothly stepped over the wooden railing and down onto the dirt and rocks on the west side of the stairs. Then he walked around behind Bridges' barracks and stood on the ground looking through the open window.

There was still a paralysis in my mind regarding what met my eyes. This was the mid '60s, before movies about aliens. My mind had locked up to a certain extent and I was unable to process everything that was going on. Unaccountably, I wasn't particularly afraid. Bridges was still screaming in terror. In a nervous but natural manner I walked outside, down the steps to my barracks and up the steps to Bridges' barracks. I steeled myself and opened the door. Inside Bridges stood screaming and frozen in terror on my right, with his back to the wall of his barracks, just this side of the window through which the guard was looking. Bridges was wearing only a towel, his boxer shorts, and his shower sandals. A second very tall chalk white guard was standing just beyond his steel two-door locker, and watching him from over the top. Three other shorter chalk white creatures, apparently women about my height, were standing in the aisle in front of door to the bathroom, apparently inspecting the building. A fourth was standing to my left just inside the outside door, watching Bridges intently. Bridges' steel locker stood on his right with both of its doors wide open. A small boy wearing a solid white jump suit was floating perhaps 4 feet off the ground in front of his locker, visually inspecting the contents.

As soon as I saw the floating little boy, I became convinced that once again my mind was playing tricks on me and all of the white creatures were pink elephants. After all, the little boy was floating some 4 feet off the ground in broad daylight. I tried speaking gently to Bridges as he stood frozen and screaming in terror. He did not respond, but he did calm down a little and more or less stopped screaming. Even though I, myself, was becoming quite frightened, it was obvious that I was going to have to go in and get him. I spoke loudly and gently to the white creatures, as though I were talking to myself in the dark. I said, "Bridges is my friend. I want to take him next door to my barracks. Take all of the time you want."

Then I walked slowly and carefully in amongst the white creatures, in much the same way that a lamb might walk in among a pride of lions. I walked over to Bridges, put my left arm around his towel-covered shoulders and said in a forceful brotherly manner, "Come on Bridges. Let's go over to my barracks."

Bridges finally stopped screaming and with my help, the two of us walked slowly and carefully over to the door, then outside, down the wooden steps, and up the next steps into my barracks. Once inside I sat down with him on the first good empty bunk and let him cry off the terror. It took a long while, probably a half hour. Through one of the windows on the western side of my barracks, I could see the procession of chalk white creatures casually making their way over to one of the other barracks. They were heading towards the barracks that Doug always claimed was haunted. I considered that fact to be proof that they were all just part of my collection of pink elephants going home to roost. A little more fresh air along with the cooler evening temperatures, and soon the blood flow in my brain would be right back to normal, or so I supposed.

After a long time, Bridges finally started to calm down and stop shaking. When he was able to speak again, he began, "What happened to the world we knew, Charlie? What happened to the world we lived in when we enlisted? Remember how it was such an ordinary world with

13

beautiful women and fast cars and nights downtown in the city that were absolutely enchanting and … and no terrifying white creatures?"

"It's still there," I reassured him. "You'll be getting discharged in a few weeks and you'll go home to Chicago and you'll see. It's still there, downtown Chicago, summer nights in Grant Park, Chicago city women who just want to make love and dance, just the way we both remember them."

"No, Charlie," he said breaking down and crying. "It's not there. It's not there anymore because the man I was isn't there anymore. When I get my discharge in a few weeks, I just want to go back to Chicago, back to that same world that we both knew when I enlisted. But the terror I felt today changed me. I can never go back to being the way I was. I am so terrified that I am not even able to go back into my barracks to get my clothes. I am so glad that you're here, Charlie. I need you to go back to my barracks and get my clothes and my wallet and my things for me. I am going to load them into my truck and drive back to Desert Center. I can't come back here, Charlie. I can't ever come back here again. The very ground in this place terrifies me."

"Sure Bridges," I answered. Then I got up and went back to Bridges' barracks. It was now perfectly empty. It took me three or four trips to collect his belongings and his duffel bag and carry them over to my barracks. Then, after he was dressed and packed, I helped him load his things into his truck, and we said our goodbyes, promising to meet again sometime in Chicago.

As he was getting into his truck, he was saying, "Thank God you were here, Charlie."

The drive back to desert Center was perhaps longer than Bridges had been expecting. In any case, he was probably too upset and shouldn't have been driving at all. Maybe something panicked him. The state police believe he had to be driving more than 95 mph when his truck slid on a curve, overturned, burned, and killed him.

I remember my loneliness, sleeping alone in my barracks, alone on base. It certainly seemed like the world that both Bridges and I knew ended that night.

Settling In

>... The city clerk quieted the crowd said:
> "Men of Ephesus, doesn't all the world know
> that the city of Ephesus is the guardian
> of the temple of the great Artemis
> and of her image, which fell from heaven?
> Therefore, since these facts are undeniable,
> you ought to be quiet,
> and not do anything rash. ..."
> ... Acts 19:35,36

A few days passed uneventfully. My life was more relaxing now that I was familiar with the ranges and had an adequate collection of supplies. Then one cool moonless windy morning I arrived out on Range Three a few minutes early. I had stayed late playing pool at the airman's club and had gotten only a quick shower, a tooth brushing, and 2 hours sleep. I had been drinking only soda pop but his morning's headache kept me from shaving. I was sleepy at the wheel for most of the drive out, and had driven off the paved road at least twice. I was draped over the steering wheel nearly asleep when my truck finally rolled to a stop in front of the generator shack. I turned off the engine and stumbled out into the cool wind, hoping it would wake me up. I was too tired to attempt to start the diesel. No matter, I was easily capable of releasing a balloon and taking a complete set of wind measurements using only my flashlight. I was afraid that I would drop and break my flashlight if I tried to carry it as I walked, so I stuffed it into my back pocket and began stumbling over to my weather shack. I looked down concentrating on the ground as I did so.

I had taken 15 or 20 steps when I noticed a tall thin man in a chalk white aluminum suit standing on the balcony of the control tower about 100 feet off to my left. He didn't act the slightest bit afraid or surprised by my presence. He stood on the wooden deck with a natural authoritative stance, watching me in total silence. He acted as if he had been waiting to talk to me. He seemed somewhat surprised when I just kept on walking. My head hurt too much to talk. As I walked, I noticed that he had a very unusual physical appearance. He was much taller than most, standing 7 or 8 feet tall with short transparent blonde hair. His blue eyes were much larger and stretched further around the side of his head than anybody that I had ever seen. His nose was similar to that of a horse, and his ears could not be seen. His suit reflected a white, aluminum sheen, but it was not emitting any white fluorescent light. It was quite obvious to me that he was real because the wooden boards on the tower balcony reacted whenever he shifted his weight.

I was so sleepy that when I reached my theodolite, I stopped to rest for a moment. I was more than 75 feet from the control tower and my head ached badly. After a glance up towards him, I stumbled over to my weather shack. My initial guess was that he must be the day's range control officer who presumably had chosen to come out to Range Three several hours early, and I must just be too tired to see straight. The ranges were scheduled to be in use today. It made sense to my tired mind, and the last thing I needed was for an officer to see me reporting for duty in the shape I was in.

I proceeded, then, to ignore this supposed range officer. I opened up my weather shack and took 2 aspirins for my headache, along with a drink of water. Then I took the morning weather report, filled the balloon, and walked back out to unlock my theodolite. All the time, the tall white man stood on the tower balcony, watching my every move.

As I was unlocking my theodolite, I noticed that my truck was the only vehicle out on the range. Whoever the man was, he had no visible means of transportation. This meant that he would need a ride in to base for breakfast. The aspirins were starting to work and my headache was diminishing. I decided that I would be better off if I made friends with the range officer. Range officers were usually bird Colonels, and an unfriendly Colonel's inspection could mean real trouble for an enlisted man like me. Therefore, I walked politely towards the base of the tower. The man just stood and watched me as I came. I stopped about 25 feet from the base of the tower. The balcony was perhaps 30 feet above me. I began addressing him as I would a bird Colonel. "Excuse me, Sir," I began, saluting him as I did so. "I am airman Baker. I am the duty weather observer out here on the ranges. It will take me another 25 or 30 minutes to finish my morning wind report. Then I will be closing up and heading back to base for breakfast. You don't seem to have a truck or anything. If you want to ride back to base with me when I go in for breakfast, you're welcome to. Mojave Wells has a nice chow hall, and it does its' best job with breakfast. I'm sure that Steve and the range maintenance men will be happy to bring you back out with them when they come at 8:00 a.m."

He seemed to find my request amusing, but he did not otherwise respond.

I continued politely, "It would be a lot more fun than waiting out here for 4 hours on an empty stomach with no coffee or anything. I can bring you back out myself, if you want, when I come at 7:30 a.m."

He seemed almost unable to contain his amusement. Eventually, he leaned over the balcony railing slightly, looked down at me and said politely, "You do not need to salute me, airman Baker. Continue with your balloon release."

"Yes, Sir," I responded. Then I turned in military fashion, and walked back to my weather shack. I proceeded with the balloon release and wind measurements. When I had finished tracking the balloon, I returned to my weather shack and completed the wind calculations by flashlight. All the time, the man remained watching me from the tower balcony. I was just finishing the computations when my phone rang. It was my friend Dwight from Desert Center. We exchanged pleasantries and I gave him the morning report. Our conversation was interrupted when Dwight received a phone call from the Desert Center base commander on one of his other lines. When it was completed, Dwight came back on my line.

"Boy, Charlie," he said, "That was the commander himself. He sure is scared as hell about something that's going on up there. He was angry that I was keeping you on the line, and keeping you from breakfast."

"Don't worry about that," I responded. The chow hall doesn't open for another hour. I'll get there in plenty of time. What reporting schedule do you want me to follow today? The first flight of planes is supposed to arrive by 8:00 a.m. Then we'll be getting planes every other hour until 4:00 p.m."

"Not anymore," said Dwight. "The base commander just cancelled all flights and all wind measurements for today. In that phone call, he said he's hoping that you'll take a nice long breakfast in the chow hall and spend the rest of the day catching up on your sleep."

"What about the range officer," I asked? "He's over on the control tower now, watching me. He doesn't have a truck or anything. How's he supposed to get back to base?"

"I don't know," answered Dwight. "Let me call the commander back and ask him."

I waited a few minutes while Dwight checked with the base commander. Then he came back on line, "I'm not sure, Charlie, but I think that you just got me in a lot of trouble with the base commander," Dwight said seriously. "The base commander almost had a bird when I called him back. He swore that the range officer for today was sitting in the command post next to him. He ordered me to get off the phone and let you head in for breakfast immediately. I'm not supposed to ask you any more questions. Whatever the situation is up there, just ignore it, shut everything down, and head in to base for the rest of the day."

"Ok," I answered. "I'm fine up here, but if you need an excuse with the base commander, tell him I was homesick as hell and needed a friend to talk to. Tell him that it was my idea to talk so long. Then, along about 7:00 a.m., tell him that I called you again from the chow hall because I still needed to talk to someone. If anyone ever asks me, I'll say the same thing. I hope that helps."

"Right," responded Dwight. "I think I'm going to have to do that." Then Dwight hung up.

I closed and locked my weather shack. Then I walked over to my theodolite, and locked it up. The man was still standing on the tower balcony watching me. Still thinking he was probably the range officer I politely walked over towards the base of the tower to the spot where I was before. I addressed him as before, "Excuse me, Sir. I'm going in for breakfast now. The Desert Center base commander has just cancelled all of the flights for today, cancelled all of the wind measurements, and closed all of the ranges. You don't seem to have any way to get back in to base. You can ride back in with me if you want to."

Once again he seemed to be amused by my statements. However, he didn't respond. The balcony completely encircled the control tower. The man stepped quickly around to the opposite side of the control tower and stood by the northeast support, apparently waiting for my next move. I wasn't sure that he had heard me, so I wasn't sure if he expected me to wait for him or not. This was a big problem because abandoning a bird Colonel in this desert would certainly get me a court martial. In confusion and some trepidation, I decided that I should use the wooden stairway to go up to the balcony and ask him. I walked over to the base of the tower stairway and began slowly climbing the stairs. I continued talking to him as if he were a bird Colonel. I was saying, "I'm sorry, I didn't hear you Colonel. I'll be happy to give you a ride in to base if you need one. It's no problem. Of course, if you have other plans, it's no problem for me to drive in by myself. I know I've been quite tired this morning, but I'm fine now."

I was about three fourths of the way up the tower stairs when the suit he was wearing began to emit a uniform thin field of white fluorescent light. Then, while hanging onto the tower support, he stepped over the balcony railing onto the air outside, in much the same manner that a man might step into a swimming pool. Then, while holding on to the tower support for balance, he floated slowly down to the ground below. He looked much the same as a man riding down on an elevator. Once he was on the ground, his suit stopped emitting the white fluorescent light. Then he proceeded to walk quickly out into the desert towards the mountains to the northeast. He seemed to be walking at more than 15 miles an hour. Within a minute or so he disappeared from sight, passing over one of the distant sagebrush covered ridges. I was left standing on the stairs, too confused to know what to do.

After some mental struggling, I decided to double check the tower and then go in for breakfast. I finished climbing the stairs and performed a quick inspection. Everything was in order, so I quickly came back down from the tower, returned to my truck, and headed back in to base. I was quite hungry. I shared the breakfast table with Steve, Doug, and Bryan. I was enjoying the chow hall bacon with my eggs, and laughing at myself as I began relating my morning experiences to my friends. They refused to laugh with me. "How tall did you say that range officer was again," asked Steve?

"Maybe 7 or 8 feet, I'd guess," I responded.

Steve suddenly became angry, and tears formed in his eyes. He stood up from the table and shouted, "I love you like a brother, Charlie, but it's only your own stupidity that kept you alive out there. When are you going to start listening to me? Don't you realize that tall son of a bitch had to have been well armed!!" Then, he stomped angrily out of the chow hall.

A few uneventful days passed as I tried to make sense of that morning's events. Then, ridiculous as the hypothesis was, I decided that the man must have been some kind of angel who had come to warn me of my impending death. I didn't think that he was one of my guardian angels. I had always lived a clean, drug-free life. However, it included soda pop, potato chips, a beer once in a while, gambling, playing pool, dancing, and otherwise having fun. Naturally

I found the prospect of dying and not making it into heaven to be quite alarming. I vowed to reform my life along stricter Christian principles. Since I was Roman Catholic, I began by going to confession. It was such a long detailed confession that the priest became impatient with me and shooed me out early. Then I implemented the practice of improving my eating habits. I began consuming large quantities of milk, vegetables, vitamins, and nutritious foods instead of soda pop and potato chips. I decided that I needed to visit each one of my friends in turn and make amends for anything I might have done that was sinful or that might have offended them. For this reason, late one afternoon after the evening meal, as Steve was leaving the chow hall, I caught up with him outside. I began seriously, "Excuse me Steve. We're as close as brothers and since I'll probably be dying soon, I want to make sure that I have made my amends for any way I might have sinned against you."

"Why do you say that, Charlie," asked Steve? "You look pretty healthy to me."

Nervously I continued, "Well, you know, Steve, I figure that man on the tower the other night must have been some kind of angel sent by God to warn me to get my soul ready for death. So I want to be ready whenever God sends his angels to come get me."

Steve put his arm around my shoulder in a brotherly fashion, and said gently, "Get all of those kind of thoughts out of your head, Charlie. You aren't going to die anytime soon. God hasn't sent what is out there. It can be put to death just like you and me. Just don't do anything rash when they come around."

Charles James Hall

Then Steve hugged my shoulder a second time and walked quickly away towards his barracks. I was so stunned I was left standing without words to respond.

By the time the weekend arrived, I had decided that the man was just the range officer and that I had been too tired to see straight. By then I was well rested. I made the long bus ride up to Las Vegas and returned to my previous habits.

Valentine's Day

. . . Then Philip ran up to the chariot
and heard the man reading Isaiah the prophet.
"Do you understand what you are reading?"
Philip asked.
"How can I," he said,
"unless someone explains it to me?"

. . . Acts 8:30,31

It was a beautiful summer. Every morning at 3:15 a.m., I sang my way out to Range Three, fiddled with the diesel engines, released my balloon, phoned in the wind results to Desert Center, re-fiddled with the diesel engines, and sang my way back in for breakfast. Within a few days I was happy and relaxed. I had become really skilled at starting and stopping the diesel engines that powered the electrical generators. Each of the two engines had 12 huge cylinders and was somewhat larger in size than an entire car. Although either one of the engines and their generators could easily power a medium sized city, I used them only to power my radio, one electric light, and sometimes the fan on my oil heater. Sometimes I started and stopped the huge diesels just for the fun of it. Of course, the small lawn mower sized gasoline engine and generator that the USAF had provided for me to actually use when lighting my weather shack was much too small to be of any interest to me. It sat in perfect working order next door in the supply shed as pristine as the day it came out of the box.

A Tuesday morning came. I had returned to my usual happy, singing self. I began, as was typical, by opening up the generator shack and starting the diesels. The generator shack was a windowless wooden structure with a gravel floor. It was noticeably larger that an ordinary 2 car garage. The two diesels with their attached electrical generators sat on concrete foundations within the shack, positioned in much the same way that one might park two cars in the garage. Across the back of the shack sat several dozen batteries that provided the power to start the diesels. There were quite a few shelves that held parts and other supplies. In particular, a large set of shelves holding many pressurized cans of ether starting fluid sat along the wall on the south side by the door. The huge tank of diesel fuel sat out back between the generator shack and the supply sheds. Beyond the supply sheds, of course, sat my weather shack.

The only doors to the shack were on the west, facing the open desert. The diesels were parked east to west, facing west. Each Diesel had its own pair of wooden doors. A wide upright section separated these pairs of doors. This section had a post that supported the weight of the ordinary peaked roof.

When I opened up the generator shack this morning, as usual, I parked my truck beside the paved road out in front of the northern set of doors. Then I opened up the southern set of doors. The doors were hinged on the side and opened outward. They dragged a little on the gravel. Consequently, opening them could be difficult. I didn't open them all the way. When I had opened the right hand door to a 45 degree angle, I fixed it into position by placing a large stone on each side of the door and called it good. I did the same to its partner on the left. There wasn't much wind this morning, so the doors easily remained in that position for the duration of my morning balloon run.

Having completed the morning run and having locked up my weather shack and my theodolite, I was in the process of shutting down the diesel engine before heading in for breakfast. Unlike many nights, I had not yet started my pickup truck.

Nothing seemed out of place when I entered the shack. With a practiced hand I turned the knobs, moved the levers, threw the switches, shut off the fuel to the carburetor, and sang while the diesel shut down. Then, still singing, I marched outside to close the doors. As usual, I began with the door on the right. It was a bright moonlit night so the fluorescent light coming from behind the door didn't seem unusual. Anyway, I was hungry and in a hurry to make it in to breakfast. In a smooth, fluid fashion, and totally occupied with my work, I kicked away the inner stone and began closing the door, swinging it towards me and to my left. The edge of the door came past me and the region behind the door came into my view. My head instinctively turned to the right and my eyes immediately fixed on the sight of a white child behind the door. He was floating in total silence about 3 feet off the ground. The child appeared to be a small, slightly heavy-set chalk white boy about 3 or 4 feet tall. He was wearing a white suit that was surrounded by a field of white fluorescent light. He looked like a small version of an American astronaut on the moon, except that he clearly wasn't human. His large blue eyes were much larger than any human's and they were molded a quarter of the way around the side of his head. I could occasionally see the decay chains from radioactive particles coming from the shoulder area of his suit. He was wearing a pleasant expression as he faced me. He was bent towards me slightly

27

at the waist with his arms outstretched to each side. He behaved in much the same manner that a child swimming in a pool might have.

I was so stunned when I saw him that there wasn't any way my brain could process the information. He floated no more than 5 feet in front of me in total silence. He floated high enough off the ground so that he could almost look me straight in the eyes. My brain really wasn't making enough connections for me to be afraid. All I could think of was, "So this is what insanity is like. They were right, you know. It's really quite painless."

The two of us remained in that position, facing each other for quite a while. The boy was apparently unwilling to turn his back or side to me and move away. For my part, I was too stunned to think of anything to do. I was certain that my brain must have suddenly begun malfunctioning. I wanted to remain holding on to the wooden shack door in case I were to suddenly collapse. I began mentally checking my body to see if my blood was flowing erratically. My heartbeat was normal, and I didn't feel any dizziness. Finally I began wondering if perhaps, some of the cans of ether starting fluid were leaking. Maybe that was the problem. The cans were in the shed only 8 feet or so away. In order to get some fresh air, then, I begin carefully backing away from what I supposed to be an ether-induced hallucination. I took 4 or 5 steps backward, until I was standing out on the paved road, still facing the child. There was a nice breeze out on the road, and I began breathing deeply, hoping to get my brain back to normal. I was still too stunned to risk turning my head to either side. Transfixed by the boy, I refused to turn my head to the left to inspect the two patches of white fluorescent light positioned side by side next to the door of my truck, some

20 feet off to my left. The boy seemed to find the entire experience to be immensely amusing and seemed to appreciate having the extra space to maneuver. Then, as if on command, while still floating, he turned to his left and floated around the corner of the generator shack. He disappeared out of sight by floating in between the supply sheds. As he did so, he was moving his arms in much the same manner that a swimmer in a pool might have.

I remained standing motionless and breathing deeply for several minutes. I was still stunned and I wanted to be sure that the blood flow in my brain had returned to normal. Out of the left corner of my eye I could see the white patches by my truck take off running towards the far side of the Range Three lounge. I didn't turn my head to look at them. With the state of mind that I was in, my brain couldn't have processed the information anyway.

After waiting and breathing the fresh air for a while, I decided that the blood flow in my brain had returned to normal. It was time to get back in to town. I began by exercising. I spent about 20 minutes walking back and forth on the paved road, breathing deeply as I did so. Then, when my appetite had returned, I returned to the generator shack and inspected the pressurized cans of ether. There were several dozen of them. Almost all of the cans were new. I had previously brought them out from the supply depot myself. None of the cans appeared to be leaking, and everything appeared to be in perfect order. However, there were two or three older cans which contained some rust around the edges. Those cans I placed in a cardboard box in the back of my pickup truck for disposal in town. "That will solve this problem," I said to myself, with obvious satisfaction. "As soon as I get my brain back to normal, I don't want this to be happening again."

29

I closed up the generator shack, started up my truck, and began heading slowly towards base. I took my good-natured time doing so. I thought of myself as carefully nursing the blood flow in my brain back to health. As I was leaving the Range Three area I stopped for a minute and looked back out over the beautiful moonlit desert. Floating out there some 5 feet off the desert, perhaps a mile away, was the little white boy. He was following the paved road towards the ammunition bunker off to the northeast. He was spread out, laying forward. In the moonlight, he looked remarkably similar to the cherubs that are typically depicted on Valentine's Day cards. As I watched him, I wasn't afraid. I was convinced that he was just a pink elephant, and that brain malfunctions of the type I must be having, were the real reason for the invention of Valentine's Day. As I placed my truck back in gear and resumed my drive in to base, I was chuckling to myself. I was saying, "I'll be darned. So that's how Valentine's Day got started. It was originally a summer holiday that began as a kind of blood flow problem in the brain." That morning I drove back in to base feeling very unusual.

Several days passed. Not much happened except that my friends Steve, Doug, and Bryan all seemed to find my "Valentine" story to be quite alarming. When I described my morning experience to them over the breakfast table, they refused to join in laughing with me. I was only half way through my description when Steve jumped up from the table screaming, "Those sons of bitches are going to kill you coming in close like that, Charlie!! Why the hell weren't you afraid? Why the hell didn't you break and run?" Then he took a deep breath, thought for a minute, and said, "I'm sorry, Charlie. Maybe that's why you're still alive." Then he stomped angrily out of the chow hall. He had tears in his eyes at the time.

Customizing The Winds

. . . Make it your ambition to lead a quiet life,
to mind your own business
and to work with your hands,
just as we told you
so that your daily life might win
the respect of outsiders
and so that you will not be
dependent on anybody.
… 1 Thessalonians 4:11,12

4:00 p.m. was rapidly approaching and the afternoon shadows were slowly lengthening at Desert Center Air Base. My dayshift as duty weather observer was drawing to a close. I was working a few day shifts before taking two week's leave. As I was posting the weather maps behind the forecaster's counter, master sergeant O'Keefe interrupted me. As the duty weather forecaster, he was just finishing tomorrow's forecast. O'Keefe was a fun sergeant to work with, and he was a veteran forecaster. As a naturalized American, he was quite proudly Irish.

"Are those the latest wind charts from Tinker Air Base you have there, Charlie?" he asked in his heavy Irish brogue.

"Yes, Sergeant," I responded. "This is the last of the set. All 18 of them have been posted. I suppose you need them to complete tomorrow's forecast."

"Yes. Tomorrow is going to be a busy day on the Mojave Wells gunnery ranges," answered the sergeant. "Some English blooded Colonel named Harrison has brought his planes here special from New York. I suppose he's pacing the hallways in the command post right now, waiting for me to phone the winds to him."

"He sure is eager to fly tomorrow," I said. "He has three complete flights of new pilots set to go up first thing tomorrow morning. I guess he's going to work them on low-level skip bombing techniques. He wants the planes to come in groups of six, right down to within ten feet of the desert before they release their practice bombs. Range Three at the Wells is going to be pretty crowded. Counting his wingman, that'll make 20 planes up there all at once."

"Isn't that just like a mad dog of an Englishman," exclaimed O'Keefe. "When he's riding me, I hope he remembers that God created two chosen races."

"Two chosen races?" I asked.

"Why, yes," responded O'Keefe seriously. "First he chose the Jews. Later, he chose the Irish. That's what the history of Europe is, you know, Charlie. First it was what the Jews were doing in Israel. Then there was Jesus and the Romans. Then European history became a history of what the Irish were doing in Ireland. No intelligent scholar ever wanted to hear about what was going on in England."

Laughing under my breath, I continued, "Well, I do know that the Colonel was born in New York City and doesn't understand the desert. What I don't know is why he is in such a hurry. Look at these wind charts and weather reports. That big weather front up north has slipped south. It has just reached Iron Mountain. It doesn't have any clouds or rain with it, but the winds up there are 45 miles per hour, gusting to 70. That front is certain to slip further south tonight. Tomorrow morning, once the evening inversion breaks, Desert Center will be receiving the same winds.

Fifteen of his new pilots will be on their first mission here at Desert Center. I wouldn't think he'd want to take off at all tomorrow. If he and his pilots are up at the Wells tomorrow when the winds start up, they'll all be in one hell of a mess. They won't have enough fuel to go to an airfield where they can land safely. In winds like that, they won't even be able to parachute out safely. I suppose you're going to tell him to cancel his plans for tomorrow, and wait a day or so until the weather calms down."

"Oh, no, Charlie," said O'Keefe. "I couldn't do that. Look at those 24 hour forecast charts from Tinker. They're all certain that the front is going to stall over Iron Mountain and then go back up north. They're all forecasting light winds for tomorrow for Desert Center."

"But what does Tinker know about anything, sergeant," I objected. "There aren't any weather stations between here and Iron Mountain except our station at Mojave Wells. Those high winds could be on us tomorrow before anyone knows what's happening."

"Don't worry about it, Charlie," said O'Keefe. "The Lord will take care of everything. Honestly, Charlie, you have to learn to relax more and just let Jesus run your life. You're too much of an Englishman, Charlie. Learn to be more like the Irish.

"Take me for example," continued O'Keefe. "I'm going with Tinker's forecast. I'm going to call up that English Colonel and tell him to expect clear skies and light winds. Sergeant Rogers will be the duty forecaster tomorrow. When he receives those 4:30 a.m. Mojave Wells winds, he can decide if he wants to change the forecast. If tomorrow is going to be a windy day, it'll show right up in those upper four wind readings from Mojave Wells."

With the clock racing, we both had to go on with our duties. I knew what I had to do. As I walked back to my barracks, I knew exactly what I had to do.

Back at the barracks, I went to the room next to mine and woke my friend McIntyre. "McIntyre. Wake up it's time to eat."

After some protesting, McIntyre finally sat up, still half asleep. He said, "I know you, Charlie. You're waking me up earlier than usual. What do you want, old boy." McIntyre was too intelligent to have the wool pulled over his eyes. He was scheduled to work the coming mid shift, midnight to 8:00 a.m. It was on this shift that tomorrow's flight decisions would be made. Much as I respected McIntyre's high intelligence, I knew that tomorrow morning he was going to need help, even if he didn't know it.

Thinking up a subtle lie, I answered him, "Well, as you know I'm working the day shift tomorrow."

"So," answered McIntyre.

"Well, I was hoping you would do me a favor," I said.

"Yes," responded McIntyre. "What is it?"

"I was hoping that I could relieve you an hour early or so, tomorrow morning. That would mean that tomorrow I would be working nine or ten hours and you'd owe me a couple of hours. I want to date Michael's sister Pamela next week, after the shift assignments change. Next week, you could relieve me for the last couple of hours on one of my shifts and I could spend that extra time with Pamela,"

"I see," said McIntyre laughing. "I'll agree to it if you promise to give her a little extra pat for me."

"Agreed," I said laughing. McIntyre sure was an easy guy to get along with.

Next morning came early. After a good night's sleep, I found myself in uniform, walking into the Desert Center weather station at 4:45 a.m. My plan was simple. The Mojave Wells weather observer was another one of my good friends named Jim Payne. He'd grown up in the desert southwest of Las Cruces so I figured he'd be up early and out at the Range Three weather shack as scheduled. I decided to phone him up and make sure that the upper four levels of his wind report contained big numbers.

I entered quietly though the front door of the weather station. McIntyre, as I had expected, was sleeping at his desk. The last forecaster had left at 10:00 the night before. Like many weather observers, McIntyre paid little attention to the rules once he was alone in the weather station.

Quietly picking up the phone on the Major's desk, I dialed the phone number of the Range Three weather shack at Mojave Wells. After 20 rings I decided that Payne, like McIntyre, was still asleep.

I signed in as the duty observer and quickly took the 5:00 a.m. weather report. I wanted McIntyre to leave before the Mojave Wells winds were phoned in, so I gently woke him and sent him back to the barracks. He always had a good sense of humor. Half asleep getting up from the desk, he said chuckling, "It's just like you, old man. You never sleep on duty. You just show up with one of those history books of yours, do all of the work as you're supposed to, and spend your spare time reading all night. You wouldn't sleep on duty if your life depended on it."

I cleaned up the paper mess the teletypes had made in the teletype room. McIntyre had left four hours of weather reports on the machines and they all needed filing in the forecaster's area. Then I needed to transmit his last three hourly reports to Tinker, along with a procedure report explaining why they were late. I needed a good excuse to cover McIntyre. After all, he was doing me a favor. I told Tinker that the communication lines had been down due to high winds. I knew it was a lie, but why burn McIntyre? He was only doing what almost all of the other weather observers were doing.

While I was waiting for Payne to phone from Range Three, I checked the winds at Desert Center. According to the chart recorder, the winds had been consistent all night. They were out of the south at 4 to 6 miles per hour, hardly anything for a pilot to be concerned about.

I went outside for a look at the sky. The air outside was cold. Obviously a desert inversion had formed. A large bubble of cold air on the ground was keeping the winds from blowing at low levels. Above me I could see wind clouds as low as 4000 feet. It was obvious to me that once the morning sun had heated up the cold air next to the ground, the bubble would blow away, and Desert Center would be subjected to the same winds that had torn Iron Mountain apart yesterday.

Going back inside, I checked Iron Mountain's weather report. I was not surprised to learn that they were also reporting light winds from the south. It meant of course, that an experienced weather observer could sleep in any kind of weather.

I knew what I had to do. I walked over to the wind recorder and changed the roll of paper. I filed the old roll with its record of the winds for the last twelve hours as per regulation. It fit nicely into a box in the back of the record storage closet. Of course, getting to the back of the records closet was always a difficult task.

Going over to the weather chart, I opened up the front glass and exposed the recording needle. It was moving now on a brand new roll of paper. Using the little finger of my left hand, I pulled the recording needle slowly and gently to the right. Soon the record showed almost a full minute of gusting winds. According to this new and fake record, some gusts were as high as 33 miles an hour. What a coincidence, I thought, laughing to myself. I'll get to close the base if this happens four times this hour. Releasing the needle, I closed the front glass door and returned to babysitting the teletype machines. Time passed. By 5:45 a.m. the winds recorded on the chart recorder showed three different periods of high gusty winds. Of course, I also had to make three trips to the restroom to wash the ink off my hands. No problem. I figured I'd get the hang of it sooner or later. Finally, at 5:50 a.m. the phone rang. Picking it up, I answered, "Desert Center weather station, airman Charlie Baker speaking."

As I had expected, it was my good friend Payne. Ordinarily, Payne would have been accompanied by Dwight, forming a two man team. However, Dwight's wife was 8 months pregnant. So Steve, the lead range maintenance man, had been allowed to substitute for Dwight. Speaking quickly, Payne said, "Charlie, I've got the winds. Ready to copy?"

"Yes," I answered. Then, speaking carefully, I said, "Before you give them to me Payne, I'm certain that your upper four levels are going to be really high. There's a big weather front over you and I'm expecting those winds to be at least 35 miles per hour."

It was obvious to me that Payne had made up the winds he was about to read to me. I figured that one made up number was a good as another. Yet, Payne, for some reason I could never fathom, brushed all of my hints aside. Continuing in a loud clear voice he proceeded to report winds of five to ten miles per hour out of the southwest for each altitude level up to 15,000 feet.

I tried to talk him out of it. I tried everything, but Payne was adamant. Those were the winds, he claimed. He'd measured them himself. I was left with no choice but to record these low values and distribute the Mojave Wells winds as required. This meant that I had to phone the Colonel at the command post and tell him the gunnery range winds were light and no danger, exactly as forecast. It was obvious to me that his plans for taking 20 planes up to Mojave Wells at 7:30 a.m. had been given a big green light. I knew what I had to do. Walking over to the wind recorder, I proceeded to get some more red ink on my hands. Then, phoning the Desert Center tower, I told the tower operator that the base was still open but that I would be closing the base soon due to high winds. We agreed that the tower would not let any planes take off unless they were heading for someplace very far away. I made certain they understood that for today, all flights up to the gunnery ranges were canceled. Being the duty weather observer did have its privileges.

I was just hanging up the phone when sergeant Rogers, the morning duty forecaster arrived. Entering the weather station, he greeted me, "Good morning Baker. What's happening?"

"Well," I answered him, "You might want to consider amending yesterday's forecast. You might want to cancel all flights up to the gunnery ranges today. There's a Colonel over at the fighter weapons school planning on taking 20 airplanes with 15 new pilots up to the gunnery ranges first thing. You probably don't want him to do it. There are an awful lot of wind clouds out there. I think that weather front north of us is a lot further south than Iron Mountain."

Sergeant Rogers walked over to the Mojave Wells wind report. After taking one look at it, he responded, "Nonsense, Baker. Look at those top four high altitude winds. They're as calm as they can be. Then look at those light winds at Iron Mountain. That front has retreated back north just like Tinker expects. There's nothing out there. We won't have any problems here at Desert Center."

"Surely you don't believe those morning winds from Mojave Wells?" I continued gently. "Payne must have confused the light on the balloon with the light bulb in his barracks."

"Why do you say that?" asked sergeant Rogers.

Rogers had just come back from two year's duty in Vietnam. One day I asked him why he always drove a new Cadillac to work? After all, he only carried six stripes. He responded by confiding in me that the club he had run for two years in Thailand had furnished him with a million dollar bank account in Switzerland. I figured he'd understand if an enlisted man had broken a few rules.

"Payne didn't phone in these 4:30 a.m. winds until 5:50 a.m.," I pointed out to the sergeant. "Those winds should have been ready by 5:00 a.m. Remember sergeant, the chow hall at Mojave Wells begins serving breakfast exactly at 6:00 a.m., and you can go over early if you want to."

"I don't get what you mean, Baker," responded the sergeant.

"His next wind measurement is scheduled for 7:30 a.m. Preparing the balloon takes about 20 minutes. Now it's at least a 45 minute drive between Range Three and the chow hall. If Payne were actually out at Range Three when he phoned in these winds, that would leave him no more than 10 minutes to spend over the breakfast table."

"I don't get what you're saying, Baker," laughed the sergeant. "Tell me. Just what is it that you're trying to say? What's wrong with spending only 10 minutes at the breakfast table?"

"Sergeant," I said gently, "We're talking about Small Jimmy Payne. I shared a barracks room with him for six months. He must stand more than 6'4" in his stocking feet. This is the Small Jimmy who weighs more than 240 pounds. He's built like a tank. There's not an ounce of fat anywhere on his body. He's nothing but solid muscle and bone. He's not a man to hurry his meals, breakfast or otherwise. Over here in our chow hall I saw him go back for seconds three times and then bitch because they ran out of fried potatoes. He was still hungry! You'd need a gun to get him away from the breakfast table after only 10 minutes! Obviously he slept in until he smelled the eggs frying in the chow hall next to his barracks. Then he woke up hungry, faked the wind measurement, and hiked over for breakfast next door. I may not know much, sergeant, but trust me, I know Jimmy Payne. There's no way he would have cut short his breakfast just to compute winds like these. If the lower altitude winds really were this calm, he'd have let the balloon go and made up the four higher levels just so he could get to breakfast on time. Whether he was out at Range Three or not, either way, these upper four levels can't be depended on. But those wind clouds I see out there at 4,000 feet can be depended on. Perhaps you might want to rethink the forecast, sergeant."

The sergeant laughed until there were tears in his eyes. "You're probably right about Payne, Baker," he laughed. "But, I really don't think we're going to get much for wind today. Look again at that report from Iron Mountain. Those winds are calm up there. The front must have gone back up north. Now you're not going to tell me that they're sleeping too."

"Well, I did phone them at 5:30 a.m.," I answered, "and nobody answered the phone. Nighttime weather observers who are awake usually answer their phones. Weather observers get so lonesome they're usually dying to talk to anyone."

Rogers, still bent over laughing, answered, "I appreciate your opinion, Baker, but I'm not changing the forecast."

I could see it was of little use. Leaving the sergeant at his forecaster's counter, I returned to the weather observer's room that housed the wind recorder. Quietly opening it's front glass door, I got some more red ink on my left hand. I was, after all, the official duty weather observer. Some things I could do myself. In a determined manner, I proceeded to file a special weather report, send Tinker AFB a procedure message, and phone the Desert Center tower on the emergency phone.

"Hello. This is Airman Baker. I'm the duty weather observer until 4:00 p.m. today," I informed the tower operator simply. "I'm closing Desert Center air base for all of today because of high and erratic winds. These winds are affecting the entire Palm Meadows valley.

"If you have any planes that need to land or take off, phone me on a case-by-case basis. Planes may only take off if they intend to fly to someplace far away such as Chicago. I don't want any planes to take off from Desert Center with the intention of landing here again today. I believe that these erratic winds make it too dangerous. I especially don't want any planes to take off headed for the gunnery ranges. It's just too dangerous."

"Roger, copy," responded the tower operator.

I continued, "Make certain the tower operators at Palm Meadows field have received the procedure message that I sent to Tinker. Make certain their tower operators understand that no airliners will be allowed to land here at Desert Center today, even under emergency conditions. Be sure to remind them that my procedure message forces them to implement stage two safety levels immediately. Remind them that stage two levels require that any airliner bound for Palm Meadows field must declare a low fuel emergency when they are down to two and a half hours of fuel. Remind them that such airliners must head immediately for the nearest safe alternate destination unless they are already on final approach. The nearest safe alternate destination is San Diego, California. Lastly, make certain they understand that no airliner may circle for more than ten minutes before heading for the safe alternate destination."

"Roger, copy," responded the operator. "You know of course, that more than 38 flights have been scheduled for the gunnery ranges this morning. Most of the guys will understand, but I've got one Colonel out there who's going to be angry when he hears about it."

"I understand," I responded. "The Colonel will just have to understand that I don't want to be looking at his guts draped over the sagebrush when I'm eating my noon sandwiches."

"Good luck, Charlie," laughed the operator. "I was working the tower that day last spring when you saved those six F105s. Don't worry, we'll close down Desert Center tight as a drum."

Hanging up the phone, I checked the clock. It was time for more ink stains. Then I washed my hands again and busied myself with my weather duties.

43

Time passed. The pleasant atmosphere of the weather station was broken at 7:15 a.m. Out front in the forecaster's room, the Colonel, his wingman, and three dozen other pilots trooped in for the flight level winds. I sat quietly listening as sergeant Rogers read them his best estimates. All altitudes were low values. The pilots carefully recorded these winds on their flight plans. They were all expecting winds of eight to ten miles per hour. Having finished their writing lessons, they trooped out to the base operations area of the building to file their flight plans. Of course, when they arrived, they received the bad news that Desert Center was closed due to high winds and would remain closed for the entire day. Soon, almost three dozen pilots could be seen trooping out the front of the building towards the bus stop. Having received the news, most of them were laughing and looking forward to spending another day relaxing downtown. The English Colonel was another matter.

"Sergeant! What's this about the base being closed because of high winds?" demanded the Colonel in a loud voice, trooping back into the weather station. "There are no winds whatever out there. Look out there at the windsock. I wouldn't make the wind out there to be more than eight miles an hour. It's going on 7:30 a.m. Now open the air base so I can get my men into the sky."

Of course, he was quite right. Sergeant Rogers, obviously taken by surprise, stuttered for a moment and came back to where I was. "Baker, what's going on?" he asked.

Standing my ground, I replied, "Well, Sergeant, I was forced to close Desert Center because of high and unpredictable winds. Here, look at the wind recorder. See, every now and then a high and unpredictable gust of wind comes through. The regulations from the weather command clearly state that the duty observer shall close the base at any time weather conditions threaten the safety of flight operations, or in the opinion of the duty weather observer, will threaten the safety of flight operations at anytime during the next two hours. So I did. Since I'm the duty observer, it's all perfectly according to regulations."

"How long do you expect to keep the base closed?" asked the sergeant.

"I am waiting for the inversion to break. Then I'll see what the winds are and decide if Desert Center can be reopened," I responded cheerfully. I added, "However, considering all of those wind clouds out there, I am expecting that it will be necessary to keep the base closed for the rest of the day."

"What about Payne at Mojave Wells?" asked the sergeant? "Has he called in the 7:30 winds yet?"

"Not yet," I answered. "But when he does, I can call you so that you can talk to him on the phone, if you'd like."

"Right. Do that," answered the sergeant. Then, returning to the forecasting station, he said to the Colonel, "You know the military, Colonel. Only the duty weather observer can close the base. Only the duty weather observer can reopen the base. He's waiting to see the 7:30 a.m. wind measurements from the gunnery ranges. Then we can talk things over and get this base opened again."

"I'll be back," stated the Colonel forcefully.

I busied myself with my weather duties and waited patiently for Payne to call. I tried phoning the Range Three weather shack myself. Still there was no answer. At 8:05 a.m. the phone finally rang. It was Payne. "I've got the 7:30 a.m. winds, Charlie," he stated authoritatively. "Are you ready to copy?"

"Jim, before you read them to me, I want to tell you that I have wind clouds all over down here. Those top four levels from the 4:30 a.m. run look awfully low. I'm willing to tell the sergeant that I copied the 4:30 winds wrong if these winds are a lot higher. So, if these wind values are kind of high, you know, like 35 or 40 miles per hour, don't worry about those 4:30 a.m. winds. We can easily change them."

"Why Charlie," said Payne laughing, "You know I'm just like you. I would never make up a set of wind measurements." Then he proceeded to read me another set of wind measurements that were identical to the 4:30 a.m. winds. Each altitude was eight to ten miles an hour out of the southwest. I pleaded with him but to no avail. I simply had no choice but to distribute the low values. Before Payne hung up, I called the sergeant to the phone. Their conversation left me without a leg to stand on. Low winds, clear skies, all gunnery ranges open. The next winds at Mojave Wells wouldn't be taken until 9:30 a.m.

While the sergeant was talking, however, I was able to get some more red ink on my fingers. The base stayed closed.

At 8:30a.m., the Colonel returned. Reading him the low wind values from the gunnery ranges was equivalent to bleeding in front of a shark. Taking him outside to show him the wind clouds that were now down to 3,000 over the mountains north of the base was a little like telling a hair-raising story to a bald headed man.

Since the Colonel wasn't in my chain of command, he couldn't order me to do anything. He knew it and I knew it. Since he was a Colonel, I couldn't actually argue with him, but I didn't have to open the base either. Once I had respectfully informed him that the base was closed and that

46

the base would not reopen until I judged that the existing weather conditions would allow his planes to operate safely, there wasn't much else I could explain to him. I did, however, stand quietly while he vented his spleen on me. Bird Colonels have big spleens. I did so for a good reason. It took time off the clock.

10:15 a.m. found me in the front office, standing respectfully in front of the Major's desk. Behind the desk stood the Major. At the next desk to the left sat Paul, the detachment records clerk. Standing beside me screaming, was the English Colonel.

"Damn it, Major," screamed the Colonel. "How much of this BS is a man supposed to take? This airman has had Desert Center closed since 6:30 a.m. He would have us believe that high winds are making flight operations dangerous. Look at those gunnery range winds! All three of these runs are identical. The 4:30 a.m. run, the 7:30 run, and now the 9:30 run are all the same. There's simply no wind out there whatever. Yet, this incompetent weather observer has my wingman, all 18 of my men, and me, sitting down in base operations twiddling our thumbs. We should be out flying. Look Major, our fighter planes are sitting right out there on the ramp all fueled and ready to go. My wingman, my men and I, none of us understand what is going on.

"I watched that windsock down at the end of the runway for a half hour. I never saw a wind higher than ten miles an hour. Yet, according to this idiot, four different times in that half hour, the winds were so strong they were blowing almost 35 miles an hour. He's got to be making them up, Major!

"We've tried everything! We've had the instrument technicians come in and check out the equipment. We've called Palm Meadows. Their winds are calm, but they're forcing all of the airliners to carry two and a half hours of extra fuel because of this airman here. We've called Iron Mountain. Their observer said they're wide open and calm. Then slammed down the phone on me. And me, I haven't found a wind high enough to launch a sparrow anywhere outside this doorway. Yet, this idiot right here has had this whole base locked down tighter than a drum since before dawn. He's even got George air base up by Barstow scared out of their wits. He phoned their tower two hours ago with his make believe winds, and got them to move to a stage one high wind alert. Because of him, right now they're only allowing two of their planes to take off and use the gunnery ranges at a time. Everybody else has to sit on the parking ramp until those first two get back. Nobody can even take off until those first two land. And Major, even that wasn't good enough for him! He went and argued with their tower operators because they are only requiring their fighters to carry 45 minutes of reserve fuel. He's trying to get them to require two and a half hours of reserve fuel too."

I quietly stood my ground. I knew well how the military operated.

"Well, airman Baker, I think the Colonel deserves an answer to his questions, don't you?" stated the Major simply.

"Well sir," I answered respectfully, "For a pilot as experienced as the Colonel and his wingman, taking off is never the problem. They can take off in any kind of weather. What I'm worried about is whether or not the Colonel and his men will have a safe place to land.

"I don't believe the Mojave Wells gunnery range winds, sir. Maybe Payne is losing the balloon against the clouds or something, but I can't believe that those winds are correct. If you would care to look out that open window, you can see those wind clouds over the mountains just north of the field. They are now down to less than 1,500 feet. As my 6:00 a.m. weather report clearly shows, four hours ago they were at 4,000 feet. According to everyone's forecast, those clouds shouldn't be there at all. Those unexpected clouds have convinced me to close the base until we all have a better understanding of what the weather is doing.

"Then sir, if you will check that little mountain off to the northeast. You see how it has a small wind cloud above it? For that mountain to have any clouds, I believe that the winds above this inversion layer have to be much higher than 45 miles an hour. As both of you officers are well aware, such high winds are quite dangerous to flight operations.

"Of course I phoned the Palm Meadows airport and George airbase, sir. I also phoned Las Vegas, Yuma, Phoenix, El Centro, Salt Lake City, and Iron Mountain a second time. It's my duty. The regulations clearly state that if I observe anything that is a danger to flight operations, I am required to notify everyone who is in danger.

"Major, that's why I closed the base. If the Colonel and his men had taken off as planned this morning, they would now be very low on fuel and just starting back towards Desert Center. If I have judged those winds correctly, the Colonel and his men would be in very serious trouble. They wouldn't be able to land. They wouldn't be able to stay flying. They wouldn't be able to parachute out."

The Colonel's face was distorted with rage. He could no longer contain himself. Screaming at the Major and slamming his fist onto the desk, he bellowed, "I want them all! Damn it, Major! This man has stripes on his arm! I want them all! Never have I seen such insubordination and such incompetence! I know what I can do with my planes and what I can't. I don't need this incompetent idiot telling me the difference! I want him court-martialed Major, and I want him court-martialed now! Those damn high winds he's reporting are all make believe!! I know we're not in the same chain of command, but you'll court-martial this yellow haired insubordinate airman now, or I'll complain up the ladder until we are in the same chain of command!"

The Colonel was just finishing this latest tirade when, at last, the inversion broke. Sounding like a line of distant rolling thunder, open doors could be heard slamming shut all through the building. Suddenly and without warning, the winds started blowing for real. As the four of us, frozen in time, watched, winds of 60 to 80 miles per hour raced across the base, tipping over garbage cans, ripping down signs, tearing down traffic lights. I remember watching a large cardboard box as it was lifted, then blown into the weather station window. Then it was carried off toward the distant mountains.

We all stood in shock and none of us knew what to say. Even I was in shock. I could hardly believe that so many weathermen had been so wrong.

While we stood there, the phone rang. Paul answered the phone and listened for a minute or so. Then he turned to me and said, "It's the Palm Meadows tower. They've just had an accident and they've been forced to close the airport. They'll need a weather report from us as part of their accident report. They report that because of the wind, three single engine Cessna airplanes that had been parked on the ramp have been blown on to the active runway. The planes were empty and no one was injured. They report that the inversion has just broken. Their winds are 60 miles per hour gusting to 85. They are ordering all inbound airliners to divert to San Diego. Because level two safety precautions were already in effect, all of their airliners are expected to make it into San Diego with no trouble.

"They report that all of their emergency equipment is available to help us if we need it. Fire trucks and ambulances are standing by, located next to their east-west runway. They want to know how many planes we have trapped aloft over the gunnery ranges and what they can do to help."

I would have answered, and I suppose the Major would have answered. But before either of us could say anything, the Colonel took the phone from Paul. Speaking forcefully into the phone, he said in an otherwise normal tone of voice, "Palm Meadows Tower, This is Colonel Harrison. Desert Center has no planes trapped aloft anywhere because Desert Center has the best weather observer in the U.S. Air Force. He'll break all the rules just to get things done right. We appreciate your offer of help, and we may take you up on it in the future. But for today, at least, you can send your fire trucks and ambulances back to their bases. I'll need a copy of your accident report as soon as it's available. It needs to be attached to the airman's commendation medal which the Major will be requesting."

Then he simply hung up the phone. It had hardly been hung up when it rang again. Paul answered. The Colonel, the Major and I waited quietly and patiently while Paul took notes. Then, after a couple of minutes, he turned to me and said, "It's the tower down at George airbase. They've just closed George. Their inversion broke about two minutes ago. Their winds are 55 miles per hour, gusting to 80. They have two fighter planes trapped aloft over their gunnery ranges. The two planes have 45 minutes of fuel left and are in serious trouble. Desert Center is the only base they have fuel enough to make it to. They called us because you're here, Charlie. George wants to know what to do?"

Taking the phone from Paul, I said calmly, "George tower, there's no chance of making a safe landing at Desert Center. The winds are too high. But, don't panic. We can get your men down safely. Tell your two planes to head as slow as safely possible, down towards El Centro, California. I know they don't have enough fuel to make it all the way to El Centro, but there won't be much wind down there. Tell your pilots to stay together and to fly directly over the city of Indio, California. Then have them follow the highway south along the west shore of the Salton Sea. Tell them they'll be landing on the highway right next to the little town of Salton Shores. The road there is flat and level. Have the state police block off the highway. They'll need a couple of experienced pilots to talk them down and help them land on the highway. It happens that we have a highly experienced Colonel and his wingman standing by. They're really good at checking winds, working with new pilots, and talking down planes. They're just perfect for this sort of thing. I'm sure it won't be any problem for them to take off from Desert Center and meet up with your planes on the way to El Centro. That way, when your planes have to land on the highway, there'll be two experienced pilots flying right beside them to talk them down safely. After your two planes are safely on the highway and the State Police have arrived, the Colonel and his wingman can continue on to Navy Mirmar at San Diego. You get your planes started. I'll get the Colonel and his wingman into the air right away."

Hanging up the phone, I turned to the Colonel and said, "They need your help desperately Colonel, you and your wingman. You can expect the winds to be 45 gusting to 60 on take off. I'll phone Desert Center tower right now and tell them you and your wingman, are cleared for takeoff. Desert Center will stay closed for another whole day so after you get those two new pilots landed safely on the highway down by the Salton Shores, you and your wingman have a couple of days in San Diego.

"By the way, Colonel, you're really good at judging the winds. Don't let all of those fake wind gusts on the chart recorder shake your judgment. Those new guys are really going to need your help when you get there."

The Colonel grabbed my hand and shaking it, exclaimed, "You're the best, airman. You're just the best." Then he hurried out to base operations. As I stood waiting to be dismissed by the Major, we could hear the Colonel. His loud strong voice carried easily throughout the building. He was happy as a lark. "Men, listen up. We don't have time to screw around. Wilson and I have to make an emergency flight down to El Centro to save the lives of a couple of new pilots trapped up there in these high winds. Gonzales! You're in command until we return. We'll be gone for two days. While Wilson and I are gone, I want you men to inspect all of the golf courses downtown. When we get back, we'll want a full report. We'll want to know about the clubhouses, the putting greens, and the condition of all those women caddies. Now get on it! That's an order.

"Wilson, tell base ops it's an emergency and we'll file our flight plans when we get back. Make sure they understand that we're bird Colonels and that we don't have time for all their silly paper work!"

Yes, the Colonel certainly seemed to be a happy man. Through the station window, I could see the Colonel and his wingman running to their airplanes. The Major finally spoke to me. He seemed unusually serious. "You better call the tower and get those planes in the air, airman Baker. Then get a hold of Payne as soon as you can. Tell him to use the weather truck and come down here immediately. I want to talk with him alone in my office."

Then, laughing a little, the Major said, "Oh, ah, and airman Baker, you get a more realistic wind gust when you use the ring finger on your left hand instead of your little finger. It's just one of those things that a man learns over the years. You're dismissed, now, airman. You may return to your duties."

Getting Payne on the telephone was a lot easier than I had expected. It was now 10:45 a.m. Of course, I was back to being alone in the weather observer's room. I was just hanging up the emergency phone to the Desert Center tower when my regular phone rang. On the other end, Payne was nearly hysterical. "Charlie, you've got to help me. I'm in big trouble up here," he exclaimed. "It's just like you said. The inversion broke and the winds must be blowing 80 miles an hour out at Range Three. You have to stop all of the planes that are coming up here this afternoon. You have to give me time to get out to Range Three and take a wind measurement. You got to stall them or something, but whatever you do, Charlie, don't let them take off!"

"Don't worry Payne," I said. "I've had Desert Center closed since early this morning. There aren't any planes coming up there for at least the next two days.

"The Major wants me to tell you that you should cancel the rest of the day's runs and drive down here as soon as you can. He seems to be angry about those three earlier runs. I think he's planning on taking away one of your stripes under an article fifteen."

"Oh, those runs," said Payne showing obvious apprehension. "Is there any way to get those back and change them?"

"I'm afraid not Payne," I answered. "But, I'll tell you what, there's a very simple way for us to get you out of this mess."

"I hope so!" exclaimed Payne, showing obvious dread. "You know the Air Force. They'll court martial me over this. Those officers will never understand why I refuse to go out onto Range Three, even with Steve along. They'll never understand how terrifying nights on those ranges become whenever Range Four Harry is walking around out in the sagebrush. One night Harry was able to surprise the two of us. Steve and I had to stand there with our backs together for a half hour while Harry just stood out in the sagebrush laughing at us."

"Don't worry," I responded. "I understand completely.

"Now to begin with, if the Major asks, I'll tell him you haven't phoned yet. I'll tell him the range crew reports that you're taking a special balloon run because the weather has changed dramatically.

"You and Steve drive out to Range Three with them as soon as you can. Release a balloon and take a real wind measurement. Of course, in these winds, your balloon is going to be blown out of sight after only three or four minutes in the air. Now make sure that your wind report ends after only three or four altitudes and states that the run ended early because the balloon was blown out of sight.

"Phone this special report in to me right at noon. I'll make sure the Major is standing right here when you phone and everything looks like a coincidence. After you read me the winds, you tell me that the reason the winds on those other runs are so low is because the winds were so strong this morning that they couldn't be measured. Tell me the balloons were blowing out of sight before you realized what was happening, and you got confused searching for them. Then tell me that on those three earlier runs, you must have been tracking stars or clouds or something. Say this loudly with emotion. I'll hold up the phone so the Major can hear it. He'll think he's accidentally listening in on our conversation and he'll believe what you're saying. That way, you'll be off the hook."

"Right Charlie. I'm going to owe you one big favor when this is over," said Payne gratefully.

"Don't worry about it. Remember your story. The high winds blew the balloons out of sight before you realized what was happening. You took a reading. Then you looked down at the clipboard as you were recording the numbers, and when you looked back the balloon was gone. When you went looking for the balloon using the theodolite, you thought you found it, but you must have been mistaken. You must have just been looking at distant clouds or something. Stick to your story. The worst that can happen is that they'll send me up there for a couple of days to train you some more and the two of us will have a good time swimming in the Mojave Wells pool.

"Remember Payne, there haven't been any airplane crashes or anything down here. Nobody has been injured. I haven't let anybody take off all morning. By now, most of the pilots are down in town having fun. Nobody's going to remember your morning winds for more than a couple of days."

"Thanks, Charlie," said Payne. Then he hung up.

The plan worked perfectly. The paper 'jammed' in my teletype machines at 11:58 a.m. so the Major was forced to answer my phones while I got some more. It was a great coincidence, and Payne got off with a serious lecture on the importance of accurate wind measurements.

By 4:00 p.m. everyone in the station was laughing happily. The TV news report showed the Colonel and his wingman from Desert Center, heroically saving the lives of two new pilots as they made a forced landing on California highway 86. It did wonders for everyone's morale. Even sergeant O'Keefe was impressed with the skill the English Colonel displayed when he chased the cars off a three-mile stretch of highway so the new pilots had a clear stretch to land on. "It was just like an Englishman," O'Keefe said, "to come right in, take over, and not depend on that nice Irish state policeman to get there in time."

Of course, the Major never did realize that I was the one who phoned the television station so the TV news cameramen could be there. We all worked hard at Desert Center. Some recognition, now and then, I figured, wouldn't hurt us. It made us all like each other better, Irishman and Englishman alike.

Shadow Run

... "It is easy for the shadow to advance 10 steps,"
Hezekiah answered.
"Rather, let it go back ten steps."
... 2 Kings 21:10

The winds were gentle that gorgeous summer day out at Range Three. The gunnery ranges at Mojave Wells were simply captivating. I had just completed my 9:30 a.m. balloon run. The ranges weren't in use so I was expecting a very easy day. Desert Center had informed me that I needed to make only one more run, the 12:00 noon run. Then the rest of the day was mine.

I was reading a book on gold and mineral prospecting. I had checked it out from the base library. Since this part of the desert was covered with many beautiful rocks and had never been adequately prospected, I imagined that if I knew more about gold nuggets I might accidentally find one.

I had always lived a clean, drug-free life. It included soda pop, potato chips, a beer once in a while, gambling, playing pool, dancing, and otherwise having fun. "Wouldn't that be a surprise if God rewarded me by leading me to a great big gold strike right out here in the desert," I laughed? "What's a summer without dreams?"

On the walls of my weather shack I had posted two highly detailed topographical maps of the valley and of the surrounding mountains. One was a flat printed wall map with elevation contours. The other was a 3D plastic relief map, also with elevation contours. The maps were very large. Each map was more than 4 feet square and showed objects separated by only a few feet. The Base supply depot had obtained the maps from the US Geological Service and surprisingly, neither map showed a section of mountains and valley that lay some 50 or 70 miles off to the north and northeast. Instead, the maps showed nothing in that area and had labeled it "Unexplored Territory".

With my library book in hand and singing one of my favorite songs, I carefully reviewed the geology of the valley around me. "There must be gold nuggets laying out there somewhere," I assured myself. "All I have to do is find them." Then I laughed some more, "According to my orders, if I find them, I get to keep them."

I studied the two maps carefully as I mentally recalled my orders. The Pentagon neurosurgeon had told me directly, "I'm going to give your commanding officer, the major, the following orders. Only you may be stationed at Mojave Wells. You will be stationed up there alone, and you will be stationed up there until further notice. You will never be ordered off the ranges, even if the ranges are closed due to an emergency.

"You may go anywhere you wish on the ranges, at anytime you wish. That includes day or night, weekends and holidays. You are also allowed to go as far out as you wish, anytime you wish. No guard is ever allowed to say 'No' to you, even at night.

"No other weather observer may be stationed with you. If you get sick, then no one may replace you. Taking the wind measurements will cease until you have fully recovered. If you have an accident when you're out there, then you must bring yourself safely home.

"If you need to be relieved for a few weeks to take your annual leave, then your friend Payne, and your friend Dwight, as a team may relieve you. This two-man team,

Payne and Dwight, must be together at all times, even to visit the bathroom. They may relieve you for no more than two weeks, once every six months.

"Under any circumstances, no married observer, other than Dwight, may ever be stationed at the gunnery ranges. Only those single observers whom I have approved may be stationed at the gunnery ranges. In every case they must be part of a two or three man team, and in every case the team may not spend more than 3 days and 2 nights at Mojave Wells, with no more than one assignment per man per year. Under no circumstances is any weather observer except you, ever allowed more than one half mile from the immediate roads between the Mojave Wells base and the weather shacks. No observer, except you, is ever allowed to visit places such as the ammunition bunkers out at Range Three or the arroyo at Range One. In addition, no observer, except you, is ever allowed to travel beyond Range Three, or to be on the road to Range Four.

Every weather observer, except you, must report immediately to the Desert Center base neurosurgeon for debriefing. They must do so upon return from any trip or any assignment to the Mojave Wells ranges. They must be debriefed, even if the trip was only an afternoon trip to deliver supplies. Upon their return, as soon as they enter the Desert Center gate, they must report to the neurosurgeon. That's everyone, including the Major and Sergeant Walters, no exceptions, except you."

"Except me?" I had asked, sitting in quiet wonderment.

"Yes," he answered. "Everyone except you. Nothing about your assignment is classified, nothing whatsoever. You have total control over everything that you see, that you hear, or that you do. The only rule is that whatever you do, you must do it alone.

You are never to report for debriefing. Whatever you see, whatever you hear, whatever you experience, you need never tell anyone unless you wish to. You may tell anyone you wish, or no one if you so wish. You may tell them every single detail and experience, as often as you wish, or you may tell them nothing. It's all totally up to you. Just remember, if you ever feel overwhelmed, if you ever feel that you need to talk to one of us about your experiences, just phone the neurosurgeon, day or night, or phone the duty officer here at Desert Center. The base medical commander, or myself, will personally and immediately come to you. There will be no questions asked. The two of us, myself, and the base medical commander, are authorized to use the emergency medical helicopter for transportation. Ours is the highest priority. We are ordered not to ask you any questions! We have been ordered not to keep any records of such meetings. You will never be criticized, reproached, or disciplined for asking to see either one of us. Do you understand your orders?"

"Yes," I had answered at the time. Now, I laughed loudly, "Yes, and I'll be keeping all of the gold nuggets that I find. I may even need the helicopter to help me bring them back." Life was good in those days.

The maps clearly showed that a number of arroyos came down from the nearby mountains and fed into the dry lakebed of Range Four. There were two places of special interest. One lay on the northeast edge of the dry lakebed. The other lay on the southwest edge of the dry lakebed. Surely, I supposed, those would be natural places for gold nuggets to collect. The lakebed was more than 5 miles across so the two places were several miles apart. So I decided that as soon as I had completed the 12:00 noon run, this would be a perfect day to go both joy-riding and prospecting for gold.

The afternoon winds were light and variable all the way up to 20,000 feet, and it was very hot. My 12:30 p.m. run measured the Range Three temperature at 112 degrees. "The temperatures out on that dry lakebed up at Range Four must be soaring to 120 degrees," I laughed to myself, "That heat will make the gold real shiny and easy to find."

I had developed the habit of carrying a second fatigue hat with me for safety. Usually I kept it in my truck. One hot day a couple of weeks before, I had put my regular fatigue hat in my back pocket while I was taking the noon balloon run. When the run was over, a gentle gust of wind seemed to come along. Then my watch stopped suddenly and my mind seemed to fuzz over for a moment. After I was able to shake off the dizziness, I found that I was badly sunburned and I couldn't find my hat. I spent so much time looking for it that I didn't get the winds phoned in to Desert Center until almost 3:00 p.m. in the afternoon. I finally had to drive in to Mojave Wells without it. The next morning when I opened up my weather shack I found my hat lying on the floor directly in front of the door.

Today, I dreamed, I would find so many gold nuggets laying out on the open desert up there that, like every true prospector, I would take off my first hat and fill it with gold nuggets to bring back with me. Then, naturally laughing, I would need to put on my second hat to protect me from the harsh desert sun. "Why dream if you're not going to dream big," I asked myself? Yes, I laughed my way through life in those days.

I took the noon meal at the chow hall and told my friend Smokey the head cook where I was going. I came back out early and brought extra water, some sandwiches, and a full tank of gas with me. My truck had a spare tire and was running in near perfect condition.

Surprisingly, Smokey had tried to talk me out of my planned afternoon adventure. I was not to be put off. As I was leaving the chow hall, Smokey reassured me. He said that all of the range rats and maintenance men were on base mowing lawns and if he hadn't seen me again by the end of evening chow at 7:00 p.m., he would assemble them and come looking for me, regardless of orders.

After finishing the noon balloon run and phoning the results in to Desert Center, I loaded my book and my other supplies into my truck, shut everything down, and headed north up the valley on the Range Four road. Because of the heat, I had both truck windows rolled down and the vents open. I had all of my food and water supplies sitting in front on the floor on the passenger side. On the seat next to me, I had placed my second fatigue hat, and I was holding it down with my book on gold prospecting.

The road from the Mojave Wells base out to Range Three was paved. However, the pavement ended when it reached the square graveled area where the Range Three buildings stood. The road north towards Range Four was nothing but dirt and rocks for the entire 20 miles or so up the valley. It began on the north side of the Range Three graveled area. It continued north between the control tower and the range billboards.

Just past the range boards was an intersection with another road that lead over to a concrete ammunition bunker located at the base of the valley's eastern mountains. This bunker road was narrow, paved, and one and a quarter miles long. When it reached the base of the mountains, it turned into gravel, turned to the north and ran for a quarter of a mile along the mountains, ending finally in front of the concrete bunker and its heavy wooden door.

I had to be very careful on the drive out to Range Four. The dirt road was rocky in some places near the top of the first ridge. However, after I made it over the first ridge it got easier, finally smoothing out and sloping down an easy hill for the last 10 miles of so. I paid close attention as I drove. I was singing loudly and traveling a good 45 mph by the time I was down the hill and coming into the Range Four building area. I was therefore, quite surprised when the engine of my truck suddenly began misfiring and running rough. By the time reached the generator shack I was traveling barely 5 mph. Then my engine quit altogether and I was forced to let my truck just roll to a stop.

The buildings at Range Four were similar to those at Range Three. They were arranged in a narrow graveled square area. There was a generator shack, a couple of supply sheds, a weather shack and a lounge building. The Range Four lounge was designed differently than the Range Three lounge and had a nearby well and indoor plumbing. Of course, one of the diesels generators had to be running in order for the pump to work.

There were also four old wooden aircraft hangers sitting connected side by side. They were positioned along the northern side of the graveled area where the gravel met the southern edge of the dry sandy lakebed. Each hanger was large enough to hold a large semi truck with a mountain-sized trailer. Each hanger had movable doors both front and back. The wooden doors hung on steel rails and were too heavy to be blown around, even in the highest winds. Just the same, they were exceptionally well maintained and something about their design made them easy to operate. Any child, it seemed, could open or close them. This afternoon the front doors to the first hanger on the left had been rolled partly open. All of the other hanger doors were closed. I found this surprising because after the morning balloon run from Range Three I had used my theodolite to visually inspect Range Four from a distance. At that time, all of the hanger doors had been rolled completely closed.

The Range Four road did not end at Range Four. It continued through the square graveled area and on between an open space between the lounge building and the aircraft hangers. It continued slightly northwest out across the dry lakebed for a half-mile or so. This strip of the lakebed was mostly open packed dirt and soft sand. Then the road turned to the north and northeast and abruptly entered a zone of unusually dense sagebrush and tall mesquite. Then it continued on across the lakebed for perhaps another 5 miles through more heavy sagebrush and tall mesquite. Finally it turned straight north and continued up the valley, up over ridges and arroyos for perhaps another 100 miles, on towards the mountains at the north end of the valley.

My truck wouldn't restart. It behaved as if its new battery was totally dead. Frustrated, I set the parking brake and stepped out onto the hot gravel. I opened the hood and checked the battery. It was in perfect shape and full of fluid. So were the belts and radiator. Swearing, I closed the hood, and took a drink of water from my canteen. Then I made the short walk over to the lounge building and tried the phone inside. The phone line was well maintained but I found it to be useless. The dial tone appeared to be overwhelmed by static. I was surprised by the way the receiver tingled in my hand. After all, I had not started the diesel generator.

I decided to open a few windows, rest in the cool interior of the lounge, and plan my next move. However, when I attempted to open the first window, the static tingling in the metal window frame was quite unnerving so I let the window remained closed. Then when I reached for the nearby metal frame chair, it too, tingled so much that I instinctively let go of it. Even the air in the room seemed to be filled with static tingling. Nervous and jumpy, I quickly left the lounge for the safety of the fresh air outside.

Outside, I was going to wait out the afternoon by my truck or over in the little used weather shack. However, as I was exiting the lounge building I caught a glimpse of a portion of a large white object sitting out on the range road as it continued to the north out across the dry lakebed. The object sat mostly hidden just beyond the wall of the thick sagebrush and mesquite that was located a half mile north along the road. The object was about the size of a large RV or camping trailer.

Because of the glare of the desert sun, the intense heat waves coming off the lakebed, and the few seconds that I had to look at it, I wasn't able to discern much. It was covered with a uniform white fuzzy haze. I could make out a few windows that reminded me of the front of a passenger train engine. It seemed to silently rise up a few feet and float slowly for a quarter mile or so, back north up the range road. Then, almost completely hidden by the mesquite, it appeared to sit back down on the lakebed. After a couple of minutes or so, the tingling in the air seemed to go away.

Curious, I took a drink of water from my canteen, adjusted my fatigue hat, put on my sunglasses, and began strolling casually out between the buildings, onto the dry lakebed. I was going to hike out to get a better look at the white object. I left the hard packed dirt road and took a direct route across the soft beach-like sand. I hadn't gotten very far when the air began tingling again. Then, as I watched through the occasional gaps in the mesquite, the white object silently lifted up, and resumed floating slowly along the road until it was more than two miles north of me. Then it sat back down on the road as before and the tingling went away.

For want of anything better, I resumed walking north in its direction. When I finally reached the wall of sagebrush and mesquite I realized how senseless it was for me to be chasing mirages out in the desert on a hot day like today. Laughing at myself then, I turned around and began retracing my steps across the soft sand back to the edge of the lakebed.

Walking in the soft sand was quite tiring. My boots sunk deep into the sand and left a very distinctive trail. When I arrived again at the opening between the buildings, I noticed the control tower. It sat a few hundred feet off to the west, just north of four more supply sheds. The range boards, ranges and targets sat out in the desert beyond it. All four supply sheds sat with their doors closed. My gold prospecting areas were too far away for me to walk to in this heat, so I decided that I would walk over to the tower, climb up the wooden stairs, and from the top, maybe get a good look at everything. So I took another drink of water, began singing one of my favorite songs, and walked over to the base of the control tower.

The control tower was similar to the tower back at Range Three. It stood 30 feet or so high with a balcony, a cab, and windows at the top. It was painted red and white and had a wooden stairway at the back that lead to the top. I was standing on the first step with my back to the supply sheds. I was just beginning to step up to the second step when an unusual gentle breeze blew some sand past me. My mind seemed to fuzz over momentarily. After a few seconds I was able to shake off the dizziness and get a new grip on the wooden railing. During the process of doing so I had gotten turned around and I was now coming down the tower. I felt thirsty again so I took another drink of water. Then I noticed that my watch had stopped. Since it was a windup mechanical watch, I rewound it, shook it, and got it running again. Then I noticed that the tower shadows had changed. It seemed as if a half hour or 45 minutes had suddenly passed. Far to the north I could see the white object sitting on the range road, now more than 4 miles away. In my mind, my memory put up one or two quick flashes or glimpses of two white things rushing up on me from behind. Then I noticed my boot prints in the soft sand. One set approached the tower from the opening by the lounge as expected. However, a second set followed from the base of the tower steps over to one of the empty supply sheds and back again. That supply shed now sat with its front door open.

The whole experience left me feeling very unnerved, so I abandoned my plan to scale the tower. I came down off the stairs and returned to the range road where it passed through the opening between the buildings by the lounge. When I arrived at the open space, I stood for a few minutes, admiring the beauty of the dry lakebed on this hot afternoon. I decided to try prospecting for gold one last time before giving up on the plan. Straight east of me along the southern edge of the dry lakebed, perhaps a quarter of a mile away, was the mouth of a very small gully that contained some colorful rocks. As I studied it through the heat waves, it also appeared to contain one or two chalk white suitcases of medium size. I decided to check it out so I turned to the east, and began walking slowly towards it through the soft sand. I wasn't singing at the time. I was following along behind the four aircraft hangers. I was about halfway past the third one when I suddenly heard an unusually loud meadowlark sound coming from behind the far eastern end of the hanger. Then I heard a second such sound coming loudly from the other side of the hanger on my right, from out on the graveled area of Range Four. Then, from out in the mesquite to my left, I heard the bark or woof of a dog. The chorus ended finally with a loud whinny sound coming from the same area in the mesquite, as if coming from a horse. Alarmed, I stopped immediately. Then from my memory another image suddenly flashed across my mind. In the image, I was standing facing the eastern wall in the supply shed down behind the tower. In the image my head was turned diagonally to the left and I was saying to someone who was standing outside by the door, "Why are you out here?"

Fear began welling up within me. I decided to leave the dry lakebed and Range Four as quickly as I could. I turned around and began hurrying back to the dirt road and the opening between the buildings. It wasn't possible to run in the soft sand and hurrying was very tiring. When I was just a few feet from the hard dirt road and the open space, I stopped to rest and plan my next moves. I decided that as soon as I got back onto the range road, I should collect all of my water from the truck and began walking back towards Range Three. Even though I could not carry nearly enough water to last 2 hours in this hot sun, let alone make it the full 20 miles back in to the Range Three area, at least it would be easy for the range rats to find me when they came out looking at 7:00 p.m.... even if I were passed out from sunstroke at the time. It wasn't much of a plan, but I was becoming too terrified to think of anything else.

Having rested then, I resumed walking. Finally, I reached the hard dirt road, turned, and went quickly through the opening between the hanger on my left and the Range Four lounge on my right. I had just passed by the open hanger door when suddenly I heard another loud meadowlark sound, another unusual gentle gust of wind passed through the graveled area, and something suddenly came up on me from behind. Moving too fast for me to react, it touched me on my left temple. Once again my mind suddenly fuzzed over and my muscles tightened. For a moment it seemed as if I was dreaming. It seemed like I was standing in a cool corner of the nearby aircraft hanger and someone was saying, "We can't let you kill yourself trying to walk in to base in this hot sun, Charlie. Just wait here in the shade for a while."

It seemed like it took me only a minute or so to shake off the dizziness, curse the heat, catch my breath, and get the blood flowing again in my arms and legs. There seemed to be a flurry of activity in and behind the last hanger on the east, but I was too dizzy at the time to turn to see what it was. I had to fight off some nausea by bending over at the waist while I practiced breathing deeply for several more minutes. Then I exercised my arms and legs by walking back and forth side to side a short distance on the gravel. Finally, after a few minutes, my mind cleared and my muscles relaxed. I stopped in the middle of the graveled square and took stock of my situation. Unaccountably, I felt perfectly Ok, perfectly alone, and I was no longer afraid. Then I noticed that my watch had stopped and, once again, the shadows had moved a very large distance. In disbelief, I turned around and walked the short distance back to the edge of the dry lakebed. The tower now cast the long shadows of late afternoon. More than two hours had to have passed while I was fighting off the dizziness. In shock and confusion and shaking my head in disbelief, I turned back towards the graveled area. Then I noticed that my truck sat in front of the generator shack with the door on the driver's side open, almost inviting me to get back in and drive it. Confused and curious, I hurried over to my truck, climbed in, and turned the key. It started immediately. Laughing, thanking God, and too happy for words, I closed the driver's side door, fastened my seat belt, turned the truck around in record time, and headed back towards Mojave wells at full speed. On the way back I visually checked my supplies. Everything was in good order except my second fatigue hat. It was nowhere to be found. It remained missing for two and a half months. Then, one morning I opened up my weather shack at Range Three and found it sitting on the floor just inside the front door. It had been washed and cleaned.

The Rabbit Test

"... As long as the earth lasts,
seedtime and harvest,
cold and heat,
Summer and winter,
and day and night
shall not cease."
... Genesis 8:22

"Fear of the dark is a desire for the mother's presence," I laughed to myself. Then I gave up on trying to start the diesel generator. For no obvious reason, it behaved as if all 20 batteries attached to the starting motor were dead. My flashlight with its new batteries was in the same state, although it had worked perfectly when I was unlocking the main range gate this morning. It was very unusual for the padlock on the main gate to be actually locking the gate. Usually it just hung unused on the nearby fence. I thought nothing of it, took out my spare key, opened it right up, and drove on through. After all, the rules did say I could go anywhere I wanted.

Then my truck engine had suddenly quit on me when I was still more than a half-mile from Range Three. I had silently trudged the distance in near total darkness. The thin sliver of the moon had just risen. It was in its late fourth quarter so there was very little moonlight. Taking the morning balloon run was going to require patience and skill, especially since my usually reliable watch had kept stopping ever since I got out of my truck.

As I came out of the generator shack I stumbled over something in the darkness. I took a bad fall onto the hard gravel. However, except for a few bruises and scrapes, I wasn't hurt. My dark green work fatigues had protected me well. I brushed myself off and sat up in the shadows next to the generator shack with my back to the shack wall. Just 3 or 4 feet from me, blocking the doorway, calmly sat the large jackrabbit that I had obviously tripped over. I immediately realized that it could not possibly have been sitting there when I entered the shack. It was one of two or three such rabbits that occasionally sat out in the sagebrush next to the graveled portion of the Range Three area. I never fed the rabbits and they were quite wild. They commonly took off running at the first sight of me. Normally, the rabbits never sought my presence. As I sat there thinking, the rabbit gently closed the distance between the two of us until it sat beside me in the shadows, just out of arm's reach. I found this alarming. "What is out there in the darkness," I wondered to myself, "that scares the rabbit so badly that it comes to me for protection? Only frightened rabbits don't run away."

Not finding any answers to my questions, I laughed off the incident, picked myself up, left the rabbit sitting where it was, and began the walk over to my weather shack. As I reached the corner of the generator shack, I began singing one of my favorite songs. Suddenly, I heard a loud whinny, as if from a horse, emanate from behind the Range Three Lounge. Then I heard a short flurry of activity from over that way. Finally the silence of the desert night returned. The whole affair made me nervous and I hurried on towards the safety of my weather shack, singing loudly as I did so. Once I was inside I left the front door and the side door open. I could perform the entire balloon run in near total darkness, but having some moonlight stream in through the open doors was a big help. It also let me keep an active lookout to help calm my nerves.

I would have phoned Desert Center for a time check but my phone was totally dead. I was back outdoors measuring the temperature of the air when something out in the desert spooked a large sea gull which had been sleeping on the balcony of the control tower. It went flying past me just above the sagebrush heading down towards the southeast, screaming alarms as it did so. Although nervous about the way the morning run was progressing, I laughed it off too. Then I went back into my shack to attach the battery and its light to my balloon. The battery was a dry chemical battery that became active after soaking in water for a minute. Each battery could be used only once. This morning, new battery and all, the process failed. Having little choice, I filled a white balloon, attached the battery with its non-working light for weight control, laughed at my non-working watch, carried the balloon out to the theodolite stand and released it. Then singing one of my usual songs to help me as I guessed at the times, I began taking the readings. This was a very difficult task because the theodolite's battery powered scale lights would not operate. There wasn't much wind and the balloon rose straight up, but without the balloon's light working I immediately lost the white balloon against the star fields of the Milky Way. The first four readings were worthless. Then, as the balloon rose above 4,000 feet, the balloon's light started working. I readjusted the theodolite and began taking actual readings as best I could. I suddenly realized that my truck, my flashlight, and my watch had all stopped working almost 4,000 feet down the road. "Is there really a force field," I wondered, "affecting everything electrical and everything metal for a distance of 4,000 feet in every direction, even in the direction straight up?"

The idea didn't seem possible. "After all," I reasoned, "my truck and its 12 volt battery had operated quite well when I went joy-riding directly underneath the high voltage electrical transmission lines which served greater Los Angeles. To overpower a 12 volt circuit at half a mile using the known laws of physics, would require a force field that was much more powerful than could be generated by Hoover dam. And if the rabbit and I were standing in such a field, why weren't we both being fried?" Laughing at myself, I decided that this was just a night full of coincidences.

When my balloon run was completed, I locked up my theodolite and trudged back to my weather shack. Performing the wind calculations without so much as a flashlight to help me was quite a feat. As I was working and sitting silently at my desk in the shadowy darkness of my weather shack, I noticed three men about my height wearing dark blue uniforms, nervously step out from the darkness behind the Range Three lounge. They walked quickly and quietly straight east, crossing the range four road and passing in front of the Range Three outhouse, stopping at last on the paved area behind the Range Three billboards. Two of them walked like older men unused to the desert. The men obviously did not wish for me to see them. One of them spent a few minutes peeking around the edge of the range boards trying to locate me. He was obviously confused as to where I might be. Based on the few muffled words I could pick up, he was apparently afraid that I might be walking around over on the other side of the lounge building. Under the circumstances I thought it best if I just stayed sitting in my weather shack, hidden in the shadows.

I quickly completed my wind calculations. With my phone not working, I made a copy of the results and put it in my pocket. I could phone them in from the chow hall as soon as I could get back in to base. I now had a decision to make. Had I been alone, I would have walked over to the lounge building and phoned both Desert Center and the chow hall. Failing that, I would have just rested until daylight, knowing that the range maintenance men would come looking for me when I didn't show up for breakfast. However, the men hiding behind the range boards appeared to me to be high ranking Air Force officers. Those officers, I supposed, had come out here in a truck and would understand my need for help with my truck. It seemed reasonable, then, for me to walk over to where they were and ask for their help. Addressing a Colonel or a General would have made me nervous anyway, but the way they continued to hide behind the range boards really made me edgy. However, it was 22 miles back in to base, so driven by necessity, I very quietly got up from my chair, stepped outside, and began walking at a reasonably slow pace over towards the range boards. I did not make any noise on the gravel as I did so. When I got to within 20 feet or so of the boards I stopped and rethought things through. I could hear them on the other side of the range boards talking to each other in low voices. One was saying, "Can you see him, Colonel?"

The Colonel responded, "No, General. He must know this place like the back of his hand. Why don't' we send sergeant Smith back over to check out the other side of the lounge?"

The General replied, "Not a good idea for Smith to bump into him in this darkness. Let's just wait here until our friends come back for us. If we have to, we can always let the other sergeants wait where they are while we fall back to the ammunition bunker since we're already here on the bunker road."

Then sergeant Smith said defensively, "I don't know how the said airman got out here, General. I personally locked the range gate as ordered.

"It's okay, sergeant," replied the general. Then the General turned to the Colonel and continued, "Colonel, what do you think of the range layout?"

"We can certainly run the project tests from here on Range Three, don't you think General?" replied the Colonel.

"Yes," the General replied, "This is just perfect. The lounge has a dressing room and a waiting room that can be used as a makeup area. There won't be any reason to move the wind measurements back to Range Four. That young airman always brings his own water with him. He doesn't need a well or indoor plumbing. We'll tell our friends they can begin as soon as they're ready."

I'd heard all I needed to hear. I was curious but as an enlisted man, I knew the General and the Colonel's business was not mine. Quietly I turned around and quickly retraced my footsteps back to my weather shack. I quietly closed the front door as I stepped inside. I couldn't lock it because, like the back door, the lock fit only on the outside. I quickly collected my spare canteen and stepped quietly out the side door into the dark shaded area next to the cable fence, carefully closing the side door as I did so. Then, I headed south along the cable fence to the back of my weather shack and continued on through the mesquite and brush that grew between the paved road and me. Through gaps in the brush and glimpses in between the buildings, I could see one of the sergeants standing just behind the southwest corner of the lounge. He appeared to be looking for someone.

I continued through the sagebrush, following down along the cable fence for almost a full half-mile before I felt safe enough to cross over to the paved Range Three road. Then, moving faster on the pavement, I hurried through the darkness until I reached my parked pickup truck. I had left it parked facing north towards the Range Three area. My flashlight still wouldn't work so I didn't expect that my truck would either. However, remembering my experience with the balloon light, I guessed that if I could manually push my truck a thousand feet or so back towards base, it would start up. First I had to turn it around.

The narrow two lane road was flat and level where my truck sat. Of course since it was only a light pickup truck, it was easy to push and a simple matter for me to turn my truck around by manually pushing it through a "Y" turn. Once I had it headed back towards base, I moved the truck by pushing on the frame next to the open driver's side door, steering the truck as I did so. After I had moved the truck several hundred feet I noticed that my flashlight was beginning to flicker when I turned it on. Excited by my success so far, I pushed the truck as hard as I could and got it rolling at perhaps 3 mph. Then I jumped in, closed the door, turned on the key, threw the truck into second gear and popped the clutch. To my immense satisfaction, after some careful nursing of the clutch and gas petal, the engine clunked back to life. The engine was misfiring but it was running. With the headlights still off, I placed the truck in low gear and, at 3 mph I carefully began heading back in to base. The further I got, the better the engine ran. By the time I had traveled another mile, the engine was back to running in a near perfect manner. I turned on the headlights, hit the gas, and soon was traveling back in to base at 50 mph. My watch started running nicely again too. Breakfast that morning tasted especially good. I went back for two extra helpings of eggs, bacon and coffee. I'd worked up quite an appetite. Smokey was teasing me as I phoned Desert Center using the chow hall phone. "If you'd made up the winds like you should have, you'd have been able to have a nice cup of coffee with me, and still phone in those damn winds on time."

I stayed late at the chow hall, laughing with Smokey. When I arrived back out to Range Three at 8:30 a.m. everything was deserted and the diesels started as normal.

A couple of uneventful days passed. I spent them singing and reading. I also brought out some mops, cleaning rags, soap, wax, and two big garbage cans of water. Then I cleaned, waxed, and polished pretty much every square inch of my Range Three weather shack, windows included, inside and out. I even cleaned the flaky rust off the helium tanks and nicely numbered them using some colored chalk that I kept in my desk. I used green numbers when the tanks were full and added red numbers when the tanks were empty. I routinely kept extensive supply logs that I shared with the Desert Center supply depot. I could identify any tank that was defective or hadn't been filled properly so the supply depot could ask the suppliers for credit. It was fun having a nice neat place of my own and it fully occupied my mind.

The morning of the full moon arrived and it was unusually windy. The sky was clouded over so not even the stars illuminated the darkened nighttime desert. Singing as usual, I made the drive out to Range Three. My truck was running perfectly. As I was coming up on the generator shack, I noticed the three jackrabbits huddled together at the edge of the sagebrush to my left. Once again they showed little interest in running away. Suspicious, then, I didn't park my truck in the usual place. Instead, I first drove slowly all around the graveled area using the headlights of the truck to illuminate all of the dark and shadowy places. Nothing seemed out of place, but it was a slow process. Some places such as the area hidden behind the outhouse, and the first ridge beyond the bunker road were especially hard to shine my headlights into. Nervous but satisfied, I drove my truck back over to the generator shack and pulled up facing the southern pair of doors. I left the headlights on, the engine running, and the driver's side door open. Then I got out and nervously strolled into the generator shack. Of course the inside of the diesel shack was filled with the usual odors of grease, oil, and diesel fuel. The wind rattled a number of the loose boards.

The headlights from my truck shone directly into the generator shack and illuminated the diesel inside, so I left my flashlight in the truck. The southern diesel started right up. As usual, I had to walk into the narrow space that was in between the two diesels in order to activate and adjust the electrical generator. This was a delicate process. The noise level in between the two diesels made my skin vibrate, to say nothing about my head and eardrums. I could hardly hear myself think. The manifolds on the diesel heated up so fast that they were already becoming red hot. To make the electrical adjustments I had to reach in between two of the red hot manifolds and adjust several knobs. I had to reach in almost as far as my elbow. The process took several minutes. Then, after the diesel had warmed up, I had to make some carburetor adjustments. I was standing there with my right hand on the knobs in between the red hot manifolds when without warning the headlights on my truck went off. I was now standing in total darkness. I couldn't hear anything but the diesel running next to me. "Who's there," I called out into the darkness? Hearing any response was out of the question. Terror began to overtake me. The only light I could see came from the red hot manifolds. "Who's there," I called again. Still nothing. I became more and more terrified with each passing second. I stood there, frozen in fear for a few minutes. The heat from the red hot manifold began cooking a spot on my right arm, bringing me to my senses at last. I screamed in pain and pulled my arm out from between the manifolds. I realized that I had no other choice but to walk out to my truck in this total darkness, and turn the lights back on, no matter what was waiting for me outside. So, steeling myself against attack, I began carefully feeling my way through the darkness towards the place where I remember the door as having been located. I continued forward in a straight line until I bumped into the front support post of the shack. I felt my way along until I made it outside. Then I followed the sound of my truck engine until I located my truck. The terror that I had to overcome every step of the way cannot be described. During that time I recited a lifetime of prayers.

Once I was inside of my truck, from memory I could locate the switch to my truck lights and turn them back on. What terrified me the most was my knowing that while I had been in the generator shack, someone had moved the switch to the off position. I decided that when I had searched the range area with my headlights, I must have upset someone and they were sending me a message. In the future, I would be very careful about not doing that again.

I sat enjoying the security of my truck for 10 minutes or so. However, I had not completed my electrical adjustments. Taking my flashlight in hand and making certain that it was working, I got back out of my truck and reentered the generator shack. In record time I completed the adjustments and double-timed back to my tuck. I drove my truck over to my weather shack and proceeded as normal with my morning wind measurements. I was still so terrified that I refused to think about the implications of this morning's events.

Desert Stages

> . . . Until you return to the ground,
> from which you were taken;
> For you are dirt,
> and to dirt shall you return."
> . . . Genesis 3:19

One summer day as I was taking the 12:00 noon run I noticed a large chalk white object sitting on the desert about a mile north of the ammunition bunker. The object was about the size of the engine on a passenger train and had similar appearing windows. It was sitting mostly hidden from view by the sagebrush-covered ridge to the northeast. The intense heat waves coming off the desert obscured any other details that I might have seen. The bunker road passed over that ridge at a beautiful viewing point that I had dubbed "The second gallery."

I was singing happy songs and curious about what it might be. After I finished my balloon run and had phoned the results in to Desert Center, I decided to hike over to the "second gallery" to get a better view of the object. I had a couple hours to kill and I expected it to be an easy walk. Collecting up my hat, sunglasses, and two canteens of water, I set off singing my hiking songs. Being young, I quickly hiked the half-mile along the bunker road. I even skipped and danced some on the hot pavement. When I arrived at the second gallery, I stopped for a few minutes and danced to the tune of several meadowlark sounds that I could hear coming from the sagebrush around me.

The view of the valley and of the surrounding desert from the second gallery was quite spectacular. However, because of the intense heat waves and the glare from the bright sunshine I still couldn't make out any details on the white object. I decided to continue my hike over to the ammunition bunker and then up the valley to see how close I could get to it. It seemed the only way to get a better view.

In the fullness of time I arrived over by the foot of the eastern mountains where the hard surface ended. Then I followed north along the hard gravel road until I had arrived out in front of the concrete ammunition bunker. It sat empty with its heavy wooden door half open.

A ridge of the mountain blocked my way directly north. However, the trail led along the base of the mountain, up over the small ridge, angling slightly northwest past some unusually beautiful mesquite and sagebrush. I proceeded far enough along the trail to the top of the ridge. From there I could get a better view of the large white object that still sat on the desert floor perhaps a half mile northwest of me. Suddenly the white object appeared to fuzz over. It slowly floated up 20 or 30 feet from the desert floor. Then in little more than the blink of an eye, it headed in a line for 5 to 7 miles, straight northwest. Then, just as suddenly, it stopped in mid air and floated back down to the sit again on the desert floor. Slowly, the white fuzz went away and through the heat waves in the distance the front windows could again be seen. It had accomplished the entire flight in total silence. Instinctively I had timed it in its flight. Less than 3 seconds had passed.

Hiking any further out into the desert in this heat was obviously out of the question. "Whatever the object is," I said to myself, "it can certainly start and stop fast enough."

I turned around and began retracing my steps the 3 miles or so back to my weather shack.

When I arrived back at the second gallery, I stopped for a few minutes to enjoy the view and take another dink of water. The view of the desert and the range areas was especially captivating. The object, of course, was too far away to see much of anything. The unseen meadowlarks were still all around me, and still singing from out in the sagebrush. Once again I did a little dance on the hot pavement as I sang one of my favorite songs.

As I took another quick drink of water from my canteen, I got to thinking about what I had seen. I mentally performed some calculations. The object had started from a standing position, traveled approximately 7 miles, and stopped again to a standing position in less than 3 seconds. That means that during its flight it was traveling at an average speed of more than 8,000 miles an hour. If it had been rocket powered, anyone on board would now look like ketchup. At that rate of acceleration, the object could reach the speed of light in less than 10 hours. Suddenly the star Arcturas at a distance of 36 light years, Bernard's star at 5.5 light years, and the other star fields of the Milky Way didn't seem so far away.

I stood there for a few minutes thinking. When the object moved it had not left behind any fuel. There hadn't been any vapor trail, any sonic boom, any bright lights, or even any sparks. One would expect to see these according to the known laws of physics. It had instead propelled itself in a manner that was totally self-contained. I realized the implications. Only a craft that is totally self-contained can make the deep space crossing between the stars. Space is so vast. Any craft that used a rocket engine and left a vapor trail would need a fuel tank the size of the moon to make it even as far as Barnard's star. Making the trip on such a rocket would be like waiting for the next ice age. Making the trip on any other kind of craft would be the same as proving Einstein wrong. And if Einstein was wrong, then why couldn't such a craft accelerate for 30 hours instead of 10 and be traveling 3 times the speed of light? Yes, Arcturas and Bernard's star now seemed a lot closer.

I turned and retraced my steps to my weather shack. As I walked, I muttered to myself, "They knew they were only going to move the object 7 miles, so they probably left it in low gear. I wonder what it could do if they were out in deep space and they opened it up." Yet, as I hiked back along the bunker road, I decided that what I had really seen was just the sunlight playing tricks on my eyes. I refused to believe that the object was real because it was much too small to make the deep space crossing all by itself. Any other conclusion was just too frightening.

Several uneventful days passed. I was down on Range One. It was another beautiful summer day and the last run of the day was scheduled to be unusually late, 3:30 p.m. When I phoned the results in to Desert Center I became somewhat miffed. The command post didn't actually want to know what the winds were. The base commander just wanted to make certain that I had actually been out on Range One taking them. Then I was told that the rest of the day was mine to do with as I pleased, as though any useful portion of the day remained. "Those damn generals act like all of the ranges are just a stage," I grumbled as I hung up the phone, "and all they want me to do is to show off my beautiful collection of balloons."

It had been a cool dry and cloudy day with a nice breeze. Now that the heat of the day had broken, just for the fun of it, I decided to take a hike out through the purple sagebrush to the edge of the arroyo that ran through the valley north of my weather shack. The idea formed in my mind so unexpectedly that I wasn't sure it was my idea at all. My friends the range rats, had said that back in the 1950's an F84 jet crashed on a training mission and that the wreckage still laid in the arroyo only a half-mile or so down from my weather shack. The pilot had died in the crash. After due consideration, I decided that I had probably gotten the idea from one of my friends. I strapped on two canteens of water, put on my leather gloves, tightened by boots, adjusted my fatigue hat, and set off hiking down the valley to see it. I was only expecting this to be a short hike that would help me get over my annoyance with the command post. I certainly didn't expect this hike to interfere with my evening meal plans.

The trail down the valley meandered through sagebrush, mesquite, and other desert vegetation. All of it was very thick and very tall. I couldn't actually hike along the edge of the arroyo, or down in the arroyo. The desert was just too rugged. So, my plan was to hike down the valley until I came to one of the rare open lanes that led over to the arroyo's edge. It was a pleasant hike and I sang loudly as I walked.

For some reason despite the isolation of Range One, it didn't seem as though I was alone. I had traveled only a couple thousand yards down the trail when I heard an unusual loud whinny, like that from a horse, emanate from behind a large patch of mesquite behind me. The trail seemed to close behind me and I became certain that I was being closely followed. Always, it seemed, they remained behind me hidden by the numerous bends in the trail or by the thick brush on my right and left as I progressed down the valley. After a while the feeling became very unnerving.

At one point I stopped, turned around, and would have gone back to my shack except that it felt as though two or three people, hidden by the brush and the bends in the trail, were intentionally blocking the path behind me. I felt as though they were herding me forward down the trail, much as one would herd a sheep or a cow. Slowly I became more and more alarmed, and began hoping that my mind was just playing more tricks on me.

After a couple of miles, I came to an open lane that led up to the arroyo's edge, several hundred feet to the north. Cautiously I left the main trail and approached the edge of the arroyo, hoping to find an unblocked return route to my weather shack. In the distance down in the arroyo perhaps another mile further on, sat a large featureless white object, almost entirely hidden by the rocks and brush. It was about the size of a large RV or a two car garage. I supposed that it must be the F84 wreckage. While I watched, it appeared to fuzz over with a white haze. In total silence it floated perhaps 20 feet up from the arroyo floor. Then, in little more then the blink of an eye, still in total silence, it traveled in a straight line down the arroyo for a distance of perhaps 7 miles. Just as suddenly, it stopped in mid air and floated back down to the arroyo floor, positioning itself behind some rocks and brush. Once again I instinctively timed it in its flight by counting, "One thousand one, one thousand two, one thousand three". It had accelerated to more than 8,000 mph and returned to a complete stop in less than 3 seconds.

The arroyo rim was so rugged that I had no choice but to return to the main trail. The path back to my weather shack still felt blocked by someone hiding behind some nearby mesquite. Now feeling quite uneasy, I decided I had no choice but to continue down the valley trail, still further away from my weather shack, hoping to find an alternate return route further on. I had hiked a very long way, perhaps another 4 miles before I found another open lane to the arroyo's edge. Now feeling extremely uneasy, I hiked up to the edge of the arroyo for another look. Once again I could see the featureless white object sitting in the distance, down in the arroyo. It sat perhaps 3 miles further down the arroyo next to the rocks and brush along the base of the arroyo wall. It was now completely enveloped by the late afternoon shadows. Through the desert haze and the deep blue desert shadows, I could see that the object sat with its front windows clearly visible, and a side door open. The door was hinged at the top and had a set of steps that folded down to the outside. There was no sign of the white haze that had previously surrounded the object.

I was mystified and confused. This couldn't be the wreckage of the F84, moving around as it did. My mind seemed to be playing tricks on me again. There was the simple fact that I had seen the craft silently accelerate to 8,000 mph in the atmosphere without creating a single shock wave, vapor trail, or sonic boom. Then the memory of the white haze crossed my mind. In order for the white haze to obscure the view of the front windows on the craft and also travel at 8,000 mph with the craft, the haze had to result from some type a force field that interacted with light, and it had to be generated by the craft itself. Space is full of cosmic radiation. Any attempt to make the deep space crossing in a craft without radiation protection would be like sleeping next to a nuclear reactor. It seemed to me as if the craft had all of the qualities needed to come here from a nearby star. Yet, Einstein forbade all of these same qualities. In the end, I shrugged off my musings and voted to continue believing in Einstein instead. There was simply no way around the fact that the craft was too small to have come from anywhere except these desert valleys.

What I needed, I decided was a good evening meal and a nice relaxing night watching television in the day room. Somehow I was going to have to get back to my weather shack and back to my everyday world.

Cautiously I returned to the main trail. I waited at the trail junction for a few minutes, thinking carefully about my next move, and trying very carefully to get a sense of the mesquite and sagebrush around me. The main trail widened at the junction and the tall brush and mesquite formed a thick wall that was more or less circular. It felt as though the unseen people following me had moved down the valley and were now hidden behind an extensive patch of large mesquite that blocked both sides of the trail as it followed on down towards the white object. It also felt like 5 or 6 other people from the craft had joined them. I felt like an actor who had been coaxed and herded on stage for an audition, or maybe like an animal in the wild being studied by a bunch of tourists. My watch stopped for some reason, and I felt a certain momentary dizziness that I quickly shook off. Then I noticed that night seemed to be setting in faster than I had expected. An image from memory seemed to momentarily flash across my mind. In the momentary image, a thin chalk white young woman who was a little shorter than me stepped out from behind the mesquite onto the trail, studied me for a minute or so, and said, "Yes, he will do nicely, but there is a problem. He is so intelligent that he can defeat our controls. He's doing it now. Here, I'll readjust them."

After the dizziness wore off, I exercised my arms and legs a little bit. I quickly shook off the images in my memory, took a nice drink of water from one of my canteens, and breathed deeply. The trail back to my weather shack now felt open. It was with a great sense of relief that I turned back up the valley. As quickly as I could hike, I returned the long miles back up the valley to my weather shack. I was singing loudly every step of the way.

In the fullness of time I arrived at the chow hall back on base. It was quite a bit past its normal closing time. Smokey met me at the door laughing, and escorted me to the nearest table. It contained a special meal that he had prepared just for he and I. Laughing he explained that the Desert Center base commander had phoned the chow hall and wanted to make sure that they kept it open for me. As I was adding the milk to my coffee, Smokey laughed, "You sure have gotten yourself into one hell of a lot of trouble now, Charlie, if the base commanding General is spending time worrying about your eating habits. That's my job. You know that General is never going to be able to cook as well as I do."

Charles James Hall

The Night the Laughter Stopped

. . . Therefore, do not worry about tomorrow,
for tomorrow will worry about itself.
Each day has enough trouble of its own.
. . . Matthew 7:34

The summer days out in the desert followed one after another in beautiful repeatable succession. Many times the 8:00 a.m. wind reports from one day to the next were so similar it was hard to tell that time had passed.

I was sitting in my chair in my Range Three weather shack one afternoon. I had some time to kill. I was looking out into the desert and enjoying the gentle winds and the music on the radio. Over the distant mountains in the north stood a few cumulus clouds, very high up. The way they drifted slowly in the bright afternoon sunshine they looked like beautiful white castles floating in the air. I was reminiscing about how much fun the last few weeks had been and how much laughter I had enjoyed. The days and nights had been quite ordinary and I had been completely alone. Even my pink elephants seemed to have floated away.

My thoughts had returned to more ordinary topics such as beautiful women, gambling, and the casinos in far away Las Vegas. I kept several decks of cards in the weather shack with me. I spent many afternoons practicing the game of blackjack and reading books on how to gamble properly. I also practiced counting cards and quickly computing the odds, all completely and silently in my mind. I had gotten so good that counting cards against a single deck was as

92

natural as eating peanuts. I could now silently count cards against a dealer using a six-deck shoe. During my last trip up north to far away Las Vegas, I had started out with $10 and won $250. I had also gotten thrown out of one of the major casinos down on the strip. It wasn't for counting cards, none of the casinos cared as long as I did it silently in my head. It was for asking if I could shuffle the deck once, something that was permitted by the rules. Once a Las Vegas card mechanic had his deck properly stacked, he could be awfully touchy about anyone else shuffling the cards. For my part I discovered that it only paid to count cards in those casinos that believed in always giving you the next card off the top.

I sat there happily remembering my last evening in Las Vegas, dancing with Michael's sister Pamela. Pamela was a little shorter than I was and a little on the thin side. She had very light blonde hair, blue eyes, and a very light complexion. She was also quite intelligent. She was so good at putting on different kinds of make-up and dresses that the first four times I dated her, I didn't realize that I was dating the same woman. She was an excellent dancer and the two of us had shared many enjoyable evenings. My good friend Michael was determined to do everything possible to get Pamela and I married. One day he had even pointed out to me the amount of money I would be paid by the US Air Force if she and I chose to tie the knot. Every time I thought of it, I had to laugh.

As I sat there, I noticed that I had a small amount of desert sand on the upper part of my boots. At first it seemed like something I should laugh off. I started to reach for the shoe polish kit that I kept with me in the weather shack when I remembered that I had just polished my boots earlier in the day. I wasn't particularly military, but I did routinely polish my boots in order to protect the leather from the harsh desert environment. A sturdy protective pair of boots was a necessity out on the gunnery ranges.

The Range Three buildings were arranged around a square that was entirely covered with hard gravel. Although the gravel and dirt was soft enough to preserve nice sets of boot prints, a hiker did not encounter much in the way of deep desert sand or very soft dirt until he had left the extensive graveled area. Areas of deep sand and very soft dirt included the area out back of my weather shack, in between the supply sheds, and the desert expanses west, east, and south of the graveled area. I had polished my shoes earlier in the day and I couldn't remember having since been in any of those areas, or having walked anywhere else in the desert. Suddenly the extra sand on my boots didn't seem so funny.

I still wondered about an early afternoon a few days before. While I was adjusting my theodolite, I thought I got a glimpse of someone walking around the southwest corner of the Range Three lounge building. I remembered walking over there to see what was going on when an unusual gentle gust of wind passed by. I had planned on inspecting the hidden area on the western side. Then I remember walking back in to the Range Three area from the western desert a few minutes later. I was singing one of my favorite songs at the time. However, in my memory, I couldn't seem to connect those two events. Something about the entire incident left me feeling worried and edgy.

I opened up my shoe polish kit and began shining my boots when the phone rang. "Range Three weather shack, airman Charlie Baker here," I answered.

It was my friend Dwight from Desert Center on the line. "Charlie," he laughed, "I just wanted to remind you that tomorrow is the end of the month. When you drive down here to Desert Center with the completed wind reports, you will be able to pick up your pay check here at the station as usual."

"Thanks for reminding me, Dwight," I answered, "I almost forgot. How are things with you?"

"Fine," he answered, "I can't talk now, though, we're pretty busy down here. I suppose you're pretty busy up there too, since you have to start filling the balloon for the 2:30 p.m. run."

"No," I answered, "It's only 1:25 p.m. and I don't start that for another half hour."

"1:25 p.m.," he laughed. "Where have you been? It's 1:55 p.m. I got to get going. I'll talk to you later." Then he hung up.

As I put down the phone, the 1:55 p.m. news came on the radio. Surprised into action, I reset my watch and began my preparations for the 2:30 p.m. balloon run. "Where could the time have gone," I wondered. I searched deeply through my mind but all I remembered doing since the last run was to walk out to my theodolite stand and back again. Then, for the next several hours my mind kept stumbling across the phrase, "… the first human we've ever seen. What do the women look like?"

A week went by. I was taking a special 7:15 a.m. balloon run at Range Three. The first flight of airplanes was expected at 8:30 a.m. They planned to practice medium altitude dog fighting so I would be the only person on the ranges for the day. The Desert Center weather station forecaster had asked for the wind report by 7:45 a.m. so he could give the pilots a dependable wind forecast before they took off. I had gotten the balloon released at 7:20 a.m., and spent 12 minutes tracking it with my theodolite. Then with my clipboard and wind form held tightly in my right hand, I began walking back to my weather shack barely 25 paces away. When I arrived at the front door of the shack, I instinctively transferred the clipboard from my left hand back to my right hand as I stepped up into the shack. I sat down in my chair and placed the clipboard on my ivory topped table. It was this table that I used to plot the balloon's track and to calculate the resulting winds.

As soon as I sat down, I realized that something didn't feel right. I felt stunned or numb in some unexplained manner. I turned in my chair, looked intently out through the open front door, and carefully studied the hard gravel outside. I tried to remember exactly everything that had happened on my short walk from the theodolite stand back to my weather shack. I could remember starting the walk with the clipboard in my right hand and reaching the front door with the clipboard in my left hand. However, there were three steps in the middle of the walk that I could not remember ever having actually taken. I was not able to remember switching the clipboard to my left hand either. Then, off in the distance to the southeast I could hear the first flight of planes approaching. Then my phone rang. It was Dwight. "Hi Charlie," he said, "You sure are late with those winds. The forecaster has been pressing me, and I've been phoning you every 10 minutes since 7:54 a.m. How are they coming?"

Stunned, I replied, "But that can't be right, Dwight. It can't be more than 7:40 a.m. right now, and this is the first time you rang my phone."

Laughing, Dwight answered, "Where have you been, Charlie? It's 8:25 a.m. You're not going to try to tell me that I don't know how to make a phone call, are you?"

Shocked and confused, while Dwight was on the phone, I quickly computed the winds I had measured. The fact that they were nearly identical to the previous day's 8:00 a.m. winds was a tremendous help.

After reading the winds to Dwight, we both said goodbye and hung up the phone. I sat for a few minutes, nervous and afraid. Checking the time on the radio, I could see that Dwight had been right about the time. I was too nervous to wonder if he had been right about the phone calls as well. Slowly I got up from my chair and stepped outside onto the hard gravel. I carefully studied my boot prints that led from the theodolite stand back to my weather shack. However, the gravel was so hard and I had made the trip so many times that I couldn't decide on much of anything. After studying the gravel for a half hour or so, I returned to my weather shack and finished the paperwork that went with the last balloon run. I spent the rest of the day nervous and edgy.

Later that afternoon, I spent an hour or so looking through my logbooks. More than sixteen observers in the years before me reported similar experiences. One observer four years before me stated in the logbook that he had a similar experience on his morning run five days previous to the entry. According to the log, on the morning run four days before the entry, just as he was closing up the theodolite, he began dreaming while still standing at the theodolite stand. He said that for almost a half hour he was unable to move his arms or his feet, although he was able to move his head and neck. He wrote that while he stood there he dreamt that a group of 6 or 8 chalk white people about his height came and stood around him, always staying more or less 30 feet away. In his dream, one of the people, whom he believed to be named "Range Four Harry", acted like a tour guide pointing out his muscles, his intelligence, his jaws, his teeth, and describing his eating habits. In the logbook he stated that the entire experience had left him panicky and terrified of the ranges so three days prior to the entry he described going in to visit the neurosurgeon down at Desert Center. He said the doctor conferred with the base commander and concluded that he was too self-centered to continue to function in the US Air Force. According to the log, he was making the entry on his last day of military duty. He said that as soon as he closed up the weather shack, he would pick up his packed belongings and drive back down to Desert Center. He said that the base commander would be giving him an honorable early discharge the following day, complete with full G.I. Bill benefits and everything. The neurosurgeon had insisted that there was nothing wrong with him and that it was perfectly OK for a single civilian man to be self-centered.

I sat there wondering if I too, would soon start becoming "self-centered."

I had settled down a great deal by the next morning. I had gotten a good night's sleep after relaxing in front of the TV. Everything at Range Three began normally. The chalk white fluorescent lights that routinely could be seen way up the valley, silently floated down as far as range four. They played in and around the range four buildings they way they always had. Then they returned back up the valley to where they had come from. As usual I wondered what they were.

Then on the 10:00 a.m. run, I had a similar time experience. I was walking from my theodolite back to the weather shack. I had taken to counting my steps as I took them. I could remember beginning step number 11 and finishing step number 14. I could not remember the steps in between. This time an hour had passed and the weather forecaster at Desert Center criticized me for being late. Outraged, angry, and deeply upset, I searched all over the graveled area, in the generator shack, and all around the supply sheds, looking for practically any sign of anything. I was screaming in loud and angry tones as I did so. There was simply nothing to be found. Nothing was out of place.

That afternoon, as I sat in my chair waiting to take the last run of the day, I devised a plan. I closed all of the doors to my weather shack. Then, in the privacy and the loneliness of the shaded interior northeast corner, I took out the jackknife that I always carried in my pocket. I opened it up and carefully placed a small notch on the outside edge of the soles of both of my shoes. Now my shoes left distinctive tracks in the soft dirt when I walked normally. Then I decided that in the future, every time I walked from the theodolite stand to the front door of my weather shack, I would intentionally alter my route. This would allow me to check up on myself. I also began writing down the time that I started walking back to my weather shack on my weather form, and also the time when I arrived back at my weather shack. One way or another, I was determined to get to the bottom of whatever it was that was happening. I didn't have long to wait.

Only a few days passed before it happened again. This time I was just finishing the last run of the day. This time as I was taking step number 12, an hour and a half passed. After phoning in the winds, and getting myself settled down, with a couple of stones in hand, I went out to find and follow my boot prints. I found them immediately by searching the soft dirt in the skip bomb area to the east of my shack. They led out across the skip bomb area to a hollow depression in the desert about a half mile southeast of my weather shack, and they also led back. Someone had been following along behind me as I walked both ways. Two other sets of tracks entered the hollow area from the northeast. They appeared to have come down from the ammunition bunker.

As I stood studying the boot prints in the soft desert dirt, an image from my memory suddenly flashed into my mind. In the image, two young women dressed as nurses and looking very human, were standing about 30 feet in front of me diagonally off to my left. One was about my height, the other was an inch or so shorter. They both looked very familiar. The taller one was saying to the other, "You must learn to talk to him face to face without using these controls. The American Generals require it. Now go on. We can't keep bringing him out into the desert like this. Overcome your fears and say, 'Hello Charlie."

In the image, the other young woman replied, "Yes, Teacher, but being this close to him is very terrifying. I am telling you, he can break out of these controls. Already I have to readjust them."

I shook the images from my mind and trudged back to my weather shack, still not knowing what to make of it all. I resolved to be even more careful. Now, in the coming days, whenever I took the wind measurements, I became even more circumspect. Now I varied the route that I took while walking back to my weather shack even more than before. Sometimes I even chose a route that took me east from my theodolite over into the skip bomb area, than south parallel to the cable fence, and then back into my weather shack through the side door. Another time I was certain that something was hiding in between the two supply sheds, so I walked backwards way out into the desert to the west, always watching the supply sheds as I did so. Then, after waiting a half hour or so, everything felt safe again so I cautiously returned to my weather shack to complete the report. On that occasion, as the late winds were being reported to the Desert Center base commander he said he had too much respect for my bravery to make any kind of statement. For 10 days or so, my carefully laid plans seemed to work.

Then one windy day even those efforts failed. It was the 10:00 a.m. run and the winds were 10 mph or so from the southeast. This meant that since my side door was on the east side of the shack, when I opened it to take the balloon outside, the wind blew the balloon around a great deal. I had perfected a special technique for taking the balloon outside and releasing it on windy days. The inflated balloon was very fragile so, using my practiced technique, I held the balloon with both hands, and jumped out the door backwards. This allowed me to use my body to shield the balloon. Then, as soon as I was outside, I jumped up as high as I could and released the balloon. This allowed the rising balloon to miss hitting the roof and the overhang on my shack.

After releasing the balloon, I quickly jumped back inside the shack, closed the side door, opened the front door, grabbed my clipboard and forms and ran out to my theodolite to begin tracking the balloon. Desert Center had specifically asked for the wind readings all the way up to 25,000 feet, which was quite a bit higher than usual. The command post had requested these upper level winds even though I had previously closed the ranges. In order to take those readings in this wind I had to pay far more attention to tracking the balloon than normal. With the winds coming out of the southeast, I also had to do so with my back to my weather shack. After taking only 5 readings, I thought I heard the sound of someone stepping on the gravel behind me. Before I could react or look around, once again a momentary dizziness passed through my mind. This time when I shook it off, more than an hour and 15 minutes had passed. The balloon was long gone and Desert Center didn't care. In rage and anger I stomped all over the Range Three area, kicking the gravel and rocks and shouting obscenities out into the wind.

My boot prints lead to an area of soft dirt next to the tall mesquite out behind my weather shack. As I stood back there studying the boot prints, once again an image flashed into my memory. Once again the image was of two young women nurses who looked perfectly human and very familiar. One was my height and the other one was an inch or so shorter. This time the tall one was standing only 10 feet or so in front of me while the shorter one was standing some 40 feet further back. The tall one was saying, "See. There's nothing whatever to be afraid of. Now come up here, look him in the face, and say 'Hello, Charlie.'"

The other nurse replied, "Yes, Teacher, but don't you see how dangerous he is? He has learned to defeat these controls! Every few minutes I have to keep readjusting them! He can break out and attack us any time he wants to!"

Then the first nurse replied, "We've wasted weeks and you still haven't talked to him. We can't keep doing this. It's OK if he breaks out of the controls. He's very gentle. He won't attack us. Now come up here and say, 'Hello, Charlie.'"

I angrily shook the rest of the images from my mind. None of them seemed to be making any sense. I stomped back to the middle of the graveled area and screamed into the wind towards the mountains to the east, "Stop this BS, now! Do you hear me? Stop it now! If there's something that you want to say to me, just walk the hell in on me when

I'm taking the balloon run and say it to my face! But stop this nonsense now!" At least the shouting made me feel a lot better. It didn't seem like anyone was listening.

A few uneventful days passed. On some of the days I was certain that I was completely alone out on the ranges. On other days, I felt certain that I was being watched, but only from afar. I didn't know what to make of it all, but finally my laugher returned. I started feeling quite a bit safer and no new sets of my boot prints appeared anywhere in the soft dirt around the Range Three area. Soon I had settled back down and my thoughts returned back to the more ordinary topics of beautiful women, gambling, card counting, and dancing with Pamela in the beautiful casinos in far away Las Vegas.

One bright moonlit morning when I arrived out at Range Three, I noticed that the northern set of doors on the generator shack were open, and some soft fluorescent light was coming out of them. As I drove past them and parked my truck, it appeared that two thin white people about my height were standing in between the northern diesel and the shack wall, as though they were adjusting the generator controls. I was still half asleep and I didn't think much about it. I was in my usual hurry and I didn't pay much attention to them.

I parked my truck in its normal position, turned off the engine, began singing one of my favorite songs, and proceeded as normal to open up the southern set of doors and start the diesel. The diesels stood taller than me so once I was inside there wasn't much about the people that I could see. Of course, before I started up the diesel, the interior of the generator shack was a very quiet place. We could have carried on a very nice conversation without ever actually seeing each other.

To start the diesel I had to take a can of ether starting fluid and walk in between the two diesels so I could spray the fluid into a place next to the carburetor. This meant that I had to turn my back to the two white people who were on the other side of the northern diesel as it sat behind me. Out of the corner of my eye, through the open northern set of doors, I got a glimpse of a third white person outside apparently standing guard next to my truck. As I began spraying the ether starting fluid into the diesel, the shorter person of the two, who was closest to the door, seemed to become very agitated and suddenly ran out of the generator shack, disappearing around the corner to the north.

After spraying some ether into the diesel, I had to quickly walk back to the front of the diesel and engage the electric starter. After the diesel started, I had to make some carburetor and fuel line adjustments. Then I had to walk back in between the two diesels to make the generator adjustments. The second white person remained behind the northern diesel while I performed these tasks, although they did appear to be slowly drifting towards the open front door as the time passed normally. As I was finishing my work and my back was still turned to the open front doors, the second white person appeared to leave the shack and also disappear out of sight around the corner of the shack to the north. The guard by the truck appeared to follow.

Now that the diesel was running, I stepped back outside of the generator shack and began thinking things through. I became very confused by what had just happened. I wondered if maybe I'd breathed in too many fumes of ether and diesel fuel. I decided that I should get some fresh air before continuing so I walked over to the sagebrush and mesquite on the west side of the road where the rabbits commonly hid. I was reassured when the rabbits ran away as soon as I got anywhere near them. There was a nice evening breeze over there. Even though I was running late, I stood and enjoyed it for a few minutes. My position gave me a good view of the Range Three area. I could see that the two white people were women. The taller of the two was standing just east of my theodolite stand, apparently waiting to talk to me as soon as I arrived over in front of my weather shack. The shorter of the two white women had retreated to the east, standing perhaps a half-mile out in the sagebrush facing me from the distance. The guard had retreated to the base of the tower. All three of them looked familiar.

I was quite confused. Nothing seemed to be making any sense and I really didn't know what to do. I still considered the white creatures to be my special collection of pink elephants, but then someone real had opened up the northern set of doors on the generator shack. As I stood there waiting for my mind to clear, the white woman in front of my weather shack began floating slowly over towards me, approaching me by way of the front of my truck. When she was perhaps 30 feet from me, the fluorescent light from her suit turned off. She stopped floating and took two or three more steps, as though she were getting used to walking normally as she came back down on the gravel. Then she stopped and said to me, using English, "Don't be afraid, Charlie. This is a beautiful evening isn't it?"

Yes," I stumbled in response. I recognized her as the leader of my pink elephants, known as "The Teacher." Despite her perfectly real appearance, with her large blue eyes, chalk white skin, and short transparent blonde hair, I didn't actually believe that she was real. I had only trained myself to treat her as though she was real in order to control my fears and get the blood flowing properly back in my brain. After all, usually when I saw her, it was at night and she was floating.

She continued, "We're leaving now. You can continue with your morning wind report."

"Thank you, Teacher," I stammered nervously.

Then the fluorescent light on her suit came back on and she began floating a few inches of the ground again. Then she turned and joined up with the guard. Then the two of them floated off towards the east, finally joining up with the woman in the distance before disappearing over the sagebrush-covered ridge off to the southeast. Just before I lost sight of them she seemed to be saying, "You see. That's what you have to do."

I was extremely confused and I remained standing there for several minutes. I wondered why my pink elephants were now disappearing out of sight by traveling over the ridge to the southeast. I thought my brain stored all of my pink elephants behind images of the Range Three lounge building off to my left. Whatever my problems were, they seemed to be spreading.

The next few days passed quickly enough. After that morning's experience in the generator shack, I took to spending my spare time cleaning up all around the Range Three area. I spent some afternoons filling in potholes, raking the gravel, pulling and removing weeds, cleaning up trash, and so on. Another afternoon I spent repairing the back of the generator shack, nailing down loose boards, and so on. As the range weather observer, I wasn't required to do any work of that type, but I was happy to do so. I considered hard work to be the best therapy. Then one sunny afternoon I began repainting and repairing the red and white cable fence between my shack and the skip bomb area. Without warning, it looked like three chalk white children floated in from the sagebrush to the southeast and began playing 200 feet or so up and down the fence from me. They were two boys and a girl. They were so happy they seemed to be having the time of their lives. One of the boys even moved one of my empty paint cans and obviously began pretending that he was me. He began imitating the way I had been painting one of the posts.

I tried to ignore them at first, but seeing the boy actually move the empty paint can left me feeling shocked and stunned. I wondered, "How sick does a person have to be before they can move an object that heavy with their mind?"

Alone as I was out in the desert, I quietly retreated to the safety of the interior of my weather shack. I sat resting in the cool breeze with all three of the doors to my shack open, listening to the radio, wondering how I was ever going to get out of the mess I was in. The little white boy floated around to the rear of my weather shack and floated in the open doorway. He happily watched me for a while, apparently waiting for me to come back out. "You go play and have fun," I said, more to hear the sound of my own voice than anything. My nerves were almost ready to break on me at the time. I sat there singing for more than another hour before the children finally went away, disappearing back down to the southeast from where they had first come.

I was very careful with myself as I finished the work on the fence. I resolved to return to my previous habits of resting, reading books, painting pictures, and practicing my gambling techniques. All work on the roads and grounds, I decided to leave to the range maintenance men. "Recovering from a bad case of exhaustion," I said to myself, "is no laughing matter."

Several mornings later I was driving out to Range Three when I noticed the lights that always came out at night and roamed around up the valley by Range Four. This morning they had come further south than normal. As I parked my truck, I noticed that the lights, instead of spending the usual amount of time playing around the Range Four buildings north of me, formed up into a line and began coming down the Range Four road towards Range Three. This morning there seemed to be more of them. Instead of the usual 3 tall lights and 3 short lights, this morning there were 4 tall lights and 3 short lights. By the time I had finished starting the diesel, I was already becoming very nervous. There was something about the determined manner in which the lights kept coming that I found really upsetting.

I opened up my theodolite and my weather shack, turned on the lights and filled the balloon. Then I recorded my temperature and air pressure measurements and released my balloon. All the while the lights kept floating towards me down the Range Four road. Terror was building within me. I finished taking my readings and retreated to a position straight west of my theodolite and just in front of my truck. I stood there in confused terror waiting for the lights to come up over the ridge. As I watched, it looked like a large fluorescent chalk white horse floated up over the ridge on the Range Four road and continued on towards Range Three, stopping at last a quarter mile north of the graveled area, all in total silence. I would have broken in panic and ran to my truck except that I was so filled with terror that I was unable to move my feet and legs at the time. All I could think of was, "So this is Range Four Harry."

Although the fluorescent light wasn't bright, it hurt my eyes when I looked at it, but I could see that what I was looking at wasn't really a horse. It was a procession with the adults floating in the front and rear, and the children floating in the middle.

While I stood frozen in terror the shorter white woman floated out from the rear group of adults and continued floating slowly down towards the graveled area. When she arrived at the edge of the graveled area she stopped and waited, looking generally in my direction. She appeared to be waiting for me to close the distance between us. I was still frozen in terror and I had given up any hope of surviving this evening.

After 10 or 15 minutes or so, the woman turned around and floated back to the group. Then, they all formed up into their horse formation again and headed back up the road towards Range Four. Another 10 or 15 minutes passed before the terror within me subsided enough for me to be able to move my feet again.

Alone on Range Three and emotionally exhausted, I quickly closed up my theodolite and weather shack and headed back into base. When I arrived on base, I drove up the chow hall, computed the winds as best I could, and phoned them in late to Desert Center. Once again, the command post didn't care. I spent the rest of the day alone out at Range Three, resting and trying to get my life back to normal.

The next morning I was an emotional vegetable as I drove out to Range Three. However, on the way out, I didn't see anything out of the ordinary. I parked my truck in the usual position, started the diesels, opened my weather shack and began the morning tasks. I was just releasing the balloon when I noticed that up the valley at Range Four, once again the lights formed up on the Range Four road and began progressing down the road towards me. Once again there were 4 adults and 3 children. Since Range Four was some 20 miles away, I supposed that I would have time to complete my 12 wind measurements and run to my truck before the lights had made it even half way. However, I was just finishing the last balloon reading when once again, the image of a giant floating horse came up over the ridge three quarters of a mile north of me. I was shocked. The lights had to have made the trip from Range Four at an average speed of almost 100 mph. Outraged, angry, and confused with myself and with fear building inside of me, I began waving my flashlight wildly. Then I began quickly marching and shouting loudly towards the procession that was floating slowly down the road towards me. I was shouting, "Don't you see me? Get back! I'm terrified of you! I'm out here trying to work!"

The forward progress of the horse slowed but did not stop. Then the shorter woman proceeded out from the rear group of adults and began slowly approaching directly towards me. While she was still a quarter of a mile away or so, she seemed to be addressed me saying, "Hi."

Abject terror and panic raced through every facet of my body. In near hysteria I turned back towards my weather shack. Dropping my flashlight and my clipboard, I broke and ran in panic back to my weather shack, vomiting out everything in my stomach as I did so. Once inside, I closed the doors and locked the side door. The front door locked only on the outside and it could not be locked. Looking out through the small front window I watched in terror as the procession of 4 adults and 3 children continued up to my theodolite stand. Then the lights in my shack went out and I could hear the diesel running without a load as the generator went offline. There weren't words to describe the abject terror I felt as I hid behind the stove in my shack begging God to let me live until the sun came up, so at least I could see who it was that would be killing me. There was no way out of my weather shack. The back door was locked on the outside. Through the side window I could see that a guard had been posted to watch the side and back of my shack. For more than 45 minutes I huddled in white terror and hysteria while the people outside amused themselves playing with my theodolite and inspecting the graveled Range Three area. Then they formed up into the horse again. I could hear the diesel come back under load and the generator come back on line. Then the lights in my shack came back on and the procession returned back up the valley towards Range Four just as they had come. I waited locked in my shack for more than an hour until the sun came up, before opening the front door and stepping gingerly back outside. I had been praying every second of the time and ignoring the phone every time it rang. I recovered my flashlight and my clipboard, locked up my theodolite, and proceeded to quickly calculate the winds in my head. When I phoned them in to Desert Center, my friend Dwight answered the phone. As I read him the winds, he sympathetically said it sounded like I was crying from terror. I didn't argue with him. We both agreed that the next wind measurement I would take would be the 12:00 p.m. noon run, and I would rest until then.

The next few days were uneventful. I had to use every mental trick I could think of, and sing practically every song I'd ever heard to rebuild my failing courage and overcome my terror. An important part of my new plan was to run, not walk, to my truck and drive at high speed back in to base at the first sign of any lights whenever I was taking the morning run. During the next couple of weeks I had to use my new running plan several times. One morning I was driving in blind terror at more than 70 mph when the truck almost left the dry paved road, sliding on one of the curves. One another I almost crashed into the Range Three gate. On one morning, however, I slipped and fell while I was running on the gravel, and I scraped my hands quite badly. On the drive back in to base at 70 mph the cuts on my hands were so painful that I was just barely able to steer the truck. Swearing in pain and reciting my prayers, I slowed to 15 mph, downshifted to second gear and began thinking things through very carefully. I was getting tired of being afraid and sick of running. It was obvious that if I kept driving in to base like this, sooner or later I would have an accident and kill myself. Then there was the simple fact, on that awful morning of terror my front door hadn't been locked. There had been nothing from keeping the people outside from simply opening up my front door and coming in to get me. I decided that if they had wanted to do me any harm, they would have done so already. That morning, I stopped my truck on the highway and turned around. That morning I said my prayers and relocated my courage.

The next morning, once again I drove out to Range Three for the morning run. This morning I parked my truck in a new position. I parked it diagonally facing the theodolite stand on the western edge of the building square. This morning, as I was releasing my balloon, once again in the distance a group of 4 adults and 3 children formed up on the edge of Range Four and began proceeding down the road towards me. As usual, they were using their high-speed formation. They were formed up into the shape of a horse. This morning I decided that I would stand my ground, even if it killed me. Once again I was just finishing my last balloon reading as the procession came up over the ridge located three quarters of a mile down the road. While saying my prayers, I picked up my clipboard and calmly walked over to the front bumper of my carefully positioned truck. Then, with my back to the front of my truck, I stood calmly and waited as the procession floated in on me. This time the procession maintained its horse formation until it was all of the way onto the northern edge of the graveled area, stopping less than 50 feet north of the theodolite stand. Although the fluorescent light was only of ordinary brightness, looking into the procession when they were that close was so painful to my eyes that it was like looking into a blast furnace. The shorter woman floated out from the rear group of adults and took up a position just east of my theodolite. While I stood reciting my prayers, one of the male guards from the procession turned off his suit, stopped floating, and walked over towards me, stopping at last when he was still 30 feet from me. Addressing me in English, he said forcefully, "Tonight you don't run away, airman Baker."

Nervous and stammering, I replied, "Tonight I don't run away. I'm tired of being afraid. I only come out here because I'm ordered to. I can't follow my orders and measure the winds when I'm running and afraid. I'm going to follow my orders like a man or die like one."

Then the guard said forcefully, "You know that if anything goes wrong with this plan we can kill you any time we want to."

Standing my ground still shaking in fear, I replied, "Yes, but I haven't given you any reason to kill me. Anyway, you haven't killed me yet, so you are probably not going to."

The guard smiled and replied, "You are quite right. We could have killed you in your shack the other night if we had wanted to." Then he turned and walked back to the procession. Stopping for a minute near the shorter woman he said, "See. Now he knows for sure that we will kill him if anything ever goes wrong. Now talk to him."

The shorter white woman replied, "Yes, father, but not tonight. I'm still too terrified of him."

Then the procession formed back up into the horse formation in much the same manner that a conductor and passengers would board a train. They proceeded to float back up the Range Four road until they had returned to the ridge at three quarters of a mile. There, they stopped and watched me from a distance as I completed my calculations and phoned Desert Center. As I was closing up my weather shack, and getting back to where I could breathe without my nerves shaking, they turned and proceeded back up the road towards Range Four.

As I drove safely back in to base, my confused and frightened mind simply couldn't process all of the events of the evening. I simply didn't know where to put any of the pieces or what to make of anything. "Perhaps some coffee and breakfast will help," I said to myself. One thing I wasn't doing, I certainly wasn't laughing.

Olympic Dreams

…After a lapse of two years,
Pharaoh had a dream.
He saw himself standing by the Nile,
When up out of the Nile came seven cows, handsome and
fat;
They grazed in the reed grass.
Behind them seven other cows, ugly and gaunt, came up out
of the Nile;
…
Then Pharaoh woke up.
He fell asleep again and had another dream.
He saw seven ears of grain fat and healthy,
growing on a single stalk.
…
Then Pharaoh woke up, to find it was only a dream.
Genesis 41:1,7

During the hot summer afternoons, Range Three could be a quiet restful place. I always kept a broom, a dustpan, and other cleaning supplies in my weather shack. I used them to keep the interior of my shack clean and military. There was a small gas stove with an electric fan that sat in the center of the shack. I kept a few boxes of long wooden matches to start it. I also kept a military first aid kit, some rubbing alcohol, and various cold medicines for use when I was sick.

The wooden floor was covered with linoleum. The entire weather shack was built on blocks and raised a few feet off the desert. If I left the front door and the side door open, the

115

floor of my weather shack could be a warm comfortable place to take an afternoon nap. I was careful to keep the linoleum floor clean, highly polished, and in good repair. I brought out a large soft pillow with two army blankets. I arranged the furniture so that I had a comfortable place to lie down in front of the gas stove. I also brought out a windup mechanical alarm clock to supplement my radio and my watch. This allowed me to set my alarm clock, position it on the floor next to my gas stove, arrange my pillow, and catch 40 winks when I needed to. I didn't usually sleep between balloon runs but I was alone so far out in the desert that on days when I was sick, the open place on the floor of my weather shack frequently had to double as my hospital bed.

On hot summer afternoons if taking a nap was a necessity, the floor of my weather shack was much more comfortable than sleeping in my pickup truck. Even so, there were a number of days when I as so sick with the flu that I had to park my truck along the side of the road, turn off the engine, and sleep sitting behind the wheel. One winter afternoon I was feverish and extremely sick with the flu and I was caught in a blinding snowstorm down on the Range One road. I had no choice but to park the truck, turn off the engine, and sleep until the storm was over. I didn't get back to base until almost midnight. Fortunately, on that occasion, I was well dressed for winter.

I was normally quite healthy but between the military way of life, mold and fungus in the barracks, and the many people in the casinos of Las Vegas, there seemed to be an unusually large number of flues and other sicknesses that year. One summer afternoon out at Range Four, I became sick so suddenly that I had no choice but to crawl up into the corrugated back of my pickup truck, uncomfortable as it was, and go to sleep in the warm sun. After three or four hours of rest, still shaky, I was able to crawl out from the back of my truck, stumble over to the driver's side, drink some water, and drive slowly back in to base.

On those times at Range Three when I did rest on the floor of my weather shack, it wasn't very often that I had dreams. Those dreams that I did have were usually those of a young man. In one of my favorite dreams I would be gambling in the casinos up in Las Vegas, winning thousands of dollars and laughing with many beautiful young ladies. I would use a small part of the money to buy a new yellow Italian sports car. In my dream it was a fast convertible. Of course, in my favorite dream I never won so much money that I was satisfied. Unlike real life, in my dream I always quit winning and the young women were never after my money or my car. Being young was such fun. The casinos in Las Vegas had a large number of different designs and themes, so my favorite dream came with many different colors, designs, and variations.

One hot summer afternoon as I was sitting in the front doorway of my weather shack alone out at Range Three, I even dreamed that I would own my own casino. In my dream the U.S. government bought it and sold it to me cheap, of course. It would be way down on the end of the Las Vegas Strip, out in the desert next to a landing strip. It would be large and beautiful and well protected. It would have a playground for children and it would entertain guests from all over the galaxy. It was a very happy dream and I just loved having it. However, even though the dream was obviously a dream, it was also unusually forceful and captivating. The dream came upon me suddenly without warning. It left me feeling numb and dizzy for almost a half hour afterwards. When my mind finally cleared, I became certain that a stray radar beam had hit me. I spent most of the next hour checking the electronics in the control tower and visually inspecting the valley around me. For all of my searching, there was simply nothing out of place.

Occasionally I would have dreams of a much different nature. Sometimes my dreams would be so vivid and realistic and come to me so naturally that, like the Pharaoh in the book of Genesis, it didn't seem as if I were dreaming at all. In one such dream that I had several times, I was an ice age hunter chasing a deer on a beautiful day by a glacier in France. Always, the deer got away and I stood wondering what the future would be like.

In another, I was in a birch bark canoe on a lake in the spring, watching a lone wild goose fly by. In the dream I was wondering where wild geese spent the summer and wishing I could follow them. On one occasion the dream was so vivid that when I awoke, I stood at the side door of my weather shack actually looking out to see if the goose was still in view. Of course, outside there was only sagebrush and sand.

One hot afternoon out at Range Three, I was once again running a very high fever with nausea and all of the usual flu symptoms. I had taken the full dose of flu medicine. After completing the 11:30 a.m. balloon run and phoning Desert Center, I had another bad vomiting attack. With my head pounding, I decided that I would just take a drink of water and rest on the floor of my weather shack instead of attempting to make the long drive in to Mojave Wells for the noon meal. I probably wouldn't have been able to keep it down anyway. I set my alarm clock to 1:45 p.m. so I could make the 2:00 p.m. run. I positioned my pillow and my blankets and lay down on the floor of my weather shack. Soon I was resting comfortably on the warm floor and appreciating the cool gentle desert breezes. My fever was intense, and I immediately went to sleep.

While I was sleeping I had another vividly realistic dream. I was a young ice age hunter in France living with my wife and son in a cave on the side of a cliff not very far from the face of a glacier. I was standing looking out over the nearby river valley wondering why the earth was such a cold and desolate place. In my dream I noted that each year the summers were starting to become warmer. Then a large section of ice fell off the face of the glacier and cascaded into the valley below me.

The dream was so vivid and shocking that I woke up suddenly, thinking that I had felt an earthquake or maybe that the ground under my weather shack had moved. Sick and groggy, I got up and stumbled around outside for perhaps 45 minutes trying to comprehend what had happened.

Then, after returning to my shack and resting for a while, I decided to take the 2:00 p.m. run a few minutes early and spend the rest of the afternoon nursing my flu. I filled the balloon and took the measurements as best I could. After 4 minutes, I lost the balloon in the sun so I just tracked the sun for 5 minutes before I was able to relocate the balloon. The resulting calculated winds were quite erratic but it was the best I could do.

After phoning the winds in to Desert Center, I was too sick to lock up and drive back in to base right away. So I decided to rest some more on the floor of my weather shack first. I ached all over and I was running a very high fever. I lay down on the floor and I had a very hard time getting comfortable.

However, as I drifted off to sleep, a few scattered memorized images of the accident I had suffered on that painful summer day when I fell on my knee out in the sagebrush here at Range Three would float into my mind. They were ordinary memorized images of that painful afternoon when I had been practicing the Olympic broad jump, slipped, and deeply bruised my left knee. The few scattered images included several from the next morning when I had been surprised and found myself standing face-to-face with Range Four Harry in the generator shack.

After sleeping for perhaps a half hour I was awakened by the sound of two people walking lightly just outside in the sagebrush. They were mostly hidden from my view by the northeast corner of my weather shack. However I did catch a glimpse of one of them. It was a USAF one star general. He was saying in a low voice, "You say he's sick. He missed lunch and he is lying in here, Teacher?"

The other, a woman, replied, "Yes, Doctor. But do not disturb him. He is a very light sleeper."

Roused from my sleep, I stuttered out, "Who's there? Please don't bother me. I'm very sick. After I rest some, I'll go back in to town."

Outside the sounds retreated several feet back to the northeast. I lay back down and resumed resting. After a few minutes, out through the front door of my weather shack I could see a thin chalk white woman about my height, wearing a white aluminum jump suit. She walked casually over to my theodolite, adjusted it, and looked through it for a minute or so. Then she resumed walking casually over towards the generator shack, finally passing from my view. I was so sick that I couldn't tell if the scene that I had just witnessed was real or a dream. I continued resting, finally drifting off again into a light sleep. Once again memorized images from that following morning when I had been standing face to face with Range Four Harry kept drifting up into my mind. After napping for perhaps another two hours, I finally woke up feeling relaxed and better rested.

The stray images from memory of Range Four Harry had aroused my curiosity. On the morning after I had bruised my knee and had encountered Range Four Harry waiting for me in the generator shack, two hours or so of time had passed for which my memory was blank. Yet, while I had been resting on this afternoon, it felt like my mind was on the verge of recalling those two hours as a series of short dreams. As I slowly got up off the floor of my weather shack that warm afternoon, there was much to be considered.

I was still very sick and shaky but at least I felt well enough to shut down everything and drive back in to town. As I was closing up my theodolite, I noticed that it was pointing towards Mount Stockton perhaps 70 miles off to the north and east. It was pointing to a place just below the upper tree line. Between the afternoon haze, the heat waves, and my blurry vision I couldn't see much of anything when I looked through the theodolite. However, I noted the settings as I was locking everything up.

The drive back in to base was uneventful. Being sick, I drove quite slowly.

By the time the weekend arrived, I was more or less over my flu and able to travel. Still curious about my dreams, I drove in to Desert Center to visit its library. The base library had several books that I found quite interesting.

As I was browsing, for some reason I found myself paging through some books on microwave radars. I was surprised to discover that if a technician is directly hit by a beam from a high powered microwave radar, he may become mildly hypnotized. Later, even if he was uninjured, he may experience difficulty remembering what happened. I noted that the width of the white pencil carried by Range Four Harry was the same as the wavelength of a high powered microwave radar. A few of the pieces of the puzzle started falling into place. Generating Microwaves also generates heat. So to increase the power of Range Four Harry's microwave pencil, one would have to make it longer or else it would burn up when it was used. It would be natural for him to be carrying several pencils of different lengths. The radar books also stated that once lightly hypnotized by a microwave radar beam, some individuals are able to break out of the induced trance by rearranging their thought processes. Breaking out of the trance appears to be easier for people of higher intelligence. Yes, I found the books on microwave radars to be very interesting. However, I did not check any such books out of the library since I had no place to keep them from prying eyes.

Most interesting of all however, were several books on hypnotism and dreams. According to the experts, if a person has been lightly hypnotized and told not to remember the events that took place during his trance, later he can break through that mind block and remember the events as a series of short dreams. According to the experts, he should go to a warm comfortable sunny place to lie down and rest. He should let his mind wander as he drifts off into a light sleep. The books stated that sometimes the process takes a couple of years of practice and it's much easier to accomplish if the individual has a high level of intelligence. However, according to the experts, subjects of all different intelligence levels who have been hypnotized, do it all of the time.

There was, of course, one obvious problem. How can a person who is drifting off to sleep tell the difference between ordinary dreams and recovered memories from past hypnotic trances? According to the experts, it's frequently not possible for the individual alone to tell the difference. Apparently many individuals, like the Pharaoh of Ancient Egypt in the time of Joseph, are never exactly sure what it is that they are remembering in their dreams unless someone tells them. After all, according to the Bible, it was the Pharaoh of Ancient Egypt who received the prophetic dream communicated to him directly by God. The dream was useless until Joseph, acting only as the messenger of God, delivered the interpretation. Even though Pharaoh was a pagan, God expected Joseph to reward him for his previous hospitality. Hospitality, tit for tat, working together to build a pleasant and sustaining world while worshipping God, is where The Bible begins.

Yes, I read those books carefully, several times. Once a person begins drifting off to sleep, their brain is free to put up any idea, memory, or dream that it chooses, real or imagined, no matter where it comes from.

The next Monday afternoon, I decided to try relaxing on the floor of my weather shack and see how much I could remember about the missing two hours that I had spent with Range Four Harry. As soon as I had completed the 12:30 run and phoned the results in to Desert Center, I began my test. I opened both the front door and the side door of my weather shack. I positioned my pillow and blankets and adjusted my radio to a nice music station. I wound and set my alarm clock to wake me for the last run of the day at 2:00 p.m. Then I lay down on the floor and got comfortable. I still had a few minor lingering effects of the previous week's flu, so no matter what happened the rest would do me good.

As I lay resting and drifting off towards sleep, I let my mind wander. The noon lunch had been very good, the afternoon summer sun was very warm, the afternoon breezes were gentle, and I was naturally a little sleepy. Out to the east in the distant sagebrush I could hear the sounds of an occasional meadowlark. I remembered that morning in the generator shack, standing only 15 feet in front of Range Four Harry. He had a pencil-like instrument pointed directly at my left temple. "This isn't going to hurt Charlie, but your generals really have to inspect that damaged knee," he said in perfect English.

I remembered that my mind fuzzed over and my muscles would not respond. Only this time, I could remember more than before. I could remember turning around, walking outside and waiting there for a few minutes while one of the other white creatures turned off my truck. Then I could remember a large white ellipsoidal craft floating in silently from the north and landing a few hundred feet away from me out in the sagebrush to the west.

Then my dream ended as suddenly as it had begun. I woke up again, still feeling comfortable and relaxed, but also feeling an unusual kind of mental exhaustion. The entire process seemed to have tired out my brain.

I didn't know what to make of my dream. I sat up, took a drink of water from my canteen, thought about things for a while. Then I lied back down to rest and try it again.

This time, however, I began having my ice age glacier dream again. Just as before it felt intensely vivid and realistic. This time the dream made it further than before. This time in the dream, the huge blocks of ice continued breaking off the face of the glacier and cascading down into the river valley throughout the rest of the afternoon and all through the following evening. A huge section of the glacier was breaking up and I was very worried about what the future would be like. Then my alarm clock rang and awakened me. As it did so, I was so shocked that for a minute I felt as if I was going to be physically thrown into my helium tank. Once again it seemed as if there had been an earthquake and the ground under my weather shack had moved. I was half asleep, groggy and confused for a long time before I could finally get fully awake and started on the last balloon run of the day. The run was very late and Desert Center was quite upset. I resolved to be much more conscientious in the future regarding my balloon schedule.

I let my brain rest for a few days. Then I tried my resting technique again. Once again I was trying to remember what had happened during the two hours I had spent with Range four Harry. This time a different set of images began floating up into my consciousness. In my dream, a young woman began leaving her position behind a desk on my right and came into the right edge of my field of vision. She was almost 6 feet tall, very thin, had an extremely light, almost chalk white complexion. She was wearing a wig, gloves, and a great deal of make-up. She was dressed very stylishly. In my dream I was immediately convinced that I was looking at a high-ranking teacher. She had a friendly feminine, almost childish giggle as she stated, "There's nothing to be afraid of, Charlie. See, I look just like you, don't I?"

Once again, my dream ended as suddenly as it had begun. As before, I woke up still feeling comfortable and relaxed, but also feeling exhausted. As before, I didn't know what to make of my dream.

Over the course of the coming weeks I practiced my resting technique. Even though the floor of my weather shack was a very comfortable place, I discovered that recovering my missing memories was a slow and very tiring process. Usually, it only paid me to make one attempt every week or so. On many of the attempts only my casino winning dreams would come to me. Sometimes I had my ice age dreams and other recurring dreams set in various times in history. On three occasions I had my casino owner dream again, complete with its sudden onset and dizzy spells at the end.

On those occasions when I could successfully remember standing in front of Range Four Harry, usually only one or two minutes of images would float up into my mind. However, it was with patience that I persevered. Finally, on one beautiful warm late summer afternoon after all of my runs for the day had been completed, I was resting and daydreaming on the floor of my weather shack. An unusually large number of images started floating up into my consciousness. They felt like the complete two hour set of missing memories from that morning in the generator shack when I was standing face-to-face with Range Four Harry. The complete set of images came to me only once. Since I had no way to verify the source or accuracy of the images, I was never sure what to make of them. Like my other dreams, all I could do was remember them and wonder.

I could remember that summer morning, walking over to the large white craft. Range Four Harry opened up a large cargo hold door that had a round glass porthole window. Then I could remember climbing into the cargo hold and sitting down while Harry closed the door from the outside. I waited a few minutes and then the craft lifted off. The vehicle rose up no more than 50 feet off the desert. I remembered watching as the vehicle floated slowly past the buildings of Range Four, some twenty miles north of Range Three, heading up the valley towards the north and east.

Finally it arrived at an underground base carved out of the side of a granite mountain.

I could remember the craft entering an auditorium sized, well-lit concrete hanger, tunneled into the western side of the mountain, and the concrete hanger doors closing behind us. Then Range Four Harry came into my cargo hold and opened the craft's door. Someone on the outside helped him. The auditorium was a normal temperature but warmer than I'd expected. It was well lit by ordinary fluorescent lights.

The far half of the auditorium was filled with 15 or 20 rows of folding chairs, separated into four sections by three aisles. The chairs were facing away from me. On my far right near the wall, facing the center of the room was an ordinary oak desk with a phone and two ordinary straight chairs.

The far half of the auditorium was wider than the near half, the half where the craft sat by the entrance. The far half was about 20 feet or so wider. This change in dimension was marked by a normal 90 degree corner.

An American three star USAF General was standing by this corner watching me. Range Four Harry, using his perfect English, pleasantly ordered me out of the craft. Having been electronically hypnotized, I obeyed without hesitation. As I did so, the three star General walked quickly around behind the 90 degree corner. I could hear his footsteps on the concrete floor as he entered another room and then still another. I could hear the general talking to someone. He was speaking with some urgency, "He's finally here. He ran later than we expected because he actually takes his wind measurements instead of making them up like the other observers do."

There was a short pause. Then the General continued, "We haven't much time to repair his knee and issue a cover story down at Mojave Wells. If he doesn't report for breakfast, his friends will notice he's gone. God, I still can't believe that he smashed his knee and did not even report for x-rays. Where do they find men like him?"

There was another short pause, then the General continued, as though talking to the high ranking lady, "Oh, yes. If his friends think he's missing or in trouble, they'll disobey their orders and come looking for him. If that happens, it'll cause difficulties."

There was another short pause, then the General continued, "Yes, Teacher. I've ordered his friends to stay back at their Mojave Wells base, but if those young airman friends of his think he's in any trouble, my orders wouldn't mean a thing. They'd all come rescue him. That's how young men are."

After another short pause, the three star General could be heard continuing, "Colonel, now that he's here, you get him ready for his knee operation. General, after you finish, we'll fly him down to Desert Center in the courier plane. As soon as you finish, I'll phone the Desert Center Base Commander and have him tell Payne to get up here for tomorrow's runs. Then I'll have him inform all of Charlie's friends that he's in the hospital down at Desert Center so they can visit him there. If he remembers anything unusual, we'll have the Desert Center doctor tell him his memory is fuzzy because of the drugs we gave him during the operation."

Harry walked me into the hanger and over to the 90 degree corner. Then he had me turn and walk around the corner and continue on for perhaps another 10 feet. I was stopped at last in front of the door to the next room. Harry then took up a military position, standing behind me on my left. Apparently he felt this position gave him a free shot at my left temple in case he felt he needed one.

The doorway in front of me was a double door, slightly wider than ordinary. The doors had been opened inward. Harry had me stand in front of the door, looking up through the right side. In front of me was an ordinary concrete step into the next room. The next room wasn't very large. It was about the same size as a doctor's examining room. It looked about the same as the emergency medical rooms at Desert Center. In the center of the room and off to my right was an ordinary medical examining table. The rest of the equipment in the room was quite ordinary. It had a medium sized X-Ray machine and the usual collection of ordinary medical supplies. Inside the room the writing on the walls was entirely in English.

On the other side of the room was another doorway. Like the first, it was a doublewide door and both doors had been opened inward. A downward sloping ramp led into a hallway and gallery beyond.

Inside the room, on the other side of the examining table stood a one star USAF General, obviously an American medical doctor. He was wearing a lab coat and surgical attire. He stood with his back to me. Standing around him and listening intently to every word he spoke, stood three tall white creatures. They were also dressed in medical clothes. They appeared to be young medical students in training. The General stood at least 6 feet tall and the three tall whites were not more than an inch or so shorter then he was. Like the other white creatures, they were much thinner than any human. Despite their height, they probably didn't weigh much more than 100 pounds. Like the others, they had blonde hair, bright blue eyes, and only four fingers on each hand.

In the opposite hallway, a tall USAF colonel, obviously another medical doctor, came walking into view from the left. He turned and entered the examining room. He came to a halt and stood waiting for orders.

The one star General was saying to his students, "We'll go next door to the library while Harry and the Colonel get Charlie up on the table. With his knee injured the way it is, he probably won't be able to step up into this examination room.

The Colonel will need the help of Harry's equipment to get him up in here and onto the table. The Colonel will take some X-rays and prepare him for knee surgery. Don't worry. We'll only be performing a minor operation. It's a shame he smashed his knee the way he did. We've all been learning so much from him but he'll heal fast. We'll have him back up here and on duty in a few weeks." Then the General and his students left the room by the other doorway and disappeared from view by turning to the right.

After they had left, the Colonel turned towards Harry and I. The Colonel then began to approach us very slowly. Apparently the Colonel had a deep respect for Harry and had no desire to do anything unexpected. While the Colonel was still more or less 15 feet away, he begin speaking to Harry in calm, smooth pleasant tones, much the way a man might speak calmly to a horse, "That equipment of yours is very impressive, Harry. It must be very effective at neutralizing pain. I see Charlie is standing there normally with his weight distributed evenly on both of his legs."

Harry waited patiently for the Colonel to finish. Apparently Harry was very experienced at dealing with humans. Speaking perfect English, Harry answered, "Our equipment is very good but Charlie is so intelligent that our equipment does not affect him in the manner which we expected. Our equipment has not been able to neutralize any of his pain."

The Colonel continued smoothly, apparently not believing the words that Harry had just spoken, "Did you have any trouble getting him onto the scout craft? I didn't see, but wasn't he limping badly when he walked in here?"

Harry responded simply, "Charlie stands normally because none of his bones are broken. Charlie walks normally because his muscles, his knee ligaments, and his other body parts are still in their proper working order. They are bruised but not otherwise damaged." Harry's stunning command of English was so perfect that he was obviously able to think in it.

"Really?" asked the Colonel obviously unconvinced.

"Yes," answered Harry. "I examined him myself while he was still in his generator shack. I brought him here because we both agreed that you needed to examine him for yourself. I believe you will agree with me that he does not require an operation."

The Colonel walked over beside me on my left and continued smoothly, "But his leg was broken only yesterday."

Harry responded pleasantly, but otherwise without emotion, "Yes, that is what we believed yesterday. After he fell, he lay in the thorns and rocks for 27 minutes and 31 seconds before he began trying to recover from his accident. It took him three minutes and 15 seconds to reposition his body and sit up. After his accident, most of the time he spent screaming unintelligibly in agony. He vomited up everything in his stomach from the pain. After he sat up, we were finally able to understand his words. He was screaming sentences in agony such as, 'my knee, my knee. I've gone and broken my knee.' Then he spent a little more than 4 minutes and 14 seconds crying from the agony of it all.

We notified your Generals immediately after it happened. We went to help him, but by the time we were able to get to where he was, he had already gotten up. He would have fought with us had we approached any closer. The Teacher is certain that he would have fought us if we hadn't stayed back from him. He's very strong willed and brave beyond description. He is a much stronger individual than any of the other weather observers that you have sent to Mojave Wells."

The Colonel thought about the words Harry had spoken for a few minutes. Then he squatted down beside me on my left and began carefully examining my cuts and bruises. After he finished with my left wrist and arm, he asked me to raise my left pants leg. Hypnotized as I was, I was unable to respond. The Colonel then asked Harry if he would ask me to raise my left pants leg so he could examine my leg. Harry made some adjustments on the electronic equipment that he carried and I found myself able to respond to the Colonel's orders. Reaching down with my left hand, I carefully pulled my pants leg up until the top of my left knee was exposed. Then the Colonel, in medical fashion, gave my left ankle and left knee a short examination. Then he thought about Harry's words. Speaking at last, and still squatting next to me, the Colonel asked, "When I was walking over here, Charlie was able to follow my movements with his eyes. Is that because your equipment doesn't work on Charlie in the same manner that it worked on the other weather observers?"

"Yes," responded Harry simply. "He is so intelligent that his thought processes are unusual for a human."

132

"Does that mean that Charlie here, may be able to remember seeing me standing in front of him when this is all over?" continued the Colonel smoothly.

"Yes," responded Harry. Then Harry inspected his equipment for a few seconds and continued, "I believe that Charlie will be able to remember most of what has happened within a few days or weeks. He'll be able to remember every detail within three to five years. It is also possible for him to break out of these controls now if he should become terrified or if he should set his mind to it. The Teacher has seen him break free from controls of this nature several times in the past."

The Colonel thought for a few minutes and then responded smoothly, "You are correct as usual. Charlie does not require an operation. I had better inform The General."

Then the Colonel rose smoothly to his feet, stepped up into the examining room and proceeded smoothly to the opposite door, walked down the opposite ramp, turned right and walked out of sight.

After a minute or so, the Colonel could be heard saying, "Excuse me, General, but there's something you should know."

"Yes, Colonel," responded the one star Medical General.

"First, Sir, I would like you to examine Charlie's wounds. It does not appear to Harry or myself that he requires medical attention. None of his bones are broken. His muscles and ligaments are all in their proper working order.

His left wrist, left knee and left ankle are all horribly bruised and very badly swollen, but they are not infected and they are healing rapidly. Otherwise, he is showing only cuts and scratches. His records show that his tetanus shots are current. The bruises, the swollen knee, the swollen wrist, and the swollen ankle mean nothing to him. He cleaned his wounds himself, probably using only soap, water, and rubbing alcohol. He had some cuts that for most men would have required several stitches. He closed his cuts by spitting on them and then carefully pressing them closed. He appears to have held them closed until they had healed well enough to stay closed." The Colonel paused for a few seconds and then continued matter-of-factly. "He'll probably spend this afternoon nursing his wounds by sunning himself and swimming in the warm outdoor pool down on base. By tomorrow morning he'll be out playing basketball with his friends and he'll have forgotten all about his fall yesterday."

"Yes, Colonel," responded the General.

"Second, Harry says Charlie is so intelligent that their electronic equipment isn't working on him in the manner that we were expecting. Harry says that the equipment hasn't neutralized any of Charlie's pain. Harry says that Charlie is walking normally and that he just shrugs off the pain. Harry also says that if Charlie becomes terrified or if he sets his mind to it, he can break out of those electronic controls at anytime as he stands there."

A short pause followed. Then the General responded, "You were correct to warn me, Colonel. We had better both check."

Then the two USAF officers appeared in the far hallway from the right and both entered the examining room. They were only half way across the room when the medical General noticed that I was able to follow his movements with my eyes. The General stopped immediately and stated to the Colonel in authoritative tones, "Harry is right. He's hardly hypnotized at all! And the way he's standing, there can't be a thing wrong with any of his bones or muscles!" Then the General half turned back towards the far doorway and exclaimed in raised tones, "Sergeant Smith! I need you in here immediately!"

Immediately a young, muscular USAF military policeman wearing eight stripes appeared from around the doorway to the right. The sergeant stepped smartly up to the General, came to attention in front of him, and responded proudly, "Chief Master Sergeant Smith reporting as ordered, Sir." The Sergeant was obviously a guard but he did not appear to be armed.

The General continued, "Sergeant, you are ordered to have that Airman under the control of you and your men at all times while he is in this facility. Do you understand your orders?"

The Sergeant responded, "Yes, Sir! May I remind the General, Sir, that my standing orders are to have the General under the direct observation of me and my men at all times and to protect the General with the lives of me and my men if necessary, at all times day or night, Sir!"

The General continued, "Yes, Sergeant, I am well aware of your standing orders. However, I am in no danger here among our tall friends. But if Charlie, there, breaks out of those electronic controls that he is under, a terrible incident might occur. I am ordering you to personally guarantee that he is under American control at all times, no matter what happens."

"Yes, Sir," responded the Sergeant, smartly! "I have received my direct orders. I will have the said airman under my complete and personal control at all times while he is in this facility, Sir!"

Still, the General did not seem pleased. He continued sternly, "Sergeant, I don't believe that you fully appreciate the situation you're facing. Charlie, here, is the most gentle and the most intelligent airman ever to be stationed at Mojave Wells. That's part of the reason he has survived out in that hellish desert longer than any other weather observer ever has. For a good many months now, he has bravely performed his military duties in an environment that has chewed up every other observer before him after just a handful of days. Alone, always by himself, he happily performs duties that have wasted even three and four man teams of weather observers in months past. Our tall friends have fallen in love with him because of his sense of humor, his intelligence, his strong will, and his bravery. If he were to break out of those electronic controls, he would probably begin by telling us funny stories until we were all laughing helplessly on the floor. Then he would probably sneak through that side door and vanish into that mountain wilderness outside. The next time any of us saw him, he would probably be playing water polo with the school children down in the pool at Mojave Wells. Usually he's like that, a big kid who has never quite grown up."

"Yes, General," responded the Sergeant.

"Or, if he broke out of those controls, he might choose to ignore all of us. He might announce that he had his military duties to perform and his breakfast to get to. Then he might step quickly through that side door before any of us knew what had happened. He would escape into that desolate mountain wilderness outside as naturally as a child heads for a playground," continued the General. "The next time any of us saw him he would be nonchalantly releasing his balloons from Range Three as though nothing had ever happened. Sometimes he's like that, a grown man with the innocence of a child."

"Yes, General," responded the Sergeant.

But Charlie, there, has another perfectly fine way of escaping from this facility, Sergeant. That way is over our dead bodies."

"Our dead bodies, Sir?" asked the Sergeant in surprise.

"Yes, Sergeant, over our dead bodies," responded the General. "Charlie can take both you and me by surprise any time he feels like it. Charlie, there, has more moves than you and I would ever dream possible. Once he sets his mind to something, he becomes the most bull-headed, single minded man that ever walked the face of God's Green Earth. If he should break free and set his mind to fighting his way out of here, he would be as tough a man as you could ever imagine."

"Yes, Sir," responded the Sergeant smartly! "I have heard the General and I understand the meaning of the General's words, Sir!"

Then the Sergeant barked a command to another guard who appeared from around the far corner on the right. "Sergeant Jones. Order Sergeant Anderson to vacate his post by the outer door immediately and assist me here in the scout craft hanger. Then you are to assume a military position here in the examination room and to stand ready at all times to assist Sergeant Anderson and myself in the event that we should need assistance with the said Airman. Remember, Sergeant Jones, there are white children in the corridor. Do not double time. Do not frighten them!"

"Yes, Sergeant," responded the second guard. Then he could be heard walking quickly down a long corridor off somewhere to the right of the far doorway.

The General seemed happier now but still he continued, "Remember, Sergeant, maintain a military position on Charlie at all times. Don't let him take you or your men by surprise!" Then the General looked at me for a minute or two, obviously deep in thought. Suddenly an idea hit him like a bolt of lightening. Sergeant, you and Harry move Charlie over to the right immediately. Have him stand facing the wall and make sure this entryway is free for our white friends to use."

"Yes, General," responded Sergeant Smith.

The Sergeant turned slowly towards Harry. The Sergeant, like the Colonel, appeared to have a tremendous respect for Harry and obviously did not wish to upset him. Like the Colonel, the Sergeant spoke to Harry using calm and smooth tones, almost as though he were speaking calmly to a horse. "Please have Charlie move ten feet to the right," stated the Sergeant calmly.

"Charlie will respond to your commands," replied Harry using pleasant matter-of-fact tones. Harry was adjusting his electronics as he spoke.

Then the Sergeant walked over to me and barked authoritatively, "Said Airman, step 10 feet to the right as the General has ordered, NOW!"

I responded by standing upright and immediately side stepped three times to the right. This left me standing facing the concrete wall and standing perhaps three feet from the wall. I had just finished when the second and third USAF guards arrived. Then the Colonel arrived at the doorway and it was obvious that the entire area was becoming too crowded for the medical General to complete his examination. The Colonel mused over the situation for a few minutes. Then he ordered me to move another 20 feet to the right and to turn right at a 45 degree angle so that I was facing into the far right corner of the room. As I waited in this position, the Colonel spoke in slightly raised tones into the examination room, "General Miles, Sir. Charlie stands ready for you to complete your medical examination."

The one star medical General calmly walked out into the hanger, stepping down from the examination room as he did so. Approaching me from behind and on my left side, the two American USAF doctors proceeded to carefully and intensely examine my entire bone and muscle structure, my back, my spine, and, especially, my left wrist, my left ankle, and my left knee. The American doctors, like good doctors everywhere, appeared interested only in my medical well-being. The three tall white medical students remained standing back by the doorway and the American Medical General showed little interest in sharing information with them.

Satisfied that my bones and muscles were in good order, the medical General, ordered me to hop on one leg, first my right and then my left. When I had finished hopping several times on each leg, The General stepped back, turned to the Colonel and stated, "I would have never believed it if I hadn't seen it for myself. That Charlie has handled all of his wounds himself. You and Harry were correct, Colonel. There isn't a damned thing we need to do for him. He doesn't even need us to put rubbing alcohol on those scratches on his back."

"What the hell do we do now?" asked the Colonel seriously. "We don't have to take Charlie back to Range Three for another hour and a half. We promised our tall friends they'd get to study Charlie up close when the operation was over. We have to keep our word."

"As usual, you're correct Colonel," stated the one star General seriously. Let me go talk it over with General Shaw.

I stood and waited as the medical General walked calmly back into the examination room and turned out of sight. The three USAF Sergeants, fine military guards that they were, assumed military positions behind and around me. All three stood ready to attack and watched me intently. If I so much as sneezed, they obviously intended to break half the bones in my body, bones that the General had just pronounced to be in proper working order.

After a few minutes, the three Generals came walking back into the hanger. Speaking to the Chief Master Sergeant, the three star General said authoritatively, "Sergeant Smith, have Charlie stand in the center of the middle aisle, just in front of the first row of chairs. Have him face the front wall. I'll inform our tall friends we're ready for them. They may inspect Charlie now. When the Teacher arrives, she will take full custody of Charlie. It appears that she trusts him. Then, you and your men will fall back to guard the side door."

The Sergeant responded immediately, "Yes Sir!" Turning to me the Sergeant gave the necessary orders. Except for Harry and the USAF personnel, the hanger was otherwise empty at the time. The scout craft remained parked near the entrance and appeared to be unoccupied.

The guards positioned me in the center of the middle aisle in front of the chairs, standing facing the front wall. The front wall was ordinary poured gray concrete and was about 10 feet in front of me. Then Harry and the three USAF guards retreated back to the 90 degree corner.

As I stood there, I could hear the three star General walking back through the examination room and into the gallery beyond. I could hear him saying, as though speaking to a lady, "Charlie is ready for you to talk to. We have plenty of time. As you heard General Miles say, Charlie doesn't require an operation so we're happy to report that he'll continue on duty at Mojave Wells just as before. We'll order him to take it easy for the next week. He should be completely healed up by then. We're all very glad that you reported his accident to us. We were all very, very lucky. I'll tell you one thing, General Miles says that Charlie is the toughest airman that he's ever seen. We're all proud that you selected him. When you finish talking to him, we'll take him back to Range Three. We would like to return him while there is still time for him to make it in for his breakfast. As you know, good food is very important to our soldier's moral."

I could hear a feminine voice respond in perfect English, "Thank you General. I'll inform our people."

The three star General walked back into the hanger, crossed the room and took a chair at the desk on the opposite wall. He specifically sat in the chair that was farthest from me. The one star General and the Colonel each took a chair on the aisle in the last row of chairs directly behind me. During the next few minutes a large number of the tall white creatures assembled in the examination room and in the hanger by the examination room door. After a few minutes, the lady could be heard coming through the examination room, through the door, and through the crowd. After she made it through the crowd and into the hanger, she stood upright and adjusted her hair and clothes in much the same way that a human lady would have. Since she was some distance behind me, I could catch only glimpses of her. She was about 6 feet tall and dressed very stylishly. She had large blue eyes, stylish blonde hair, and a complexion far lighter than any human. She was wearing a long sleeve dress with a high neck. Her outfit was attractive but it wasn't the least bit revealing. Her outfit

141

included gloves, nurse style white nylons, and a substantial amount of make up. For shoes she was wearing flats.

The Lady crossed the hanger in ordinary fashion and took up a position at the desk on the far wall. She remained standing behind the chair next to the three star General. After a few moments, she began to address the crowd using perfect, beautiful English, without any contractions.

She began by giggling a little and laughing happily. She said in a raised voice, to the crowd behind me, "This is Charlie. He is the airman who saved the life of my little girl down at Range One. He is the one who found her when she was lost and freed her from the thick sagebrush. Remember, we must not frighten him. He speaks only English and he frightens very easily. You must speak English when you are in this room and you must understand English to be in this room or in the examination room." The manner in which the crowd reacted convinced me that the lady held a very high rank.

The crowd then appeared to separate into two groups. One group entered the hanger and began taking seats in the chairs behind me. The other group thinned out and returned into the examination room. When everyone had finally gotten to their destinations, she turned towards me and began, "Charlie, we were wondering how you chose your name?"

I was still electronically hypnotized and unable to answer. I could move my eyes some and my neck a little bit. I felt as though I might be able to move my left arm if I tried hard enough. After waiting a few seconds, the lady appeared to realize I was unable to answer. From her left sleeve, she took a pencil-like electronic instrument similar to the one Harry carried, and pointed it at my exposed right temple. In a few seconds, I found myself able to speak. I was also able move my head and neck from side to side. The situation I was in seemed to greatly amuse her and she responded by giggling for a few minutes. Then she repeated the question, "Charlie, we were wondering how you chose your name?"

I could just barely see her by straining to turn my neck and my eyes as far to the right as I could. I responded calmly, "It would be less frightening if I could see you as I was answering the question."

This seemed to greatly amuse her. She giggled happily some more. Then she left her position behind the desk and came into the right edge of my field of vision until she was standing only 5 or 6 feet in front of me, off to my right. I noticed that she assumed a position that still left Harry with a clear field of fire in case he should feel he needed one. She was almost 6 feet tall, very thin, had an extremely light, almost chalk white, complexion. Upon finally getting a good look at her, I was immediately convinced that I was looking at a Teacher. She had a friendly, feminine, almost childish giggle as she stated, "There's nothing to be afraid of, Charlie. See, I look just like you, don't I?"

I responded, "Yes. Of course, you don't look exactly like me because I'm a man and you're a woman."

With this, the lady and everyone in the room behind me, including the American officers, began laughing like there was no tomorrow. It took a long time for the laughter to die down. Then she pleasantly repeated her first question, "Charlie, we were wondering how you chose your name?"

Not sure how to answer the question, I responded, "My mother and father chose my real name when I was born.

The lady continued with the next question, "We were all quite worried about you, Charlie. Yesterday, you fell very badly out in the desert. We all believed that you had broken your left leg and your left knee. However, your doctors tell us that today your left leg isn't broken. We are all wondering what happened."

Not sure how to respond, I struggled for words, "Well, at first after I fell, my leg hurt a lot and I thought it was broken, too. But after a while, I saw these white seagulls. They scared me into getting up and walking it off."

The lady and the crowd were laughing even before I had finished. The part about the white seagulls seemed to especially amuse them. After the laughter subsided, the lady continued, "Seriously, Charlie, you should be more careful when you are alone out in the desert. There are many dangerous animals out there. There are coyotes, stray dogs, rattle snakes, and bumble bees. You go out there every morning completely unarmed. You do not even carry a gun in your truck."

I responded, "I could be more careful, I suppose. But I'm used to being alone out in the desert. I'm not afraid of the darkness or anything and there isn't anything out there I can't handle alone." I wondered how the lady knew that I never carried a gun in my truck.

For some reason, my ordinary response was met with more laughter. Then the lady continued her pleasant questions, "Charlie, you were born in Wisconsin. There are no deserts or mountains in Wisconsin. Wisconsin gets very cold. It rains and snows there. Humans usually stay in the climate where they were born. Yet, you are perfectly at home, alone out here in this desert. You know you are a very unusual person. You are not the slightest bit afraid of breaking you leg when you are alone so far out in this desert."

I was surprised that she knew so much about me. Watching her reactions, I became completely convinced that I was talking to a very high-ranking teacher. Her childish giggling convinced me that she must spend a large portion of her time teaching children. "Well, I'm a young man, and strong. Even if I fell and broke a bone, it would heal quickly," I responded in a matter-a-fact manner.

Still she continued her questioning, "Broken bones are very dangerous. You should be more careful. One time, when I was a little girl, I fell and broke my left leg. It took more than five of your years for it to heal. It was very painful. Both my mother and father were very worried about me."

I wasn't sure how to respond. "Oh, I'm a young man. If I broke a bone, it would just heal right up in a couple of days. I'd be back on my feet before anyone even missed me." I stammered.

The young lady and the crowd behind me found this noticeably amusing. The Teacher continued, as though teasing childishly, "My bones take five years to heal. Yours take only a few days. Charlie, why do you suppose that your bones heal up so much faster than mine?"

I puzzled over this for a minute or so. Then I answered in a pleasant and authoritative manner, "Well, of course. You see, you're a beautiful young woman. I'm a strong young man. A young man's bones just naturally heal up much faster than the bones of a young woman."

With this, the Teacher, the Generals, and the entire room behind me broke into hysterical laughter. Harry, the USAF guards, everyone was just absolutely hysterical with laughter. The three star General took a handkerchief out from his rear pocket and began wiping his eyes and forehead because he'd been laughing so hard. The Teacher and some of the white creatures began making a series of barking sounds. Then some of them began whinnying like

145

horses because they were laughing so hard. The laughter continued for a long time. When the laughter had begun to die down, no one in the entire crowd behind me was still sitting down. Everyone was up and moving around. Only the three star General was still sitting, holding his sides in laughter as he did so. Still laughing, the Teacher began speaking loudly to the crowd, she said, "See, I told you that talking to Charlie was going to be fun. He isn't anything like the other observers before him."

Then, the Teacher turned to me. She was smiling and still laughing. Between giggles, she stated in a beautiful feminine voice, "No, Charlie. That isn't the reason that your bones heal up so much faster than mine." For the first time, I wondered if she was really human.

The Teacher addressed the crowd behind me, "We have several more minutes before we must return Charlie to Range Three. We promised the American Generals that we would not make him miss his breakfast. If any of you would like to ask him questions, you may do so now. Remember, all questions must be in English."

One of the female creatures in the back asked what breakfast was. The Teacher responded, "Charlie eats more times in one day than we do. He eats a meal in the morning which he calls breakfast. Breakfast is very important to him. Then he eats again at noon. He calls his noon meal dinner. He eats a third time in the late afternoon about sundown. His late afternoon meal he calls supper. Because he's a young man and still growing, usually he eats again at night just before he goes to bed."

After a short pause, another female creature that sounded somewhat older than the Teacher, asked, "Does he enjoy coming out into the desert at night?" She seemed to be afraid of me and hid noticeably behind the others as she asked the question.

The Teacher responded, "Charlie understands English and he is very brave. It will not frighten him if you ask him yourself."

Upon hearing this, the older woman appeared to become somewhat braver, and restated the question, this time addressing it directly to me, "Charlie, do you enjoy coming out into the desert at night?"

"Yes," I responded evenly. "The desert is very beautiful, especially on warm, summer moonlit nights. I enjoy the desert very much and I enjoy looking at the stars during the night time."

The older lady appeared to find my answer quite interesting. She paused, and then continued the questioning, "Charlie, how does it feel to be a grown human man out here under the stars, alone, at night?"

I answered without giving the answer much thought, "The stars are so beautiful that frequently I just stand and look at them for a long time. On some clear moonless summer nights I get so caught up looking at stars such as Arcturas, that I almost forget to take the wind measurements."

A ripple of emotion passed through the crowd when I mentioned the star Arcturas, some 36 light years away. After a short pause, the older lady asked with some surprise, "Teacher, does Charlie know where we come from?"

The Teacher replied, "No, not quite, but he is close. Charlie is extremely perceptive and he thinks things through so carefully that he is able to discover things that other humans would miss. Unlike most other humans, he is so open to new ideas that he has almost figured out the physics of how our scout craft works. Remember none of the

American scientists have been able to accomplish anything even close to that, and that's one body of knowledge that we haven't shared with the American Generals. The American scientists are still wasting their time trying Einstein's approach, and pretending that our ships can not travel faster than the speed of light."

With that statement, the American Generals seemed especially impressed.

Then the Teacher said, "Just one more question. It has gotten late and we have to take Charlie back so he can have his breakfast."

A young mother, about the same age as the Teacher asked, "Charlie spends so much time alone out in the desert. The desert and this mountain base are so boring. There's nothing whatever for us women with children to do while our men are off working. Does Charlie ever get bored like we do? Does he ever feel like going into town and shopping and doing exciting things the way we would like to?"

The Teacher replied, "Yes. Charlie feels that way on many days and he goes in to town quite often. I would like to get my pet project started so that we young mothers with children could do more exciting things. I wish we could go into town and go shopping like Charlie does. To do so, however, we have to get over our natural fear of humans and we will have to learn how to blend in with them in a crowd of shoppers. I believe that we can learn that from Charlie. His ability to quickly adjust his actions and his way of thinking so that he blends in with the people around him is especially impressive and also very easy for us to monitor."

The young mother began laughing and stated, "So, Teacher, you're saying that if we're nice to Charlie, perhaps someday he can take us all shopping for clothes."

Then a gentle laughter from the crowd filled the hanger and the three star General stated, while wiping tears of laughter from his eyes, "This airman can do anything we ask him. He can even take young mothers shopping for pretty dresses."

The gentle laughter continued for a while. Then the Teacher stated, "It is late. We have to end our meeting and take Charlie back to Range Three. Perhaps we will be able to do this again sometime. Thank you everyone for coming."

The crowd filed out of the hanger, back through the medical examination room, and disappeared out of sight, leaving only the Teacher, the Generals, Harry, and the guards in the hanger with me. Once the hanger was empty, the three star General turned to the other two generals and said authoritatively, "That Charlie is the bravest man that I have ever seen or heard tell of. Maybe we should consider having him take some of those women shopping. With him as the tour guide, no one would ever suspect."

Then Harry had me turn around and walk back over to the scout craft. He opened the door to the cargo hold, had me get back in and sit on the floor. Then he closed the door. In a few minutes, the hanger doors opened. Then the craft powered up and we lifted off, all in total silence. As the craft headed back towards Range Three, through the porthole I could see that we had been in a small hanger on the western side of one of the mountains at the far northern end of the valley.

In the fullness of time, I found myself, once again standing in front of the diesel generator in the generator shack at Range Three with Harry standing slightly behind me. Harry said, "Charlie, you are the strongest human the Teacher and I have ever seen. I want you to stand here and sing the first two verses of your favorite song. Then you may wake up and continue with what you were doing."

I began singing my favorite song. Then Harry pointed his short white pencil directly at my left temple and activated the instrument. I felt a certain dizziness and confusion pass through my mind. A gentle early morning breeze seemed to pass through the generator shack. I continued to sing my song for two more verses. Then, I remember suddenly having full control of myself again. Harry was nowhere in sight and everything at Range Three was back to normal.

After finishing my dream, I remember waking up naturally on the floor of my weather shack that warm late summer afternoon. I was well rested but my mind felt exhausted. Many days, perhaps a month would pass before my mind felt recharged enough to think about what had happened. Some days it felt as though the subconscious part of my mind was busy and that it had a great deal of furniture to rearrange. Other days it felt like it was joining things together. Finally I felt as though my memories were reconnected and whole again. Finally, I felt relaxed again. Finally, at last, the ranges were filled once again, with the sounds of my laughter.

A Day With a View

"... The Lord is my light and my salvation --
Whom shall I fear? . . ."
Psalm of David 27:1

"Charlie, I wonder if you'd do something for me and the rest of the boys," said Steve as he mixed his fried eggs in with his hash browns. It was a perfect summer morning and breakfast was unusually well prepared. The Mojave Wells chow hall had been designed back in World War II to accommodate several hundred soldiers. Now with only 17 men stationed at Mojave Wells, the chow hall generally ran close to empty. Usually at chow time, the handful of men who were present for duty responded by huddling close together around a few special tables close to the windows. This morning was no exception. Steve, Doug, Bryan, and I had all joined tables for breakfast. The talk turned naturally to the ranges because even in the chow hall, always there was the ranges, always there was something, something that waited and watched from afar when a man was out there in the loneliness of the ranges. Every man at Mojave Wells knew that he desperately needed the help of every other man if he was to survive a trip out onto the ranges.

"Why, yes, Steve," I happily responded. "Anything. What is it?"

"I want you to keep a close watch on that ammunition bunker out at Range Three," said Steve thoughtfully and carefully. "Don't ever go over there, especially when you're out there alone. Just tell us guys if you ever see anyone over there."

151

"Yes, Steve." I said, "Why? Did someone get lost over there?"

"No," answered Steve thoughtfully. "But a couple months ago when your friend Payne was up here, before he had his accident and all, and before your friend Washington was up here and got himself burned up in the forehead, someone opened the lock on that ammunition bunker over there by the mountains at Range Three and borrowed one of the flares and one of the flare guns that we used to keep in the bunker over there."

"And you want to make sure that it doesn't happen again?" I asked instinctively.

"No," said Steve. "Since then I've been careful to keep the bunker empty so I'm not expecting that it will ever happen again. I'm expecting that whoever took it will be returning it one of these days and I want to be sure to go get it when it shows up again."

Confused, I stammered, "I don't understand, Steve. Are you suggesting that some two months ago when Payne was up here, that he took one of those flares and flare guns and has been keeping it from you ever since?"

Steve smiled and slowly shook his head no.

I continued, "I know Payne. He's as honest as a judge. I honestly don't think Payne would ever take anything like that and surely you're not suggesting that I ever took the flare gun, are you, Steve?"

"Oh, heck no, Charlie," Steve responded, laughing some. "And, anyway, after your friend Washington got himself burned and the Desert Center Base Commander and the rest went through all that trouble to pick you, they've damn near given everything out on the ranges to you. You could take all the damned flares out there anytime you wanted to and we all have standing orders from the Desert Center Base

Commander to just go get more from Desert Center and not ask you so much as a single question about them. Not that me or any of the boys care, Charlie, but ever since you came up here this time, Desert Center has been treating you like you're some kind of Teacher's Pet." Then Steve paused for a minute to let his words sink in. Then he laughed some more before continuing. "As for Payne, I'm absolutely certain that he didn't take the flare or the flare gun. When he was up here, he was so afraid of Range Three that the only times he ever went out to his weather shack, were during broad daylight when either Doug or I or one of the boys were with him. You'd have had to shoot him to get him to go over there to the ammo bunker alone. There's no way in hell he could have taken it."

"I've always wondered about that, Steve." I responded. "I mean Payne grew up in the desert. He couldn't possibly be afraid of the desert itself, or the openness, or the loneliness or any of that. He's so big and muscular, he can't possibly be afraid of any man that walks or talks. I've always wondered about the story he told me about his accident and what he saw out there that had him so terrified."

Steve paused for a minute, choosing his next words carefully and slowly. He continued, "Well remember, the boys and I were all out on the ranges that day and we all saw what he saw. Payne was definitely telling the truth. Whatever is out there, the boys and I have noticed that you're the only man that has ever been stationed up here that it hasn't terrified off the ranges. To a man, we don't think you should be spending so much time alone out there on the ranges, Charlie. We think you should be more like Payne. He would never go out there at night and he would never go out to Range Three without one of us along with

153

him. We give you our word that if you are ever out there and come back terrified, every man here will support you. Every man here will understand anything you feel like telling us."

"Thanks, Steve," I said. "I really appreciate it and I want you to know that I will always help any man here anytime you need it. But what I don't understand Steve, is why you're expecting the flare gun and flare to pop again after being missing for more than two months."

"Well, see Charlie," responded Steve in a slow and guarded fashion, "There's cycles of things up here at the Wells. Sometimes things up here, curious things, like your toothpaste and aftershave bottle, well, they disappear, and then reappear in a couple of days. Then other things, useful things, like your favorite pencil and that pair of work gloves out in your Range Three weather shack, well, they disappear, and then reappear in a couple of weeks. Other things, scientific things, like that spare weight you use when filling the balloons, or that plastic ruler you use to compute the winds, well, they disappear and then reappear in a couple months. Once in a while, beautiful things like that painting you made which hangs on the wall of your Range Three weather shack, they disappear and reappear in about 6 months. Some things, like that completed weather reporting sheet of yours from last spring and that cardboard box with your cola and sack lunch in it that vanished on the same day, well, they've been known to reappear two and a half years later. The things that disappear generally reappear in about the same place and in the same condition that they were in on the day the disappeared."

"And since the flare and flare gun might be thought of as a scientific curiosity, you're expecting it to reappear after being missing for about two and half months," I interjected.

"Right," smiled Steve. "So be sure to keep a close watch on that ammunition bunker and let us know if you see anything over that way. When the flare and flare gun show up, we need to retrieve them. The Sergeant is very particular about the safety hazard involved when anything is lying around out in the desert."

"I sure will," I answered. "There's been a lot activity over that way these last few days. I was just over there looking in that bunker last Friday. There's a single flare and a flare gun in an open cardboard box sitting on the floor of the bunker. It must be the one you're thinking of. That cardboard box appears to be one I put in my garbage can out at Range Three last week, so they probably haven't been back too long."

"Activity?" asked Steve in a nervous, surprised fashion. "You were over to that bunker just last week checking on activity? The boys and I haven't been over to that bunker in several weeks."

"Well, quite a few things have been happening over that way, Steve," I responded defensively. "Yesterday during the morning run, there was a guy, tall and white, wearing a white fluorescent jumpsuit. I saw him walking up along the eastern edge of the valley. He came up from the direction of Range Two and walked north along the edge of the sagebrush. When he got to the ammunition bunker, he stood in front of it for a half a minute and pointed this pencil like object at it. The door to the bunker sprung open part way and he walked inside. That door is 6 feet high. He had to stoop a great deal to get inside so I estimate that he was about 6 feet six inches tall and he was real thin. Once he got inside, he turned around and stood bent over, looking at me through the open door. It's about a mile and a quarter over there but it still made me feel uncomfortable. I hurried through the rest of my work and phoned Desert Center. He was still watching me when I locked up and left to come into breakfast. While I was finishing my duties, two other shorter adults joined him. One of them seemed to be a woman with a small child. They all just stood over there and stared at me."

Steve, Bryan, and Doug exchanged furtive glances. It made me nervous. I continued, stammering somewhat, "Well, that whole stretch of desert out there is a little screwy. There was the noon run last Wednesday out at Range Three. As you know, it's been real hot and the ranges were closed. You know, come to think of it, ever since I came up here this time, it seems like the ranges are almost always closed. Anyway, I had already been in for the noon meal and I had just come back out. I was taking the temperature. The temperature was already more than 110 degrees. I noticed something out of place over there along the bunker road. It was chalk white and seemed to be watching me from behind the sagebrush on that low ridge about three quarters of a mile over to the northeast."

"Didn't that terrify you?" asked Steve in brotherly tones.

"No, not actually," I responded. "There seemed to be three or four of them over that way. It was so hot with the heat waves and the glare of the sun and all, I couldn't see them very well, so I wasn't sure what I was looking at. At first I supposed that it was three or four sea gulls perched on the sagebrush. Then I remembered that sea gulls do not perch on sagebrush the way a sparrow might and I started getting really curious as to what it might be.

"Well, whatever it was stayed over that way watching me from a distance while I took the noon balloon run and phoned it into Desert Center. I had become really curious as to what it might be. I came out of my weather shack and I was walking over towards my theodolite. I was going to point my theodolite over that way and see if I could get a better view of it. As I was looking over that way, I noticed that the heat waves coming off the pavement on the bunker road were so intense that my theodolite wouldn't be of any use. I stopped and thought things through for a minute. I decided that since I was probably just dealing with harmless sea gulls, I should just get a couple of canteens of water and walk over that way to check things out. I'm used to the desert and three quarters of a mile isn't that far if you're careful. Well, I swear, Steve, whatever it was must have been able to read my mind because as soon as I had decided to hike over that way, they hit the panic button. I mean it was just like sounding the fire alarm. They all took off running back towards that depression up along those mountains towards the northeast.

"That made me even more curious, so I walked over to my truck, got my canteen belt and a couple of full canteens of water, fixed my fatigue hat, and set out walking over in that direction. It was a beautiful day. The pavement on the bunker road was hot and sometimes I had to walk in the sand along side the road because my shoes got so hot. That slowed me down quite a bit, but after a little while and a couple of drinks of water, I was over by the sagebrush where I'd seen them. While I was still a half mile away or so, I could see one of them hurrying out from the ammo bunker and heading on up along the base of the mountains towards the north-northwest. I couldn't get a very good look at them. They were solid chalk white and because of the distance, the glare of the sun and the heat waves there wasn't much to see. I suppose they must have been sea gulls or something because they were moving almost 30 miles an hour as they were hurrying to get away from me.

157

Well, I walked all around over by the stretch of sagebrush along the bunker road where they had been, looking things over. The sagebrush wasn't broken down or anything. The desert soil is soft over there. The thing I found curious was that in and around the sagebrush there were at least four or five different sets of boot prints. Some were the size of adults but at least one of them was the boot prints of a small child. It couldn't possibly have been made by any of us guys."

"Didn't you find that curious?" asked Steve in a guarded fashion.

"Yes, Steve." I answered. "I found it real curious because I keep seeing the same kind of boot prints out in back of my weather shacks and the Range Three lounge, down at Range Four and all over. As long as I was over there and didn't have anything to do, I decided to check the ammo bunker. I was taking my time in the hot sun and it took me another half hour or so to get over that far. As I was walking up on the bunker, I noticed this big white object sitting on the desert floor up along the mountains north-northwest of me. It was about a half a mile away from me at the time. It was about the size of the diesel engine on a passenger train. It was solid white and had wrap around windows and everything, but it didn't have any wings or visible engines. Between the glare of the sun and the heat waves, I couldn't see very much. What ever it was, it didn't glint in the sunshine or anything. Well, the thing made me really curious, so I took another drink of water and rested while I stood in the shade of the ammo bunker and studied it for ten minutes or so. I couldn't make out very much at that distance so I decided to walk up that way and get a closer look. Well, when I had closed the distance to about a quarter of a mile, suddenly it seemed to turn on. It's appearance changed. It suddenly took on a fuzzy white appearance all over itself. Then it suddenly rose up about 20 feet and terrain followed out into the desert towards the northwest. When it got about five miles from me, it stopped suddenly, and set down on the desert again. The fuzzy white field around it went away and things seemed to return to normal. It terrain-followed the five miles at an average speed of more than 200 miles an hour. The thing I still can't get over though was how quickly it could speed up and slow down. I calculated that if a fighter jet were to speed up or slow down as quickly as that object had, the pilot would have experienced more than 10 times the force of gravity. Most pilots black out at 5 g's and many pilots would be risking death at 9."

"So what ever it was, it could not have been carrying human beings or have been made here on this earth. Is that right, Charlie?" Steve interrupted.

"Well, yes. I guess I would have to agree with what you just said, Steve." I slowly stammered in return. "But if that were the case, what would it be doing watching me out on Range Three?"

"That's a good question," replied Steve smiling.

"Well, anyway," I continued, "Five miles was too far for me to walk in the hot sun, so I turned around and walked back to the ammunition bunker. I wanted to rest in the shade for a while. As I was walking slowly back there, the white object fuzzed over and then suddenly lifted of. It terrain followed up the valley until it disappeared from view out in the glare of the sun and the heat waves.

When I got to the bunker, I saw that the front door was propped partly open. Someone had used a rock and an old metal chair and a short piece of wood to hold it about half way open. The skill with which they had positioned the board was really impressive. Inside in that cardboard box sat a single flare and the flare gun. It was pretty hot inside, so I stayed outside and rested in the shade for a while. Then I put the metal chair and the board back inside in the ammo bunker, closed the door and walked back to my weather shack and the Range Three buildings."

Steve sat thinking things through for a minute. Then he spoke, "Well, if that flare gun and flare is back, then the boys and I will come out and get it first thing next Monday after breakfast. The Ranges will be open then, and we'll make it a fast trip."

"I could get it for you if you want, Steve," I volunteered. "I have lots of free time. It wouldn't be any trouble for me whatever."

"Oh, no," answered Steve emotionally. "Not in hot weather like this. There's too damn much that goes on out there in hot weather. You better let me and the boys handle it."

"OK. If you want, Steve." I said.

The next Monday morning the ranges were open. I was just preparing for my eight o'clock balloon run out at Range Three when Steve and the Range Rats came out to get the flare and the flare gun. They brought three power wagons and I was struck by the technique Steve used. One power wagon, two new Range Rats, and Toni, waited idling back by the Range Three gate. One power wagon with Doug at the wheel waited idling in front of my weather shack. The third, with Steve and Bryan, cautiously made the trip down the bunker road and up along the base of the mountain. Reaching the ammo bunker, they turned around and were facing back, before Bryan stopped the truck. He waited with the engine idling while Steve cautiously got out, entered the ammo bunker, retrieved the flare and flare gun and hurried back to the waiting truck. I remember wondering what Steve and Bryan were afraid of. They certainly were used to the empty, open desert. There was something about the entire episode that just didn't seem to be adding up.

Once Steve was back in the truck, Bryan hit the gas and came barreling back down the bunker road. Reaching the Range Three buildings, he slowed to ten miles an hour and shouted to Doug, "We got the flares, Doug. They're out there today. Steve saw them south of the bunker, down in the brush. Hurry! Let's get out of here. Only Charlie can handle them when they're in this close." Then Bryan hit the gas and headed down the road towards the Range Three gate. I wanted to question Doug about what Bryan had said, but he just revved his engine and hit the gas too, leaving me alone in beautiful, splendid silence.

The remainder of the day was agreeable enough but for some reason, a curious fascination kept forming in my mind. Try as I would, I couldn't shake it. I became fascinated with the prospect of exploring the north end of the Mojave Wells valley all by myself. Time after time I found myself looking at the distant majestic mountains that formed the north end of Mojave Wells. Some of them stood as far as 105 miles distant. I decided that I would ignore the danger and go exploring up that way at my first opportunity. I expected to have to wait some time for a suitable opportunity but to my surprise, I had hardly finished arriving at the decision when Desert Center phoned me with the information that the Ranges would be closed for the next two days. Desert Center needed only a 4:30 a.m. run and an 8:00 a.m. run. According to the duty weather forecaster, the Desert Center Base Commander himself on the phone, made it perfectly clear that after completing the 8:00 a.m. run, I was completely free to do anything I felt like doing, anything at all. I was stunned. I stood for several minutes holding the phone in my hand. The phone call came so soon after I had made the decision to go exploring that I decided that it wasn't a coincidence. I became convinced that there was something up the valley that I need to inspect.

The next day was a very hot day. I had prepared well. I had packed the front seat of my pickup truck with extra water, canteens, and extra food. I informed The Desert Center Weather Station that I would be driving north up the valley so everyone would know where to search if I didn't report back by 8:00 p.m. in the evening. Before leaving Range Three, I rolled down the windows on both sides of my truck so I had plenty of fresh air.

The drive north to Range Four was pleasant enough. I was singing my summer songs as the truck bounced along. The dirt road was wide, reasonable flat, and easy enough to follow as it headed north across the dry lakebed of Range Four. As the road was leaving the lakebed, I happened to glance over through the open truck window on my right. Something over there along the base of the mountains caught my eye. The mountains were probably a mile and a half distant. It took a few tries to locate the object. I first located it floating a few feet off the ground, concealed in one of the canyons a mile or so east of me. It was large, white and egg-shaped. In the bright sunlight, the heat waves and the haze, I couldn't make out any details. I supposed that it was just some kind of large white seagull so I ignored it.

After several miles across the lakebed, the road left the floor of the Mojave Wells valley and headed gently uphill through the tall sagebrush and cactus. The road stayed generally in the middle of the valley for a few miles. Then it

162

angled slowly towards the higher ground on the west side of the valley. After driving many miles, the terrain became rougher. A series of dry arroyos now came down from the mountains to the west and joined together to form the larger arroyo that the road followed for many more miles. As I drove north past the entrances to these arroyos, I would sometimes stop on the main road and enjoy the beauty of their upper reaches. Sculptured over the ages by the summer winds and the desert rains, covered with sagebrush in bloom and mesquite clinging to their walls, they could hardly have been more beautiful. I was enjoying the beauty of one of the larger of these, many miles north of Range Four when I noticed an unusual structure part way up one of the canyon walls. It was an aircraft hanger sized opening with concrete walls and vertical concrete doors. The arroyo ran east and west. The hanger had been tunneled into the southern side of the arroyo, totally concealing it from the outside world. Curiosity overcame me. Without thinking of the obvious danger, I parked my pickup truck by the side of the dirt road, turned off the engine, grabbed my canteen belt with two canteens of water and began hiking up the arroyo to inspect the structure. It wasn't far up the arroyo, perhaps only a half a mile. The base of the entrance was about 15 feet above the arroyo floor. Only a vehicle capable of standing stationary in the air could enter it. It was about 100 feet wide and 40 feet high. The hanger doors opened in sections but they were currently closed. Except for the thick concrete there wasn't much else to be seen. I noticed a path leading from the floor of the arroyo up to the top of the canyon. Up on the canyon rim was another entrance with a thick wooden door set into a thick concrete frame. My curiosity was rapidly getting the best of me. It was with considerable excitement that I climbed the path, arriving finally at the thick wooden door on the top. It was painted in battleship gray and closed at the time. The door was unusually tall. I estimated the height of the door to be almost 15 feet tall and was hinged on the right. At first glance, the door and the concrete appeared to be featureless, but when the light reflected off the paint properly, the faint outline of a series of hieroglyph like pictures could be seen. The hieroglyphs were perhaps visible under ultraviolet light. One, I remember looked like an icon of the sun. Another appeared to be the icon of a dry river valley.

Without thinking, I carefully opened the door. It opened with unusual ease. I found this surprising, considering the door's location and it's obvious exposure to the wind and to the desert elements. Inside was a long, clean, featureless concrete stairway that led down into the rock, until it reached the level of the floor of the concrete hanger. Down at the base of this long stairway stood a similar looking door, also closed. The door and doorway at the bottom also appeared to have several hieroglyphs partially concealed by their heavy gray coats of paint.

I was too apprehensive to go through the open door and enter the exposed stairway. I stopped to catch my breath in the hot sun, take a couple drinks of water and to think things through. I spent a few minutes collecting my thoughts and my fears. I was totally alone, with no help coming any time soon if I got in trouble. I had really wanted to inspect the north end of the valley. Across the valley in the distance, in one of the canyons in the mountains to the east, the white object was apparently still floating there, paralleling my every move. After giving the matter due consideration, I decided that I would continue inspecting the valley north of me. I would wait and inspect the concrete hanger on the way back if I had the time.

Singing in the sunshine then, I closed the door, quickly retraced my steps back down into the arroyo, back down the dry arroyo to the edge of the road, and back across the dry sandy dirt to my parked truck. It started as expected. Soon I was back in high gear and once again heading north.

The road continued on through the sagebrush on the west side of the valley and remained generally up hill. It was a beautiful drive. Soon the stunning view of Mojave Wells valley appeared in the distance behind me. I was still singing to myself. Thoughts of the white object no longer crossed my mind. I supposed it was far behind me. Then I noticed it changing canyons in the nearby mountains on the far side of the valley. Still singing, but curious now, I began monitoring its movements as it terrain followed along the base of the mountains to the east.

The road continued slowly up hill as the miles passed beneath the wheels of my truck. It soon became patently obvious that the white object was intent on paralleling my every move and it obviously had no intention of breaking off the pursuit. As soon as I realized this, I began feeling ill at ease. The ability to parallel has been the basic defensive military maneuver since the last ice age. If the white object was paralleling my movements, I said to myself, "What's it defending? After all, it hadn't chosen to defend the concrete hanger."

More miles slipped by as I thought things over. The white object was making me more and more nervous as it continued to parallel my movements. Then, slowly but surely, the white object started lagging noticeably behind me, always staying in the canyons and valleys along the base of the mountains to the east. Mentally I divided the bottom of the truck window on my right, into sections. Good weather observer that I was, I began estimating the angle which the white object was maintaining on me. First it stayed directly opposite me. Then it lagged five or ten degrees behind me, then fifteen. Soon it was lagging almost thirty degrees behind me.

As I was wondering about the meaning of this, I noticed a second identical white object terrain following down the mountainside northeast of me. Like the first, the second object terrain followed along the base of the mountains east of me, until it stood some thirty degrees northeast and in front of me. Still new to the ranges, I wondered what it all meant.

By now I was some forty or fifty miles north of Range Four, and the road was becoming rough and narrow. I drove on for a few more miles wondering about what I had seen. Finally topping a ridge, I made my decision. With both white objects now paralleling my every move and keeping me bracketed between them, I decided that men smarter than me knew how to stop their trucks on narrow dirt roads and turn around. It seemed like this would be a good time for me to start learning from others. Finding a suitable place to turn around was no easy task. The road was now very rough and quite narrow. I was driving slower now as I studied the ground. Suddenly, on my left, I passed a wide sandy area. There clearly visible in the sand were the boot prints of several adults. This really surprised me because I was so far out in the desert. I wondered how people could possibly be this far out in a seemingly deserted desert valley?

Up ahead the dirt road crossed a wide flat arroyo. At last, I had a place wide enough to turn around. I pulled my truck up into the entrance to the arroyo and carefully turned around. It was a considerable accomplishment. I had to make effective use of the reverse gear. I was quite proud of myself when I finally had my truck turned around on the dirt road and headed back towards Range Four. There was just barely room enough to fit my truck between the rocks, the sagebrush, and the soft sand. The view of Mojave Wells valley in the distance was absolutely breath taking that summer day. I remember sitting breathless for several minutes, stopped in my truck, just enjoying the view.

Slowly I nursed my truck a little ways down hill, heading south, back down towards Range Four. After about a quarter mile, I got back to the sandy area. I was intensely curious about the boot prints. The two white objects were holding their positions in the canyons east of me and my curiosity temporarily overcame my fear. Being alone, I carefully stopped my truck on the incline, set the brake securely and turned off the engine. My truck came to a stop on the dirt road perhaps 300 feet north of the sandy area. I had plenty of gas but I didn't want the engine to over heat while idling in the hot sun. My truck was quite dependable. I had no worries about it starting again. I got out of my truck and placed a large rock in front of the back tire to make sure the truck didn't roll on me. Then I took one of the jars of water out of my truck and took a long drink. Then I carefully refilled my canteens. The air up here along the mountains was cooler than it had been down in the desert below. Just the same, I could probably have fried an egg on the hood of my truck. I returned the water jar to my truck and put on my canteen belt. It was heavy and awkward, with its two canteens but I didn't mind. I didn't intend to walk very far.

Slowly and carefully, I walked over to the sandy area and began following the boot prints. Most of the boot prints seemed human enough but the shape of one set of prints was unusual. That unusual set of boot prints was identical in shape to the boot prints that I had frequently seen in the soft dirt around my weather shacks. They weren't like any human footprints I'd ever seen. The heel part of the boot was almost the same size as the front part of the boot, i.e. the part of the boot that was in front of the instep.

Inspecting the boot prints was interesting. The scenery was breath taking. The winds were cool and pleasant. I was singing to myself and gazing over towards the two white objects that were still on station in the canyons a mile east of me when my consciousness was suddenly invaded by a man pleasantly shouting at me. Coming to my senses, I turned and looked back up the road to the north. There, where the road crossed the wide flat arroyo, two grown men stood hailing me. One of the men was young, probably in his early twenties. The other was much older, maybe forty-five. Both men were wearing featureless black uniforms and both men were very well armed. Both wore 45 caliber automatic revolvers and carried many rounds of ammunition in their ammunition belts. The nerves in my stomach tightened when I realized they were obviously guards and they obviously had questions for me to answer.

I started to return to my truck but the younger guard shouted in very authoritative tones for me to stay standing where I was. Both guards had their revolvers drawn. I stood motionless and waited as the guards approached me slowly. The younger guard came first while the older guard trailed behind him, and to his left by ten feet or so. Not wanting to be gunned down so far from the casinos in Las Vegas, I froze into position and shouted back pleasantly, "Yes, I am standing still. I am waiting here. I am not armed."

The younger guard circled me to the west, in military fashion, and stopped finally, facing me, standing some eight feet or so from me. I rotated so that I was facing him, showing my right side to the older guard. I was too nervous to do much else at the time. The older guard stopped on the road, standing some twenty feet or so north of me. Both guards continued to hold their guns drawn, although their guns were not actually pointed at me.

The younger guard began pleasantly enough. "Who are you?" he asked in friendly, but stern tones.

It was obvious that both of their guns were loaded and both of them were in positions that would give them as many clean, clear shots at me as they felt they needed. Having been taken completely off guard, I was almost too nervous to respond to the question. Stammering a great deal, I responded, "I'm the weather observer from down in the valley. You can see my weather shacks at Range Three and Range Four out there in the distance. I was just inspecting the Mojave Wells valley and the mountains. I didn't mean anyone any harm."

Neither guard seemed impressed by my words. The older guard spoke in experienced, and authoritative tones, "We don't give a damn about that. The man asked you who you are. Now tell him! Who are you?"

Shaking some now, from nerves, I responded, "I'm Charlie Baker. As you can see, I'm an Airman First class. Here, I'll show you my military id and my dog tags." I turned slightly as I reached for my wallet. Out of the corner of my eye, I noticed the second white object maneuvering slowly, over along the mountains northeast of me. The second white object, the younger guard, and myself, had all been previously positioned more or less in the same line. This apparently had caused the second white object some problems. It began slowly maneuvering towards the north, still staying along the base of the distant eastern mountains.

It seemed apparent to me that it, too, was searching for a clean, clear firing position.

Nervously, I took my military id out of my wallet and tried to hand it to the younger guard since he stood closest to me. He refused to reach out to accept it, or even to gaze at it. Speaking to me sternly, but still in friendly tones, he said, "I'm not allowed to look at that. That's your military id. Now I'm asking you again. Who are you?"

"But I just told you, didn't I?" I stammered nervously in answer.

The two guards exchanged glances and generally ignored my words. Then the younger guard spoke again, "Someone sent you out here, didn't they, Charlie."

"Yes," I answered humbly. "I'm assigned to the weather detachment down at Desert Center. I'm the duty observer up here at the Wells. You can check with my commander, the Major. He'll tell you who I am."

The younger guard continued, "And whoever that was, did they give you a name?"

"Well, yes." I responded shaking visibly from nerves at the time. Out of the corner of my eye I noticed the second white object still slowly maneuvering, apparently still seeking an acceptable firing position.

Neither of the guards seemed to care. The younger guard persevered slowly, "Has anyone down at Desert Center ever called you anything else? Has anyone down there ever sat down to talk to you and said, 'This is your name?'"

Desperate and sweating from fear and tension, I would have made up any lie to satisfy them. "Well, yes," I instinctively blurted out. Then I stood wondering what I had meant by my answer.

"And what was that name?" asked the young guard in pleasant, stern, and authoritative tones.

170

With my brain racing in fear, I desperately searched for an answer. Stammering, stuttering, my lips and throat dry from nerves and the hot sun, I instinctively responded, "Before I came up here, the observer before me got burned real bad out here. So the Desert Center Base Commander ordered the Desert Center base hospital to go through this big inspection process. They had this guy wearing a gun, who pretended to be the base psychiatrist, sit down and talk to me on a weird Wednesday afternoon just before Easter about a month ago." As I was speaking, the younger guard made impatient, rotating motions with his left hand and said sternly, "Come on, Charlie, Get it together. Hurry it up. Out with it. Who'd he say you are?"

Almost down to whining and not believing the answer myself, I responded, "Teacher's Pet."

The two guards stood motionless, just staring at me, apparently numbed. Although my answer had apparently touched one of their nerves, their stares did nothing to help mine. I anxiously tried to explain. I continued, "He said that if anyone ever asked me, I should say that I was a friend of the Teacher. Then he told me that I was 'Teacher's Pet.' I don't know what it means but he had it placed in my personnel records that are locked in up this special safe down at Desert Center. He said I could go anywhere I wanted whenever I wanted, day or night, and that no one would ever stand in my way or order me off the ranges. The only rule was that whatever I did, I had to do it alone. I have to be completely alone when I come out to the ranges in the morning. I have to be completely alone when I drive back into base in the afternoon. In between, I have to be completely alone whenever I go anywhere out on the ranges, and see, here, today I'm obeying the rules. See, I'm

171

out here today all by myself. See, I'm not a danger to anybody. I'm totally unarmed and completely alone."

The two guards finally caught their breath and exchanged meaningful glances. The older guard continued, again using slow friendly tones, "What did he say your name was, again?"

Desperate to keep from being shot, I would have said anything to make them happy, anything at all. Sweating nervously, I repeated myself, trying hard to show my obvious sincerity, "He said the observer before me had gotten into trouble and had been burned real bad, up here in the forehead. He said I was special. He said they were picking me because I had proven myself to be a friend of the Teacher. He said I should be proud of my name and I should always remember that I was the only one who had ever been chosen. Then he gave me my name. He said I was 'Teacher's Pet'."

The older guard slowly put away his revolver and spoke to the younger guard, "Sam, if that's true, we had better both put away our guns."

The younger guard slowly lowered his revolver and returned it to his holster. Then he stood relaxed with his right hand resting on the handle of his gun. Speaking to the older guard, he said, "I don't know, Kelly. I'm not sure I believe him. He seems sincere enough, but this must be just another one of General Shaw's security tests. Who ever Charlie is, he sure as hell can't be the real Teacher's Pet. If there were a real Teacher's Pet, he would be back in D.C., way in those back reaches of the Pentagon, and acting way different than Charlie, here. You know Kelly, deep down, I've always believed that Teacher's Pet was just some made up name General Shaw uses when he wants to test our security responses. Teacher's Pet has such a high clearance,

I don't believe there ever could be a real one." Up the valley, I noticed a third white object, identical to the first two, slowly terrain following across the valley floor, perhaps a mile north of us. Like the second white object, it, too, seemed to be maneuvering for a clean firing position.

The older guard shook his head slowly, "Oh, there has got to be a real one somewhere, but I always figured he was somewhere up at home base. The security awareness paperwork that we got from Captain McCoy when we were assigned out here last month, had the name 'Teacher's Pet' in red and purple at the top of the list. The way General Shaw has been testing us ever since, convinces me that something big is in progress. But I agree with you, Sam, whoever Charlie really is, he sure as hell can't be the Real Teacher's Pet."

The younger guard nodded his approval and then continued with his friendly but authoritative questioning, "When The General runs a security test, he gives his substitute Teacher's Pet a red and purple striped id to carry. Were you given such an id to carry? Were you sent out here to test our security awareness by General Shaw?"

"No," I answered, trying to show my honestly. "I don't even know who General Shaw is." Watching the third white object in the distance continuing to maneuver slowly for a clean firing position wasn't doing anything to make the questions easier to answer. I carefully stepped backward two or three steps so that the older guard to the north of me, blocked the third object's line of fire. Then I slowly moved two or three steps to the right to keep the younger guard and myself both in the second white object's line of fire. The older guard appeared to take note of my movements and moved his right hand closer to the handle of his gun.

The younger guard also reacted to my movement and moved his right hand somewhat, so that he had a better grip on the handle of his gun. Then the younger guard continued his careful probing, "Or maybe he gave you an arm band with red and purple stripes, real bright, that you're supposed to be wearing when you come out here?"

"No," I responded humbly.

The younger guard stood shaking his head. The older guard took up the questioning, "Were you maybe sent up here by that damned bird Colonel, that older security officer down at Desert Center who's such a stickler for the rules?"

Again, I shook my head slowly and answered, "No. I'm not in security. I'm a weather observer and my duty is to take the daily weather reports out on the gunnery ranges."

The older guard continued, "You've never met General Shaw, but you still say you're Teacher's Pet."

"Yes," I answered, stuttering some in fear. "That's what they told me to say. You can ask my commander, the Major. It's right there in my personnel file. I saw it myself. It says that anytime anyone asks for my identification, I am authorized to respond verbally and identify myself as Teacher's Pet. I am also authorized to identify myself as a Friend of the Teacher." My eyes naturally followed the third white object as it floated silently west of the dirt road, a mile north of me. I could see that no matter how I maneuvered, it would soon have a clean, clear, unobstructed field of fire at me. It would have me cleanly singled out from the two guards.

"Well, tell me, Charlie," the older guard continued. "You look like a nice enough young man. If you aren't up here testing our security responses, what would a nice young airman like you be doing, driving around alone in this part of the desert on a hot day like today anyway?"

"Well, it's a nice day and Desert Center told me I could take the day off. The ranges are closed, and I was kind of bored with nothing to do and with my history books and all, so I decided to drive up here and take a good look around, you know, enjoy the scenery. I thought I'd make it a nice day with a view," I responded.

The two guards snickered in response. Then the older guard continued probing, "You have the day off. You were a little bored, so you just decided to drive way the hell up here and enjoy the view."

"Well, yes," I answered, defensively. "I'm a weather man. I've gotten used to doing everything out here alone." I glanced over at the third object as it continued to slowly maneuver. However, the first object to the southeast remained stationary. It was apparently satisfied with its' line of fire.

The older guard continued his probing, "You know, Charlie, when I was young, if a young man was a little bored and had some time on his hands, he'd get himself a six pack of beer and sandwiches, maybe even a picnic blanket, and call his girl friend. I don't remember ever meeting a young man quite like you, one that would pass up an opportunity to party with his girl, just to drive way up here, out into this hellish desert, just so he could enjoy the view."

"Well, I was curious," I answered slowly, groping for words. "I was looking for foot prints and tracks and anything that seemed out of place. I wanted to check up on Range Four Harry. I wondered if he'd really been up this way like they say." Then I paused for a moment to take a deep breath. My gaze naturally fell on the third white object still slowly maneuvering in the bright sunlight to the north and west of me. Through the heat waves and the glare and

175

the haze, I noticed that, like the first two objects, sunlight would not glint off its dull white exterior.

The two guards just stood there staring at me, looking stunned and frozen. Off-balance and still groping for words, I continued slowly, trying desperately to offer an explanation that the guards would accept, "I'd heard tell that Range Four Harry, every now and then, has caused some of my friends a great deal of trouble. I kind of thought it would be a good idea if I came up here and tracked him down. I wanted to meet with him in person and check up on what I've been hearing first hand. I hoped that if Harry knew I was out here checking up on him, that it would cut down on some of Harry's nonsense and some of his horsing around."

The young guard reacted almost instantly when I'd finished speaking. "Damn it, Kelly! That proves it! I knew he was from Pentagon security. Otherwise, why would he be out here checking up on Range Four Harry?" My words appeared to have touched a deep nerve and the younger guard continued angrily. "Charlie has got to be up here on account of that damn circus we had out here last week. He's got to be from General Shaw's office, or above, or something. I'll bet he's up here checking so he can bust that arrogant Chief Master Sergeant Smith they've been sending out here to test us. Charlie is such a nice guy, he probably just doesn't want to tell us all of his plans or who sent him and stuff. I knew your bitching to old Harry would have some effect somewhere. It might even be that Range Four Harry's sent him."

Then the older guard chimed in angrily, "You damned right, Sam! That circus last Wednesday was nothing more than a damned disgrace. The way they rated you and me as failing that stupid test and rating that Chief Master Sergeant as winning perfectly. That was some more of Old Harry's horse-shit!" Then the older guard turned slightly towards me and continued, angrily, "That substitute Teacher's Pet that General Miles sent up here last Wednesday, came driving up here in a truck that looked just like yours, and he looks almost just about like you too. He wasn't wearing that armband like he was supposed to in the inspection script that Miles made up. He wouldn't stop when we shouted at him or do anything like he was supposed to. He was honking his horn and screaming obscenities at us like 'You can't make me stop, you stupid sons-a-bitches'. Then after Sam and I shot out the front tires on his truck to make him stop, he got out laughing, saying he was going to screw us good, and started calling Sam and I every dirty name he could think of. He wasn't nice and polite like you. He didn't identify himself as the substitute Teacher's Pet or as being from General Miles' office or anything like he's supposed to."

"Yah," exclaimed the younger guard angrily. "I wanted to smash his face up against one of those rocks over there. "Sam there, couldn't take it any longer." The older guard continued.

The younger guard then caught his breath, and continued angrily, "He wouldn't even stand and fight me like man. As soon as I began my swing at him, he fell to the ground, right about where you are. Then he lay there for at least two minutes before he pulled that red and purple arm band out from his pocket and identified himself. He began by saying he was acting out General Mile's security inspection script and pretending to be the Real Teacher's Pet, like his saying that he's authorized to substitute for Teacher's Pet is supposed to make everything all right. I'm so glad to see you out here checking up on him."

The older guard then interrupted angrily, "You can tell General Shaw and General Miles and Old Harry, that we're both still mad about the way we got screwed last week. Both Sam and I have been having a real hard time handling it. That Chief Master Sergeant was laughing at us like we were the scum of the earth. He was pointing his finger at us, and teasing us, and everything. He said that we had failed the security inspection miserably, that we were getting awarded a perfect zero, and he was awarding himself a perfect 100." As they talked, I could see that the third white object appeared to have located an acceptable firing position, about three quarters of a mile slightly northwest of me. Once again, it now had me cleanly singled out from the two guards.

The young guard continued, "You're right. That was one awful screw job. Before that guy opened his mouth, Kelly and I had both our guns drawn and zeroed in on him. He wouldn't have had a snowball's chance in hell of escaping. We had him dead in our sights. Sam was zeroed in on his head and I was zeroed in on his heart. If he had so much as sneezed we'd had at least ten shots in him so fast it would have made Satan proud. Kelly and I were so upset. We walked that jerk up the arroyo to our guard station and phoned Captain McCoy. The Chief Master Sergeant phoned General Shaw's office up at home base. It's just over those mountains behind us. General Shaw collected up General Miles, Captain McCoy, Old Harry and some guards, and came down here to clean house. Kelly and I showed them. We walked them right out here, right out to where you're standing, and showed them. Those are Old Harry's boot prints, the unusual ones that you were looking at when we came out here just now. We showed them how we had that substitute Teacher's Pet face down in the dirt right about where you're standing. We told them what a jerk he'd been. We told them that we should have been rated at least 75 and him the zero because when the test ended we could have riddled him with a dozen bullets and there wasn't shit he could have done in return. Like you, he wasn't even armed."

The younger guard stopped momentarily to catch his breath. The older guard continued, "But General Shaw agreed with the substitute Teacher's Pet from General Miles' office. Shaw insisted that Sam and I should be rated a zero and that other jerk should receive a perfect 100. Then I tried to explain my case to old Harry. You know how General Shaw and General Miles always suck ass on that quiet, stand-offish white Harry. I tried to reason with Harry. I figured that if I could get him on my side, then General Shaw would change the rating. But Old Harry agreed with Chief Master Sergeant Smith. Harry said the Real teacher's Pet is too valuable for us to ever draw our guns on him. He said if the Real Teacher's Pet were ever killed, he could never be replaced. Old Harry said that if Sam and me had been facing the Real Teacher's Pet, once we actually pointed our guns at him, or once he fell to the ground, both of us would have been killed instantly, before we were even aware that we were being fired on. He said those were the direct orders he'd received from the Teacher. He said both Sam and me would have been killed without warning and that neither of our guns would have ever fired.

"I was so angry! How can anyone be so stupid? Teacher's Pet would have had to kill both Sam and I right out of a clear blue sky for that to happen. I tried to reason with Harry. I asked him, 'How the heck are Sam and I to know what to do if the Real Teacher's Pet ever does show up? Neither Sam nor I have ever seen him. But before Old

Harry could answer my question, General Miles came down on Sam and I like we were scum. He screamed at us like we were nothing more than water boys. He said that Old Harry wasn't to be argued with, that if the Teacher ordered us killed before our guns could fire, then that was exactly what would happen."

Out of the corner of my eye, I could see that the second white object, like the first and the third, appeared to have found a suitable firing position. The younger guard continued, "Then Chief Master Sergeant began taunting Kelly and me, saying, 'See, I told you so. It was all in the test script just like I said. See, I won.' Then he laughed in our faces. General Shaw and General Miles just stood there laughing, and let him tease us, saying it was good training in case the Real Teacher's Pet should ever show up."

Then the older guard chimed in, "So you see, Charlie, or whoever the hell you really are, when you get back to wherever you came from, you tell them. Sam and I are people! In the future we expect to be treated like people, just like you've been doing!"

Nervous, wanting to keep the conversation going and keep the gunplay to a minimum, I tried to sympathize with the guards. "Well, I certainly agree that the real Teacher's Pet should ask General Shaw to be more considerate of your feelings during these tests," I stated simply.

The younger guard responded by gleefully exclaiming, "See, Kelly, we got him to admit he's lying, and that means that you and I are winning this security test! This week we're going to get us a real good high score! See, he's sympathizing with us. That proves he's lying. I told you he couldn't possibly be the Real Pet. See, I told you someone had to have sent him out here to check up on last week's test."

The older guard responded, "You're right, Sam. You had him spotted all along. You hold him here while I go call Captain McCoy and General Shaw. We'll get us our high grade and get to the bottom of this all at the same time. We're not going to fail this week's test. We're not going to get screwed this time. This week we're going to get us that high rating we deserved last week."

"But I'm not out here testing the security," I pleaded. "There's no reason for you to phone YOUR commander. He'll just phone MY commander and that'll just get ME screwed. I don't know why you couldn't just let me go. I'm not hurting anybody. I'm only the weather observer. I was just out here enjoying the scenery. I'm not even armed."

The two guards chuckled gleefully. The older guard responded pleasantly, "Don't worry, Charlie. Sam will hold you here while I go make the phone calls and get to the bottom of this. Now don't go trying to run off or anything, and make Sam have to shoot you. I will say this, Charlie, you'd better be from somebody's security office because if you really are just the range weather observer like you say, you're going to be in one hell of a mess, driving around this stretch of desert, pretending to be the real Teacher's Pet like you were. Once the real Teacher's Pet catches wind of that, I wouldn't be in your shoes for all the tea in China." The older guard turned and walked back up the road towards the wide arroyo. He could be heard whistling and chuckling and humming to himself as he walked. He was obviously having a pretty good day. When he got back to the wide spot in the road, he turned west, into the arroyo. Following up the arroyo for a quarter mile, he disappeared from view behind some rocks and sagebrush.

I stood quietly for a few minutes. The younger guard, with his right hand resting on the handle of his revolver, watched my every move. A morbid, anxious, angry sickness began building deep down in my stomach. The three white objects remained on station, motionless in the distance. The day with so much promise had started so beautifully in the morning. Now it was turning out to be a complete disaster. The phone call to the unknown General Shaw seemed certain to result in a phone call to the Desert Center base commander, then to my commander, the Major. They would all realize that I had been out joy riding in my truck. By sundown, they would be taking turns screwing me for sure, if the guards didn't shoot me first, if the white objects didn't fire on me in the meantime. There weren't words to express my emotions. Standing there in quiet desperate anger, I decided that at least I would maneuver so as to make their job as hard as possible. Slowly I stepped backward until my truck was blocking the field of fire from the third white object. I slowly stepped to my right again, until the young guard, the second white object, and myself, were again all in line, thereby re-blocking the field of fire from the second white object. I realized that the first white object could still cut me down anytime it felt like doing so but there wasn't anything else I could do.

As I expected, the second white object began immediately maneuvering to clear its field of fire. The young guard, however, remained standing where he had been. I wondered. The young guard could clearly see that the second white object didn't have a clear field of fire at me. He was obviously well trained. I wondered why he, too, didn't move, or order me to move, to clear the field of fire for the second white object. After all, I wondered, the guards and the white objects were working together as a team, weren't they?

Then I noticed that the third white object, whose field of fire at me was now blocked by my truck, remained motionless where it was. Again I wondered. It seemed happy where it was. Yet, the only thing it had to fire on was the young guard, himself.

Trying to control my fear, my anger, my emotions in general, and without giving my questions much thought, I asked the young guard, "Does Harry's appearance seem unusual to you?"

"Not too much," responded the guard. "Although he's so thin sometimes his clothes seem to hang on him. The way he walks through the sagebrush can be pretty comical. You get used to it, to seeing him, and being around him. I always figured that he must be from somewhere back east because he's so proud of the way he speaks perfect English. One time I asked him when he'd learned to speak English, and he claimed he'd learned to speak it some 200 years ago. His skin is so white he must be suffering from some kind of skin disease. Some days when he and General Shaw show up here, Old Harry's skin is just pure chalk white."

A gentle gust of wind came up from the hot, distant desert floor. It swirled and danced and tossed some dust and dry leaves around and between the younger guard and myself. It seemed to be whispering friendly desert messages, placing pleasant feminine-like thoughts in my mind, thoughts that didn't seem to be my own, calming me down, reminding me of happier times, telling me that everything was going to be OK, until, after a few minutes, the wind escaped from us, playing as it left, heading uphill towards the mountains to the north and west. The wind distracted me for a time, and it seemed to carry the guard's words with it as it left. My mind seemed to go into a slight daze. The guard's words seemed so light and so meaningless that I happily ignored them, and, for a time, I cared only about the messages that seemed to be written in the wind. They seemed to be asking me pleasantly if I wanted the guards alive. From deep within me, I seemed to be singing happy songs in return, answering "Yes, Oh Yes. Oh, I know they're jerks, but they're harmless, happy jerks. That's what this world needs is more harmless, happy jerks."

Coming back from my wind song and my desire to let my soul leave my body to go out playing in the sunshine and out in the wind, I motioned slowly with my arm towards the first white object, and asked, "I wonder what that white thing is, over there against the mountains."

The young guard smiled knowingly, and answered without taking his eyes off me and without actually looking at the first white object, "You see there, Charlie. That's the second time I caught you lying."

"How's that?" I asked.

"The real Teacher's Pet wouldn't have to ask. He would know what that was. Now you can see why Kelly and I knew right off that you couldn't possibly be the real Teacher's Pet."

"I don't understand," I responded.

"Well, see, Charlie," the young guard answered patiently. "A month ago when Kelly and I and Captain McCoy were assigned out here, General Shaw, and General Miles, and Old Harry came out here to give us our orientation briefing. We were standing right about where you are now. Captain McCoy asked the same question, 'What are the white things?' General Shaw ordered us to ignore the white things. He said they were just large, white, sea gulls, and we should never go chasing after them. Then Captain McCoy pointed out that they would have to be the largest sea gulls ever recorded. At this distance, for a sea gull to look that large it would have to have a wingspan of at least 60 feet. Captain McCoy said he wished he could see a sea gull that large close up. That caused General Miles to just come unglued. He just went ballistic. The General said that the only human being he knew of, who should ever even consider walking up to one of those sea gulls out in the desert, was the real Teacher's Pet, and HE was too intelligent to try anything that stupid. If we guards were to try walking up to one of those white objects we would be killed instantly. Well, see, Charlie, if you were the real Teacher's Pet as you've been pretending, you'd already know what those white objects are because you would have already seen them close up."

"But in my records that my commander, the Major, showed me, it says that I am authorized to identify myself as the Teacher's Pet," I responded meekly.

The young guard smiled knowingly and responded, "You might be right, Charlie, but there has got to be some kind of mistake somewhere because you sure as hell aren't the real Teacher's Pet. I don't mean to insult you, Charlie. You're really the nicest guy Kelly and I have ever met, but you can't be the real Teacher's Pet because you're so ordinary, so common. The real Teacher's Pet is special and you're nothing special. Kelly and I, we've met them all, astronauts, test pilots, and sons of senators. Many of them are very nice people but every one of them is special. They know they're special. They think they're special. They act special. They tell us they're special. If Kelly and I were to stop any one of them like we stopped you, today, why, every one of them would tell us to get screwed and get the hell out of their way because they're in the middle of doing something special. After telling us their name, not one of them would even stop to give us the time of day. Not one of them would talk to us politely, or care about our problems like you, Charlie. That's why I say, and I don't mean any insult, Charlie, but you're not special. That means you can't be the real Teacher's Pet because nice as you are, you sure as hell aren't anything special."

I watched the second white object as it slowly settled into its newly found firing position. Then I continued slowly, "So you say the real Teacher's Pet is special?"

"That's right, Charlie. You can't even imagine how special he is." The young guard responded. "When we were getting our orientation briefing last month, General Shaw was trying to explain how special the Pet is. The General said that if the real Pet wanted to see the moon and the stars, The Teacher is so much in love with him, she would carry him right up into the night time sky and show him the stars close up.

"Then Old Harry said that in the last 200 years there has been only one Teacher but never before has there ever been a Teacher's Pet. He said the Teacher tried more than a hundred times to find someone suitable for her pet project without success. He said General Shaw and the Teacher together, tried more than forty different individuals and they all failed. Shaw and the Teacher had given up trying when one day, just by luck, the real Teacher's Pet happened along. According to Harry, the real Pet, just as luck would have it, also happens to be absolutely perfect for the Teacher's pet project, for their electronics and all. I guess they're able to communicate with him in more ways then they ever expected. Then, I guess, the Pet turned out to be such a nice likable guy that the Teacher went and fell in love with him, too. Now, Old Harry says, the Pentagon Generals and the Teacher are both learning so much, so fast, from the Pet project, that the history of the entire world has already been changed for the better. Old Harry says they've all learned more by studying the Pet and his reactions for the last few weeks than they had learned by studying the entire human race for the past two hundred years.

"So, you see, Charlie, you see how special the real Pet is. You see how special the real Pet must feel. You see how arrogant the real Pet must be acting. But you aren't anything like that. You're too nice. You see why both Kelly and I knew right off that it couldn't be you."

"So what you're saying is that I'm in deep trouble because I'm too nice," I asked. "Well, yes, Charlie. I guess you could say that," answered the guard pleasantly.

"What do you think they'll do to me?" I asked soberly.

"I don't know for sure, Charlie," responded the guard sympathetically. "It probably depends on what the real Teacher's Pet decides. General Miles says that the real Pet is a hell of a nice guy. However, when he decides that he has to fight or feels threatened, he's just fearless. Miles says the real Pet is so intelligent that you never know what he's thinking or how he's going to react or when he's going to attack."

"How long will it take to find out?" I asked, more to keep my dejected spirits from totally collapsing, than anything.

"Oh, we'll have a good idea as soon as Kelly returns," answered the guard, seriously. "Kelly gets real bored out here. It takes a good court martial or something to get his spirits up. If he comes back walking slowly, that would be a real good sign for you. I expect, though that he'll probably come back running. I expect General Shaw will probably give you two years in that chicken wire brig they have down at Desert Center. As far as the Pentagon is concerned,

I'll recommend to General Shaw and General Miles that six months in the brig would be plenty for a nice guy like you. Maybe I can work up some sympathy for you. Shaw and Miles are both pretty nice guys. I'm expecting they'll both go for it, unless the real Teacher's Pet votes them down. But, you know, Charlie, I really don't know what they'll do to you. People have been killed who've seen less than what you've seen today. Pretending to be the real Teacher's Pet, out here in this stretch of desert, is a mighty serious offense."

"But I haven't seen anything and what about my records?" I asked desperately. "It says right there in my records I'm authorized to identify myself as Teacher's Pet."

Before the young guard could answer, the older guard could be heard shouting and running down the arroyo. Both the young guard and I turned to watch him as he came running desperately down the arroyo towards the dirt road. "God, Charlie, it's worse than I thought," the young guard exclaimed. "They really mean to screw you. I've never seen Kelly run so fast."

My stomach became filled with a sick, sinking feeling. I had to fight hard to resist the urge to just sit down in the dirt and vomit into the desert. In the distance, the older guard continued shouting, running, and stumbling down the arroyo towards the dirt road. At first the distance was too great to make out his words. Despite the distance, I could see that he wasn't armed. He had apparently left his gun and his ammunition belt back at the guard station. As he got closer I could make out a few of his words. He was shouting, "Sam! Sam! Back the hell away from him, NOW! General Shaw's orders! Don't touch your gun!" Then the older guard had to slow to catch his breath for a minute of so, before running some more.

The wind and the distance prevented the younger guard from hearing Kelly's words. The younger guard shouted back, "He's not that bad a guy, Kelly. He's just a little screwed up. We could maybe let him off with just a good beating and some time behind the chicken wire. He's been nice and polite all the time you were gone."

The older guard resumed running some more and shouting, "Back away from him, Sam. Back away from him NOW! HE IS THE PET, the REAL ONE, just like he says!! General Shaw was shouting at me on the phone. Shaw says he's not the substitute. He IS THE REAL TEACHER'S PET!! We're ordered to take one good look at him so we'll know him by sight if we ever see him again, and we're supposed to help him any way he asks of us. Then we're ordered to get the hell out of his way and get back to our guard station. They sent him up here 'cause Old Harry wanted us to meet him up close. They wanted us to see who the real Pet is, so we didn't shoot him by accident! I'm telling you, Sam, he is the REAL TEACHER'S PET! Reaching the dirt road, the older guard stopped and bent over, trying to catch his breath.

After a few minutes, the older guard straightened back up, and began walking slowly along the side of the road towards us. "I'm ordering you, move your right hand away from your gun, NOW! Use your left hand to slowly unbuckle your gun belt and let it fall to the ground. Then back slowly away from him. Sam!! I'm telling you, both of our lives depend on it!"

The younger guard slowly complied, moving his right hand out away from his body and, using his left hand, let his gun and gun belt fall to the desert at his feet. Then he slowly took three steps backward away from it. Turning back toward me, the younger guard responded, "I don't see it, Kelly. I don't see how Charlie, here, could ever be the real Teacher's Pet."

The older guard continued to approach us, catching his breath, stopping at last when he was standing only twenty feet or so from me. He looked me over intently. Then he began shouting at me emotionally, "Why the hell didn't you tell us, Charlie? Why the hell did you let us risk our lives like this? We should have known. There isn't anybody but you would have the guts to drive around this desert on that shitty road like you were doing, stopping your truck and inspecting the bunker down in that arroyo like you were doing, just to enjoy the scenery! Why the hell didn't you tell us that you are the real Teacher's Pet?"

Still shocked, confused, and off-balance myself, I meekly responded, "But, I did tell you that I'm the real Teacher's Pet, didn't I?"

The younger guard shouted emotionally to the older guard, "I'm asking you, Kelly, how the hell can Charlie, here, possibly be the REAL Pet?"

The older guard shouted at me, emotionally, "Show him you're THE PET! Tell Sam why you been moving around slowly, right out here in front of us, right out here under the very guns of those three heavily armed white gun ships that have us surrounded. Tell Sam just what the hell you've been doing right out here in front of our eyes while we been asking you questions!! Tell him, Charlie!!"

Stumbling a little for words, I responded, "I didn't want them to fire on us. They obviously aren't willing to fire on both you and me, so whenever I could, I've been keeping their lines of fire blocked. I've been doing that by keeping you guards, me, and the gun ships all in the same lines of fire."

Then Kelly shouted at the younger guard, "See, Sam, see. That proves it! When I got back to the guard shack, the phone was ringing off the hook and General Shaw was screaming at me. He said the only reason that both you and I were still alive was because the real Pet was intentionally risking his life for us by purposely blocking the lines of fire from Old Harry's gun ships. When Old Harry saw him do it, he figured that Charlie, here, wanted the both of us kept alive. He says that if the real Pet, here, hadn't done that, both you and I would be nothing but dead meat by now because of the way we had our guns drawn!"

The younger guard suddenly realized that the older guard was right. Sam jerked his head up and to the left. The third white object was now resting on the road, facing us in perfect firing position, some three quarters of a mile to the north. The heat waves and the hot summer sun's glare obscured some of its exterior details but it's military intent was painfully obvious. It was solid white, and ellipsoidal, with a molded flat bottom, and a row of large, airplane style windows on both sides. It showed no wings or exterior controls, and had no visible undercarriage. It was about the same size and shape as the diesel engine on a passenger train. Its' windows on the front were also similar to the windows on the front of a passenger diesel. It had obviously found a perfect firing position, floating silently some two or three feet above the dirt and the rocks at a place where the road topped a small ridge some three quarters of a mile north of us. In the distance, through its front windows, could be seen the faces and upper bodies of what appeared to be two chalk white human-like creatures sitting in the pilot and co-pilot seats. The veins in Sam's neck bulged, and he screamed, "Kelly, you're right! Whatever they are, they've got us surrounded. Those gun ships can cut us down anytime Harry gives the order!" Then, turning towards me, the younger guard screamed, "Charlie! Why didn't you tell us? How else were we to know that YOU ARE THE PET?"

"But I did tell you," I responded meekly.

The older guard stepped back away from me and shouted emotionally to the younger guard, "We gotta get out of here, Sam. Unless Charlie here needs something, we gotta get back to our station. General Shaw and the rest are coming down here from their base. They're sure going to be mad when they get here. They sent Sergeant Smith on ahead and he'll be here any minute now. We got to get back to our station up the arroyo. Take one last good look at Charlie and let's get out of here, NOW!"

"Right!" screamed Sam. He took one last good look at my face, turned towards Kelly and shouted, "Let's go!" Then the two guards began double timing up the road towards the dry arroyo. When they reached the entrance to the arroyo, they stopped to catch their breath before turning in to the arroyo. Kelly exclaimed, "Sam, there's Sergeant Smith now, waiting for us up by the sagebrush in the bend. We better get our stories straight or we'll both get screwed for stopping the Pet like we did."

"You're right," answered Sam. "Let's say we were just making sure the Pet was all right because his truck was stopped on the dirt road. Remember we can pass a lie detector test. He stopped his truck of his own accord, and remember he never did tell us his real name, and neither one of us ever actually looked at his military id."

"Right," answered Kelly. "And then once we stopped him, he's such a nice likable guy. We'll tell them that we were just having fun talking to the Pet and getting to know him better. He showed us that we were treated fairly in last week's security exam. They'll love that stuff for sure."

The two guards walked off. I remained standing where I was for a few minutes. It was a beautiful day and I was in no hurry. I enjoyed watching the wind as it played with the purple sage flowers in the plants near me. While I waited, the third white object, positioned on the road some three quarters of a mile north of me, slowly lifted off, turned slowly away from me. Then it began terrain following across the valley towards the mountains to the northeast. The remaining two white objects remained on station in the canyons to the east of me. After a few minutes had passed, I decided it was time for me to head back to base. I walked slowly to my parked truck and removed the rock from behind the back wheel. I climbed into my truck, started it, took a drink of water, and began heading slowly back towards Mojave Wells some forty or fifty miles away.

The two white objects paralleled me for twenty miles or so. Then the second white object began slowly trailing behind, always staying in the mountains and canyons northeast of me, until it could be seen breaking off the quiet game of pursuit that it had played for almost half a day, silently terrain following, at last, back towards the mountains in the distant northeast. The final white object continued paralleling my movements as it had done before, until I reached the dry lakebed that was the Range Four gunnery range. There, the first white object took up a position at the mouth of a canyon at the base of the mountains east of me. It appeared to watch me from a distance as I, in my truck, continued across the lakebed in through the buildings at Range Four. It stayed on station in the canyon as I continued up the road back to Range Three and on back into Mojave Wells. It was now late afternoon and I would be getting back into base just in time for supper.

I took my time at supper. It had been a long day and there was much to be considered. Later in the evening, after the sun had set, I found myself sitting on the wooden steps to Steve's barracks. The evening was beautiful and cool. I was sitting looking north, up the valley. In the distance I could see the dim white fluorescent light given off by the first white object as it remained on station at the entrance to the canyon so many miles north of me. Steve came by and we talked for a while. Then I pointed out the white object to Steve and mused, "I wonder why it's still out there, Steve."

Steve thought for a minute and then answered, "Remember how you always equate emotions to actions, Charlie?"

"Yes," I said.

"Well, it's obviously waiting there for something, isn't it Charlie?" stated Steve simply.

"Yes," I answered slowly.

"And it can see you just as easily as you can see it. Isn't that right, Charlie?" asked Steve carefully.

"Yes. I suppose so," I answered.

"Well," Steve continued knowingly, using his north Georgia drawl, "Remember which emotion you always say goes with that action, that action of waiting."

"You mean love?" I asked in surprise.

"Yes," answered Steve simply. "You always say that love waits. You always say that love watches from afar and waits. So, according to you, Charlie, if it's waiting there and watching from afar, then it's waiting for a view of someone it loves."

Truck

> . . . As they walked on conversing,
> a flaming chariot and flaming horses
> came between them,
> and Elijah went up to heaven in a whirlwind.
> . . . 2 Kings 2:11

It was the tail end of another warm summer night at Range Three. I was having fun taking the morning balloon run. I was singing my favorite songs and listening to my radio. When the noise from the diesel was added in with my loud, off-key singing, I probably wouldn't have been able to hear an army tank if one had driven by.

A crescent of the moon remained above the horizon. I had parked my pickup truck in the usual place just west of the generator shack opposite the northern set of double doors. This meant, of course, that I couldn't actually see my truck for most of the time that I spent taking the morning run and performing the other tasks in the weather shack. As was common, I had left both windows on my truck rolled down for ventilation.

On this morning I had just locked up the weather shack and I was walking over to my truck to go in for my morning breakfast. As I rounded the corner of the generator shack I was struck by the observation that my truck appeared to have been moved. I was certain that I had left it parked opposite the northern set of doors where the front bumper and the hood would have been visible from the theodolite stand. Now, however, the truck sat parked opposite the southern set of doors, totally hidden from view by the generator shack. I was surprised and I thought it was just me being absent minded.

I always set the brake and left my truck in gear when I parked it. This morning however, I found my truck in neutral with the parking brake off. Just the same, the ground all around the Range Three area was reasonably level, the truck could not have rolled by itself.

I became even more confused when I studied the tire tracks in the dirt. The dry hard gravel and the pavement on the Range Three road had preserved very little in the way of the truck's tracks. The few it had preserved suggested that the truck had been lifted off the ground, carried back down the road for a ways, and then rolled in neutral with the engine off, back to its present position. If the few tracks were to be believed, an adult had been pushing it from behind the back bumper. There were also two sets of small boot tracks suggesting that after it stopped, two children had gotten out of the truck and ran off into the mesquite maze behind the sheds and shacks that formed the southern portion of the Range Three buildings.

After standing perplexed for a few minutes, I decided to chalk the entire episode up to poor lighting of the tracks and me being absent-minded. I shut down the diesel and drove back in to breakfast still wondering about the incident. For one thing, there was the matter of my pickup truck's weight. Could it actually have been lifted off the ground and carried or floated back down the paved road? The pickup truck weighed at least a ton and a half empty. No matter how it was accomplished, only an adult living in a world of science undiscovered by Albert Einstein could have pulled it off. Their only motive would be that they were playing with their children. Parents would never allow children to play with my truck in unsupervised manner since the children might hurt themselves. After a few miles, I shrugged off the entire train of thought since it seemed so impossible. Even so, the entire episode convinced me that I should start paying more attention to the details surrounding my truck.

A couple of nights passed. I continued to park my truck in its usual location. Then one morning as I was getting into my truck to go back in to breakfast, I noticed that the door to the glove compartment was open. There wasn't much of anything in the glove compartment but I was certain that I always kept it closed. I got back out of my truck and checked the surrounding dirt for tracks. Once again from the few tracks that were visible, it appeared that two children had come out from the mesquite behind the sheds, approached my truck, one on each side, and jumped up into it through the open windows. Another set of tracks suggested that a third child also came out from the mesquite and jumped up into the bed of my truck. Once again, after some momentary confusion, I decided that I must just be absent minded and misreading the few tracks in the dirt. After all, the windows and the bed of my pickup truck were at the normal distances above the ground. I didn't see any way that children could have gotten into my truck to play with it. Anyway, why would their parents be bringing them out here to Range Three to play? Why wouldn't they just take their children into Los Angeles where they would certainly find a better amusement park?

A few more nights passed. As before, on three of four of the nights as I closed up to go in to breakfast, I noticed that my truck didn't seem to be parked in exactly the same position that I had left it. On one of those nights, I actually tried myself to lift the front bumper of my truck. I came away convinced that a ton and a half of truck is really a ton and a half of truck. On another of those nights I tried lifting the back bumper and came away with the same conclusion.

One morning I marked the position of the rear tire with a medium sized rock. As I was taking the morning run, I was certain that I heard the driver's side door on my truck slam closed. When the morning run was over and I returned to my truck, the front bumper of the truck now sat more than 10 feet south of the rock. Not willing to accept the obvious conclusion, I decided that the gentle five mph morning winds had probably just blown the two pound rock out of position.

Then, one morning with only a thin sliver for a moon, I parked my truck in its usual position and proceeded as normal with the morning balloon run. The afternoon before I had driven in to Desert Center to pick up an extra wrench from the supply depot. It was to replace a wrench that had suddenly turned up missing the day before. I hadn't yet begun to fill the helium balloon when I remembered that I had left the new wrench on the front seat of my truck. It seemed only natural, then, to walk back to my truck to get it. So, singing one of my favorite songs, I stepped out from my weather shack and began walking back over to the generator shack to where I had left my truck parked. There seemed to be a sudden intense flurry of activity and dim fluorescent lights coming from the mesquite behind the supply sheds as I did so. To my surprise, when I rounded the corner of the generator shack, my truck wasn't there. It was sitting more than a quarter of a mile back down the Range Three road. The moonlight was reflecting dimly off its windshield, headlights, and chromium covered front bumper. In the distance, I could see a small, chalk white boy wearing an astronaut type suit that gave off some dim fluorescent light. He was floating 4 feet or so above the back bed of the truck. He appeared to be floating reluctantly over towards the sagebrush to the east.

I was mystified and surprised by the sight. However, since my truck was parked so far down the Range Three road, there wasn't time for me to walk down to retrieve it and still release the 4:30 a.m. balloon on schedule. So, swearing a little bit, I turned around and trudged back to my weather shack.

I made the balloon run as scheduled, completed the calculations, and phoned Desert Center. This naturally took the usual amount of time. Then, I locked up my weather shack and my theodolite and set out to retrieve my truck. I supposed it had just rolled of its own accord back down the level paved road. I was expecting my truck to be some distance down the road so I wasn't paying much attention to where I was going as I rounded the corner of the generator shack. My dark blue truck was sitting there, in its usual position hidden in the darkness. Not seeing it in time, I walked directly into the front bumper, banging my right shin quite badly. The sun was already coming up before I was ambulatory again. By the time I got my bruises tended to, my wounds licked, and the diesel shut down, I had developed quite an appetite for breakfast. As I sat on the front bumper of my truck rubbing my right shin and licking my wounds, I noticed that my walking full speed into my truck had not caused it to roll. Therefore, I questioned whether or not I had actually seen it parked so far down the Range Three road.

For the next two weeks or so, I took to parking my truck right next to my weather shack and driving between the generator shack and my weather shack. This wasn't because of any concerns that I might have had for my truck. It was because my shinbone was bruised so badly that it was hard for me to walk between the generator shack and my weather shack.

During those two weeks the end of the month came. As usual I collected up my completed wind and weather reports and made the long drive in to Desert Center. As I was picking up my paycheck, Master Sergeant Walters noticed that I was limping quite badly and wondered why. I tried to explain to him what had happened. However, before I could finish, he began teasing me in a fatherly kind of manner. He asked if I had really been stone sober at the time. He noted that if a man has too much to drink, it's only natural that he would forget where he'd parked his truck. Frustrated and embarrassed, I decided to just forget the whole thing as soon as my bruises would let me.

Later, my good friend Dwight reminded me that no one else but me should ever be driving my Mojave Wells weather truck even if they out-ranked me. Then he thought for a few minutes and stated seriously, "You know, Charlie, maybe you should check the old Range log books. I remember a few years back, the observer Jackson used to claim every now and then, stuff like that would happen to him, even when he was on the wagon. Maybe you weren't as drunk as Sergeant Walters thinks you were."

As I drove back to Mojave Wells, I made a mental note to remember that none of the boot prints that I had found in the soft dirt surrounding my range weather shacks, had been made by anyone I had spoken with today.

When my cuts and bruises were finally healed, I returned to my previous practice of parking my truck next to the northern set of doors just west of the generator shack. Now I was careful to park my truck far enough forward so that I could easily see the hood and driver's seat while I was taking the balloon reading, or if I chose to stick my head out the front door of my weather shack. I developed the habit of always parking my truck in the same spot and using the line of buildings as a gauge to tell if my truck had moved.

Several more uneventful mornings passed. My truck no longer moved around as it had been. As the days passed I settled down and got used to concentrating on my morning wind measurements.

Then, one moonless morning I was just finishing my calculations and preparing to phone Desert Center. I was singing. I had my radio playing loudly, my front door open, and the lights in my weather shack turned on. I wasn't paying much attention to anything outside. Suddenly, once again the image of a giant floating horse came up over the ridge three quarters of a mile north of me on the Range Four Road. It appeared to be traveling towards me in total silence at more than 45 mph, and this time it didn't slow down. It just continued smoothly through the Range Three area at the same high rate of speed, turning smoothly to avoid the theodolite stand and my truck and continued on towards base on the Range Three road. Looking directly at it when it was in that close was like looking into a blast furnace, but it appeared to be two young women, side by side, in front, three children lined up in the middle, and two male adults side by side in the back. They were bent forward and all holding on to each other in the same manner that a group of skiers might have. The women in the front were bent forward and formed the head, front, and fore feet of the horse. They seemed to be responsible for steering the formation. The back of each of their suits emitted a long narrow zone of dim fluorescent light and wispy radioactive particles. This gave the horse formation the appearance of having a broad beautiful mane along the top of its neck. It appeared to steer itself by turning its head. The three children were floating higher off the ground then the adults and formed the middle of the horse in the formation. The last two males had suits that emitted a narrow deep zone of dim fluorescent light and wispy radioactive particles. This zone formed the apparent tail of the horse formation and also pushed it forward. All of the people in the formation were intensely happy and laughing. As they passed by, they appeared to be having the time of their lives.

I was so taken off guard and they went by so fast that it took me quite a while to get over my surprise. Although I'd seen variations of the horse formation before, looking at it was so painful to my eyes that I spent most of the next few minutes just trying to get my normal vision back. After a while, perhaps 20 minutes, my eyes stopped hurting. I stepped out of my weather shack to take a good look around and to try to get over having been so startled. Outside, everything was perfectly normal. The horse formation was now several miles away down in a clear stretch of the valley. It was heading back north towards Range Four. It was traveling almost 100 mph at the time. It behaved just like a group of skiers out having fun.

A few more uneventful nights passed. I was still parking my truck in its usual place by the generator shack. I had my radio on loud and I had the lights in my weather shack turned off. I was standing by my theodolite and therefore, it was probably very hard to see me from a distance. I was just finishing my balloon readings when something in the distance down in the valley towards the base caught my attention. Once again it was the high speed horse formation. This time, it traveled down the longest of the Mojave Wells runways at more than 100 mph, perhaps even 150 mph. Then, slowing to about 70 mph or so, the formation turned and began returning up the valley following the Range

Three road. It had to rise up to 12 feet or so off the desert for a short distance to clear one of the airfield fences as it did so. Even though the buildings on the south side of Range Three blocked my view, I stood transfixed, waiting as it sped up the road towards Range Three. Then moving at least 70 mph it traveled past my parked truck and smoothly maneuvered between my theodolite stand and the Range Three lounge, turned onto the Range Four road and sped off up the road towards Range Four in the distance. Once again, looking into its dim fluorescent light close up was like looking into a blast furnace. When the pain finally left my eyes I decided that I had seen the same four adults and the same three children that I'd seen before. They were in the same formations as before, laughing themselves silly and having the time of their lives. They had come to within 40 feet of me as they passed by, all in total silence. As they were passing by, I was struck by the observation that if I hadn't seen the horse formation up close before, I would almost certainly have believed, like Elisha in The Bible, that I was looking at two flaming horses pulling a flaming chariot.

Later, as I drove back in to base for breakfast, my mind was unable to comprehend what to make of it all. I refused to believe that people wearing suits that float could be real. Yet, the pain in my eyes was very real. Therefore the light produced by their suits was real. Therefore their suits were real and they were real. Then there was the fact that normally light as dim as the light produced by their suits was not painful to look at. Light that dim could only be painful if each individual photon of light was carrying hundreds or thousands of times more energy than Einstein said was possible. In order to carry that much energy, there would have to be more physical structures within a photon of light than any human physicist had ever considered. Of course, the people I had seen clearly weren't human. They didn't have to feel limited by Einstein's reasoning.

In the end, I shrugged it all off. I didn't know what to make of what I'd seen so I returned to singing my songs and hurried on in to breakfast.

A couple more uneventful nights passed. I was in the process of taking the morning run and my truck was parked in its normal position. I was taking the balloon readings at my theodolite stand when once again I noticed the high speed horse formation down the valley. As before, the four adults and three children had apparently been playing down on the Mojave Wells runways and were heading back north up the Range Three road towards me. This time as I watched, the formation slowed to perhaps 20 mph. They reduced the power of their suits as they approached the graveled area. They continued straight north, staying west of the lounge building. Then they continued around the west side and the north side of the Range Three area, joining up finally with the Range Four road. Then, once again they turned up the power of their suits and sped off towards Range Four to the north. The sagebrush, mesquite, and other obstacles on the north side of the graveled area appeared to cause them a great deal of trouble. One of the lanes through the sagebrush appeared to be far too narrow for two adults to float through side by side, and with their suits turned down, they did not appear to be able to rise above the tall sagebrush the way they might have otherwise. Their ride was so bumpy that I was surprised they had made it through to the Range Four road. It seemed as though they had gone through a great deal of trouble just out of a consideration for me. I stood there thinking things through for a long time. Whoever they were, we seemed to share a large number of basic human emotions.

A few more uneventful nights passed. I had just finished taking the morning balloon readings and I was locking up my theodolite. Down towards base on the Range Three road, once again I could see the high speed horse formation coming towards me. This morning, using the range roads, it had made the long run down to Range One. It was just now returning back up the valley.

I had long since gotten over my fear of the horse formation. In a natural manner I continued locking up my theodolite. Then with my clipboard in hand I began walking back to my weather shack to complete the calculations. I was about half way there when the horse formation pulled up and stopped next to the sagebrush just west of the Range Three lounge. They made no attempt to hide behind the lounge. Rather, they floated back and forth in the open area straight west of me. They had all turned sideways so that they were facing me. They all seemed as happy as a bunch of clowns. The way they oscillated slowly forward and back next to the line of sagebrush reminded me of a charioteer farmer trying to hold his horses while parked next to a corn field.

Even though I was still confused by it all, and still unsure about the reality of the horse formation, I did have to laugh to myself as I walked back to my shack. It didn't seem like anyone had ever lived in a screwier world than I did. Later, as I was phoning the results in to Desert Center, I laughed to Dwight, "If I told Sergeant Walters about what's been going on tonight, he'd really think I'd been drinking."

We shared a good laugh and then I began closing up shop and heading in to breakfast. I did have a slight problem, though. The horse formation still floated over by the sagebrush to the west. They still floated in line, side by side, laughing and talking silently to each other while watching my every move. I wasn't afraid but their actions did make me feel very self-conscious. Although they had turned down the power to their suits, looking over at them still hurt my eyes. I had parked my truck in its normal position so to get my truck I was going to have to walk over to within 20 feet of the formation. The whole thing made me feel quite awkward and I decided to stall for time. I sat down in the front doorway of my weather shack, began singing some of my favorite songs, and waiting until they chose to go on their way. Peering through the white fluorescent light, I noticed that one of their children was unaccounted for. Of the three children who had been with them when they arrived, the little fat boy was now nowhere to be seen. Since they didn't seem worried, I saw no reason to feel worried either.

I sat there until the early stages of dawn were showing in the eastern sky. Finally, driven by hunger, I got up and finished closing up my weather shack. Then I walked slowly over to the generator shack and shut down the generators. I walked carefully to my truck and climbed inside. I started my truck and very carefully backed it several hundred feet down the road before turning around and heading in to base. All of the time, the horse formation floated silently back and forth watching me as I left. As I drove back in to base, it seemed like I was running more of an amusement park than a military weather station. In order to avoid awkward situations in the future, I decided that for the next few days, at least, I should park my truck in a less exposed location.

A couple of uneventful weeks went by and the memory of the high speed horse formation drifted from my mind. I was young and it was easy to devote my thoughts to fast cars, gambling, and young women, not necessarily in that order. I had taken to parking my truck in a new location next to the front of the supply sheds, halfway between my weather shack and the north end of the generator shack. One warm morning I had just begun taking the balloon measurements. I had parked my truck as usual, with both windows rolled down. I was standing by my theodolite resting my eyes between readings. My truck was parked facing to my left perhaps 70 feet away from me. I was gazing over towards my truck when suddenly and without warning; two smiling happy chalk white children came silently trotting out from between the two supply sheds. They were both wearing chalk white suits that gave off a thin zone of white fluorescent light. The thin little boy stopped by the passenger side of the truck, the far side, and floated up into the passenger seat through the open window. The other little boy, who was somewhat fatter, ran around the front of the truck to the driver's side. In a single fluid motion he floated up through the open window and settled into the driver's seat. Then a third child, a little chalk white girl, came trotting out from the same alley and jumped up into the bed of the truck. Then the little fat boy proceeded to pretend that he was driving the truck while the other children proceeded to pretend that they were riding in the truck while it was moving. The three children clearly weren't human.

I was far too stunned and taken off guard to be able to process anything that I was looking at. I remember saying to myself, "For a man going nuts, I'm sure doing it in style." I wasn't the slightest bit afraid or even curious about the sight I was witnessing. I was so certain that my brain was malfunctioning that I did not even speak or call out to the children. It was time to take another reading, so in the most ordinary and normal manner imaginable, I returned to looking through the theodolite and taking the next reading. When I returned to looking at my truck. The children were still in it, still playing as before. This process continued until I had completed taking all of my balloon readings. Except for the children playing silently in my truck, nothing seemed out of place.

After I had taken my last reading, I locked up the theodolite and stood thinking, watching the children for a minute. They seemed to be having a good time, and they certainly appeared to be perfectly real. After a few minutes, I began very slowly walking over towards my truck to get a closer look at what was happening. I had gotten about half way over to it when the fat little boy in the driver's seat looked over at me. Then the other two children jumped out of the truck and went trotting back down the alleyway between the two supply sheds. They disappeared out of sight into the thick mesquite behind the buildings. The fat little boy, in a reluctant manner floated out the window on the driver's side, then down to the ground. Then he too, trotted around the front of my truck, over to the alleyway and disappeared into the thick mesquite behind the buildings, all in total silence.

I stood there stunned, confused, and relieved that things had returned back to normal. My brain was so locked up that the only time I could remember ever having seen the three children was on that summer day several months before when I had been painting the cable fence posts. Since I had considered them to be pink elephants then, it was only natural for my mind to revert to thinking of them as pink elephants now. How could real children float in and out of my truck, or play in total silence?

The rest of the morning run proceeded in a normal and uneventful manner. By the time that I was driving in to base for breakfast, I was convinced that all of the events of the morning had just been another blood flow problem in my brain. "Things like that can come and go at anytime," I reassured myself.

A couple of uneventful days passed. I continued to park my truck in its new location by the supply sheds. On this morning, however, I had not rolled down the window on the passenger side of my truck. Only the window on the driver's side was rolled down. Once again, I was standing by my theodolite and had just taken the first reading. I was looking at my truck when, once again, the three children came trotting out of the mesquite, down the alley between the two supply sheds, and began playing in my truck. This time, however, since the window on the passenger side was closed, the thin little boy was unable to get inside. He tried jumping up to the window several times and then gave up. He returned back down the alley to the thick mesquite. The little girl jumped back out of the truck and followed him. This left only the little fat boy sitting at the driver's seat, pretending to drive my truck.

As before, I was taken completely off guard. I wasn't afraid, but I was too stunned and surprised to be able to think much of anything for a while. As before, I proceeded with my normal routine of taking the balloon measurements and resting my eyes by watching the little fat boy play in my truck. After I had taken all of my readings, I locked up the theodolite and stood looking at the little fat boy. He was having so much fun that it seemed a shame to disturb him. Anyway, I thought, maybe my blood flow problem would heal faster if I just ignored it and let it play it self out.

So this time, I picked up my clipboard and walked back to my weather shack. After finishing my calculations, and phoning Desert Center, I shut down my weather shack and went outside to lock the front door. The little fat boy was still playing in my truck. The little thin boy had joined him and was now sitting in the passenger seat. While I was locking the front door, the two boys in turn floated out the driver's side window, floated down to the ground, and took off trotting down the alley between the two supply sheds. I stood there for a few minutes wondering why both boys had had to use the single open window. If this was really my brain malfunctioning, I wondered, why couldn't the thin little boy just float through the closed glass window? Isn't one brain malfunction as good as another?

A few more uneventful days passed. I continued to park my truck in its new location by the supply sheds. On this morning, however, I rolled up all of the windows on my truck as I parked it. I did so intentionally, wondering what would happen if my brain began malfunctioning again. Once again, I was standing by my theodolite and had just taken the first balloon reading. I was intentionally keeping a careful watch on my truck. As suddenly as before, the three little white children came trotting down the alley between the two supply sheds. The little girl had no trouble jumping up into the back of the truck. However, this time I noticed that with both windows closed, neither of the two little boys could make it into my truck to pretend they were driving it. I was still confused and still I didn't have the faintest idea what was going on. Everything was still happening in total silence. It seemed only natural for me to begin walking very slowly over towards my truck. The little girl jumped out of my truck. Then she and the thin little boy went trotting back down the alley way between the two sheds. The fat little boy, however, just began playing in front of my truck and on the other side. I was in a bit of a hurry to get back to my balloon readings. Without really thinking much about things, I opened up the door on the driver's side and rolled down the window. Then I closed the door and walked back to the theodolite to continue with my readings. The little fat boy, obviously very happy, trotted around to the driver's side, jumped and floated up through the open window and began pretending he was driving the truck. I continued with my balloon readings. I rested my eyes by looking over at my truck in between, as normal. The little fat white boy picked up my spare fatigue cap that had been lying on the front seat, put it on backwards as I sometimes did, and appeared to be pretending to be singing the way I did when I drove. My mind could no longer process any of the images that I was seeing. The little fat boy was pretending to be me while I drove my truck. To my stunned, defenseless, and confused mind, this proved to me that everything I was seeing was just a brain malfunction. When I had completed my last balloon reading, I locked up the theodolite and walked calmly back to my weather shack. After completing the calculations and phoning Desert Center, I laid down on the floor of my weather shack for 20 minutes or so and rested. I decided that my brain was so messed up, I just didn't know what to do anymore.

Then with my empty stomach reminding me that it was breakfast time, I got up, closed and locked the weather shack. I walked very slowly over to my weather truck. The little fat boy was still playing inside. When he saw me approaching, he reluctantly took off my cap, and floated out the window to the ground below. However, he obviously did not want to quit playing. Instead, he jumped up into the back of my truck, and then down to the ground behind it. I sat down on the front bumper of my truck for a while waiting for him to go away. He wouldn't. I slowly got up, walked around to the driver's side, and got into my truck. I rolled up the window and rested some more while the little fat boy played in the back of the truck, behind the truck, and then around in front of the truck.

Finally, after I had been waiting for perhaps an hour, and with the sun already well above the horizon, the little fat white boy reluctantly went trotting back down the alley between the two supply sheds and disappeared into the thick mesquite. I was, by now, hungry as the devil and frustrated from waiting. Before starting the truck, I got out and checked all around it to make sure that there weren't any children in hidden places. Then, with my stomach growling, I climbed in and drove back in for breakfast. I was so hungry that I didn't even bother shutting down the diesel. As I drove back in to base, I decided that I had no choice but to return to the practice of parking my truck back over by the generator shack as I had been doing before. Only now, I would be very careful to keep both of the windows rolled up.

A couple more uneventful weeks passed. Mentally I struggled with my conclusion that the white children who had been playing in my truck were not real. On the one hand they had looked so real and acted so real. On the other hand they had worn suits and floated, and they obviously weren't human. For a number of days, it was a coin toss. Then one morning with a very nice moon, I was seated at my ivory topped table calculating the winds. The balloon run had proceeded on schedule and everything out at Range Three had been the picture of ordinary. I happened to glance up and gaze through the small window in my weather shack that over looked the table. The window was on the western side of my weather shack. Though the window I could see the little fat boy floating by, as though drifting on the wind. The little boy was very high up, perhaps as high as 30 feet and he had his suit turned up to a high power. He was floating towards the south into the wind. He was high above the roofs of the two supply sheds that sat next door. He was lying down the way a swimmer might float in a pool, and he was looking directly at me.

The entire experience didn't frighten or alarm me. I did not even go outside to check further on what I had just seen. Instead, seeing the little boy floating so high up and against the wind totally convinced me that my brain was periodically malfunctioning and that none of the children had been real. I sat quietly and calmly waiting for my brain to return to normal. I decided that if my medical problems continued much longer, I would have no choice but to visit the hospital at Desert Center and request a complete medical checkup.

The weekend came. It was about 2:00 p.m. on Saturday and I was alone on the Mojave Wells base and alone in my mostly empty barracks. I had been resting for an hour or so in my bunk after taking my noon lunch. I decided to get up, take a shower, and take the bus in to Palm Meadows. I was singing one of my favorite songs as I undressed, picked up my towel, and went walking casually down to the bathroom and showers. I had previously noticed that the screens wouldn't stay on the window to the bathroom. Several times during the past month I had picked up the screen from where it sat outside on the ground, leaning against the side of the barracks, and put it back into position on the window. This was a very difficult task because the barracks was raised and built on the side of a reasonably sloping hill. The base of the window was more than 8 feet above the ground outside.

Today, as I entered the bathroom I noticed that once again the screen had been removed and the window was wide open. I took off my shorts and hung them, along with my towel on one of the wooden pegs, and strolled smoothly into the walk-in shower room. The shower room was built for at least six men. It had no windows, only one entryway. Since the lights were off, it was fairly dark inside. Still singing, I turned on the first shower and began showering. I had only just begun when I noticed the same two chalk white little boys floating at the far end of the shower room in perfect silence, barely five feet from me. The two of them were both facing me. They were floating high enough off the floor so that they could look me more or less straight in the face. Both of them were making slow motions with their arms and hands, similar to motions made by swimmers who are floating upright in a pool.

I was so taken off guard that, once again, my brain simply couldn't process the information. I wasn't frightened or even surprised. I just stood there looking back at them, totally unable to comprehend what was happening or to think of anything. They seemed to find it all very amusing. After standing there perhaps five minutes, the water from the shower began to make the skin on my shoulders noticeably tender. Without thinking about much of anything, I turned off the shower and continued standing there watching the two boys. Then the thin little boy, as if on command, bent forward as a swimmer might have and began floating towards the entryway next to me. While I stood more or less still, he floated by me through the entryway back into the bathroom, passing within a foot of me. Then he turned and watched me while the fat little boy also bent forward and floated past me through the entryway, making swimming like motions as he did so. He was so close that I was actually looking down on him from above as he passed by less than two feet from my nose.

My mind was unable to organize even a single thought as the two of them floated by me in complete silence. The two little boys seemed to find the entire episode to be intensely amusing. Once back in the bathroom, they floated over towards the open window in much the same happy manner that two children would get off a roller coaster. Wet and naked, I slowly stepped out from the shower room into the bathroom watching them as they floated towards the open window. Through the window I could see three tall chalk white adults, Range Four Harry, the Teacher, and a young male guard, all looking at me and laughing like this was the best fun house ride in the amusement park. My mind was still totally non-functioning. I just stood there in surprise as the two boys floated out the window and the entire group of white creatures went skipping and laughing through the bright sunshine over to the row of large old trees that lined the road to the motor pool northeast of my barracks.

With my brain still numb, I carefully returned to the empty shower room and finished my shower. I decided that I was in such bad shape that I should schedule a medical exam down at the Desert Center hospital as soon as they had an opening. After all, how could any children that a man saw floating in the shower room be real?

However, there was one question that I couldn't shake from my mind for the rest of the afternoon. Why would any parent, real or imagined, allow their child to come alone into my bathroom if they didn't trust me completely? I had stood for perhaps five minutes in the hidden confines of the shower room with two small boys. It wasn't just that I hadn't panicked. Neither the boys nor any of the others had panicked either. After all, when I had to go get Bridges from the barracks next door, I had to walk him out between the adults as well as walking him past the floating little fat white boy. The entire experience left me feeling like my brain had just been scrambled. As I was walking to catch the bus into town I remember saying to myself, "I must really be sick. Now my pink elephants have learned to trust me just like I have learned to trust them."

The following Monday afternoon I had just finished the last run of the day. Range Three was showing off its late summer foliage. Before phoning the Desert Center hospital and making an appointment, I sat mulling over in my mind what I was going to say. I supposed that I would need some brain x-rays and other tests. While I sat thinking I decided to check the old log books for ideas. I came across the following series of entries from an observer a few years before me:

"Range Three, Monday 18 June 1962 9:30 P.M. This place terrifies me. I was in the weather shack computing the winds for the 4:30 a.m. run. I thought I saw a radioactive horse float down the road from Range Four and began playing with my truck. It looked like some children were pretending to drive it. The horse pulled my truck three miles down the road towards town and left it there. I became hysterical and locked myself in the weather shack. The Range Rats just now brought my truck back to me. It wasn't damaged. I'm driving in to Desert Center to request an immediate transfer."

"Range Three, Tuesday 19 June 1962 10:30 a.m. I drove in to Desert Center yesterday afternoon and requested a transfer. I told my commander about the horse. My commander refused my request and wrote me up for drinking while I was on duty. If I'm late with any more winds he'll start disciplinary action to have me discharged. I don't know what I'm going to do. I'm so terrified of this place, I just can't come out here for the morning run anymore."

"Range Three, Thursday 21 June 1962 11:00 a.m. This is my last entry in the log. Yesterday, while I was filling the balloon for the 8:00 a.m. run I saw a white woman about my height standing outside in the sagebrush by the side door of my weather shack. She didn't look human. I became so terrified I couldn't move. She said she was sorry the children had caused me so much trouble with my truck and promised that it wouldn't happen again. When she left I panicked and drove in to Desert Center to see the neurosurgeon. He said I can receive any transfer I request, or an honorable discharge if I want it, but I won't receive any disability benefits because there's nothing the matter with me. I said, "What about the horse?" and he said, "So you saw a horse." Afterwards my commander called me in his office and screamed at me for an hour. He said the base commander had ordered him to tear up the disciplinary notice that he had given me and recommend me for an award for bravery. I just can't take this place. It's driving me nuts. I've requested a transfer to Hawaii so I can rest. The neurosurgeon says that I can leave tomorrow."

I put down the logbook and thought about things. I decided the neurosurgeon was right back then. There wasn't a mark on me. What's the hurry? With a renewed purpose, I got up from my chair, closed up my weather shack and drove back into base. The Desert Center hospital would always be there.

The next morning began as usual and I parked my truck in the usual place. There was a good deal of moonlight and I was running a half hour late, so I skipped starting up the diesel. Consequently, it was a very quiet night. I was in my weather shack putting helium in the balloon when I heard the front door of my truck slam shut. Nervous about the safety of my only means of transportation, I shut off the flow of helium, got up, stepped outside and began walking slowly over towards the generator shack. As soon as I was outside I saw the Teacher and Range Four Harry standing side by side over by the sagebrush line on the west side of the graveled area. They were standing out in the open looking at me and made no effort to conceal themselves as I approached. When I got beside the northwestern corner of the generator shack I could see the three children playing in my truck as before. Tonight one adult was standing beside the door on the driver's side. All of the white creatures stood silently looking at me. Apparently none of them knew quite what to say. It was, after all, my truck.

I found the entire situation to be quite intimidating and the presence of the children convinced me that my brain was once again malfunctioning. However, the truck was my only means of transportation and I did need to keep it safe. In a nervous, almost wimpy manner then, I began talking. It took a great deal of courage to speak so I was very slow in starting. I wasn't actually addressing them so much as I was addressing the sagebrush in the open area west of the buildings. I wasn't even looking at them at the time. I said, "Please don't damage my truck. I am not able to float as

218

you are. My truck is the only way I have to get back in to base to eat my breakfast. Please be careful with it, and please leave it in the same place as you found it when you are through playing."

Then I looked at them one last time before turning and retracing my steps back to my weather shack. The looks in each of their eyes appeared to be looks of immense respect. That was the last evening that anyone ever again touched my truck.

Two Games on One Board

"Reach down your hand from on high;
deliver and rescue me
from the mighty waters,
from the hands of foreigners . . ."
Psalm 144:7

It was a beautiful Wednesday morning at Range Three. I was sitting quietly in my weather shack, listening to my radio, and reading a book on the history of the west. The radio was tuned to one of my favorite popular music stations. They were playing the songs I referred to as my sunshine songs. Both the front door and side door of my weather shack stood open. The clipboard holding my completed weather reports hung from a nail on the wall, swinging slowly back and forth in the soft summer breezes. Range Three was in use that day. Consequently, Steve, Wayne, Doug, three other range rats, and a bird Colonel, the range officer were out on the range. The three power wagons that the range rats used sat parked out beside the Range Three lounge. Doug and the bird Colonel were in the nearby control tower talking to the airplanes.

Sometimes, through my side door, I would watch the current group of six F-105 fighter planes as they took turns bombing and strafing the targets out in the desert to the east of my weather shack. The radio announced the time. It was 11:00 a.m. I didn't have a balloon release scheduled for another hour. The current group of planes was scheduled to spend another 25 minutes practicing low level strafing runs. Putting my book aside, I decided to walk over to the Range

Three lounge. It would be fun talking to my good friends, Steve, Wayne, and the other range rats. What else was there to do until Jesus comes, I asked myself? I put my book aside, stood up, went outside, and began crossing the open square that separated my weather shack from the lounge. Halfway across the open area, I stopped for a few minutes and watched the current flight of F-105s as they practiced skip bombing. One by one, the planes would level off and come in low over the skip bomb practice range. Sometimes they would come as low as 4 feet off the desert before releasing their practice bomb. One of the pilots was obviously quite new and, after releasing one of his practice bombs, he made the mistake of watching the bomb skip towards its target instead of watching the path of his airplane. As his F-105 sunk slowly towards the barren gravel covered desert below him, I could hear Doug in the tower shouting into the microphone, "Pull up!! Pull up!! Sparrow four, you're too low!! Pull up, now!!"

The tail of the F105 was barely 18 inches off the desert when the pilot nosed up. Then the pilot hit his afterburner and blasted small rocks and gravel for several hundred feet in all directions as his plane finally headed back towards the skies where it belonged.

Laughing, and shaking my head a little, I said to myself, "Boy, he sure was lucky." I turned back towards the Range Three lounge, intending to finish my happy journey. Then, I heard the telephone in the tower ring. Thinking, at first, that it was the phone in my weather shack, I stopped and listened. My friend Doug answered it.

"Range Three tower, range rat Doug speaking." There was a short pause. Then Doug shouted into the phone, "Yes Sir! and slammed down the phone. Turning to the bird colonel next to him, he shouted, "That was the Desert

Center base commander himself. He has declared a range emergency! Condition RED!! We are ordered to close and evacuate the ranges under emergency conditions, NOW! All planes are ordered off the ranges immediately. They are ordered to come to less than 100 feet off the desert and to immediately head down the valley to the southeast and return to Desert Center. After landing at Desert Center, the pilots are ordered to remain immediately beside their planes. They are to speak to no one, not even each other, until they have been individually and personally debriefed by the Desert Center security officer."

"Roger," answered the bird colonel without hesitation.

As the Colonel began relaying the orders to the planes, Doug ran outside to the balcony around the outside of the cab on the control tower. He shouted to Steve and the range rats in the lounge, "Range emergency. Condition RED! Desert Center base commander's orders! Evacuate immediately!"

Steve, without hesitation, shouted to Wayne, and to the other range rats with him, "Wayne, Gary, take power wagons two and three and get the hell out of here, now! I'll stay with wagon one and bring in the Colonel and Doug!"

Without hesitation, Wayne and the other range rats ran from the lounge, out to their two power wagons. They climbed into the wagons the way firemen load onto fire trucks. Spinning the tires on the soft gravel, they accelerated past me as they headed into base. Steve, likewise, went running to the remaining power wagon. Starting it, he pulled it up along side of me, and screamed to Doug, "Come on Doug! Let's get the hell out of here, NOW!!"

Doug came running down the steps of the tower. However, when he reached the ground, he did not head

Charles James Hall

immediately towards the power wagon. Instead, he went running at full speed over towards the range boards. Since the range had been in use, they were currently in the "white" position. Doug began moving the boards to the "red" position, i.e. the range closed position. Seeing him in the process of doing this. Steve screamed, "To hell with the damn boards, Doug. You know the rules! Get the hell into the truck, NOW!! Let Charlie close the damned boards."

This surprised me, since I was completely unaware that those were the range emergency closure rules. As I stood there in surprise, I shouted to Steve, "I have to leave too, don't I?"

The Colonel was still in the tower screaming into the radio microphone, "Sparrow four! Get the hell off the ranges, NOW! This is an emergency! The condition is RED!! The ranges are closed! You are ordered to head immediately down the valley towards the southeast. You are ordered to come below 100 feet immediately and head down the valley!"

Looking towards the east, I could see the new pilot as he slowly headed north up the valley along the base of the mountains to the east. The other planes had already evacuated the range, leaving the new pilot alone. His wings were wobbling in an unusual manner. He seemed to be nervous and on the verge of losing control of his plane. Then I noticed that Doug had stopped moving the range boards to the "red" position, and was standing next to the far range board looking up the valley. Then Doug shouted, "Hey! There's something white up there, sitting on the desert!"

Steve screamed at Doug, "To hell with it, Doug!! Damn it!! To hell with it!! Forget the damned range boards. Get the hell back into the wagon, NOW!!"

Then I heard the bird Colonel screaming into the radio microphone, "Sparrow four! Did you hear your orders? Get the hell out of there now! This is an emergency! Get the hell off the ranges!! Head down the valley to the southeast immediately!!"

As I watched, the F-105 turned slowly, came down to perhaps as little as 25 feet off the desert, and headed down the valley to the southeast. The pilot seemed dazed or stunned. He was flying very slowly and still didn't seem to have his plane under complete control. Then the bird Colonel came running down the stairs of the tower. Reaching the ground, he ran to the waiting truck, hastily climbed into the back seat of the power wagon and slammed the truck door. Then he shouted to Steve, "Let's GO!!"

Steve was still waiting for Doug who still stood over by the range boards watching something up the valley. Steve screamed at Doug, "Doug, for God's sake, let's get the hell out of here, now! To hell with it! Let Charlie handle it! Damn it, COME ON!! NOW!!"

Surprised, shocked, and confused, I shouted to the bird Colonel through the open windows of the power wagon, "Colonel, I've got no orders. I'm supposed to leave too, aren't I?"

To my shock and surprise, the bird Colonel whom I had never seen before and have never seen since, looked me straight in the eyes and asked calmly, "You're Airman Charlie Baker, the range weather observer, the one they call Teacher's Pet, aren't you?"

"Yes, Colonel." I shouted, wondering for a minute how he knew who I was. After all, I was only an enlisted man wearing three stripes and he was a bird Colonel - and I wondered how he knew I was "Teacher's Pet". I continued, shouting, "I've got no orders. I have to evacuate too, don't I?"

To my absolute surprise, the bird Colonel said, "No. The last orders which I personally received from the Desert Center base commander made it clear that range closure orders do not apply to you, even if it is an emergency closure. None of us at Desert Center have the authority to order you off the ranges. You are to carry on with your normal activities, according to your normal orders."

I stood there in shock, and near disbelief. The Desert Center base commander was a two star General. He could give any order he felt like to an enlisted man like me. Ignoring an evacuation order from a commanding General would certainly get a man court-martialed. Doug came running back from the range boards, leaving two of them in the "white" position. Steve was screaming at him, "MOVE IT, Doug. Damn it! MOVE IT!"

Doug flung open the truck door next to me, jumped in, and slammed close the door. Steve threw the truck in gear and spun the wheels as he raced out of there. I was left standing alone in total confusion. "Surely the evacuation orders must apply to me, too, don't they?" I asked myself.

I decided that I had better check with Desert Center so I turned and ran back to my weather station. Picking up the phone, I dialed the Desert Center weather station. After a few rings, my friend Dwight answered.

"Charlie, it's good to hear your voice," exclaimed Dwight. "What can I do for you?"

"Dwight!" I screamed into the phone. "The Desert Center base commander has just declared an emergency and closed the ranges. But the range officer said the orders don't apply to me. I don't know what the hell is going on! I don't know what I'm supposed to do! I'm supposed to evacuate too, aren't I?"

"I don't know, Charlie," replied Dwight. "I haven't heard anything. Sergeant Adams is the forecaster. I'm sure he hasn't heard anything either, but I tell you what, Charlie, just wait a minute. I'll have Sergeant Adams check with the command post."

"Right, Dwight," I answered.

I waited on the phone for almost 10 minutes before Dwight finally got back to me. "The range officer was correct, Charlie. Both Sergeant Adams and I spoke with the Desert Center base commander personally. He said that the Pentagon has declared a range emergency and that the emergency is in progress. He said other than that, he had no information that he could provide to us. He said that he communicated with the Pentagon. He said a three star General in the Pentagon verified that range emergency orders. Range closure orders do no apply to you. You are ordered to carry on with your normal activities. He said that the usual orders applied, namely that only you alone are allowed to be out there. No one else can be with you. Other than that, your orders are to 'carry on'. The command post suggested that you shut down the radio in the control tower and move the range boards to the "red" closed positions, but only if you feel like those are sensible things to do. The base commander said that if you choose to cancel all balloon runs for the remainder of the week, you are free to do so. If you are willing to take a 2 o'clock balloon run today and follow the regular schedule tomorrow, the command post could use the wind information. They suggested that you keep your truck in good working order. They also suggested that you monitor your fuel gauge, watch your tires and carry a spare. Remember, when you're out there, no one else can come out to get you, even if your truck were to break down or your life were in danger. Other than that, Charlie, have fun and enjoy yourself."

Still confused, I stammered into the phone, "It's because I'm the duty weather observer up here, isn't it?"

"No," responded Dwight. "According to the base commander, the Pentagon made it explicitly clear. The range closure orders apply to every man, woman, and child at Mojave Wells, and everyone at Desert Center except you. He referred to you by your name, Charlie Baker. He also referred to you as "Teacher's Pet". He said that was the decision the Pentagon made when they chose you. The Desert Center base commander also reminded us that no one at the Desert Center weather station is ever allowed to visit you at Mojave Wells, or inspect your facilities out on the ranges. None of us is ever allowed in your barracks or even to meet with you in the parking lot by your Mojave Wells chow hall. We sure as hell aren't allowed to ask you any questions about today. The base commander swore he'd personally court-martial any one of us including the Major himself, if we ever violated those orders. He also made it clear that if anyone of us ever went out on the ranges where you are, even if your life were in danger, he guaranteed us five years in Leavenworth. I'm telling you, Charlie, the Pentagon really means it when they say that no one but you is allowed out there while the ranges are closed."

"Thanks, Dwight," I replied, confused, and stumbling for words. "I better go now, and close down the control tower. Tell Sergeant Adams that I'll give you those 2:00 p.m. winds and the regular schedule tomorrow."

"Right, Charlie," answered Dwight. "Be careful and take care of yourself."

Charles James Hall

With that, I hung up phone. Stunned and confused, I didn't immediately go out to close down the range. Instead, I sat down in my chair and tried to grasp what had just transpired. The bird Colonel had been ordered off the ranges but I, an enlisted man, had not. The pilots who were all officers, had been ordered off the ranges but I had not. Then there was the question, "What had Doug seen sitting on the valley floor, north east of here?"

Yes, for a long time I sat there in my chair in quiet, beautiful solitude, looking out through the open front door to my weather shack, quietly listening to the radio. There was much to be considered.

Another one of my sunshine songs came on the radio. Another series of gentle summer breezes rustled the papers inside my weather shack. It seemed natural for me to turn my gaze to the beautiful desert stretching north up the valley from Range Three. The buildings of Range Four, some twenty miles distant, shimmered through the noonday heat waves. On the dry lakebed beyond the distant range four buildings, several dust devils played patiently among the loose tumbleweeds and sand. Some fifty to seventy feet high, created as creatures of the summer sunshine and heat, the dust devils playfully tossed sand in and around the distant patches of dry sagebrush. Yet, beautiful as the scene in the distance was, there was something about the view that felt out of place. Out on the dry lakebed in the distance, playing in the sunshine and in the haze and heat waves and in among the patches of sagebrush, one of the dust devils appeared to have stumbled across a large white solid object. Several times I tried to look away but the image of the playful dust devil in trouble kept drawing my gaze back to the dry lakebed to the north. It took a long time, maybe twenty minutes of watching the heat waves, the sunshine,

228

the dust devils, the noonday haze, before I realized that the solid object interfering with the path of the dust devil was real. "Yes," I whispered to myself, in disbelief, "There is something real out there in the sagebrush."

Slowly, in deep thought, I rose from my chair, stepped out into the hot desert sun, and walked to my theodolite. Carefully, I moved my theodolite into position and focused in on the distant object. It took a few minutes to get a decent view of the object, hiding as it was out in the haze and the heat waves. The object sitting on the surface of the dry lakebed was about the size of the engine on a passenger train. It was solid white and ellipsoidal. On the front, it had windows similar to the windows on a passenger diesel. I watched it for a few minutes. Then to my surprise, the object appeared to become aware that I was watching it. First a field of some type appeared to form around the object. Its surface features blurred over until it had a uniform solid white appearance. This made it look something like a giant white egg hiding in the sagebrush. Then it rose up a couple feet off the dry desert lakebed and floated backwards several feet so that it was better hidden in the sagebrush and sand. Parts of it were still visible above the sagebrush. It repeated the maneuver two or three times but parts of it still remained visible in the distance.

Curious, I paused to mull things over. Whatever the object was, I decided that it couldn't be the object that Doug had seen. Doug had been looking over towards the mountains to the east when he claimed he'd seen something. With curiosity building within me, I left my theodolite and walked slowly over towards the range boards. Arriving at the place where Doug had been standing, I shaded my eyes from the glare of the sunshine and began studying the base of the mountains to the northeast. Out there, about three miles distant, sitting on a gentle gravel slope near the base of the mountain, was a second white object. The second object was virtually identical to the first one. This second object was sitting stationary, directly on the desert. Its features were not fuzzed over by the presence of a white field. For this reason I decided that the power plant on the second object must have suffered some kind of mechanical failure.

This second object was facing north, away from me. The rear of the object did not have any windows or features. The door to the east was open. Standing on the desert studying the craft, some 10 or 15 feet from the raised door, I could see a tall adult chalk white creature with three chalk white children. As I watched, the adult and three children went back on board and closed the door. Then the surface of the craft momentarily became covered with a white fuzzy field of some type. The outline of the craft momentarily became indistinct. Then, just as suddenly, the outline of the craft became distinct again and the white field went away. After a couple of minutes the door reopened. The tall white adult and the three children came back out into the desert and took up their former positions some 15 feet east of the craft.

As I scanned the scene north of me, the first white craft sitting on the dry lakebed, then moved forward a few feet. This apparently gave it a better view of the second craft. My eyes caught sight of a third craft. It was terrain following along the base of the mountains northeast of me. When it was about five miles north of me, it turned east and crossed through a pass in the mountains so that it was now out of sight in the valley east of me. Nothing much seemed to happen for the next three of four minutes. Then, I could see the third craft re-cross the mountains south east of me, down by Range Two. It came down a road from that distant valley and passed through the Range Two area. It slowly followed along the base of the eastern mountains until it was just a half-mile or so, from the second craft. It passed within a mile and a quarter of me as it did so. There was a small ridge in the desert between Range Three and the mountains to the northeast. The third craft appeared to intentionally set down on the desert in such a manner that this ridge blocked my view of the third craft. Then the adult tall white creature and the three children walked over towards the third craft.

As I stood there wondering what would happen next, I noticed that a second adult tall white creature had disembarked from the third craft. This third creature proceeded to take up a position just behind the ridge, perhaps a mile distant, between the distant craft and me. This second adult was obviously assigned to guard me. He proceeded to very intensely keep track of my every move. He seemed awfully nervous. Even slight movements of my head or hands would cause him to change position. His presence caused me to feel a great deal of confusion. Things just didn't seem to make any sense. I wondered, 'Why guard me at all. Why do they want me out here but under guard? Why didn't they just order me off the ranges in the first place?'

The presence of the guard made me a quite nervous but I was young and becoming more curious by the minute. Since nothing much seemed to be happening in the distance, I decided this was a good opportunity to close down the range. I felt that this would let the guard settle down and perhaps help me by increasing my life expectancy. After all, many guards are well armed.

I proceeded to move all of the range boards to their red, closed, positions. Then I walked slowly and calmly over to the Range Three tower. After I climbed the stairs, I walked into the cab on the top and turned off the radios.

The tower gave me a better view of the second and third craft in the distance. A mechanic had disembarked from the third craft and had begun working on the disabled craft. He opened up three large panels on the back of the disabled craft. The panels opened upwards. This gave the disabled craft an appearance similar to a large city bus with an engine under repair. Under the panels could be seen a huge number of windings similar to the windings on an electromagnet. The first craft was still semi-hiding in the sagebrush on the dry lakebed. Now it rose up several feet above the sagebrush and began slowly floating over towards the disabled craft. I estimated its speed to be little more than 30 miles per hour. Like the other craft, the first craft did not raise any dust or make any sound as it flew. The first craft floated over to within 30 feet or so, west of the disabled craft and set down on the desert. When it sat down, it floated gently to a stop in much the same way that a leaf might fall from a tree, reaching, at last, the ground below.

Another mechanic, carrying something that looked like a tool case, disembarked from the first craft and joined the other mechanic. The third craft, with the mechanics standing clear, now rose and floated over to within 30 feet or so east of the disabled craft. Then a fourth craft could be seen terrain following along the base of the mountains to the northeast. The fourth craft arrived at the scene and set down out of sight, behind the ridge to the northeast. Two more mechanics carrying tool cases disembarked for the fourth craft and joined the other two mechanics. Then the adult white creature along with the three children changed from the third craft to the fourth craft.

By now the heat waves coming off the desert floor were obscuring many of the details of the scene in the distance. I walked back around to the south side of the tower. I noticed that the guard responded immediately by changing his position. He proceeded south also, taking up a position three quarters of a mile down the road to the ammunition bunker. I could see that he was carrying a weapon of some type in his left hand. Still, I wasn't afraid. Despite the fact that all of the white creatures walked somewhat differently than humans do, I supposed they were just USAF guards who weren't used to walking in the desert or through sagebrush. Still curious about the scene out in the desert northeast of me, I decided to get a closer look. So I walked down the tower stairs and back to my truck. I took the jar of water from the truck and began walking north down the road to Range Four. This seemed to catch the guard by surprise. He reacted immediately. He fell back behind the ridge and began paralleling me, always staying about half way between the craft and me. After walking perhaps a mile down the Range Four road, I reached the high point in the road. From there, I turned northeast into the desert and began walking slowly towards the four craft that sat on the desert floor, over by the base of the mountains. Although I was now leaving the dirt road behind me, it was an easy walk, and generally downhill. The guard continued his policy of staying about half way between the four craft and me.

Since this desert slope was fairly rugged, it was necessary for me to do a certain amount of zigzagging down the slope. Time after time I expected the rough terrain would force the guard to stand aside and let me brush past. Yet, time after time, the guard fell back in front of me. Always he paralleled my every turn. The guard was quite

233

agile. I noticed that he was capable of moving two or three times faster than I was. By the time I was about half way down the slope, it was apparent that I would never be able to out distance or out maneuver him.

It was a hot day so I decided to take my own good-natured time making the hike. I changed to zigzagging a short distance and then stopping, occasionally taking a drink of water. I'd watch the scene in the distance for a few minutes. Then I'd hike some more.

Before long, I had closed to just less than a mile from the four craft. Now the guard changed his tactics. He retreated to a small hillock, less than a quarter mile in front of me. The terrain in his vicinity contained several large rocks. The guard could have avoided these rocks by falling back closer to the craft. Yet, even though falling back to this particular hillock caused the guard a great deal of trouble, he did so in an unusually deliberate and intent manner. I thought this over carefully before taking the next three of four more steps forward. When I did so, it was immediately obvious that this time, the guard had no intention of falling back any closer to the craft. He began holding his ground. Still curious, I cautiously began closing the distance between the guard and myself. The guard watched my every move, and bravely stood his ground.

Then I stepped forward some more until I had closed the distance between the guard and myself to less than a hundred yards. The guard began smoothing the ground on which he was standing. After making sure his footing was secure, he came to a full upright position. He was obviously ready for battle, and he obviously wanted to be certain that I saw him.

After giving the matter some thought, I carefully took another three or four steps forward. Still the guard stood his ground. He visibly gripped his weapon more tightly. Then he turned slightly so that he was facing me straight on. He stood approximately six feet tall with chalk white skin and short blonde, almost transparent, hair. His large blue eyes had a noticeably pink tinge and wrapped further around the sides of his head than the eyes of a human do. With his thin chalk white body, he seemed right at home in the hot desert sun. His weapon consisted of a short chalk white tube about 18 inches long. He was obviously very skilled in handling it.

I thought about things carefully for a few more minutes. In the distance, repair work on the downed craft continued uninterrupted. The tall white adult and the three children stood a few feet northeast of the fourth craft, watching the guard and I, as we performed our careful waltz in the sagebrush.

In the distance the mechanics had opened up a row of outside panels on the rear portion of the downed craft. They were hinged at the top. The scene wouldn't have appeared very different if I had been observing a group of mechanics repairing a disabled city bus. The downed craft had a double hull type of construction and did not appear to carry any fuel tanks. Instead, underneath it appeared to contain many sets of field windings that appeared very similar to those commonly found on electromagnets. It also contained several pairs of black boxes that appeared to function as batteries. The entire inner hull was surrounded by one of these protective sets of windings and battery pairs. The windings were constructed using many thousands of long thin plastic strands. The strands were clear or white in color. Like the windings on an electromagnet, the strands appeared to start from one of the two batteries, then wind around things such as the inner hull, and end on the second of the two batteries in the battery pair. Between the two hulls was space enough to hold perhaps a thousand miles of such strands.

The windings were not constructed with copper, so presumably the batteries could not have been ordinary electrical batteries. I supposed instead that the batteries must generate streams of some type of sub-atomic particles, or perhaps light photons. The entire resulting design seemed pretty self-evident. The windings that carried the resulting particle streams, were obviously used to lift and propel the scout craft, streamline the craft so it could accelerate beyond the speed of light, and also to control the levels of gravity inside the craft as it accelerated and traveled. I guessed that if American scientists could identify a sub-atomic particle that produced reverse gravity, no matter how short lived it might be, along with the fiber optics strands to carry the particle, they could probably construct an entire such craft in a few weeks. I wondered why American scientists were only trying to build more powerful sub-atomic particle accelerators. It seemed obvious to me that American scientists should also be trying to build simple battery-like generators of ordinary particles such as mesons, baryons, and pions, including particles that are electrically neutral. Then, using streams of such particles, they should construct devices with many windings, similar to electromagnets and study how such devices behave. It seemed to me that such devices could be used to streamline a spacecraft and propel it beyond the speed of light, showing the limitations of Einstein and his theories. Of course, such devices would have many other uses as well.

In any event, the downed craft sitting in the distance had clearly overheated on this hot day and suffered a melt down in some of its windings. Apparently the sub-atomic particles that were used to power the craft routinely undergo radioactive decay and heat up the windings as they do so. Since ordinary plastics begin to melt and soften when heated to perhaps, 1000 degrees Fahrenheit, the mechanics' problems were quite obvious. The mechanics were beginning the process of surgically removing the damaged windings so they could later be replaced with new ones. It was obviously going to be a very long and tedious process.

The previous behavior of the scout craft now made complete sense. When the craft originally began to overheat, the pilot had set it down immediately on the desert to allow it to cool off. Then, once it was cool, he was hoping that enough of the windings were still working well enough to allow the craft to return to its repair hanger. So he tried powering it up again. The USAF naturally wanted all of its airplanes out of the area since the scout craft pilot knew in advance that he would have very little control over his craft once it began powering up again. The attempt to power up had failed. Now it was time for the repair crew to have fun.

Still, I wanted to get a closer look at the craft in the distance. They were so different from anything I'd seen the United States Air Force fly. I carefully took another three or four steps forward and stopped. The guard, still wearing a pleasant expression, brought his weapon slowly to his chest and gripped it with both hands. Although the weapon was still pointed towards the sky, I understood exactly what the guard meant. He obviously wanted me to see that he was well armed with a very long weapon.

I thought about things carefully for a few more minutes. The guard in front of me obviously intended to defend the hillock, probably to the death if necessary, and he had obviously assumed a firing position. Out in the open, I would make a very easy target. I decided that I had pushed the guard about as far as he was willing to be pushed. Feeling alone, naked, and unarmed, I decided my life would be longer and happier if I retreated to the safety of the ridge behind me. Without turning around, I stepped backward, retreating back up the hill behind me for several feet. The footing wasn't the best and I had to do so carefully. Then I stopped and waited. The guard on the hillock responded by lowering his weapon back to his left side. Breathing a little easier, I carefully turned back towards the dirt road on the hill. Slowly and carefully, I picked my way up the hill until I was standing back on the dirt of the Range Four road. I turned at last to view the four craft sitting on the desert floor in the distance. I noticed the guard hadn't followed me but instead remained standing relaxed at the hillock. Unnoticed while I had been climbing the hill, the craft in the distance had been joined by still a fifth craft. This fifth craft was just floating to a stop, 50 feet or so north of the disabled craft. A second guard disembarked from this fifth craft, while the tall white adult and the three children hurried over to board it. The tall white adult in the distance stopped for a few minutes to communicate with the second guard. Through the heat waves, the bright sunshine, and the light haze, I could see the tall adult point out my position on the hill to the second guard.

Once the adult and the three children were on board the fifth craft, it departed as silently as it had come. It quickly followed the terrain along the base of the mountains to the northeast until it reached a pass in the north end of the valley some forty miles or so north of me. Then it gained altitude and headed up towards the mountains in the distant northeast.

The second guard moved quickly through the sagebrush until it stood next to the first guard. The two tall white guards were obviously completely at home out in the hot sun. This second guard was slightly smaller than the first and because of the manner in which it moved, I decided that it must be feminine. As the two guards stood side by side, the feeling that they were brother and sister momentarily overwhelmed me. I immediately became convinced that this younger guard was equivalent to a young girl in the eighth grade. I couldn't help but feel that she had come to protect her older brother by playing games with me. Yet I found these feelings to be intensely confusing. Why, I wondered, would the U.S. Air Force use girls as young as the eighth grade as guards? And why guard me at all? Why not just order me off the ranges as everyone else had been ordered off the ranges?

My empty stomach reminded me that all this hiking had caused me to miss my noon meal. I checked my watch. It was past 1:30 in the afternoon. A sinking feeling filled my stomach when I remembered that I had also missed my 12:30 balloon run. I took a quick drink of water, turned, and began hurrying back down the dirt road towards Range Three. The second guard paralleled my movements with the ease of a hawk following a rabbit. She had obviously been chosen for her speed and agility. She was much faster then the first guard had been. She was obviously capable of running down the Range Four road many times faster than I was, and it was immediately apparent she could maintain that speed for miles. Running from her was pointless as a field mouse trying to outrun a hawk. I quickly found myself wondering how any human could be that fast. It was painfully obvious that she was so fast I would be totally helpless if she ever decided to attack. After thinking things

x

Charles James Hall

through, I decided that since she currently appeared to be in a happy, playful frame of mind, I could best show a high level of intelligence by keeping her that way. So I returned to walking at a natural pace and began singing some of my happy desert sunshine songs. Even though my singing was way off-key, the second guard seemed to enjoy it, so I sang loudly as I walked. I sang songs to the sunshine. Then I sang songs to the mountains, then to the desert and to its flowers. In the end, I even sang a few songs to the second guard, now easily pacing me at a quarter of a mile. I looked silly enough, I suppose, singing in the sunshine, but I didn't mind. I didn't call it being silly. I called it 'Staying Alive'.

In the fullness of time, I found myself back at the northern edge of Range Three. I was still singing while I walked. The second guard had been paralleling my movements by staying about a quarter mile out in the sagebrush east of me. As I reentered the graveled area at Range Three, I began feeling somewhat safer. I ended my song and stopped singing. This seemed to have an immediate effect on the second guard. Moving at nearly full speed, she quickly closed the distance between us, coming in suddenly and in near silence up to the cable separating the graveled area from the skip bomb area. She stopped finally at a point less than 70 feet southeast of me. She did so with breath taking speed and I was too surprised to do much more than stop in my tracks. She seemed to be saying playfully, "See. Here I am, you can keep singing."

She stood an inch or so shorter than I did. Her bright blue eyes and short transparent blonde hair sparkled in the bright summer sunshine. She was totally unafraid of me. She was wearing a suit that appeared to have been made from some type of aluminized canvas. The suit contained an open helmet that appeared to contain some type of built-in

240

electronics. The footprints she left in the soft dirt were clearly visible for the next several days.

Wearing the suit, she seemed almost unaffected by the earth's gravity. Sometimes she bounded more like a deer or an antelope than she actually ran. Sometimes she appeared to be actually floating. It was painfully obvious there was no point in my becoming afraid. She could move so fast that she could kill me with impunity anytime she felt like it, anytime at all. I finally regained my breath and spoke to her. I knew I was holding my life in my hands. I was gambling everything on keeping her happy. I said in pleasant laughing tones, "You sure are in a happy mood today. You must enjoy being out here in the sunshine."

She turned her head slightly towards me and gave me a very large smile. Then she seemed to regain her composure, turned, and just as suddenly as she'd come in, she retreated perhaps a quarter mile, back out into the desert.

Controlling the nerves of fear in my stomach, I walked naturally back to my weather shack. Once safely inside, I sat down in my chair to rest, and to enjoy the shade and the cool breezes, and its safety for a few minutes. The first guard had returned to his previous position just beyond the distant desert ridge. He could be seen watching me from a distance of about a mile out in the desert, northeast of my weather shack. The second guard, who had paralleled my movements in playful fashion, now stood more or less a quarter mile out in the sagebrush, northeast of my weather shack. She stood apparently waiting for me to come out again and play.

Playing out in the sunshine with the second guard was definitely the last thing on my mind at the time. My mind turned at last, to the business at hand, the business of saving my life. Picking up the phone, I called Desert Center. It was obvious that the 2:00 p.m. run would be coming late and the missing 12:30 run must certainly concern them. I thought I'd better account for the missing 12:30 report. My friend Dwight answered the phone. He was in his usual good mood. Yet, I was surprised when he informed me that the Desert Center command post had phoned the forecaster at 12:30. The forecaster had been reminded that it was OK with the base commander if I chose to cancel the 12:30 winds and the 2:00 p.m. winds. The Desert Center weather station had been reminded of the standing order never to ask me any questions about what went on at Mojave Wells. "But how did the Desert Center base commander know at 12:30 that I was going to be missing my 12:30 winds? I don't normally report them until five minutes to one." I asked defensively. Dwight didn't know, but I wasn't surprised. Nothing about this day seemed to be making sense. It didn't seem like the U.S. Air Force was even running the ranges any more.

Nervous and defensive because of my failure to take the 12:30 winds, I told Dwight I would hurry and take a wind measurement, even if it was going to be awfully late. I hung up the phone and quickly inflated my balloon. Then with my clipboard in one hand and the balloon in the other, I backed out through the side door and headed for my theodolite. The second guard, in quick, playful fashion, closed in behind the range boards and watched me as I took the winds.

When the run was over, I hurried back to my weather shack. As I was performing the calculations, I noticed that the second guard had moved. Now, in happy, playful fashion, she was hiding behind the Range Three lounge. As I watched, the first guard retreated out of sight behind the desert ridge.

Quickly, I completed my calculations, and phoned them in to Desert Center. Then, singing loudly for self-defense, I locked up my weather shack, shut down the diesel, started my truck, and headed in to base. As my truck began heading down the Range Three road towards base, in the mirror I could see the second guard. She stepped out from behind the range three lounge and stood watching my truck as I disappeared down the road.

The drive back to base was an unusual one. My experiences out in the desert had left me feeling stunned, extremely confused, and very tired. I spent most of the drive denying the reality of the day's events. When I got back to my barracks, I lay down in my bunk and slept until it was time for the evening meal.

The food that evening was unusually good. I remember going back to the chow line twice for more. I was just finishing my evening meal when Smokey came over smiling. "Charlie", he said, "I've got Steve on the phone. He's over in the orderly room covering for the sergeant of the day until eight tonight. He said he wanted to talk to you for a little while, and challenged you to a quick game of chess."

"Sure," I laughed. "Tell him I'll be right over."

The walk over to the orderly room went quickly enough. Steve greeted like the near brother that he was. The chessboard was already set up. Steve had taken white and already made the first move.

I had just barely sat down when a young USAF Captain came out from the back room. Before Steve or I could shout, "Attention!" the captain spoke, "At ease, men. Carry on with your game."

The captain was wearing his dress blue uniform and carrying a soft briefcase of the type that lawyers frequently

243

carry. He took a chair in one of the corners, took out a pad of paper, and apparently began quietly completing some paper work.

Steve spoke to me using the same tones that a brother might use, "You know, Charlie, you were out there at Range Three today, with the rest of us when that emergency happened."

"Yes, Steve," I responded, taken somewhat off balance.

"Now, I am not asking you any questions about anything that you might have seen or done after the boys and I left. I know quite well that damned Desert Center base commander doesn't want me or anyone else asking you any of those kind of questions. So don't go telling me anything that would upset that damn base commanding General down at Desert Center," stated Steve. "I'd just forget it all right away, anyway."

"Yes, Steve," I responded. "I understand."

Steve continued, "That damn Desert Center base commander has our friend Doug in the brig down at Desert Center and he's planning on court-martialing him. He's mad as hell because Doug took so long getting into the power wagon this morning. I sure as hell don't want that damn General getting mad at me too."

"Yes, Steve," I answered. I noticed that the Captain in the corner seemed to be taking notes as Steve spoke.

"Well, Charlie," continued Steve, "I'm going to be driving down to Desert Center later this evening to visit Doug. I was wondering what you thought of the way the boys and I evacuated the ranges this afternoon. You know that you and I are closer than any two brothers so you can tell me anything that damn base commanding General allows. Do you think Doug was slow or spent any time looking at anything, or saw any unusual stuff when he was getting to the power wagon?"

I sat and thought for a minute, as I watched the Captain in the corner taking notes. 'So officers can play games, too,' I thought to myself. "Well honestly, Steve, I don't see how you and Doug and the range rats could have gotten off the ranges any faster than you did. First, that F-105 with the new pilot, sparrow four, damn near flew himself into the ground. The tail of his F-105 couldn't have been more than 18 inches off the desert when he hit his after burner. When he pulled out, he blasted rocks and dirt and sagebrush all over hell. His plane must certainly have been damaged when that happened. Whether sparrow four was actually damaged or whether that new pilot was just afraid it was damaged, makes no difference because it meant that the new pilot had lost confidence in his plane.

After that happened, I thought his flight commander made a bad mistake by not coming along side and visually inspecting sparrow four. From the point of view of both Doug, and the new pilot that F-105, sparrow four, could very well have been seriously damaged when the emergency was declared. At first, it appeared that was what the emergency was all about. Sparrow four could have had sagebrush, dirt, or rocks plugging the intake turbines, and have been on the verge of catching fire. Neither the pilot nor Doug had any way of knowing if that F-105's engine, fuel tanks, or control surfaces were intact, operating correctly, or about to break away. Before the pilot could regain his confidence, the emergency was declared. Then sparrow four was abandoned by his flight leader and by the rest of the planes in his flight. It appeared to me that sparrow four was on the verge of crashing over by the ammunition bunker east of us, and that Doug was standing

245

ready to rescue the pilot. Doug sure as hell wasn't disobeying the base commander's orders or wasting any time looking around. There were so damn many heat waves coming off the desert floor, Doug wouldn't have been able to recognize his own mother if she had been out in that valley today. But if that new pilot, sparrow four, had been forced to bail out of his F-105 at that low altitude, over there by the mountains, that new pilot's life would have depended on Doug showing us where he was, and getting over there in time to rescue him. I would say that Doug was just covering for the mistakes made by the flight commander. I think that flight commander should have been doing a much better job of looking after his men. As soon as Doug was sure that the new pilot's life wasn't in danger, he hit the dirt running to get back to the power wagon."

Steve's face began molding into a faint smile. Like me, he was an enlisted man. He always felt better whenever an officer could be shown to have made a mistake. He waited for a minute or so before continuing, apparently to give the Captain time to finish his latest round of notes. Then Steve asked, "So, Charlie, you're saying there wasn't anything out there for Doug to see that he probably hasn't seen already?"

"Oh, hell yes!" I answered. "There wasn't anything to be seen up the valley except heat waves and haze. Since Doug wears glasses, he wouldn't have been able to see anything through the glare of today's sunshine. You know Doug has always respected and obeyed the Desert Center base commander's orders. Doug was just standing ready to save the pilot's life, in case sparrow four crashed. You and I both know it's the duty of enlisted men like Doug to protect their officers when they're out there on the ranges. If I were the Desert Center base commander, I'd want to ask the flight commander why he didn't come alongside sparrow four and visually inspect the F-105 for damage, before allowing the training flight to continue. I would think the flight commander should be doing a better job of looking after his men. Anyway, that whole valley north of us was nothing but heat waves and haze. That new pilot was having so much trouble with his F-105 at the time, if there had been anything out there in the haze to see, neither the new pilot nor Doug would have had the time to look at it."

Steve sat there smiling, apparently thinking of his next move. After a few minutes, the Captain appeared to finish his notes, closed up he brief case and quietly left. He too, was smiling. Steve waited a few more minutes. Then he stood up suddenly and exclaimed happily, "I've got to get going, Charlie. I've got to get down to Desert Center, down to that chicken wire brig, and let Doug know that you've just saved his sweet ass. As for this night, looks to me like you've set a new record, Charlie. You've won two games while playing on only one board." Then, he hurried out the back door, laughing, happier than I'd ever seen him.

The downed craft would sit there on desert floor with mechanics feverishly working on it, at night under lights when necessary, until the following Monday morning. Then, as I was preparing for the 4:30 a.m. run, in the distance, I could see the damaged craft finally lift off. Then two of the other craft immediately came in along side it, one on each side. They proceeded to shepherd the damaged craft slowly up the valley, back to its mountain base in the distant north. Watching the three craft slowly terrain follow up the valley was one of the most unforgettable sights I have ever witnessed.

The Journey

…At present we see indistinctly,
as in a mirror,
but then face to face…
. . . 1 Corinthians 13:12

It was a beautiful summer evening as I stumbled towards my weather truck. The early first quarter moon had just risen and the tips of the sagebrush glistened majestically in its light.

As my feet struck the gravel-covered ground in front of my barracks, I noted that it was only 3:15 a.m. on this warm Monday morning. I was leaving for the morning run a few minutes early. The barracks poker game the night before had run late and I was very short on sleep. I decided I would take the morning balloon run earlier than usual. This would give me time to catch a nap between runs. All I had to do was stay awake in the meantime.

I knew I had stayed too long at the poker table while I was still only halfway to my truck. Only the strong wind blowing at the time kept me awake until I reached my truck. As I started my truck I was already afraid that I had pushed my body too far.

The drive out to Range Three was uneventful. I was half asleep at the wheel for most of the way. I was startled suddenly by a gust of wind as my truck was approaching the Range Three buildings. I parked my truck in front of the generator shack, but I was too tired to line it up properly in front of the shack's doors. No matter, I thought as I fell out of my truck, falling onto my hands and knees on the gravel outside. I got up slowly and brushed myself off. My truck engine was idling and the headlights were on. I'd set the brake. I was annoyed with myself when I noticed that I was parked in front of the wrong doors but I was much too tired to move the truck. Shrugging it off and grabbing my flashlight I stumbled over to the southern set of double doors on the shed. Lifting the bar, I opened the two doors to 45 degree angles and went inside.

Certainly everything inside seemed normal. The warm winds shook the shed doors a little and pieces of dry sagebrush scraped up against the outside of the shed but there was nothing in particular that I found alarming. Without paying much attention to my surroundings, I went to start the diesel. It performed normally. As it was starting up, I was surprised because the lights on my truck went out. No matter. I lit my flashlight and continued my work. There was nothing out here to be afraid of.

My work continued. I was making the adjustments to the generator settings when I first noticed it. A little fuzzy patch of white fluorescence appeared on the very lower outside edge of my vision in my right eye. I supposed that it was a piece of white thread or cloth in my right eye and I brushed it away with my sleeve.

I finished the generator settings and turned towards the door. There to my surprise, the fuzzy white patch had reappeared. Only now there were three patches, two in my left eye and one in my right. Soft fuzzy fluorescent white, they hung on the edges of my vision. They drifted out of my field of view before I could focus in on them. For a minute it looked like they were waiting outside in the darkness for me. I stopped and thought about things. Tired and run down, I decided that my eyes must have been playing tricks on me.

Charles James Hall

I walked slowly to my truck. As I did so, the white patches reappeared and then drifted around behind me. I decided the white patches must result from some kind of problem with my eyes because the patches had to drift against the wind to do so.

I turned off my truck. It didn't seem safe to drive with my eyes giving me problems the way they were. As I did so, I was surprised to notice that the switch for the headlights had already been moved to the off position. Too tired to think much about it, I began the short walk to my weather shack. As I did so, three times I stopped suddenly to check my vision. Each time, two blurry soft fluorescent white patches would silently float into my vision on my left and a third on my right. Then just as slowly, they would float back around behind me.

I became quite annoyed with myself. Everything was happening in total silence so I decided that I hadn't been taking good care of my body. I knew my eyes were bloodshot so I decided that I must be bleeding inside my eyes or maybe, I wondered, I might be having a problem with my retinas. I chastised myself a great deal. A weather observer needs good vision. I enjoyed my life and wanted it to continue unchanged. I decided I needed sleep and lots of rest to let my eyes heal up. There was just one disturbing fly in the ointment. The fourth time I stopped to rest my vision, only one white patch appeared on my left and two appeared on my right. I wondered, if bleeding inside my eyes causes the white patches, how could patches of blood change eyeballs that fast?

As I took my balloon run the patches were still there, dogging my every move. Sometimes there were three on my left, sometimes the same three were on my right, and sometimes they didn't seem to be there at all. Sometimes they seemed to be hiding behind the generator shack, other times behind the range lounge, but always they stayed out of my field of direct vision. Always, if I turned towards them they would float around behind me, or behind a building out of view. Always they did so in total silence.

As I finished my balloon run and started up my truck, one of them drifted in behind it and stayed there for a while. I had to wait at least five minutes until it was gone before I was willing to back out of my parking place. By the time I had driven back to base for breakfast, I was convinced that my eyes were in terrible shape. Never once had there been anything to focus in on. Never once had I actually seen anything other than blurry white patches at the edges of my field of vision.

After breakfast I rested a while and began a program of eating properly and taking things easy. I decided that I needed to visit the Desert Center base hospital so I called them and made an appointment for the coming Friday. My body needed vitamins, I told them, and I wanted a doctor to check out my vision. Then, with lots of hand wringing and anxiety, I began counting the days until I could get there.

Friday seemed like the proper time to visit the Desert Center hospital. I had already reserved a ton and a half truck at the Mojave Wells motor pool for my use on Friday. I needed to visit the base supply at Desert Center and check out more balloons, batteries, and helium cylinders to re-supply my weather shack.

The rest of the daylight runs that Monday passed without incident. As I closed up for the day, I took one last look around my shack. It was nearly spotless. When I was tired, I frequently slept on the floor of my shack, so I kept the floor washed and well waxed. It gleamed in the sunlight. The door in the back was closed and locked. The helium cylinders were stored in the back and separated into full and empties. All of their safety chains hung neatly in place. The oil stove in the center was clean and shiny. My weather tools along the western side of the shack were well polished and neatly arranged. The blank weather forms were neatly stacked alongside the completed ones. My radio had been turned off and sat quietly on its shelf. Along the eastern side of the shack, the metal tools, balloon measuring weights, wrenches, pressure gauges, and hoses sat neatly in their storage bins. The spare balloons, night batteries, lights, and twine all sat neatly arranged on the shelves under the window on the east. The double wide door on the east side stood open, as did the front door on the north. It was a beautiful, peaceful afternoon and a soft afternoon breeze was blowing through the shack.

Yes, I was just starting to close the doors when it struck me. Looking again at the battery storage shelf, the problem was as plain as the nose on my face. There were only three more balloon batteries. I checked my logbook. I had taken an inventory of my supplies just the previous Friday afternoon and recorded it in my logbook. Clearly written there, in large black ink, was the number five. I had used one battery this morning, as I did every morning. The conclusion was inescapable. Four batteries should have been setting on the shelf.

I searched everywhere in my shack. The fourth battery simply wasn't there. I checked the inventory in my logbook. Nothing else was missing. I was dumbfounded. It meant that I wouldn't have a battery with which to take the Friday morning run. Who could possibly have taken my battery, I wondered. I always kept my weather shack locked, and none of the range rats or cooks would have taken a battery without telling me. I was left feeling totally mystified.

That night, I went to bed at 6:30, right after I finished the evening meal. The following morning, now Tuesday, still tired but feeling better, I again left a little early for the morning run. Everything seemed to be proceeding normally and my vision seemed to be greatly improved. By the time I had finished taking my balloon readings, I still hadn't seen any white patches on the edges of my vision, and I wondered if I hadn't been too hasty in making my doctor's appointment. Then, as I was writing down my last reading and securing the theodolite, it happened again. On the very edge of my vision on my left side, appeared two blurry soft white fluorescent patches. Once again, they floated out of my field of view whenever I tried to focus in on them. One appeared to be tall and I came to believe that it was hiding around the corner of the Range Three lounge. The other, a small white patch, appeared to be floating out towards me. I now felt certain that I needed my vision checked, but I was struck by how tired the small white patch seemed to be. It seemed to be having trouble keeping up with me as I walked towards the shack, and it seemed as though it felt very sad because it was so tired. I found myself stopping and waiting now and then, just so it could catch up behind me, even though I couldn't see it, or focus in on it. By the time I arrived at the front door to my shack, I felt as though it had left me, in exhaustion, and returned to the other side of the range lounge. I had no idea what to make of it all.

The remainder of Tuesday passed without incident, and without any more eye problems, as did Wednesday, and Thursday. After finishing the last run from Range Three on Thursday, I made the long drive down to Range One to pick up a battery for the Friday morning run. It was a beautiful drive and certainly nothing appeared to be wrong with my eyes. Friday came. Using the battery, I took the Range

Three winds on time, and phoned in the weather report at 5:00 a.m. as expected. Everything seemed to be in order but my eye problems started up again. This time, they started early. This time at 3:15 a.m., as I was shaving, alone in darkness of the barracks bathroom. It made me glad that today I would be seeing the doctor at Desert Center. Still I wondered. My eyes never gave me problems when I was driving my truck, even on bumpy roads. They never gave me problems when I was away from the Mojave Wells area, even when I was tired on the darkest nights. Why would they sometimes give me problems when I was well rested and standing quietly out in the desert at Range Three?

Once the daylight runs were completed, I picked up the ton and a half truck from the motor pool and headed for the supply warehouse at Desert Center. Then, with the truck carrying six weeks worth of balloons, twine, batteries, and helium, I headed over to the Desert Center Base Hospital.

The medical exam went smoothly enough, including the eye exam, but believing my eyes were bad, I was extremely nervous. When it was over, the doctor and I sat down in a room in the back for a heart to heart talk. The doctor was a bird colonel and probably pushing 45. I was totally unprepared for his assessment.

He began, "Charlie, let me say that before anything else, I'm a doctor. You can tell me anything in privacy and confidence." Then he waited as though he were waiting for me to confess something.

"Thanks, doctor," I answered, "I'm concerned about my eyes. I'm sure that I've been bleeding internally inside my eyeballs, or maybe one of my retinas is loose or detached."

"Oh, don't give me that bullshit again," responded the colonel. "You have the most perfect set of eyes I've ever seen. With eyes like those you could count specks of fly shit on the ceiling in total darkness at a hundred yards. Here, using my magnifying scope I checked every square inch of both of your eyes. They're absolutely perfect. You eyeballs are perfectly shaped. There's no evidence of any damage whatsoever. You have the widest field of vision of any person I've ever seen or heard tell of. And what's this bullshit about detached retinas? You couldn't have found a chair in the reception room if your eyes were that bad. Yet here you are driving a ton and a half truck all over the Mojave like it was a toy tricycle. Now what the hell is going on man? Are you just trying to get out of work so you can go back East and see your girl? Well, I'll tell you one thing, airman, it'll be a cold day in hell before you get medical leave out of me with eyes as perfect as yours."

"But my eyes have been giving me problems, sir," I stammered, defensively. "I'm sure there's something medically wrong with them."

"Bullshit! Absolute bullshit!" exclaimed the colonel. "There's nothing whatever wrong with your vision and there never has been! Whatever it is that you've been seeing is real! You don't have any evidence whatever of ever having bled internally, or ever having had any bumps or bruises, or ever having had any eye problems whatever. Now get the hell out of my office and don't come back until there's something medically wrong with you."

Well, there's no arguing with an angry bird colonel. Leave his office, I did. I was practically running at the time. I was in a cold sweat as I drove the truck back to Mojave Wells. Every turn of the wheel I was afraid the Colonel would want more than the pound of flesh he'd already extracted.

Once at the Wells, I drove back out to Range Three. The truck needed to be unloaded before I could return it to the motor pool. It was already late in the afternoon as I carefully rolled the last helium cylinder from the back of the truck into my weather shack. I was under severe time pressure, knowing the chow hall wouldn't stay open forever, so I cared only about getting my supplies safely locked into my weather shack. I intended to unpack and stow them away in the morning. I secured the helium safety chain and made one last trip from the truck to my shack. Nestled in my arms were the last of many boxes of balloons and of the expendable balloon batteries. Setting the last box on the floor of my weather shack, I quickly retook my inventory. My inventory of such balloon batteries had now swelled to 251, and therein laid the problem. I'd brought only 250 from Desert Center. When I had locked up the shack earlier today after the last run, the battery inventory had been zero. Yet, there on the shelf in plain view, setting in the exact same place that I had last seen it when I'd taken the inventory one week before, sat the missing balloon battery. In the sunlight reflecting on my well waxed floor were the dim outlines of boot prints where someone had come in my front door, placed the batteries on the shelf and left again. The boot prints were about the same length as mine.

Stunned hardly describes my reaction. I was so deeply affected that I was afraid to even touch the battery. I locked the doors to my weather shack, started up the truck, and headed for the base chow hall. As my truck sped towards town, my mind struggled to make sense of the day's events. Over and over, I ran through my memories of the eye problems I'd been having. Much as my mind recoiled from the idea, the conclusion was inescapable. The fuzzy white patches had to be real. The drive back to town was a long cold, sweaty one, indeed.

All through the following weekend my mind fought with the conclusions that I had reached. Emotionally, I wanted more than anything else for the white patches to be nothing more than eye problems. Logically, however, I realized the Colonel was right. There wasn't anything whatever the matter with my eyes, tired or otherwise. So it was with considerable apprehension that I waited for Monday morning. Steve and each of the other range rats repeatedly offered to accompany me on the morning runs but I turned them down. I realized that whatever I faced out on the ranges, sooner or later, it would force me to face it alone. It might as well be sooner.

Monday came. It was with considerable fear that I arose at 3:00 a.m., dressed and shaved, and began the long, lonely drive out to Range Three. Shrinking from every shadow and jumping in fear at every gust of wind, I started one of the diesels, turned on the lights, filled the balloon, and made the morning run. I was about half way through taking the balloon readings when I paused for a minute to ponder the situation. There was no way around one simple fact. This morning I was perfectly alone, perfectly, absolutely alone. I tried over and over to get the white patches to appear but absolutely nothing out of the ordinary happened. There were simply no white patches to be seen. This discovery could hardly have been more stunning. Whatever it was, it came when it wanted to come, and it left when it wanted to leave. Whatever it was, it had to be intelligent!

I finished the balloon run at a leisurely pace, realizing that on this morning, nothing unusual was going to happen. Having finished the run, I phoned the results to Desert Center and headed into base for breakfast. Along the way, I calmly counted the days. I had seen the white patches the previous Monday, Tuesday, and Friday mornings. I

257

remembered having seen Steve count days in pairs before scheduling trips out to Range Four. I counted the days as Steve had done. It meant that the previous Monday and Tuesday were days when they had come. Then the previous Wednesday and Thursday were days when they stayed away. Then Friday and Saturday were days when they came again. Finally Sunday and this Monday morning were days when they had stayed away. I concluded that if my analysis were correct, the next day, Tuesday, the white patches would be waiting for me out at Range Three for sure.

Later that morning, I was sitting in my weather shack. Both the front door and the side door were open, letting in the morning sun and some cool breezes. I had a couple hours between runs and my friend Steve had come out to see how things were going. Taking the spare chair myself, and giving Steve the best chair, I proceeded to tell him about the battery. It still sat on the shelf, untouched since its return. I pointed out to him that it hadn't just been returned, but it had been returned to the exact position it was in when it was taken. I also pointed out to him that in order to return it, someone had to open one of the locked doors, and then re-lock it when they left. Steve listened patiently as though understanding what was happening. Then he asked a simple question, "Charlie, do you remember when that school teacher over here at the Mojave Wells grade school called you up on this phone?"

"Yes," I responded. "That was only a month ago."

"Do you remember what she asked you?" continued Steve.

"Yes," I answered. "She wanted to borrow one of my batteries and light bulbs for use in school. She said they were very educational, and she wanted to show them to her entire class of grade school children."

Steve continued, "And didn't she say that she'd give it back to you when she'd finished with it?"

"Well, yes, Steve," I answered defensively, "but surely you're not implying that the Mojave Wells grade school teacher came way out here more than twenty miles into the desert on a government air base, broke into my weather shack and took it, are you?"

"No," answered Steve patiently, "I don't want to scare you, Charlie but you know a week ago Saturday, Tony and I happened to meet the Mojave Wells grade school teacher down at the hamburger stand in town."

"You did?" I answered showing obvious surprise.

"Yes," answered Steve. "She's young and quite a looker. You know me, Charlie, I've been out here on these ranges for several years and good looking young women out here are pretty hard to come by. Just as a way of meeting her, we asked her if she still wanted to borrow one of those batteries of yours. You know what she said? She said she never phoned you. She didn't even know that you were out here."

"But, but," I stammered, "If that's true, so who was talking to me on the phone? I mean, Steve, the young woman on the phone didn't give her name, but she clearly identified herself as the Teacher. She had a young and feminine voice. She spoke perfect English and didn't use slang or contractions."

Steve thought for a minute and then answered slowly, "Look at how that battery is setting on the shelf, Charlie. It's setting perfectly positioned in the middle of that open shelf."

"Yes," I responded. "That's the exact same position it was setting in when it was taken. You and I would have a hard time replacing it that perfectly."

259

"That's my point," said Steve. "Which ever teacher phoned you and took the battery in the first place must be quite intelligent. This shack is way out in the desert, Charlie. Just to get here, she must be able to easily travel long distances quickly. What's more, Charlie, she must have spent a good deal of time studying you while you've been out here alone in your weather shack. I'm not trying to scare you Charlie, but this teacher seems to know you pretty well."

"I don't see why," I answered.

"Well, consider this," answered Steve, "No question about it, grade school children find your batteries to be educational. Now whichever teacher brought the battery back and placed it there on the shelf in the same place it was before, did so because she knows that you're naturally a very neat person. She must have wanted to keep you happy. She must not have wanted you to become frightened or worried about the safety of your supplies. I mean after all, she could have just destroyed the battery or thrown it away or placed it on the floor or something."

Steve paused for a minute, waiting for his words to sink in. Then he continued, "You see, Charlie, those other guys that Desert Center sent up here didn't have this kind of problem. Oh, don't get me wrong. They've all had their problems and I mean big ones. But they never had a problem quite like this one. They never had anyone who liked them. Yes, as I see it, your problem appears to be that you're the first one they've ever sent up here that the Teacher likes.

"Now there was Roger, for example, three years ago. From the first day he was up here, he had problems. He kept claiming that he'd seen things waiting for him out in the sagebrush, and then he'd accuse the range rats and me of playing tricks on him. Then, like most of them weather observers Desert Center sends up here, he got to where he wouldn't come out here on the ranges unless one of us range rats or a cook maybe, would come with him. Well, one time he had been missing his plastic ruler for a few days. Then, one morning when I was with him, he found it lying on the ground out there by the side door. Well, he was such a messy person that he just thought he'd dropped it there. I pointed out to him that it'd rained the night before, and it'd still been raining some when he and I had started driving out to the ranges. I picked up his ruler and showed him that the ground underneath the ruler was wet, but the topside of his ruler was dry and spotlessly clean. It proved, I told him, that someone had to have placed it there just before he and I arrived. He stood there dumbfounded while I concluded that whoever had placed the ruler there, must certainly be out in the sagebrush right at that instant, watching us from the distance. Since both he and I were certain that all of the other range rats and cooks were sleeping back in the barracks and there weren't any lights on in any of the houses down in the town of Mojave Wells, I concluded that whoever was watching us was not someone who lived in the Mojave Wells base area.

"Well, I tell you Charlie, he became real panicky for a while. Then he'd never come out on the ranges at all, even if one of us range rats came with him. He'd sit down in the barracks and make up his winds, just like the rest of them observers always used to do. Then his Master Sergeant from Desert Center caught him doing it. They'd have sent him to the stockade if the cooks and I hadn't covered for him."

I sat quietly as Steve paused to take a deep breath. Then he continued, "Then there was that black guy, Kenneth, they had up here maybe eight summers back. They tell me that one warm day in the fall, he was missing his cap. They say he'd looked everywhere and hadn't found it. He went poking around out in the sagebrush northeast of here 'cause he thought maybe the wind might have blown it up that way. As he was searching for it, he discovered that something was watching him from way out in the sagebrush. He said it was barking at him, like a dog would, and he panicked. He took off running back to his weather truck. When, it wouldn't start, he jumped out of the truck and took off running for town. The boys who were here before me, say they picked him up maybe five miles down the road or else he'd never made it to town, the heat and all. He was another one that wouldn't ever come back out here, even if the range rats came with him. But, you know, Charlie, those range rats that were here back then, claimed when they opened up this weather shack two days later, that his cap was laying right there in the middle of the floor.

"So you see, Charlie, whoever took your battery must have gotten here long before the both of us. Whoever the Teacher is, she must know about those other guys and must be trying real hard not to frighten you."

"I see what you're saying," I responded. "You're saying that whoever she is, she must want to keep me feeling the way I did on the day she took it."

Steve continued, as though he knew the answer to the problem, "Exactly. So what teacher do you know of, who knows you real well and who's trying real hard not to upset you?"

I thought about what Steve had said for a few minutes. Then, suddenly, my mind made the connection. Finally, at last, I stopped denying reality as I had been doing for such a long time. "And you're also asking, Steve, is what group of grade school children do I know, who find the areas around my weather shacks here at Range Three, out at Range Four, and down at Ranges One and Two, to be educational places to play?"

"Exactly," responded Steve, obviously knowing the answer to his question, "What group of children would that be?"

Before I could answer, the last group of planes ended their training flight and left the range. Steve raised his huge lanky frame up from the chair that held him. He turned to me, as friends do and said calmly, "Remember, Charlie, whoever the Teacher is, she must like you. Otherwise you'd be dead already."

"Dead?" I responded.

"Yes," answered Steve slowly. "Dead from fright. Make no mistake. The Teacher is well armed. She's not afraid of anything. Think of all the times you've been out here alone. You've been out on these ranges alone, day and night, more times than all of the other weather observers in the last 10 years have, total. Anytime at all, the Teacher could have come up behind you, fired on you, or just scared the living hell out of you if she'd wanted to. She used to do that to those other guys, you know. A lot of those guys Desert Center sent up here left this place running down the road at night, screaming their guts out in terror. Sooner or later, damn near all them made the trip into town on foot, wild eyed, screaming, and refusing to ever come back out here. One I saw a couple years ago had his arms covered with radiation burns. The Teacher could do the same thing to you too, if she wanted to. She could do it anytime, Charlie, anytime at all."

Then Steve said goodbye and left to lead the Range Rats as they scored the targets. As he left, I was indebted to him. I was no longer afraid. For the first time, I understood what

I would be facing when I drove out to Range Three for tomorrow morning's run.

The drive out to Range Three on the following morning was surprisingly pleasant, considering what I was facing. I realized that as long as I stayed calm, I had nothing to fear. I now realized that if I didn't panic, I wouldn't be in any danger. I spent most of the drive enjoying the desert's beauty and singing to myself. When I reached the Range Three buildings, I intentionally parked my truck in the same position it had been in on the Monday when I'd first seen the white patches. Turning off my lights, turning off my truck, and armed only with my flashlight and a song, I got out of my truck and headed for the generator shack. Turning my head just slightly to the side as I walked allowed me to glimpse three small fluorescent white patches floating silently out towards me in eager fashion from behind the Range Three lounge.

"Ah, the welcoming committee," I said to myself, "Heading out to ride their favorite pony."

I opened the doors to the generator shack, same as before, and slowly headed in to start the generators. Singing aloud to myself, and moving at only half my normal speed, I proceeded to start the diesel and make the necessary generator adjustments. I was really surprised to find that one of the white patches had floated into the shack, and persisted in staying just behind me on my right. Whenever I raised my right arm, it would float in under it, so I was frequently afraid to lower my right arm back into its normal position for fear of touching the white patch hiding behind me.

The generator running, and followed by one of the white patches, I slowly but surely headed towards the door. As expected, two white patches were waiting outside for me, hiding behind one of the generator shack's doors. Once outside, and still singing aloud to myself, I began walking slowly towards my weather shack.

When I reached my weather shack, I opened both the front door and the side door, turned on the lights, and began filling the balloon. I was running ten minutes early or so. Once the balloon was ready, I sat down in my chair and thought about things for a few minutes. So far, except for a few glimpses of the white patches floating on the very edges of my vision, I hadn't actually seen anything. Whatever was out there in the desert, was watching me in total absolute silence. Whatever it was, it certainly meant me no harm. Over the last few weeks, as Steve had pointed out, it could have killed me or scared me to death, many times over, had that been it's intention.

I felt certain that the three white patches were real, and were floating out in the desert east of my weather shack, waiting for me to emerge with the balloon. If my feelings could be depended on, I decided that what was outside in the desert watching me would be the alien equivalent of three grade school children. What kind of creatures could they be, I wondered. After thinking carefully, I decided the three white patches must be the same kind of creatures as Range Four Harry. It had been several months since I'd seen Range Four Harry and making the association was not as automatic as one might think.

"How many of them could be waiting for me out there," I wondered. I decided that no intelligent creature would bring a group of children to this desert without also bringing a teacher to look after them. The phone call suggested that this teacher must be a young adult female who spoke perfect English. Such a teacher would naturally want a young adult male to accompany her because if perhaps one

265

child were injured, she'd need his strength to care for the injured child, and she'd also need help with the others. These two might also want someone else to drive the bus while they helped the children. The bus driver would probably want a mechanic to come along in case the school bus needed repairs. It was, after all, a desert out there, and such repairs could easily be a two man job. Since the driver and the mechanic would have to stay and protect the craft, and the Teacher and the male assistant would have to stay with the children, they'd probably need at least one more person, a communications officer, to hold it all together. That was after all, what Range Four Harry's job had been. So I decided that waiting for me outside in the darkness was probably at least five other adult white patches.

I decided that the Teacher might be out in the desert close to my side door, close to where the children must be waiting. Since I'd gotten a glimpse of the children floating out from behind the Range Three lounge, I expected the other four adults to be hiding behind it, guarding the logical path of retreat.

Well, my thought processes in order I decided the time had come to introduce myself to the class. Since I had to go outside to prepare the theodolite anyway, I picked up my pencil and clipboard and singing one of my favorite tunes, I stepped out the front door and began walking slowly towards my theodolite stand in front of my weather shack.

Along the way, I remembered that Range Four Harry had brought with him a set of electronics that allowed him to communicate with me just by thinking. He was after all, the communications officer. So I decided to pay careful attention to my thoughts as I walked. Sure enough, the air outside of my weather shack seemed filled with thoughts. As I walked, my mind became filled with thoughts that I didn't believe were my own. Thoughts like, "What is he doing now? Where is he going? When is he going to release the balloon?" Still, there was absolutely nothing out of the ordinary to be seen.

I opened up the theodolite and left my clipboard and pencil by it. I returned to my weather shack. Then I took hold of the balloon and carried it outside. I walked back over to the theodolite stand where I released the balloon. Dogging my every step were the three small white fluorescent patches.

I decided to stand with my back to the theodolite while I was passing the time in between readings. Then, when it was time to take the readings, I would slowly turn around, adjust the theodolite, take the readings, and return to standing with my back to the stand. After doing this several times, I intentionally turned around suddenly to see what was happening. There, less than three feet from my nose, was one of the children looking through the eyepiece of my theodolite. If I hadn't been expecting it, I'd have probably died from the shock.

The suit he wore gave off a soft white fluorescent light and allowed him to float three or four feet above the ground. It made him look like a small version of an American astronaut on the moon. He wasn't any more than three feet tall and appeared to be having the time of his life. Reluctantly pulling himself away from the eyepiece, he floated back down towards the ground and quickly slipped back around behind me on my right.

Although my nerves were quite jangled by the whole experience, I did have to chuckle. It's just like a bunch of children to organize a game of hide-and-go-seek. I took the next balloon reading, only this time, instead of turning slowly to the left and standing with my back to the theodolite, I did something different. I decided it was time to meet the Teacher.

The Teacher, I reasoned, might be standing somewhere behind me. It seemed logical that she might have assumed a position that allowed her to remain in constant communication with the children. After giving the matter due thought, I reasoned the Teacher might logically be standing by the northeastern corner of my weather shack.

So, turning to my left, I quickly turned around completely. I wanted to first see what all three of the children looked like up close. Standing exactly behind me, looking up at me with both eyes stood a little girl. She was obviously the same little girl that I had rescued from the sagebrush down on Range One, a year earlier. Next to her floated the little fat American Astronaut and beyond him floated a thinner, more scholarly little boy. Like the other children, the little girl was wearing a suit that gave off a soft white fluorescent light and allowed her to float a few feet above the ground. She had been standing there, stooped down with her knees bent. As soon as she saw me looking down at her, she blinked her eyes and began floating slowly around behind me, towards my left. It seemed as if she was laughing as she did so.

Then, I looked up quickly and scanned the sagebrush next to the northeastern corner of my weather shack. My efforts were rewarded. Standing there watching me, was the Teacher. Obviously she was the same type of creature as Range Four Harry. As I expected, she was a young female adult. She stood just under six feet tall. She had pure chalk white skin, large intelligent blue eyes, and noticeably wide slits for her eyes. She wore an open helmet. Her hair was almost shoulder length. Her hair was so blonde that it was almost transparent. She also wore a suit that allowed her to float a foot or so off the ground. Like the other suits, the Teacher's suit gave off a soft white fluorescent light. As I had expected, she was equipped with the same type of electronics that Range Four Harry had.

As I studied her, a pleasant thought entered my mind. "You are not supposed to know that we are here."

I responded by thinking slowly, "Well I do now. It is OK with me. You may bring the children here. They appear to be having fun."

"Thank you," she responded. Then she floated slowly out of view behind my weather shack.

Having located the Teacher, I now turned slowly back to my right and began looking for her assistant. He was standing by the corner of the Range Three lounge, right where I expected him. Behind him I could see two other similar creatures. All three of them were obviously male. Each of them stood more than six feet tall. The three of them floated there in plain view for several minutes before finally floating back behind the Range Three lounge. Their reasons were plain as day to me. They obviously wanted me to understand that they were not the slightest bit afraid of me. They obviously wanted me to understand that the Teacher and the children were well protected. I rewarded their efforts. I expected that their suits would be equipped with the same electronics as the Teacher's. As I studied them, I thought slowly and clearly, "Your children are in no danger. I would never harm them. They may play wherever they want to. I will do everything in my power to protect them."

A single clear thought came back to me. "So will we," it said, "So will we."

I had the balloon readings that I needed, so I picked up my pencil and clipboard and began walking slowly back towards my shack. My nerves were quite shaken at the time, so my walk was unusually slow. Ordinarily I would have locked up my theodolite but under the circumstances, I left it as it had been so the children could watch the balloon through it. When I got back to my shack, I carefully moved the table that I used for my calculations, across the shack so that I could sit with my back to the big side door as I calculated the winds. That way, the Teacher and the children could look over my shoulder and watch me as I computed the winds. The children didn't seem very interested in the calculations. Through the front door of my shack I could see them spending most of the time carefully playing with my theodolite.

Once my calculations were finished, I phoned the winds in to Desert Center. My phone had a huge amount of static in it and getting the wind information in to Desert Center was quite a problem. Naturally, I made no mention of the aliens and their children. When I finished the phone call to Desert Center, the children were still playing with my theodolite. I didn't want to disturb them.

I waited as a great deal of time passed. Not wanting to miss breakfast, reluctantly, I moved my table back to its normal position, locked up my weather shack, and shut down the generator. The children were still fascinated with my theodolite, so I left it uncovered and unlocked. I informed the Teacher of my need to go to breakfast and said goodbye to the Teacher goodbye. Then I started up my truck and headed in to breakfast. When I returned two hours later, the place was deserted. The theodolite had been carefully covered and locked for its own protection. There could no longer be any doubt. My vision was perfect, and the white patches were also perfect, perfectly real.

The Fathers

... "So I say to you:
Ask and it will be given to you;
seek and you will find;
knock and the door will be opened to you;
for everyone who asks, receives;
he who seeks, finds;
And to him who knocks,
the door is opened.

Which of you fathers,
if your son asks for bread,
will give him a stone?
Or if he asks for a fish,
will give him a snake?

If you then,
though you are evil,
know how to give good gifts to your children,
how much more then,
will your Father in heaven
give good gifts
to those who ask him?"
... Matthew 7:7-11

Some days it seemed as though, by joyfully singing to the Lord, I could communicate with everything under God's creation. That's how the world seemed to me this beautiful morning, as I headed on out to Range Three for the morning wind measurements. It would still be more than three hours before the sun came up. The nighttime desert sky with its majestic starlit dome seemed to form a perfect starlit bond between the heavens and myself. I was happy and I was also at least an hour early. With my window rolled down, I was singing one of my favorite rock songs while my truck plunged on towards Range Three. I was singing as though there might exist a coyote somewhere, or maybe a jackrabbit, which needed to know how little I could carry a tune. Consequently, as my truck reached the Range Three buildings and pulled to a stop close to my weather shack, I guess I wasn't really surprised they were waiting for me. For a minute, I thought maybe I'd been singing too loud and maybe they had come to quiet me down. I almost started my truck and drove back in to base. When I didn't see the Teacher or the children, I became extremely afraid. I was well aware that the males were perfectly capable of killing me anytime it pleased them. At first, I wasn't sure they wanted me to be out there so early. I tried to restart my truck several times and gave it up when the battery appeared to be perfectly dead. I had come to understand that with their electronics, they could turn my truck on and off at will.

They didn't close on the truck but stayed a few hundred yards back out in the desert to the northeast and waited for me. After a few minutes of fear, I decided that they meant me no harm and just wanted to talk. Still feeling a great deal of apprehension, I waited a few minutes more before opening my truck door and getting out. Once outside, my foot had just touched the ground when I first began receiving thoughts from a young male. "You have nothing to fear," he said.

I couldn't tell where he was located at first, so I began studying the desert out to the northeast. About a quarter mile down the road that ran over to the ammunition bunker, I could see two tall white fluorescent patches and several smaller ones. South of these, directly east of my weather shack, about a quarter mile out in the sagebrush, I could see a tall white fluorescent patch waiting, along with a shorter one. Another pleasant thought entered my mind, "No, not over there. Up here."

I looked around some more. Then I saw him, the one known as the School Bus Driver. Like Range Four Harry, he had floated up to the upper northeast corner of the range billboards. Leaning over the top of the billboard, he had a good view and a clear field of fire, should he decide he needed one. The white suit that he wore gave off a soft white fluorescence and his electronics let us communicate easily, just by thinking.

Once I saw him, I thought pleasantly and somewhat nervously, "Oh, there you are. What can I do for you?"

He responded, "The Teacher would like to let the children come over and play where you are. Is that all right with you?"

"Yes," I responded, "As long as they don't interfere with the work I do."

The tall white creature responded, "Before they come again, the Captain, my brother, and I want to make sure you understand that if you do anything that harms them, we will kill you."

"I understand," I responded.

"We know you do," he responded. "But we want to make certain you understand that you are helpless against us."

"I understand," I answered again.

"We wish to make certain," he responded pleasantly. "Some of the other humans think that they are safe if they carry guns against us."

"I never bring a gun when I come out here into the desert," I answered. "As you can see, I do not have a gun in my truck or anywhere in my weather shack."

"We know," he answered. "You should carry a gun, you know, to protect yourself against the snakes and coyotes with rabies. There are many of them out here. But, we want you to see for yourself how helpless you are against us, even if you had a gun."

"How do you intend to do that?" I asked.

The white creature responded, "We want you to throw stones at me, and see if you can hit me."

"I have no desire to harm you," I said. "If I am able to hit you with a rock, won't you be injured?" I asked.

"That's what we want you to see for yourself," he replied. "We know you are more intelligent than any of the other humans that we have met. We know that once you have seen how impossible it is to hit me with a rock, you'll understand that nothing you can do will harm me. Go ahead, pick up some rocks, and see if you can hit me," he challenged.

Looking down by the metal pole that held my theodolite, I noticed a pile of smooth pebbles that the white people had apparently placed there. Picking up several, I threw a stone at the School Bus Driver. Having no desire to harm him, I didn't aim right at him. I tried, instead, to bounce the rock off the billboard right next to him. To my surprise, the rock, didn't make it even half way to the billboard. Once it was air born, it behaved as though it were moving through sticky molasses, and fell smoothly back to the ground.

274

He laughed at my apparent "weakness". "You see," he said, "You're totally helpless against us. Try again."

Again and again I threw stones at the billboard that held him. Not once did any of the rocks reach the billboard. Soon my arm was tired and I gave up throwing rocks at the white creature. It was clearly a waste of time.

"We have seen you throwing rock after rock at the billboard in the past. Every time you could easily hit the billboard where I am now." He said, "Why do you suppose that you can't hit any of the billboards now?"

"I don't know," I answered. "The stones don't seem to be flying the way they are supposed to. Whenever they get close to you, they seem to slow down and fall to the ground."

"It is because of the suits that we all wear," he responded. "I am wearing one. So are the Captain, my brother, the Teacher, and all of the children. As long as we are wearing these suits, we could walk right up to you and do anything we wanted to you. You would be totally helpless against us. You could not lay a hand on us in return. Do you understand?"

"Yes," I responded, "and if I should ever get out of line, you would burn me the way you burned Washington. I would be burned for life."

"Yes," responded the School Bus Driver. "But you're mistaken about Washington. He was not burned for life. The weapon we used on him caused him great pain and terrified him, but it didn't do any lasting damage whatever to him."

"But they tell me he's never recovered. They tell me he's damaged for life," I responded.

"We have told you the truth. We seldom lie, even though we know how to," answered the School Bus Driver. "The

Teacher told us that you think of him often, so last night we went to his home town back east, and talked with him. I dressed up like a school bus driver, and the Teacher dressed up as a young nurse. It's her favorite disguise. He did not know who we were. He was enjoying himself in a hamburger stand with a young lady friend of his when we walked in. We talked with him for more than a half hour. He could hardly have been healthier. He was just pretending to still be injured so that your government would give him his promotion and money for the rest of his life. He said he learned how to do that from you."

"Well, knowing that he's OK makes me feel better," I answered, "But I'm not certain that's what I taught him."

"The Teacher says the children are getting impatient to come and play where you are," continued the School Bus Driver. "Is it OK to let them come in now?"

"Yes," I answered. "I need to unlock my weather shack, and take my morning wind measurements."

"Before the children come," continued the School Bus Driver, "Range Four Harry's aunt and daughter want to come and watch you, also. Is that OK with you?"

"Yes," I answered. "I do not feel afraid when either you or the Teacher are here. As long as you or the Teacher are here, you may bring anyone you want to, anyone at all." As I said those words, it never occurred to me that he would take me exactly at my word.

Seeing the conversation had ended, I proceeded to my weather shack and began unlocking the doors. In the desert to the east, I could see Range Four Harry's aunt and daughter began slowly floating towards me through openings and pathways in the sagebrush, until they were only fifteen or twenty feet away. They assumed a position by the northeast corner of my weather shack, just on the other side of the wire cable that marked the boundaries of the skip bomb area. This position formed a kind of spectator's gallery and gave them a perfect position from which to view the entire process of measuring the winds. It let them view me opening the shack, inflating the balloon, releasing the balloon, taking the wind and temperature measurements, performing the calculations, and phoning the results in to Desert Center.

As Range Four Harry's aunt and daughter floated in the gallery in total silence, it was obvious to me that they still regarded me with a great deal of apprehension. I had to laugh a little, at the ridiculous situation I was in. They show up with the high technology. They prove they can kill me anytime they want to. I can't do anything whatever in return, and they're afraid of me. It's just my luck to be living in such a screwy world, I laughed to myself.

I wasn't sure if I should start up the diesels. Since they were at home in the starlit night and I was too, I decided to perform the wind measurements just using my flashlight for light. As the wind measurements proceeded, Harry's aunt and daughter continued to watch me, floating motionless in a stately manner in the gallery, saying nothing, and content to quietly monitor my thoughts without responding with any of their own. As I was recording the measurements using my theodolite, I turned to them, and by thinking pleasant thoughts, offered to let them view the balloon, and use the theodolite, the way the children had done. Receiving a response for the first time, the aunt turned to the teenage daughter and offered to let her do so. After mulling things over for a minute or so, the daughter and the aunt decided that coming any closer would be too frightening and declined. I guess I must have looked like a giant hairy monster to them.

Behind the aunt and the daughter, back a quarter of a mile in the desert; I could see the Teacher and three children waiting their turn. In the distance towards the east, I could see two tall white fluorescent patches waiting by the ammunition bunker at the end of the paved road. Another group of large and small white patches waited further north, up along the foothills of the eastern mountains.

As I was walking back to the weather shack, having just finished taking the last wind measurement, the Teacher and the children became impatient with Harry's aunt and daughter. Apparently the rules imposed by the Captain allowed only one small group to approach me at a time. He appeared to be afraid that if too many of them approached me at one time, I would panic as the other weather observers had done, and the situation would become uncontrollable. He also appeared to be afraid the combined electric field from too many suits would damage my nervous system. I hadn't yet closed up my theodolite and the Teacher wanted to let the children look through it. Apparently Harry's aunt and daughter also wanted to continue to watch me perform the calculations. I helped the Captain settle the argument by offering to leave my theodolite uncovered. I also offered to stay in the weather shack by myself while the children played with my theodolite outside. This seemed to settle the argument. As I entered my weather shack, the three children, followed by the Teacher, floated gracefully across the desert. The Teacher assumed a position in the gallery area, staying behind Harry's aunt and daughter while the three children flooded over the open area around the theodolite. As before, the three children were the little girl, the little fat boy, and the thinner, more scholarly little boy whom I had nicknamed the little young Einstein. The combined effect of all of their suits and communication electronics caused me to feel a great deal of mental confusion. For a short while, I found it hard to keep my own thoughts straight from theirs. The Teacher appeared to sense that this was the case and responded by sending two of the children back into the waiting area, out in the desert to the northeast. It made a big difference and my nerves seemed to settle down noticeably.

When it came time to phone Desert Center with the results, my phone was completely unusable. The static on the phone could hardly have been louder. The best I could do under the circumstances was to tell the white creatures what my results were and explain to them that I would phone the results in to Desert Center as soon as I was able to. Range Four Harry's aunt seemed to find the calculations quite interesting but the daughter and the children showed little interest in them. Harry's daughter seemed to be spending most of her time enjoying the beauty of the evening in much the same way that a teenage girl might have.

Eventually I had completed all of my work. I needed only to phone Desert Center and drive in for breakfast. Neither my phone nor my truck would work while all of these tall white people stood watching me so with nothing else to do, I sat down in the front doorway of my shack and waited for them to make the next move. Harry's aunt asked me a few questions about my work and what it felt like to be a human male. I'm not sure I answered her questions very well but I did the best I could. In the end, both Harry's aunt and his daughter appeared to have overcome their fear of me and were now both settled and calm.

Without further ado, the aunt and daughter slowly turned and began floating away from me. Soon, I could see the two of them floating gently across the desert, then up to the paved road, and finally they floated slowly and gracefully down the paved road towards the ammunition bunker northeast of the Range Three area. I noted that they hadn't greeted me when they came, and they hadn't said goodbye when they left. I guess that is their way.

Then the Teacher summoned the last of the children. The child was her own little girl. The two of them floated slowly and happily back across the desert to the northeast. Finally, and without saying anything whatever, the School Bus Driver floated and climbed down from his place on the billboard. Reaching the ground, he retreated gracefully back down the road to the ammunition bunkers that lay along the base of the mountains to the northeast. Once the entire procession had reached the area of the ammunition bunker, one and a quarter miles away, I decided to try my phone. Desert Center still needed to receive my results. Now, the phone worked OK, although the static was still quite noticeable. I locked up my shack and started my truck. In the distance, up along the foothills of the mountains northeast of my shack, I could see the last few groups of white fluorescent patches as they floated north over the ridges, disappearing at last, into a valley some three miles north east of my shack.

I stood for a long time, quiet and motionless in the beautiful starlit desert night. It took a long time for my mind to grasp what had just happened, and for its lesson to sink in. The lesson was the children. No matter what they were, no matter whom they were, no matter where they had come from, their fathers had worked hard to bring them across mile after mile of empty worthless desert. Their fathers had broken all of their rules. Their fathers had carefully laid their plans. Their fathers had taken risks unimaginable. Their fathers had gone through more labors than they could ever describe just to give their children a few good gifts. More than high tech suits, more than warmth, more than protection, safety, training, good food, good drinks ... the fathers had also given their children another gift. They had let them play with me and my balloons. Their fathers had given them the gifts of fun and happiness just because their children had asked for them. Their fathers had proven they were willing to give their children every good gift their children asked for. ... How could God, then, who made both them and me, be any different?

Charles James Hall

Sunshine Sleuthing

>. . . Saul said to Jonathan,
>"Tell me what you have done."
>Jonathan replied,
>"I only tasted a little honey
>from the end of the staff I was holding. ..."
>. . . 1 Samuel 15:42,43

"Don't move, Charlie," said Clark firmly. "I know it's your move, but just wait a minute."

"Sure, Clark," I answered. "What is it?"

Clark leaned over the chessboard as he reached into the bottom shelf of his locker. There his hands found a large shoebox full of cookies. Retrieving the box, he sat it carefully on the bunk next to him. Taking out exactly one large chocolate chip cookie, he handed it to me.

"Here, Charlie. I want you to just sit there quietly looking at the chess board while you eat this cookie," he said thoughtfully.

"Man, this cookie is delicious, Clark," I exclaimed. "Your mother certainly knows how to cook."

"You're right there, Charlie, she sure does," Clark responded. "Now, I don't care if you are rated as a chess master, and if you are rated as the seventh best chess player in the U.S. Air Force, and I know you've won every other chess game we've ever played, and I know you almost have this game won, too, but this time I have a new strategy that I think is going to work on you."

"Really, Clark?" I answered. "What is it?"

282

Clark responded proudly, "I'll give you two cookies for that rook, but it has to be my move!"

I could see right off that Clark had me. Piece after piece I sacrificed to the needs of my stomach. I held out for four cookies for the queen, and bravely tried to hold off checkmate with just the bishop before selling him out too, for a cookie and a half.

Clark nearly laughed himself silly as he proudly exclaimed, "Checkmate!" At the time, I was laughing too. You see, I was eating his last cookie.

"Well, Charlie, I knew I'd take you one of these days," laughed Clark. "I'll tell you what, tomorrow as soon as you finish the last afternoon run, why don't you drive in here to the POL (Petroleum Oils and Liquids) office where I am, and let's play another game of chess. I think I can win a second game. You see, my mother sent me another box of cookies."

"I'll be there at two sharp," I laughed. Then I said good night and left for my barracks.

The next afternoon, as I was finishing the afternoon run out at the Range Three weather shack, three four wheel drive pickup trucks carrying range rats pulled up outside. Out jumped Steve and Doug. Tall, young, strong, and healthy, they came forcefully into my weather shack. Steve greeted me happily, "Charlie, the boys and I are driving up north to pick up some empty napalm tanks that some idiot pilot dropped there by mistake. Now where is that mirror or whatever it is that you were wondering about the other day. We'll get that for you while we're up there."

"That's nice of you," I said. Then I took them outside into the bright sun light. Pointing straight north to the slopes of the mountain some 70 miles in the distance, I said, "You see that reflection about half way up that mountain side?"

"Yes, I see it," said Steve. "It's up there on that mountain."

"Yes," I said. "Here, I'll mark it for you, on your map. I've always wondered what that was. It never moves, so it must be a mirror or something laying on the slopes of that mountain."

"You must be right, Charlie. That's just a mile or so farther than where we're going. It won't be any problem. We'll get it for you, whatever it is," said Steve.

"That's really nice of you guys, but don't take any risks up there on my account. I measured the distance using my theodolite. Its 72 miles from here so if you can't get to it, just forget it," I said. "It's not that important to me. It's just that every morning when I look up there, I see the sunlight reflecting on it and I was just wondering what it could be."

"We'll see you later," chimed Steve and Doug as they started their engines. Soon their trucks could be seen raising dust clouds several miles up the valley.

I was running a little late so I hurriedly phoned in my results, locked up my weather shack, and raced in to base. I still needed a bathroom stop and gas for my truck from the motor pool. Finally, at 2:30 p.m., a half hour late, I pulled up in front of the POL shack that sat next to the Mojave Wells runway. Clark manned it alone.

I was embarrassed by my tardiness. I hadn't meant to keep one of my dearest friends waiting. I guess I expected to find him angry or at least upset. Instead, I found him sitting with his head in his hands, crying in loneliness. When he saw me coming in the door, he couldn't restrain himself. Loneliness had destroyed his last defenses. He leapt to his feet and momentarily hugged me as though I were a cross between Santa Claus and Jesus. He blurted out, "It's good to see you."

Then, after a bit, still in tears, he walked quickly around the POL shack to the bathroom in the back. I waited. I could hear that he was still crying. Eventually he returned, smiling, somewhat more relaxed, and ready to play chess.

It was now past 3:00 p.m.. I was unwilling to take Clark's cookies with the afternoon almost spent. I decided to save them for an afternoon when we could play longer. On the other hand, I was unwilling to beat my good friend Clark in a game of chess under these circumstances. After giving the problem due consideration, I decided the best course for Clark would be for the two of us to talk about home and our experiences here at Mojave Wells.

Pushing the board aside, I asked him, "How are things back in Boston, Clark? Will you be going home for Christmas?"

Cheering up, Clark responded, "Why Yes, Charlie. I'm looking forward to seeing my two girl friends Jeannie and Mary Ann. Jeannie is the girl from next door. She's the one my mother wants me to marry. Mary Ann is my old high school sweet heart. I'm in love with her but I think she's dating another man. I don't know what I'll do, Charlie. It's a tough problem and I'm going to have to give it some thought."

"Well, two women can certainly keep a man busy," I laughed. "I hope you're taking vitamins."

"Yes, I am," he answered, pointing to a big bottle of vitamins sitting on the shelf over his head. "But that isn't what I need to talk to you about today, Charlie. I need your help out on Range Four. You're the only one I trust, and I have to tell someone."

"What is it, Clark?" I answered. "You know you can tell me anything."

"Well, something happened the last time I was out there. I've tried telling some of the other guys, but I just couldn't. When I tried to tell Steve, he just said, that I had no business going out there alone in the first place. He said it was too dangerous and that I shouldn't want to know the answers to my questions. Then I didn't know what to say next."

"Well you can tell me, Clark," I responded, "You can tell me anything. I've seen so many things while I've been out there. Most of them, I've never had the courage to tell anyone either, so you know I'll understand, Clark. I'll understand anything."

Clark continued nervously, "Well, tell me Charlie, what happened that time Steve always talks about, out at Range One? The most I ever got out of him was that one time last summer when you were cleaning and scrubbing the Range One weather shack, you were out there alone, singing and humming songs. Steve and the Range rats were over at Range Two at the time. He swears that he saw a chalk white person with blonde hair, standing up in the sagebrush down on Range One. It was watching your every move. He and Doug were afraid that it was going to attack you, like it did Sullivan. They tried to come down there to save you but they were too terrified to come any closer than the Range Two road junction."

"I remember that day," I answered. "I remember how surprised I was to see them when I was driving in to base. They must have waited at the road junction for more than two hours while I finished cleaning my shack. I didn't even know they were there and I never have understood what they were so frightened about. I mean, when I was working, every now and then I heard a coyote or a dog barking out in the sagebrush. Then a couple of times I heard what sounded like a horse whinnying out there. Of course, I always hear meadowlark sounds out there. I just supposed it was some local guy out hunting with a horse and some dogs. I forgot that this is a fenced government reservation and that we are the only guys ever allowed out there.

"When I first drove out, I spent a few minutes looking out in the sagebrush. I could see something white or blonde in the distance. After I'd been there a few minutes, I just figured that if it hadn't attacked me by then, it probably wasn't going to. So I just went on about the business of cleaning my weather shack and I forgot about it."

With that, Clark seemed to relax noticeably. He continued, "I see why Desert Center picked you, Charlie. Really I do. That's why I need you to go with me out to Range Four. I need you to follow along with your truck as I drive out with mine."

"Of course, Clark," I answered. "It's no problem whatever. When would you like to go?"

"Next week but, I need to tell you why first," said Clark. "You see, something terrifying happened to me the last time I went out there. I have to tell someone, and I have to tell you before we go out there."

"Now's as good a time to tell me as any, Clark," I responded, leaning back in my chair.

"You see, Charlie, one of my duties is to fill the diesel fuel tanks for all of the diesel generators out on the ranges. I'm required to visit each tank at least once a month, and fill them whenever it's necessary.

"Filling the tanks at Range Three is not usually a problem because most of the time, you're out there. Even that I have to be careful about. Two months ago I made the mistake of going out to Range Three when there was no one else around. It was that day when you were sick. You phoned Desert Center and canceled the afternoon runs. It was about two in the afternoon. I swear, Charlie, there was something else out there with me. I don't know what it was but I was anything but alone. I didn't even bother checking the tanks. I just climbed back into my truck and got the hell out of there."

"Really, Clark?" I asked innocently. "I wonder what it could have been." I didn't have the courage to tell him that I was only pretending to be sick that day. As I had been looking into my theodolite taking the 11:00 a.m. balloon run that day, I suddenly became dizzy. When my mind cleared, my watch had stopped, I was standing six feet from my theodolite, and I was missing 45 minutes of time that I couldn't account for. As I struggled to clear my mind, I became convinced that eight or ten people were watching me from behind the Range Three lounge. The whole episode intimidated me because the group appeared to include a three star Air Force General. I phoned the Desert Center weather station to report my partial wind run and pretended I was sick. To my surprise, the Desert Center command post had already reported my 'illness' to the Desert Center weather station. I was left holding the phone wondering, "How did they know?" I hurriedly locked my weather shack, shut down the diesel, and headed into base.

Putting a calm smile on my face, I waited for my good friend Clark to continue.

"I don't know what was hiding out at Range Three the day I was out there, Charlie, but whatever it was, it was hiding inside the generator shack, and in around those storage buildings next to your weather shack. I was really scared. I packed up and left in record time. That's why I always phone you now, before I come out there," continued Clark. "Going out to Range Two and Range One is no

288

problem. Whenever I need to go out there, I take Bryan, the Air Policeman, and Mark from the motor pool. We always go out there together. Mark takes the wrecker. Bryan takes his police car. Of course, I take the semi-tanker parked out there on the ramp.

"Bryan goes out there first to check everything out while Mark and I wait at the road junction. If he says it's OK, I go out with the tanker while Mark waits at the road junction with the wrecker. Since Bryan's car and Mark's wrecker have CB radios in them, we can all stay in communication. Bryan, of course, always goes out there well armed. Usually he takes along his 50 caliber rifle as well as his pistol and his 30.06 deer rifle. Last time we went out there, he was carrying more than a thousand rounds of ammunition in the car with him.

"We always time Bryan. If he is ever out of communication with us for more than 30 minutes, we're supposed to go back into base for help."

"When Bryan goes out there, is everything always OK?" I asked.

"Usually, but not always," answered Clark. "Last spring, right after the warm weather started up, we tried three different times to go out to Range Two, and twice we tried to go out to Range One before Bryan would OK it."

"Why did Bryan say he turned you back on those times?" I asked.

"He wouldn't say. One time when he got back to the road junction, he just sat in his car looking dumb founded. He was saying, 'I just don't believe it. I just don't believe what's out there.'

"Another time, he let us come out but only after he'd walked around the open area in between the buildings, shooting his pistol in the air.

"Another time, when we were out at Range One, I was only half finished filling the diesel tank when he spotted something way out in the sagebrush coming towards us. He fired the rifle over its head to drive it off. We abandoned the tanker and came back to base just using the police car and the wrecker. Then we went out the next day to get the tanker."

"Did Bryan ever say what he saw out in the sagebrush?" I asked.

"Not really," responded Clark. "At the time, I couldn't understand what he was saying. At first it sounded like he was saying that he saw a white woman with blonde hair walking towards us.

"Another time, Mark said he saw the same woman way off in the sagebrush, up on the slopes of one of the mountains."

"Perhaps she just wanted to talk," I responded.

Clark continued, "I don't know. We were all too scared to stay around and find out.

"Well, anyway, Bryan, Steve, Doug, Mark, and all of the Range Rats agree that I should only go out to Range Four with the tanker if the Range Rats are out there or if I take you with me."

"I'm happy to go out with you, Clark. I understand why they would suggest that you shouldn't go out there unless they're out there, but I'm surprised that they suggested that I go with you," I answered.

"Steve, Doug, and Bryan all agreed on that," continued Clark. "They all agreed they don't really feel safe themselves, when they are way out on the ranges unless you're out there somewhere with them. Steve, himself, swears that one morning he got up real early before dawn and was driving out to make sure you were OK. When he got close to Range Three, he claims he saw Range Four Harry watching you from the sagebrush while you were releasing a balloon. He says you weren't afraid or anything but just went on about your work."

"Well, I wouldn't say I wasn't afraid," I protested. "But what was watching me wasn't a man, it was a young woman. I was convinced that if she meant to hurt me or scare me, she would have silently slipped up behind me and just done so. I first saw her as she was coming down the Range Four road. She was doing so in such an open and obvious manner that I decided her intentions must be peaceful.

"She kept her distance so I just went on about my business of taking the morning wind measurements. I was quite nervous at the time so I spoke to her. I shouted over to her pleasantly, 'I won't hurt you. You can watch me if you want to but don't come too close because you frighten me. Please stay back in the sagebrush until I can calm myself down. Then you can come in closer.'

"Well Clark, she responded in English, 'Yes, we'll stay back in the sagebrush until you tell us we can in where you are.'

"Now she comes from time to time. She calls herself the Teacher. I guess I wouldn't be able to pronounce her real name. She said that it sounds sort of like a horse whinny followed by two short dog barks.

"Usually when she comes, she waits a little ways out in the sagebrush and calls to me by name. After we have exchanged greetings and I have my nerves under control, she comes in close to where I am and we talk while I work. She says that she and the other young mothers have nothing to do for amusement up on the mountain base and that everyone gets very bored. Apparently the American

Generals decide what clothing styles the women get to pick from in their little commissary up on the mountain. Naturally, all of the American Generals are old men so all of the women's fashions look like worker's overalls. She says all of the women get so frustrated because they have to ask the American Generals for everything. Then when it comes it is always in white and the design is so plain.

"On a few nights we talked about the city of Las Vegas. She seemed especially interested in the location of some shopping centers and women's clothing stores, along with the prices of dresses, shoes, and children's clothes. A few weekends ago when I went up to Las Vegas, I spent some time looking at women's dresses, prices, and fashions. She had been wondering how much money a good shopping trip would cost. I wanted to be able to answer some of her questions. Money, time, distance, none of those seemed to be a problem for her. She believed that she and the other young mothers could just walk into a casino and win however much money she needed to pay for everything. She just wanted to have some idea of how much that would be.

"Apparently her eyes are a little bit more sensitive than mine. She said that she is able see some infrared and some ultraviolet light. Therefore every card in a deck of cards looks different to her, even if she only sees a small portion of the card. I found that quite surprising, but she pointed out that some humans who think they are color blind, actually just have eyes that are much more sensitive to infrared and ultraviolet light then hers are. I guess back in World War Two, the British had identified a group of such 'color-blind' humans who could never be fooled by German camouflage netting.

"We both concluded that she and the other women could just dress up to look like humans, and then all go shopping in the evenings in Las Vegas. Even if they didn't have their disguises perfect, no one would every notice them. So many people coming out of the casinos are half drunk and dressed weird anyway. If anyone ever challenged them, they could just say they were entertainers from some show down on the strip. I mean, who would ever go into a woman's dress store expecting to run into a group of alien women shopping for clothes?

"Her favorite colors seemed to be pink and green. I assured her that pink usually went with white, and green usually went with white, but that pink and green didn't necessarily go together. I assured her that I'd seen many pretty dresses in all of the colors in the shopping centers up in Las Vegas.

"On another night she seemed especially interested in the location of city parks in Las Vegas. She was wondering if there was a park where the children could play at night while the young mothers went to see the shows in some nearby casino.

"I assured her that there were several, and I told her where they were located. Not unexpectedly, I had to give her directions from the airport.

"Usually our conversations are quite short and she asks all of the questions. Every now and then she will say something unusual, but not very often. One night she said that her parents first brought her out here to this desert valley when she was a little girl and they were still the same height as me. I guess when their people reach old age, they start slowly growing taller and their bodies become more fragile. Eventually they become so tall that their bodies fail them and they die.

Charles James Hall

"She said that she was already equivalent to a teenage girl when the first white people came with their wagons. One of her funniest experiences, I guess, was one night she tried to talk to a group of pioneers who were camped around the springs up in Las Vegas, but they just thought they were looking at the ghost of some dead human bride and they all panicked.

"Anyway, Clark, I want you to know that you can trust me as a friend. I swear I've never told anyone about those experiences before today."

Clark listened politely and quietly, as though he didn't believe me. Then he responded, "Well, Charlie, I don't know what to say. You have spent an awful amount of time alone out in that hot desert. However, Steve, Bryan, Doug all agree that whatever it is that's out there, it doesn't intend to hurt you or scare you like it did all of those other weathermen who came out here before you. Steve says he's certain of it but he won't say why."

"I appreciate your concern for my safety, Clark," I responded. "There's really nothing out there in the desert that I ever need to feel afraid of. Really, I could hardly feel more to home when I'm out there."

"Well, I'll tell you this much, Charlie," said Clark thoughtfully. "I can see why you're the only weather observer Desert Center is willing to send up here, anymore. Now, I have to tell you what happened to me the last time I went out to Range Four. You have to know why I need you to follow me out there the next time I go.

"Remember how you told me about those times last summer when you would go out to Range One and you would see that large white object out in the sagebrush. Sometimes it was way down in the valley. Other times it was hidden in behind the buildings of Range Two?"

294

"Yes," I answered, "Several times I even saw it over behind the ammunition bunker at Range Three. There was a time when I wondered what it was, but I don't concern myself with it anymore."

"Well," said Clark, "I saw it out at Range Four parked in one of those old aircraft hangers."

"Really?" I exclaimed in surprise.

"Yes, really," answered Clark seriously. "It was last May. I had to make the monthly diesel fuel run out there, so I picked a nice sunny day when I thought the Range Rats were going to be out there. I tried phoning first but the phone out at Range Four wasn't working. It was full of static.

"I decided to go out there anyway. I took the noon meal early and left with my diesel semi-tanker about noon. The engine had just been tuned up and I swear that when I started out, that engine was running perfectly.

"When I headed north from Range Three along that gravel road that leads out to Range Four, the truck was still running perfectly. As I came up over that rise, I was singing and happy. Then the radio in my truck started going to hell on me. Soon I couldn't get any of the radio stations like I usually can. All the radio would put out was static so I turned it off.

"Everything looked normal. As I got closer to Range Four, I could see that there wasn't anyone out there. The Range Rats were looking for stray practice bombs way out to the west. There wasn't any way I could turn the tanker around on that gravel road so I just kept driving on towards Range Four.

"As I got closer and closer to Range Four, my truck began running worse and worse. The engine started miss firing and coughing. When I got right up to the buildings, my truck was just barely able to go forward. I figured I better turn around and go home but just as I got by the diesel tanks, my truck engine quit running completely. When the truck stopped rolling, I was so angry I got out and pounded on the truck door. I hurt my hand and I was swearing. I tried and tried to start the engine but that truck engine wouldn't start. It acted like the battery was totally dead. I was madder than hell with myself. I stomped into the Range Four lounge to phone for help. That damn phone was nothing but static. You couldn't dial it or anything.

"I figured that I might as well fill the diesel tanks while I was there. I figured it would lighten the load. That way, if I could get the engine started, it would make it easier for me to get home.

"I unwound my fuel hose and put it into the first diesel tank. The tank was only a quarter full and my hose went all the way to the bottom. I went to start the gasoline engine on the trailer that operates the fuel pump. That damn engine wouldn't start either. It works like a lawn mower engine. You have to pull the cord to start it. I must have tried for more than a half hour but it wasn't even close to starting.

"As I was standing there swearing at pretty much everything in sight, I suddenly realized that I wasn't alone. I suddenly realized that something else was out there with me."

"Something else?" I asked.

"Yes, something dangerous as hell was out there with me," said Clark seriously. "You know how Range Four is like Range two? They both have those old aircraft hangers. Range One and Range Three used to have them too but the ones on those two ranges were torn down back in the fifties.

"Well, I heard something growl in behind those hangers. I became afraid. Immediately I began climbing up on the fuel tank to retrieve my hose. I was going to rewind my hose and take off running to get the hell out of there. As I was retrieving my hose, I noticed that there was something hiding in one of those hangers, watching me. All of the doors to those hangers were closed. Sounds were coming from the hanger closest to me. You know, it's the one with that pile of junk wood and iron that someone piled in there?"

"Yes," I answered.

"Sometimes it sounded like a coyote growling at me. Sometimes it sounded like a horse. Other times it sounded like two children giggling at me. At first I was afraid to come down off the fuel tank. Then, after I had sat up there for 20 minutes or so, I realized that I was out here, more than 45 miles from nowhere. Whatever it was, I knew I was going to have to face it alone.

"I got down off the tank and quickly found an old piece of two by four to use as a club. Then I stood with my back to my truck and began shouting out real loud, 'Come on out and face me. I know you're in there. I'm ready for you.'

"Whatever it was, it wouldn't come out. So I figured I was probably facing a coyote. I started feeling braver. I decided to scare it off so I slowly walked towards the hanger, shouting all of the time. As I was carefully sliding open the front door to the first hanger, I got a glimpse of two little white children slipping out through a crack in the door on the other side. Their skin was real chalky white and they had real blonde hair. Then I could hear what sounded like an angry coyote growling and barking from the last hanger over. Through the gaps in the wood, I could see something large and white parked in the end hanger. It looked like the fuselage of a medium sized airplane but it didn't have any wings or any tail surfaces. Inside the hanger, standing along side it were several people but I couldn't see them very well. They were tall, white skinned, and real thin. They looked like they hadn't been eating very well. They had blonde hair and blue eyes. I'm certain they saw me. They looked like they might be Swedish, but they must have been mutants because they had real sharp bony claws on the ends of their fingers.

"Well, I tell you, Charlie, I became absolutely terrified. I didn't make any sounds, because I realized that those bastards had the power to kill me and no one would ever have the faintest idea what happened to me. I just took off running as fast as I could."

"Where to, Clark?" I asked. "You were out on Range Four. There's no place to run to. There's no place to hide. The day you were out there, it must have been 110 degrees in the shade. You were in a life and death situation."

"No crap!" continued Clark. "But I was damned if I was going to just stand there and go down without a fight. I took off running back down the road towards Range Three. I still had my cigarette lighter with me. I figured that if I could get far enough away, I could stop and set the sagebrush on fire. After all, being in POL, I am sort of an expert on fire. I was even thinking of setting the diesel tanks on fire but I decided that I didn't have enough time for that.

"I ran until I was tired. Then I kept walking as fast as I could, back towards Range Three. At the time I wasn't looking back towards Range Four. Whenever I looked back, it slowed me down so I just kept walking and running as much as I could.

"I must have walked or ran for at least an hour in the hot sun. I was getting really tired and really thirsty. I always carry something to drink with me in the truck but that was at least five miles back there. I was getting exhausted so I found a spot in the shade of some sagebrush and sat down to rest.

"As I was resting, I studied the buildings in the distance. Suddenly I noticed that there was something different about them. Before, all of the doors to the hangers had been closed. Now, both the front and back doors to the last hanger were wide open. It was almost as if the white people who had been there, wanted to make sure I saw that the hanger was now empty and they had gone!

"This caused me a lot of anxiety. I could see that I was never going to be able to walk back to base in that hot sun. I realized that whether I liked it or not, I was going to have to go back to Range Four for the water in my truck. I studied the Range Four buildings for a while, until I became convinced that whoever had been there, had left. Having no other choice, I picked up some throwing rocks and a strong piece of sagebrush to use as a club. I began walking slowly back towards my truck at Range Four. I decided that when I got there, first I'd get a good drink of water. Then I planned to signal for help by starting a good diesel fuel fire.

"It took me a while to get back there. I was exhausted from the afternoon sun. I'd stop every half mile or so, to make sure the buildings were still deserted. It was late in the afternoon when I finally got back along side my truck.

"When I got to my truck, I quickly climbed in and locked the door. Then I found my thermos jug and spent the next 20 minutes slowly sipping water.

"When I was feeling better, I started feeling braver. I decided that I would get out and start a great big diesel fuel fire, real smoky and everything so that whoever saw it would know I needed help. Just for the hell of it, I decided to try to start my truck one last time. I tell you, Charlie, I could hardly believe it! My truck started right off. The battery was charged and everything.

"I didn't know what to make of it! I almost broke my leg getting out of my truck. I rolled up my fuel hose as fast as I knew how. I left the tanks the way I found them. I didn't feel like taking the time to fill them. I locked the diesel tanks shut in a flash. Then I climbed back into my truck as fast as God would let me and I headed on out of there. Man, I turned that truck around like there was no damn tomorrow and I floored that thing heading home. At the time, I wouldn't have stopped even if the trailer had come off the tractor. All the way home, that engine ran just perfectly."

"That must have been really terrifying, Clark," I said. "You're lucky to still be alive. Did you recover all right from that long walk in the hot sun?"

"Yes, I did Charlie," answered Clark, "but it took me a couple of days before I started feeling better and my sun burn was a while healing up."

"When would you like to go out to Range Four, Clark?" I asked. "I can go out with you anytime my balloon schedule permits it. When we go out, do you want me to go first?"

"No," said Clark. "I'll go first. I want you to park about three miles back down the road. I don't want you to come into the buildings. This time, if I get in trouble, I want a truck waiting for me down the road when I come running out of there."

"Whatever you want, Clark," I responded. "When would you like to do it?"

"How about next Wednesday," asked Clark? "I've checked the Range schedule. Range Three has lots of flights scheduled but Range Four won't be in use. I can bring my tanker out there as soon as the 10:00 p.m. flights end. The next flights aren't scheduled until 1:30 p.m. in the afternoon. That'll give us more than two and a half hours to drive out to Range Four, fill the diesel tanks, and drive back. Will that fit in with your balloon schedule?"

"Sure, Clark," I answered cheerfully. "I'll just tell Desert Center that I need three hours to do some maintenance on my theodolite or something." Then, after pausing to think for a moment, I continued, "Oh, I know. I'll just tell them the truth. I'm tell the Desert Center base commander that next Wednesday at noon, I'm escorting you out to Range Four to insure your personal safety while you refuel the diesel tanks. Once the base commander has been informed, he'll tell anyone that cares. It'll all be OK. The base commander can't possibly say no. After all, my standing orders from the Pentagon say I can go anywhere I want, anytime I want. They know I always keep them informed if anything dangerous, weather wise, ever develops up here. I'll make the phone call to the Desert Center base commander tomorrow between balloon runs."

With that, the two of us were in perfect agreement. Our meeting ended with the two of us counting the days that would pass until the following Wednesday.

It was early the following afternoon when Steve, Doug, and the rest of the Range Rats came driving out to Range Three. I was sitting in the doorway to my weather shack when their three four wheel drive power wagons came skidding to a stop in front of me. Steve jumped out and triumphantly held up an old milk bottle.

"Here it is, Charlie," he exclaimed proudly, as he handed it to me. "It's all yours."

I carefully took the bottle from him. It was labeled "Tonopah Diary, 1912". The label was molded into the very glass. The glass was no longer clear. It had lain in the desert

301

sun for so many years that the very glass was now a beautiful shade of faded violet.

"It's beautiful, Steve," I exclaimed. "It was so nice of you and the Range Rats to get it for me. I hope you didn't have to go out of your way to get it."

"No," answered Steve seriously. "It was real easy to find. It was sitting up on an exposed ridge, right where you marked it on my map. Doug and I left the rest of the Range Rats down in the valley with the power wagons. We walked up there to get it. It's really a beautiful view from up there. Doug and I could see everything in the valleys all around. We could see your weather shack here at Range Three and everything down here in the valley. But, I tell you, Charlie, if that bottle had been sitting even another 100 feet further up that slope, Doug and I would have left it there and come home without it."

"Really?" I exclaimed.

"Damn straight," Steve answered. "Walking up that slope to get it was one of the scariest things Doug and I have ever done together. I tell you, Charlie, it couldn't possibly have been dropped there by accident. Whoever put it there must have done so to make that mountain stand out from the other mountains around it. The mountain it was sitting on is all honeycombed with old mine shafts and tunnels. I tell you, Charlie, every step Doug and I took got scarier and scarier."

"How come, Steve?" I asked.

"There's something hiding in those mine shafts up there, Charlie. I don't mean one or two things. It's like an entire small town of ghosts and white things dug in up there. Doug and I must have seen a dozen of them up there peeking out at us. There was probably another 50 we couldn't see barking and growling at us. There was so much barking and

302

growling coming from up by that peak, it sounded like there was a whole community of prairie dogs or coyotes hiding up there. Once Doug and I got our hands on that bottle, the two of us high tailed it out there just as fast as we could go."

"I really appreciate the trouble you and Doug went through to get this bottle," I said. "What do you suppose could be hiding up in the mountain?"

"I don't know, Charlie," answered Steve. "But I tell you one thing, there's no way in hell Doug and I are going to go back up that last slope to find out.

"Well, the Range Rats and I have to get some sleep, Charlie. We didn't get back until after midnight last night."

With that Steve strode proudly out of my weather shack and back to his truck. Soon, the three trucks could be seen disappearing down the road back to base.

After they had left, I carefully inspected the bottle, turning it slowly in my hands. It actually had an unusual shape for a milk bottle. I noticed that when the sunlight struck it, no matter how it was turned, it reflected the sunlight in all directions. Considering how it reflected the sunlight, I wondered if it actually was an old milk bottle, or if it had been intentionally made to look like one. In any event, it was unusual and absolutely beautiful. After giving it some thought, I proudly positioned the bottle on the shelf next to my radio. I wasn't surprised when I later checked the history of Nevada in a large reference book in the library. According to the Nevada State Historian, the city of Tonopah didn't have a dairy in 1912. Its first dairy wasn't founded until after 1930. Yes, there was a lot about the bottle that made it unusual.

The days passed quickly. The following Wednesday dawned clear and hot. It was 10:45 a.m. when the last of the morning flights left Range Three. One of the new pilots had almost flown his F105 into the ground. Some of the sagebrush was still burning after having been ignited by the flames from his afterburner. The range officer canceled the remainder of the strafing runs so the Range Rats could put out the burning sagebrush. This allowed Clark and I to start for Range Four earlier than planned.

The desert was majestic and castle-like as it shimmered in the hot morning sun. Clark's semi-tanker was fully loaded with diesel fuel. It rode heavy to the ground as his diesel tractor pulled it onto the gravel road that wound its way up the valley to Range Four. The big tanker threw up a huge cloud of dust and spewed rocks for a quarter of a mile behind it. It was only with difficulty that Clark got his rig up to speed. Because of the dust and rocks, I let the rig roll on ahead for several miles in front of my pickup. Soon Clark and his rig were more than three miles ahead of me as I followed patiently along behind.

Having nothing better to do, I decided to just take my time and enjoy the drive. I could see the mountains on each side of the road, but Clark's huge dust cloud prevented me from seeing the buildings of Range Four that lay up ahead. I slowed still more until Clark's rig had rolled on some five miles in front of me.

The road climbed slowly up hill for several miles before topping a rise in the desert and snaking its way slowly down the long ten mile downgrade into the Range Four buildings. As Clark's truck pulled further ahead of me, the Range Four buildings became visible, shimmering in the hot desert sun in the distance. I studied the buildings carefully as my truck rolled on towards Range four. Everything looked normal. It was immediately apparent that the buildings that lay in the hot sun in the distance were quite deserted. Still, as Clark's tanker pulled into the building area in the distance, I did notice something unusual. The back door on the far hanger, the one in which Clark had claimed he had seen the mutant Swedes, was standing open. The hanger was obviously empty and that was the problem. The hanger wasn't used anymore by the Air Force. When I had been out to Range Four only three weeks earlier, all of the hanger doors were closed. I felt certain that if the Range Rats ever had a reason to open the hanger doors, they would have also closed them. As I stopped my truck on the gravel road, I wondered.

From where I stopped my truck to the buildings in the distance, was a good five miles. I'd promised Clark that I wouldn't shut my engine off so as I waited, I let my engine idle. No problem, I thought. I had a full tank of gas.

The road was only one lane wide where I stopped and I could see that in order to turn around, I was going to have to drive closer to the Range Four buildings that lay up ahead. I decided to wait until Clark had finished filling the diesel tanks up ahead. I could solve that problem once he had his truck running again. At the time, everything seemed normal and I wasn't in any hurry.

As I sat there, I studied the mountains to the east very carefully. Several desert canyons cut deeply into them. In the hot noon day sun there really wasn't anything whatever to be seen other than rocks, sagebrush, sand, and some occasional mesquite.

It was a pleasant wait and the time seemed to pass in a carefree manner. In the distance, Clark had just finished filling the last of the three diesel tanks. It had taken him quite some time so I concluded the tanks must have all been bone dry. Clark started up his truck. It was obviously riding much higher than it had coming out. I decided this would be the best time to drive the remaining five miles into Range

Four to turn around. My truck engine was running fine and so was Clark's. I figured this would clear the road to make it easy for Clark to return to Range Three. Clark didn't see things that way. As I pulled in between the buildings of Range Four and brought my truck up next to his, he was shouting at me, "Get back, Charlie, get back. Didn't you see it?"

"No, Clark," I answered. "What should I have seen?"

"That thing," he answered. "Didn't you see it? It was sitting in that far hanger over there. When I came over the rise, it saw us coming and went out the back door. Then it headed for those mountains up the valley."

"What did it look like, Clark?" I asked.

"Just like it did before. I'll tell you more about it when we get back in to base, Charlie, but I'm not hanging around here. I'm afraid it might come back. Let's get the hell out of here," shouted Clark.

With that, Clark gunned his rig and began heading out from between the Range Four buildings. Within minutes, his huge tanker was spewing gravel out over the desert and raising huge clouds of dust as he headed up the road, back towards Range Three. Not wanting to follow too closely because of the dust and gravel, I waited at Range Four. It took some time for Clark's truck to put the necessary distance between his truck and mine. As I sat in my truck with my engine idling, I studied the four hangers. Each hanger was large enough to hold a large semi with a mountain-diesel sized trailer.

Inside the first hanger sat an ordinary looking pile of old boards. Outside on the end of the hanger sat a second pile of similar boards. I thought about it for a minute. Then it struck me. The boards in the pile outside the hanger rattled and shook with every gust of wind but the ones inside the hanger sat motionless. The boards in the pile inside the hanger fit together so snugly that they were obviously capable of carrying a great deal of weight without moving. The conclusion was inescapable. Someone had intentionally constructed the pile inside the hanger to look like the boards had been randomly piled there. Who would care what a pile of old boards would look like? After all, this is more than forty miles out into the desert and on a desolate government reservation I thought about it some more. The boards were piled in the hanger that Clark said he had seen those two children hiding. I remembered my own childhood, growing up in Wisconsin. I remembered how much fun I'd had playing on my father's woodpile. Is that what's going on, I wondered. After all, Clark hadn't said that he'd seen mutant scientists studying the desert. Had Clark inadvertently stumbled onto a playground for second graders? Is it that he hadn't hurt the children, so their parents hadn't hurt him?

I studied the pile of boards some more. From my new perspective, their use soon became apparent. The builders clearly wanted their children to enjoy the fresh air and the exercise. The boards in the front of the pile clearly formed a child-sized jungle gym. The ones in the back clearly formed a child's playhouse. Playing in the shade inside the unused hanger, the children were protected from the hot sun in the summer and protected from the cold wind in the winter. I was stunned by its intelligent simplicity.

Time was passing and Clark's truck was already several miles up the road to Range Three. The engine of my truck began missing on one of its cylinders so I decided I had better head back to Range Three, too. Putting my truck in low gear, I carefully circled the Range Four buildings and headed back up the road towards Range Three. My truck engine seemed to lack power.

The road back to Range Three continued slowly up hill for the first ten miles. I remembered distinctly taking the grade at 45 miles an hour in high gear when returning from my previous visits. Now, however, after down shifting to second gear, I found myself down shifting again into low gear. Although the slope of the hill could hardly have been gentler, I now found my engine missing so badly that I could no longer make any headway up the grade, even in low gear. I was forced to shift into neutral and just hope my engine would keep turning over.

Up ahead, some seven miles in the distance, I could see Clark's truck slowing down also. As I watched, his truck finally crawled over the peak of the rise and disappeared down the other side, leaving me sitting in my truck in quiet, splendid, if somewhat noisy, isolation.

Then my engine quit all together. A slight shudder seemed to pass through my body and my vision momentarily went out of focus. Blinking a little, and wiping some dust from my eyes, I started my truck engine up again. It just barely started and I was forced to nurse the gas pedal carefully to keep it running.

My engine could hardly have been hitting on more than three of its eight cylinders. I remember how foolish I felt, sitting there in the bright sunlight, just trying to keep it from stopping again.

Then, to my surprise, I noticed that the parking brake was set. This surprised me greatly because I was certain that I had released it when I had initially started up my truck and I was certain that I had not been driving my truck with it on. I must have sat there for more than five minutes, wondering what was happening. My mind seemed to be momentarily filled with glimpses and memory fragments. I seemed to remember reaching up and pushing a button, and a wall or something covered with hieroglyphics. Then I remembered opening a cupboard and looking at some food containers that looked like gray pudding stored in sealed plastic bags. But most of all, I was certain that an aircraft or something, had come alongside my truck, and flared out as though landing.

Then I started feeling really unusual. I searched my emotions and my memories. I decided that the last time I'd felt that way was during a thunderstorm when I was eight years old. A bolt of lightening had struck a tree near me that summer when I was eight. While the bolt of lightening exploded the tree into smithereens, I had been unable to move because of its electric field. Now, on this clear bright day in the desert, I found myself feeling as if lightening was striking next to me again. The tingling in my nerves told me exactly where the lightening would be found. Just barely able to move my muscles, I turned my head towards the mountains straight east of me. There, about three quarters of a mile in the distance, floated the cause of my problems. Large, ellipsoidal, and dull white, looking like the featureless fuselage of a medium sized passenger liner, with no wings or tail surfaces showing, it floated silently in the desert valley in the distance.

I watched the craft for the next twelve or fifteen minutes, all of the time trying to keep my truck engine from quitting. Slowly, silently, effortlessly, and patiently, it floated back and forth, inspecting every square inch of the valley before settling down behind some rocks at the mouth of the valley. It was featureless and solid white. It wouldn't glint in the bright noonday sun. As it floated over the soft ground, it didn't raise any dust or move the branches of the nearby sagebrush. The rocks and sagebrush next to it were not bent or distorted in any manner. Despite the strong electric field that I was experiencing, the craft did not give off any stray electrical discharges, sparks, or betray any evidence of the immense amount of power that it obviously commanded.

It was immediately apparent that the U.S. Air Force had not built it. Its occupants obviously did not wish for anyone but me, to know they were landing there. Yet, this too caused me some problems. "Why me?" I asked myself. After all, on the one hand they were hiding their craft behind the rocks that formed a barrier across the mouth of the valley. This meant they did not wish to be seen. Yet, even a blind person could have seen me sitting there in broad daylight on the Range Four road, desperately trying to keep my truck engine running. Creatures that intelligent, that xenophobic, that circumspect, could hardly have missed seeing me in my distinctive blue and white topped weather truck, parked in the most visible location in the entire valley. Surely they realized that if they had waited only another ten minutes to begin their landing procedure, I would have already disappeared over the top of the rise and no one would have seen them land.

"Surely they had to have known in advance that I would have to stop here on the road and wait for them to land," I said to myself. "Surely they had to have known that I would see them. Why me, and just me?" I wondered. "And how would they have known I was going to be out here on the Range Four road today at noon? The only person I'd told was the Desert Center base commander." After thinking about it for a couple of more minutes, the answers came to me. I concluded that the Teacher must be on board. I concluded the occupants were intentionally showing their craft to me. Surely the Teacher, with her electronics, must have realized that I often wondered where they came from and how they got here. "Perhaps she wished to reassure me that she and the children weren't dangerous mutants as Clark and the others had made them out to be." I speculated to myself. "She had, after all, always wanted me to enjoy their presence when they came. Reassuring me that they were perfectly ordinary alien creatures with perfectly ordinary feelings of love, hate, fear, and anger, made that a lot easier. Perhaps she worried that if I thought she and the children were dangerous mutants, the children would lose their favorite pony and no longer feel welcome on their favorite playground." As I sat there, I wondered to myself.

After the alien craft had dropped out of sight behind the rocks in the distance, my truck engine continued to misfire for another five minutes. Then, suddenly, it started running perfectly again. Moving the gear shift to low gear and releasing the parking brake, I spun the tires on the loose gravel and soon was traveling 45 miles an hour up the grade towards Range Three. I gave no thought to walking the three quarters of a mile across the desert to where the craft had landed, Teacher or no Teacher. I felt that I was increasing my life expectancy by simply driving my truck back to Range Three.

The remainder of the trip back to Range Three passed quickly. I felt a little dizzy, and now and then I had a slight sensation of nausea. Other than that I felt normal. My mind kept filling with stray thoughts and memory fragments. I remembered the Teacher greeting me as I stood outside my tuck. She was saying, "We wish to show you the inside of our scout craft. We're quite proud of it. We have to use the electronic controls so that you do not accidentally touch any of the buttons. Do not worry. As soon as you are back in your truck, you will be able to remember everything."

I remembered asking, "Where do you come from?" I remembered the Teacher smiling and answering, "From our

311

base up on the mountain. Remember, we took you up there one time."

I remembered continuing the questions, asking, "I mean, what star does your planet revolve around?"

The Teacher, still wearing her same pleasant smile answered the question with a question, "Do you know the names that we've given to the stars?"

"No," I answered.

"So if we told you, you still wouldn't know which star it was, would you?" responded the Teacher pleasantly.

For a few moments a peculiar dizziness seemed to flood over my mind. I was forced to slow down for a bit as I struggled to clear my mind. Breathing deeply, I slowly shook my head from side to side several times. Suddenly my mind cleared. Suddenly my thought fragments linked up like a group of broken country roads forming themselves into a long wide highway. Finally, I could remember everything. It took a few minutes to suppress the shock and get hold of myself. With great difficulty, I re-focused my mind on my driving.

With my truck engine now running perfectly, I sped up the gravel road, topped the rise, and continued on to the Range Three buildings. There, waiting to meet me was Clark, Steve and the other Range Rats. Each was desperately worried for my safety. The view from where they were parked in their trucks had not allowed them to see the white craft but when Clark had arrived back at Range Three and described the problems he was having with his truck, Steve had properly sounded the alarm.

As soon as I arrived back inside the graveled square of Range Three, I pulled my truck to a stop. Steve jumped from his parked power wagon and ran over to meet me. He obviously expected me to be burned or breaking down from fear. Throwing open the door to my truck, and seeing that I was untouched, unharmed, and unafraid, Steve exclaimed forcefully, "Charlie, are you all right?"

"Why yes, Steve," I answered. "Why wouldn't I be?"

Steve continued, shouting anxiously, "How can you possibly not be scared after an experience like the one you've just been through? Clark told us how your truck was forced to stop out there on the upgrade, fifteen miles back. He saw their craft come along side your truck. Charlie, they had you stopped out there for more than half an hour."

"An hour, Steve?" I asked in surprise. "But it's only 12:25 p.m.," I answered, showing Steve my watch.

Steve shouted back, holding up his watch as he did so, "Twelve twenty five, my ass! It's five minutes to one. Here, Charlie, look at my watch. Look at all of our watches! You was out there with them for more than an half an hour!"

In surprise, I responded, "Five to one? But that can't be, Steve. My watch is never that wrong."

Steve looked me in the eye carefully. He lowered his voice and said slowly, "They're out there today, aren't they, Charlie? Clark saw you getting out of your truck back there as he was coming up over the grade. He saw you out there next to their craft after it set down. They're out there in the sunshine, aren't they? You've seen them, haven't you? You've seen them good, up close and in the sunshine, like Doug, Bryan, and I did two summers ago. You were up real close and they were standing all around you, weren't they? You saw them like we did, didn't you! Only you didn't get to face them with us Range Rats there to back you, like we did! You were alone, weren't you? Those white bastards from the distant stars made you walk in among them alone, didn't they?

"You didn't have anyone to guard your back like Bryan, Doug, and I did, did you? We had each other the day they had us trapped out on Range Four, the day we surprised them while they were having a picnic out in the sun. That day there was no place for us to run. That day the three of us all put our backs together and stood our ground praying out loud while they surrounded us.

"But those white bastards are treating you different then they treated us, aren't they? That's why those damn American Generals picked you isn't it? That's why you're the only one that can ever come out here some days, isn't it? It's because you never panic when you're forced to face those damned white bastards alone? Isn't it, Charlie! I'm right, aren't I? DAMN IT, I'M RIGHT, AREN'T I!!

"It's because those damned white bastards and those damned American Generals want you and those white bastards to get so used to being around each other that both sides trust each other, isn't it? That's what this is all about, isn't it, Charlie? It's not about friendship, or love, is it? It's about trust! Because both those white bastards and those damned American Generals want to get beyond dealing with each other through their stupid military treaties and secret government alliances!! It's because both sides want to get to where they can trust each other, isn't it?

"It's so those creatures and the American government can form a permanent bond, a public relationship, isn't it? And that's what you and the Teacher are, aren't you? You're the first two, the first chalk white bastard and the first human who've ever trusted each other, aren't you? You two are teaching everyone else how to trust each other, aren't you?

"They were out there in the open today because now they've begun teaching their new arrivals to trust you, and now they have to prove to you that you can trust all of them too, AREN'T THEY! That's what you found when you walked around to the far side of that white scout craft of theirs, wasn't it! You found four or five new white creatures just standing there looking at you, DIDN"T YOU!

"That's why you always have to be alone, even if you're dying out here, isn't it? If you need help you have to get it from them and if they need help they have to get it from you, isn't it!

"That's why you were the only human allowed out here that hot day when their scout craft overheated and burned up half of its damn field windings, isn't it! It was because if they had needed any repair parts or food or supplies from the base at Mojave Wells, they would have had to ask you for them, WOULDN'T THEY! It's got to be that way because their Generals and our Generals require it, DON"T THEY! It's the only way for our two peoples to build trust, ISN"T IT!

"That whole thing is true, isn't, Charlie!! Tell me, Charlie! It's all TRUE, isn't it!!"

Steve looked me in the eye for a few seconds. I didn't have to answer. Good friend that he was, he knew the answer was 'Yes'."

Then Steve said slowly and seriously, "I love you like a brother, Charlie. You just remember what trust is. All of those chalk white bastards come here well armed. Each one of them has to learn not to kill you the first time you make an ordinary human mistake. I pray to God they're all good students."

Then Clark, running over from his 18-wheeler shouting excitedly "Is it true, Charlie. Are you really all right? You really haven't been touched?" Then looking at me, he continued, "It's true. They never laid a hand on you. They

315

didn't burn you or anything. I knew they were out there somewhere when my truck started acting up, just like before. I just barely made it over that rise. I had to shift way down into low gear and floor it or else they'd have stopped me too."

Not sure how to react, I replied calmly, "Thanks, guys. I really appreciate your looking after me the way you do. Don't worry, I'm fine."

Then Steve responded in low and serious tones, "Just the same, Charlie, I want you to know for the future that if you hadn't topped that rise when you did, every man here was coming out to get you. We'll do the same in the future, too. If you're ever out there and you don't come back when you're supposed to, we'll always come for you. We won't let anything stop us."

"Thanks, Steve," I responded thankfully. "I'll remember that. I want you to know that I deeply appreciate it, and that I'll always come for you, or any man here, too. I want you to know that I'll come alone, if necessary, for any one of you."

Then Bryan asked, "How much time do we have before the next flight of planes arrives up here? The duty range officer said they had taken off from Desert Center about fifteen minutes ago. They should be arriving any minute."

Doug responded, "I'll go ask him."

While we all waited, Doug climbed out of his power wagon and swiftly climbed the steps to the Range Three control tower. The duty range officer met him about half way down. After a short discussion, Doug, looking confused, walked slowly back to us.

"He said the planes have just arrived," said Doug as he pointed to a flight of six F105 fighters in the distance. "But he also said that the Desert Center base commander, responded to a request from the Pentagon and has canceled all flights over the gunnery ranges for the next two weeks. Desert Center refused to give anyone a reason. The only person who'll be allowed out here for the next two weeks is Charlie, there, the duty weather observer."

"Charlie?" exclaimed Clark.

"Yes," answered Doug. "He said that Charlie should continue to take the weather measurements, as always. The orders from the Desert Center Base commander are that Charlie can come and go out here, anywhere he wants to, anytime he pleases, but no other person is allowed out here for the next two weeks."

"Charlie?" exclaimed Clark again. "Why Charlie? Why the weather observer if they're not flying any planes?"

Then Steve answered him, "Don't worry about the reason, Clark. Charlie already knows the reason. He and those white creatures have business to attend to, all by themselves, out there in the sunshine."

Charles James Hall

Lilies of the Field

... "Consider how the lilies grow.
They do not labor or spin.
Yet I tell you,
not even Solomon in all his splendor
was dressed like one of these.

If that is how God clothes the grass of the field,
which is here today,
and tomorrow is thrown into the fire,
how much more will he clothe you,
O you of little faith! ..."

... Luke 12:27,28

A week or so passed. The ranges were quite peaceful and very little out of the ordinary happened. I made a supply trip in to Desert Center. While I was there I purchased another pair of paint by number scenes. They were fall mountain scenes and I greatly enjoyed painting them while I passed the time between balloon runs. This increased my inventory of great art paintings to four. When these two were completed, I proudly hung them on the wall next to my first two. The four paintings would never be worth much money, but I liked them.

I also checked out some more books on western history. I found the history of the Oregon Trail and the Pacific Northwest to be especially interesting. I wanted very much to visit the Whitman National Monument outside Walla Walla, Washington, and see the house where Narcissa Whitman proudly lived with her missionary husband

Marcus Whitman. If Narcissa had married the first man who asked her, she might well have become the First Lady and wife of an American President. She could have been hosting formal dinners and dances in the White House. Instead she lived in a log cabin, buried her child alone in the wilderness, and suffered murder at the hands of a group of angry Indians. Before dying, she learned that her husband and children had all been murdered the day before. Of course, if she hadn't married Marcus Whitman, there would not now be a national monument dedicated to her memory, and to her suffering. Neither would there be a copy of The Bible translated into the language of the Cayuse Indians and written in her own hand. One of the passages in Luke 11:4 begins, "Forgive us our sins, ...". I suppose the angry Indians may have read that passage in their own language before they murdered her. God works in mysterious ways.

As I put down the history book, I suddenly noticed something about the life of Narcissa Whitman that had previously escaped me. Marcus had been able to bring not more than a couple hundred pounds of equipment and tools with him when he and Narcissa and his twelve year old son walked the hundreds of miles on foot from St Joseph, Missouri to what is now Walla Walla, Washington. Yet once they arrived they needed tons of supplies in order to stay alive. This included the material for the clothes on their backs and the shoes on their feet. Almost everything had to come from the land, and the Indians that were around them. To obtain these things, they had to trade knowledge in return. Usually, all the Indians wanted in return was the knowledge of how to make guns and weapons.

Looking out into the desert to the east of me, I suddenly realized that the tall white beings that I frequently saw out there, such as the Teacher, were in virtually the same position that Narcissa Whitman was. To build even a small scout craft of any design would require many tons of supplies. It would require that far more industrial material be assembled in one location than could ever be brought here from the next star over. Many ordinary chemicals such as sulfuric acid would be needed, but they are naturally so dangerous to all living beings that they could never be transferred over such a vast distance. Chemicals of that type would have to be obtained from the local natives. All the tall whites would have to offer in return was knowledge of science and technology.

Yes, I decided, the tall white beings must be under tremendous pressure to share their science and technology with us, all along a broad front of topics, in order to receive a wide variety of supplies from the U.S. Government in return. Yet, the Teacher was annoyed because she and the young mothers were not able to obtain pretty dresses from the USAF, or a wider variety of children's clothes. The American Generals must be terrified by the tall whites and be only willing to discuss advanced space based military hardware; a topic that the tall whites would naturally have little interest in discussing since it might be used against them.

And likewise, the U.S. Government must be under tremendous pressure to receive scientific and technical information from the tall whites so that it can maintain the American way of life and keep America's enemies at bay. Yet, once the Teacher and her white friends had arrived here on earth, they must have found dealing with humans as difficult as Narcissa Whitman had found dealing with the American Indians. After all, my close friend Bryan felt justified in walking around the desert with a loaded 50 caliber rifle, shooting at a woman dressed in a nurse's uniform without even asking her who she was, if she needed help, or where she was from. If he had succeeded in murdering her with a bullet, he would probably have celebrated in much the same manner that the American Indians celebrated after murdering Narcissa with a tomahawk.

As I stood that afternoon looking out the side door of my weather shack, I got more than a good look at the winds, the sunshine, and the weather. That afternoon, I got a new view of the landscape.

A few afternoons later, I had just completed the noon run out at Range Three. The front door and the side door stood open and the gentle afternoon breezes cooled my weather shack nicely. On the slope of the mountain that sat at the northern end of the valley, some 70 miles away, I noticed that once again, after an absence of a week or so, a glass bottle lying in the exact same position as before was reflecting sunlight and glinting in the bright sunshine. I turned the radio to a nice music station, took a big drink of water from my canteen, and sat down to enjoy the music for a while. After just a minute or two, I could hear some meadowlark type sounds coming from out in the sagebrush, and the Teacher speaking loudly to the young girl who was her teenage cousin. She obviously intended that I should hear them. She was saying, "Isn't it a wonderful day. I wonder if Charlie's here."

I had to laugh to myself as I got up from my chair. A few weeks before the Teacher and I had agreed that she could come visit me anytime she wished, and she could bring any of her friends that she wished. All I asked was that they remain a hundred feet away or so, and call to me to make sure that I saw them, before coming in close to where I was. I explained that since they were naturally so quiet, I was afraid that if they came up behind me and surprised me, I would jump in surprise and accidentally bump or injure one of them. The Teacher had been laughing at the time, and had readily agreed. I had been afraid that they would feel offended but the white females were like children who never grew up. Like everything else, they turned it into a game and soon had a great time playing it.

I stepped outside through my front door and greeted her in return. "Hi Teacher. I see that you and your cousin are having fun this afternoon. You can come in as close as you wish. I just finished the noon balloon run and we can talk if you want."

"Yes," she giggled in return. Then she and her cousin crossed over the cable fence that marked the boundary to the skip bomb area and closed the distance between us to less than 10 feet. I noticed that both of the women were wearing ordinary white nylon nurse's uniforms, complete with solid white stockings, nurse's caps, white gloves, white nurse's shoes, and long sleeved dresses. They had also put on makeup and wigs. They stood in front of me looking just like two nurses. I guessed the purpose of their wigs was to conceal their communication equipment. About half a mile off to the northeast, I could see their white scout craft sitting parked with the door opening onto the bunker road. I concluded that they had come to trust me a great deal. I had come to trust them in return.

"My cousin and I are going up to Las Vegas this afternoon, to go dress shopping. How do we look?" the Teacher continued, giggling childishly.

I saw immediately the point of the visit was for me to critique their disguises. They had obviously brought the scout craft in close because the two women couldn't walk very far in this hostile desert while wearing those disguises.

"You two look just perfect," I answered. "Remember you can go anywhere you want to in Las Vegas wearing a nurse's uniform. You can gamble, play blackjack, go dress shopping, anything.

With that the Teacher and her cousin went half skipping back to the scout craft. It seemed as if this was the first time in a long time that they were going to be able to choose their own clothes.

In the fullness of time, the scout craft lifted off and continued on down the valley to the southeast. I returned inside to my desk and sat down to think about things.

That morning I had watched for a few minutes as one of the tall white beings had walked up to the ammunition bunker that sat along the base of the mountains to the east. He had walked up out of the desert valley, entered the open bunker, and stood stooped over looking at me. I also noticed that as he walked up the long sloping grade, he walked differently than a human would, and also very differently from the way that the regular white beings would. He walked very awkwardly, as though he was stepping from one lily pad to another lily pad, always standing perfectly straight up as he did so. Since these types of behavior on the part of the experienced white beings were quite unusual, I concluded that the particular individual must have just recently arrived and had not yet become used to the earth's gravity, or to being around humans.

I thought about that for a few minutes. I decided that particular tall white being must have just arrived from a planet that had a much stronger field of gravity. Such a planet would have to be significantly larger than the earth. Therefore, he must have just arrived from a planet that had no flying birds or insects, and had a higher air pressure.

323

My mind wandered some more. It seemed reasonable that such a planet would probably also have a higher average temperature, probably no oceans, a few large lakes, and many large desert areas. If I assumed that the planet he had just arrived from, was the home planet or similar to it, then it would make sense that the tall white beings enjoyed the hot desert summers here on earth, and usually stayed indoors during the cold wet winters. It would also make sense that the Teacher considered the earth to be a cold and desolate wilderness.

Of course, this raised the question, if the earth is so cold to them, why come here at all? I thought about that for a while. I remembered learning that the sun is located in the middle of a very large otherwise empty bubble in space. Most stars occur in groups with another star located within 2 light months of themselves. The sun however, is the only star in a bubble of emptiness that is more than 10 light years across. Suddenly, the pieces of the puzzle were fitting together. If the tall white beings inhabited planets on several sides of the bubble of emptiness, they would want very much to maintain a supply and repair facility on earth, the only available island refuge in the middle. The pieces to the puzzle were fitting together.

My mind ran back over what had happened the day that they had me stopped out on the Range Four road. After Clark and his POL truck had cleared the top of the grade several miles ahead of me, they had brought their scout craft alongside my truck, intentionally stalling my engine and forcing me to stop. I could clearly remember everything, including the manner in which their scout craft flared out as it came alongside of my truck, and then set down in the desert just one or two hundred feet a way. I could remember waiting in my stopped truck for the scout craft to finish shutting down.

The craft sat facing in the same direction as my truck. The only door opened. It was on the opposite side. The Teacher and Range Four Harry came out to greet me. They said they wanted to introduce me to some of her friends and show me the inside of the scout craft. They apologized for having to use the electronic controls on me, but said it was only so that I didn't accidentally touch any of the various buttons and switches inside. Then they promised me that I would be able to remember everything that had happened as soon as I was back in my truck and driving again.

The three of us walked around to the opposite side of the craft. Standing there in a receiving line were five white beings whom the Teacher introduced as having just arrived on earth for the first time. Like many young new arrivals, they stood and moved very stiffly, as if nearly frozen in fear. For this reason, it wasn't possible for me to tell if they were male or female, so I assumed that they were all young males. She said that they were college students who had come here to study the English language and American culture. They would be visiting here in the valley for only a very short time. They were a little bit shorter than the Teacher and they were quite afraid of being very close to me. None of them were willing to stand even as close as 20 feet. As the teacher introduced me, they nodded silently in turn, and then stepped back away from me until they were all standing perhaps 70 feet back out in the sagebrush. Their movements were quite awkward and it was obvious that they were still getting used to the earth's gravity.

I noted that each of then was wearing a nametag on an otherwise featureless white nylon jump suit. The new jump suits certainly appeared to be standard USAF issue. The names on the tags were printed in English and in pink lettering against the usual white background. I wondered if this meant that their parent star was an older star, such as a red star, that gave off most of its light in the pink region of the color spectrum. Since our sun gives off most of its light in the yellow region of the spectrum, normally washing out the contrast between pink and white to the human eye, I concluded that their eyes were much more sensitive to color that human eyes are.

The names printed on their name tags were names such as, "The Hiker", "The Walker", "The Climber", and so on. From this I concluded that each of them, like the Teacher, had chosen simple American names for the benefit of the American Generals. This got me to thinking. Their names seemed to me to be US Army oriented, more so than US Air Force oriented. Suddenly it made perfect sense. The personal communication equipment and the personal weapons that the tall whites carried, was of the type that U.S. Army soldiers would carry into battle. It was not of the type that USAF pilots would carry. The tall whites, in return for a base with supplies, were willing to share their Army related technology, but not necessarily their deep space related technology. Our hydrogen bombs, after all, were stable and space transportable. The new arrivals then, must be first meeting me as part of their preparation to meet with the American Army Generals. Then they could begin exchanging communication technology at Army weapons labs. Both sides would benefit.

Suddenly I also understood why they were showing me their scout craft. The new arrivals wanted to monitor my reaction to the various plastics and other ordinary building materials and non-military devices so they could prepare a list of Technology Transfer topics for the Generals on both sides to agree on in advance. Yes, one guinea pig that could be trusted to be honest could have a lot of uses.

After introducing me to each of the new arrivals in turn, the Teacher and Range Four Harry began showing me the inside of the scout craft. The design of the craft was similar to that of a large motor home. Inside, the craft was divided into two distinct parts. When coming in the door, directly in front of me was a large panel with many buttons, and a wall that divided the craft into a front part and a back part.

The front part was similar to the cockpit and inside of a small twin engine airplane and took up approximately one third of the interior space. The front part was large enough to stand up and walk around. There were two seats in the front for a pilot and copilot. The Teacher informed me that both she and Harry were excellent pilots. Behind them was a curved row of five ordinary molded seats for passengers. None of the seats came with seatbelts. It was immediately obvious that the tall whites had constructed the entire craft using parts and supplies obtained from the American industrial sector, albeit using their own special kind of know-how. The molded seat nearest me, for example, still contained its American mold markings. Although I was allowed to look briefly into the cockpit area, the Teacher and Harry were not particularly interested in showing it to me. The Teacher said that there wasn't much of anything in the cockpit that I would understand, anyway, except the switch that turned on the outside lights. She was most interested in showing me the living area portion of this flying RV, especially her dressing table and mirror where she put on her nurse's disguise.

The back half had some hammock style bunks, a kitchen area on the left side when facing the front, two microwave ovens, and a bathroom with a door for privacy in the back left corner. There was a standard RV style booth with a table and bench seats on the right next to two large viewing windows. On the left side of the craft there was another window. Along the ceiling on both sides were overhead storage compartments virtually identical to similar compartments on ordinary RVs.

Neither of the two microwave ovens had doors on them. Instead of a mechanical door, it was obvious that a different kind of force field formed the door and prevented microwaves from escaping from the oven and entering the living area when the oven was in use.

The Teacher proceeded to proudly show me her dressing table, lights, and mirror where she put on her makeup and nurse's disguise. It was really quite ordinary and could have come from any American department store. Apparently she was quite conservative in her disguises, although her makeup did seem to be in extremely short supply. One of the things she seemed proudest of was that she had gotten the American Generals to provide the mirror, the makeup, and the other parts. She apparently hadn't had much freedom of movement until she had done so. Evidently the American Generals originally believed that none of the tall white females should ever leave the mountain base. I understood the American Generals believed that female beings that have traveled several light years to get here, should not get bored stiff spending the next five years penned up on 200 acres of granite mountain land.

The Teacher also very proudly showed me the hammocks where the children slept when they became tired. Evidently taking care of the children was a big part of her life. Her description even included how she positioned them so they could look out the window as sleep overcame them.

I remembered asking the Teacher, "Where do you come from?" I remembered her smiling and answering, "From our base up on the mountain. Remember, we took you up there one time."

I continued the questions, asking, "I mean, what star does your planet revolve around?"

The Teacher, still wearing her same pleasant smile answered the question with a question, "Do you know the names that we've given to the stars?"

"No," I answered.

"So if we told you, you still wouldn't know which star it was, would you?" responded the Teacher pleasantly.

I had to laugh at myself. The tall whites loved to out think me. Evidently it was easy enough for them to do. I remember the Teacher opening up one of the top storage compartments. It was filled with several ordinary vacuum-sealed plastic bags, each one filled with a gray pudding type material. The Teacher informed me that those were ready to eat meals for the children, although occasionally the adults ate them too. I remember expressing surprise that there wasn't more food on board. She informed me that the whites don't eat anywhere near as often as humans do, so it wouldn't be a problem on this short trip. However, when they do take longer trips, they naturally load more food supplies.

Then I asked Range Four Harry if they took this craft on long trips very often. He replied that he had taken it to and from the moon a few times, and to mars and back, once. However, he said that its propulsion system wasn't very reliable and that he greatly preferred to use it only for short trips around the valley. He pointed out that all power system repairs had to be made from the outside, and that such repairs could only be performed properly when the craft was sitting inside a hanger. He also pointed out that the craft's design did not leave him with any place to store spare parts. He said that he personally only felt comfortable traveling into space in a large craft with many spare parts and whose design allowed all repairs to be made from the inside.

I asked him if this craft could exceed the speed of light. He replied yes, its design would enable it to travel much faster than the speed of light, but he was quite emphatic that no one with any common sense would use this craft to travel that fast because it was too poorly constructed. He said that the one time that he took it out to the planet mars, he had accelerated to 40 percent of the speed of light and he didn't like the way it behaved so he slowed back down. He pointed out that even at 25 percent of the speed of light the craft is covering distance so fast that if anything goes wrong, it would be too difficult for his friends to locate the craft in space. He said that the larger craft have many more safety features than this one. Features such as emergency beacons, backup power supplies, and so forth.

Then, with the tour ending, the three of us went back outside. While I stood stationary, each of the five new arrivals in turn, walked up to within 20 feet of me and said in English, "Hello, Charlie". Then they stepped back away from me. Each of them was obviously very frightened of me.

The Teacher and Harry bid me good-bye and I returned to my parked truck. I climbed inside and waited until the scout craft had lifted off. Then I remembered resuming my journey as before.

Yes, it was a relaxing afternoon in the desert. As I got up and began preparing to take the last balloon run of the afternoon, I remembered wondering if the Teacher and her cousin were going to be shopping for more kinds of makeup, as well as for dresses and shoes.

Good Samaritan

…He answered:
"'Love the Lord your God with all your heart
and with all your soul
and with all your strength
and with all your mind.';
and,
'Love your neighbor as yourself.'"

"You have answered correctly," Jesus replied.
"Do this and you will live."

But he wanted to justify himself,
so he asked Jesus,
"And who is my neighbor?"
. . . Luke 10:27,29

It was a warm Tuesday morning out at Range Three. It was specifically only three days past the full moon. Consequently, the desert and the mountains were bathed in soft beautiful moonlight as I quietly left my barracks and headed for my weather truck. I was well rested, well fed, and otherwise feeling great. I had even won a few dollars playing blackjack on my weekend trip up to Las Vegas, so naturally I felt as if I was in enlisted man's heaven. My truck started smoothly and I had fun singing my favorite songs as I brought my truck onto the Range Three road and headed on out, alone as usual, into the nighttime desert.

I was still a mile or so from the Range Three buildings when I noticed one of the larger white scout craft parked out in the desert. It sat on the ridge a mile and a half northwest of the Range Three lounge. It appeared to be one of the larger 'bus' type scout craft and it sat out there at a slight angle, facing me as I approached the buildings. All of its doors were closed, and it was completely powered down.

The 'bus' design had several rows of seats for passengers, along with a row of medium sized windows on both sides. All in all, the interior of the 'bus' design was very similar in many respects to the interior design of many twin engine commuter aircraft. Of course, it was wider, taller, and it had much more space. This one appeared to be able to hold, perhaps, 20 passengers.

Although I held a deep respect for the white beings and also for their ability to kill me if they ever became panicky, I was no longer afraid of them. Consequently, I continued with my duties just as I would have if the range area had been deserted. However, I knew that if I started the diesel and turned on the generator, the stray electricity would interfere with their microwave based communications. Since I didn't need any additional light on a beautiful night like tonight, I decided to proceed with my morning balloon run using just the moonlight and my flashlight for lighting. I parked my truck by the generator shack as usual and sang loudly as I walked over to my weather shack and began opening it up as usual.

I was opening the lock on my shack when I noticed that the large scout craft had powered up a small amount and floated over to an open place only a couple hundred feet or so west of the lounge building. I watched as it sat down on the desert in an unusually slow and careful manner. It appeared to be heavily loaded with passengers. I could not see any American military or anyone I recognized on board. However, I could see the pilot, the copilot, and several of the passengers looking at me through the various windows on the craft as it gently set down.

I wasn't surprised, then, when a few minutes later as I was beginning to fill my balloon I saw one of the chalk white guards step slowly and carefully out from behind the lounge building and take up a post standing at the base of the control tower facing me. Using his right hand, he motioned for the others to come as well. Then four or five other tall white beings stepped out from behind the lounge building as carefully as if they were stepping into a gorilla cage. They distributed themselves on both sides of the guard. They all kept a close eye on me as they inspected the plants, the dirt, the wooden steps, and everything in general in the area surrounding the base of the tower. Another three or four remained peeking at me from around the northeast corner of the building. They were obviously too afraid of me to come out on stage. There seemed to be another dozen or so white beings behind the lounge who were so terrified of me that they were only willing to peek out occasionally to see where I was and what I was doing. Except for the guard, they all behaved as though this was the first time they had ever been on earth and I was the first human they had ever seen. This appeared to include the pilot and the copilot. They were out inspecting the sagebrush and dirt around their craft, also looking as if this was their first trip to earth. All in all, the scene was actually quite comical, especially since the USAF weather training school hadn't prepared me to be a major attraction on a chalk white vacation plan.

The one thing I did notice, however, was that none of the white beings were paying any attention to the guard. The guard was taller than most, standing perhaps six and a half feet tall. I had seen him several times over the course of the last year, and tonight he appeared to be extremely ill. He had always been friendly and the two of us had learned to trust each other. He appeared to be the only member of the group who spoke English. Like the Teacher, whenever he brought a group of tourists around I knew that I was in no danger. Tonight, as I proceeded with my balloon release and my wind measurements, the guard's extreme illness obviously became worse and worse.

When I finished taking my balloon readings, I began walking back to my still darkened weather shack. I could see all of the tall white beings except the guard, re-boarding the scout craft. The guard was still standing at the base of the control tower. While I watched, the guard finally collapsed from his illness. He slid and sat down to the ground and remained sitting with his back to the tower and his arms and legs out in front of him, looking much the same as a sick collapsed chicken. He was obviously unconscious and in need of immediate medical attention.

However, none of the other white beings were aware of his plight. Off to the west, they continued loading the white scout craft and obviously making plans to lift off, leaving the guard behind. Their copilot was already closing the passenger door from the outside. I tossed my clipboard into my weather shack and began walking quickly over towards the fallen guard. I began calling out to him, "Do you need help? You look as if you are very sick."

He was obviously totally unconscious and in need of immediate medical attention. I walked over to the guard, as he lay there helpless. I could see immediately that his friends were totally unaware that he was sick and still laying there. Somehow I was going to have to keep the scout craft from lifting off and get his friends to come back for him.

Quickly I double timed past the doors and windows of the northern end of the Range Three lounge. Out to the southwest of the building, perhaps 200 feet to the southwest, the scout craft was just starting to carefully lift off. It was facing away from me, and no one was looking my way. I realized that I was taking my life in my hands by approaching the craft and its group of new white beings, but the guard's life depended on it. I ran up alongside the pilot's window and began shouting, "Your guard! Your Guard! Don't leave without your guard." The nose of the craft continued rising up as the craft continued its slow lift off. Then I realized that no one on board understood English. The pilot looked over at me as I was jumping up and down less than 20 feet from the craft. He obviously intended to continue lifting off.

Suddenly an idea came to me. I decided to pretend that I was injured. I placed both of my arms around my waist and doubled over, pretending to be in intense pain. The slow lift off of the craft stopped momentarily. Then, with the pilot watching me, I stood up and using my arms and hands began making motions over towards the Range Three lounge building. I did this several times while the pilot watched me through the cockpit window apparently trying to determine what was going on. Then, as I watched through the passenger windows, a commotion ran through the group as they began discovering that the guard wasn't on board. The craft began slowly setting back down onto the desert. Now, I stood up and walked quickly over to the southwest corner of the lounge building and stood out in the open where the pilot could see me. Then I continued making motions with my arms and hands directing the pilot's attention towards the hidden northeast corner of the lounge, next to which the guard lay collapsed. The scout craft finished setting down on the desert and powering down. It immediately became apparent that the new white beings were too afraid to open the door and come out with me standing so close. Therefore, in a very obvious and open manner I turned my back on them and began walking back over to my weather shack. I glanced behind me every few steps to make sure that they were going to get out and go get their sick guard.

When I got back to my weather shack, the guard was still laying collapsed at the base of the tower. I sat down in the front door of my weather shack to reassure the new beings that it was safe for them to go tend to their guard. However, all of them were too terrified of me to come out from behind the lounge. Three or four of them would peek at me from around the northeast corner of the lounge while they called to the unconscious guard. I was obviously in the way of their rescue effort. I decided that it would be best for them if I walked further away so they could find the courage to go get the guard. So, with my flashlight in hand, I very obviously stood up slowly, walked east to the skip bomb area, and began walking slowly southeast out into the desert, away from the Range Three graveled area. I was singing loudly as I did so. It wasn't until I had walked more than a quarter mile down to the southeast that a few of the new white beings found the courage to come out from behind the lounge and began tending to the fallen guard. The first one to come out appeared to be their pilot. I continued walking further on until they all felt safe coming out to help. Then from the base of the mountains to the north, I saw another scout craft moving quickly down the valley towards Range Three. It continued until it was only a couple hundred feet north of the control tower before sitting down quickly in the desert. Still a third craft also came down the valley and set down just a couple hundred feet west of the second. Soon there were perhaps 30 or 40 white beings around the guard working on him. They carefully picked him up and laid him down on his back. They took off part of the top of his clothing and appeared to be giving him something like a blood transfusion.

After perhaps an hour, there came a moment when the new pilot of the first craft appeared to be standing outside the group talking to one of the taller, and therefore older, white medical personnel. The pilot pointed towards where I was standing in the distance, and said something. Then, the white medical doctor appeared to shake his head in surprise and respect. The doctor seemed to be wearing the electronic communication equipment and for a few moments I could receive the scattered fragments of his thoughts. He seemed to be saying to the pilot, "That is one brave individual. If he hadn't stopped you when he did, the guard would have died. This disease is usually fatal, but fortunately we caught it in time."

The pilot appeared to be responding, "He sure is brave. I didn't understand at first. My copilot was the first one to understand and stopped me from firing on him."

Then the doctor replied, "It's a good thing your copilot stopped you. The Teacher and the American Generals would have all had fits if you had killed him."

Then, while the doctor gave the directions, the white beings carefully picked up the fallen guard by grabbing on to his arms and legs. Then they carried him very carefully over to the third white craft. Through its open door I could see that the third craft was very obviously an ambulance. Then the doctors climbed on board the ambulance and it lifted off. It headed off slowly to the north, back towards the mountains at the north end of the valley.

338

Then the white beings all returned to the remaining two craft and they departed as well. This time, however, before the new pilot of the first craft departed, he first made a complete and full search of the entire Range Three area. He even checked inside of my weather shack, around the supply sheds, and inside of the generator shack. From the distance I noted that he no longer appeared to be afraid of me. As he was checking the various buildings, he frequently had his back towards where I was standing. It didn't appear to concern him in the slightest when I moved around. I guess that's what trust is all about.

After the white craft had lifted off and the Range Three area was deserted again, I walked back to my weather shack. It was dawn and the morning sunrise was beautiful. By now I was getting very hungry. I quickly completed my wind calculations and phoned Desert Center. Dwight answered the phone. He was laughing and very happy. He was saying, "Charlie, you're so late with the winds, to hell with them. The command post doesn't care. I don't know what went on up there this morning, but the Desert Center base commander phoned us way back at 5:00 a.m. and ordered us to send you in for breakfast just as soon as all of the commotion that went on up there was finished. Smokey in the chow hall has a real nice special breakfast fixed for you this morning. Just shut down and go in and get it."

A little over a month went by. It was a beautiful sunny morning. The ranges were closed and I was driving back out for the 8:00 a.m. run. As I was taking the balloon out to be released, I noticed that, once again, a large white scout craft of the 'bus' design had parked a couple hundred feet west of the Range Three lounge. As I stood holding my balloon, waiting the last few minutes until it was time to release it, the same tall white guard who had previously

339

collapsed at the base of the tower stepped out from behind the lounge building. This time he walked slowly towards me until he stood facing me less than 20 feet away. He appeared to be recovering, but the lingering effects of his illness were still clearly visible.

Then the occupants of the craft, about 15 in number, along with the Teacher and an American three star General all stepped out from behind the lounge building and formed up into a long broad line across the northern portion of the graveled area. They stood facing me. I noticed that a few of the white beings appeared to be many of the same doctors who had worked on the guard when he was sick. Since I had long since gotten used to trusting the Teacher and the guard, I wasn't the slightest bit afraid. I stood naturally, waiting for them to finish moving into their positions. The General was too far away for me to salute him. I greeted the guard. I said, "Good morning. I am glad to see that you are recovering. I was very worried about you."

The guard smiled, and said, "Thanks, Charlie. I owe you my life. If you should ever need help, you may ask for me. You may call me 'The Tour Guide.'"

I thanked him. Then, without further ado, the procession and the guard returned to the scout craft and lifted off, leaving me to enjoy the remainder of the day in solitude.

Landing Lights

... The fifth angel sounded his trumpet,
and I saw a star
that had fallen from the sky to earth.

The star was given the key
to the shaft of the Abyss.

When he opened the Abyss,
smoke rose from it
as the smoke from a gigantic furnace.

... Revelation 9:1,2

"Nice theodolite," stated Doug. "Mind if I look through it?"

"Go right ahead," I replied. "I've already phoned my 8:00 a.m. winds in to Desert Center. I have at least an hour to kill. Here, I'll show you how to use it."

"I already know," replied Doug proudly. "I learned to use this thing when we were making up winds for Sullivan."

"Really?" I replied. "You know how to take the azimuth and elevation readings? You can remove the lens cap, clean the lenses and everything?"

"Of course," replied Doug with obvious pride. "I know how to turn the scale lights on and off for night readings, and how to adjust the magnification from 10x right up to 500x power. I can also level the theodolite before using it. All of my readings are accurate and reproducible. The only reason I had to make up the winds was because I didn't know how to do the calculations. Of course, I can't play with the theodolite anymore like I used to. None of us have a key for the padlock. You always put your own locks on your weather shacks and your equipment. Now, no one but you has any of the keys."

"It's just a bad habit, I guess," I laughed in reply. "I just like to keep track of my equipment out here on the ranges."

"One thing I noticed, Charlie," continued Doug thoughtfully, "is that whenever you finish using the theodolite, you always move it to azimuth 90, elevation zero. Why is that?"

"It makes it easier to put that big thick metal cover over the theodolite when I'm locking it up. See, if I point the theodolite towards the east and crank it down, I can put on the cover quickly and easily." Then I showed Doug how I put on the cover. "Remember, I'm out here on many very dark nights. Frequently I'm sleepy or in a hurry to get in to breakfast. So it's another useful habit I developed."

"That's really clever of you, Charlie," replied Doug.

Doug and I both noticed our good friend Wayne. He was ambling over from the Range Three lounge.

"Hey, Charlie, can I look through that thing for minute, too?" asked Wayne eagerly.

"Sure Wayne," I answered. "Some of the trees up on Big Bear Mountain there to the east, are beautiful this summer."

"That's not what I want to look at," replied Wayne. First he adjusted the theodolite to a high magnification. In a deliberate manner, he cautiously pointed the theodolite towards the base of the mountains slightly west of north from Range Three. Then he began carefully scanning a region of desert some 35 miles north of the Range Three buildings.

"You have the elevation way too low," I cautioned Wayne. "You won't see anything down that low except sagebrush. If we knew where to look, maybe you could see the planet Venus in the day time."

"To hell with Venus," replied Wayne in friendly tones. "I'm looking for Range Four Harry."

Laughing at what I believed to be Wayne's practical joke, I replied, "What would Harry be doing up that way on a nice day like today?"

However, neither Wayne nor Doug, were laughing. Wayne carefully focused in on a distant arroyo winding its way east from the base of one of the distant mountains to the northwest. Wayne stepped back from the theodolite and motioned me towards the eyepiece. "Here, Charlie take a good look at that," he stated.

Looking through the eyepiece, I studied the distant arroyo for a few seconds. Backing away from the theodolite, I turned to Wayne and laughed, "That's a pretty good practical joke, Wayne. There's so much haze this late in the morning, a man would have to have x-ray vision to see anything important. What should I see, Range Four Harry waving at me?"

Neither Wayne nor Doug joined in the laughter, though. Wayne replied, "No, of course not, Charlie. You should record these theodolite readings. Then, at night when you're out here alone and the air is clearer, you should move the theodolite back to those same readings and keep track of what happens up in that stretch of desert."

Seeing how serious both of my friends were, I decided to humor them. Taking a pen and a piece of scratch paper from my fatigue pocket, I recorded the theodolite readings. Putting the pen and paper back into my pocket, I continued laughing, "See, just to make my friends happy, I've recorded the readings. Shows you the kind of guy I am. Now, when I do look through the theodolite, what should I see, Range Four Harry having a picnic?"

Still serious, Wayne and Doug exchanged glances. Then Doug continued, "You can call it Range Four Harry's picnic area if you want to, Charlie, but the Range Rats call it his playground. Whenever we see him up there, he frequently seems to be looking for something.

"You see, there's something very real hidden in that arroyo up there that is right next to that playground area in the sagebrush. You can't see it from here, but that arroyo is one of the hidden places in this valley where Harry likes to come out of. There's other places, like the springs over those mountains to the west, but that arroyo up to the northwest is one of his favorites."

I still wasn't sure just what point my friends were trying to make, "But there's nothing up that way except sagebrush and sand. If Harry likes that valley he must be part jackrabbit."

"You don't understand, Charlie," cautioned Wayne. "There's a concrete bunker up that way. It's dug into the side of that arroyo. You can't see it from here but Doug, Steve, and I have all been up there. We'd take you up there and show it to you, but Steve says it's just too dangerous. He won't let any of us range rats get anywhere close to it."

"You say there's an old ammunition bunker up that way?" I asked. I silently wondered if it was the same bunker I had come across that day so many months before when I had driven up towards the north end of the valley. I had never mentioned that bunker to anyone. It was very seldom that I described my experiences, even to my closest friends. I was actually very close-mouthed and quite defensive because it always seemed to me as if my friends were much

344

braver than I was. It seemed as if they had been everywhere and seen practically everything. The day that I had visited the bunker, for example, I had been too afraid to open the lower door and look inside. Now I was too embarrassed to admit that I'd been afraid, so I preferred to play dumb and pretend that I didn't know the bunker was there.

"No," answered Wayne. "That's not what I said. It's not an old ammunition bunker. It's obviously been there for many years, maybe more than 100 years. It isn't anything left over from World War two. Steve thinks it's an underground aircraft hanger with underground living facilities. We stumbled across it one day two years ago when we were up that way with Steve."

"What's it like?" I asked innocently.

"The hanger part has concrete doors that open to the arroyo. The hanger entrance is maybe 100 feet wide and 40 feet high. The entrance faces north, so you can't see it from here," responded Wayne. "The hanger entrance does not sit at the base of the arroyo wall. Instead, The entrance is itself located 15 or 20 feet up from the sand in the arroyo. Only a vehicle that can stop in mid air and hover, like a helicopter, can use the entrance. The arroyo is probably 100 or 200 feet wide there, so vehicles that are fairly large can use the hanger.

"Up on top of the arroyo, there is another tall, wide, concrete doorway with thick wooden double doors. The doorway is maybe 10 or 15 feet high and 10 feet wide. It's set back into the next set of rocks so it can't be seen from here, either. The day we were there, the door up on top wasn't locked. When we first discovered it, we thought as you do. We thought it was an old abandoned ammunition bunker. Steve waited in the power wagon and kept the engine running. Steve stayed on the radio to Bryan, the Air

Policeman. He stayed in town at the base motor pool. Doug and I went to inspect the hanger. Steve insisted that only one of us go inside, so Doug kept the door open up on top while I went down inside. I really had to hurry because Steve refused to give us much time to inspect the place. He said it was too dangerous being that close in to Harry. He insisted that if I were out of sight or if we were out of communication for more than 15 minutes, the Air Policeman would declare an emergency and send help.

"Inside there was a long stairway down to an inner door into the hanger. The place must have been built for really tall people because all of the doorways and hallways inside were at least 15 feet tall. The inner door to the hanger wasn't locked either, so I opened it up and went inside. The hanger was probably 600 or 700 feet long. That day, the hanger was empty. There was still another concrete door inside the hanger that appeared to lead to some living quarters, but that door was locked tight as a drum. I'm certain there was someone in there behind the door though, because I could hear sounds through the concrete. They were the kind of sounds that horses and birds might make, whinnies, meadow lark sounds, and things."

I stood quietly, remembering the afternoon when I had been out exploring that arroyo myself.

"The lights were on in the hanger. It had lighting panels in the ceiling but I couldn't tell if the lights were fluorescent or not. We never did figure out where it was getting the electricity. The thing about the hanger that I still can't get over though, Charlie, is the writing on the walls. The writing was entirely in hieroglyphics."

"You mean like the Ancient Egyptian hieroglyphics?" I asked, "Like the ones found in the pyramids?"

"Yes," answered Wayne. "Only there were a lot more of them. Some were simple. Some were very complicated. There were all different kinds. Of course, I can't read hieroglyphics, so I don't know what they said. Some of them must have been pretty simple, though. For example, one set was next to an arrow that pointed to a fire extinguisher."

"I saw the hieroglyphics, too," chimed in Doug. "They were on the doors and hallways. They were everywhere."

"The hieroglyphics were painted entirely in bright pink with a white background," stated Wayne. "I tell you. Charlie, the whole experience scared us silly. I was happy as hell to get out of there."

"Me, too!" added Doug. "You should have seen Steve once we got back into the truck. He was certain that we were being watched from one of those mountains north of here. He had that power wagon floored coming out of there. He hasn't been anywhere near that arroyo since."

"Well, I'll remember that it's up that way," I stated.

We were all young men. The conversation turned naturally to Las Vegas dancers, beautiful young women, and cars. It was Monday, and each of us had weekend adventures to share. Soon it was time for Wayne and Doug to return to picking up 40 pound practice bombs in the hot sun. The time for my 10 a.m. run came. The desert heat was soon above 110 degrees. After finishing my balloon run, I was happy to return to reading one of my history books in the cool interior of my weather shack. It was a pleasant day in the desert and it passed quickly enough. Without thinking much about things, I placed the paper with Wayne's theodolite readings on a shelf in my weather shack. When my last run was completed, out of force of habit, I returned my theodolite to its 'close down' readings, 90 degrees azimuth, 0 degrees elevation. I placed the cover over it, and locked it securely. Everything seemed normal as I closed down the diesel and headed into town.

After the evening meal, I walked over to my friend's barracks to talk with them some more, but they were all too exhausted from the hard day they had spent picking up practice bombs in the hot desert sun. They had worked an extra couple of hours in the distant valley to the west. They were all in their bunks, exhausted, and sound asleep by 8:30 p.m. I had a tremendous amount of respect for them. They had one of the most demanding assignments in the US Air Force.

A couple of mornings later, the Teacher, the three children, and the two young male guards were playing on the Range Three graveled area, as I was finishing up my morning balloon run. This night the two guards had taken up military positions just northeast of my theodolite stand, in front of the Range Three billboards. The Teacher was standing 50 feet or so east of me near the cable fence. She was enjoying herself watching the children as they played on the wooden steps of the stairs to the control tower. Tonight the children had shown little interest in my theodolite. After I had written down the last readings, I picked up my clipboard and walked slowly over to where the Teacher stood. Then we talked while the children played.

"Until I met you and your people, I always thought that the Earth was the only inhabited planet in the universe," I continued.

"Why did you think that?" she asked playfully. "When you look up at the sky at night you can see thousands of stars. On our planet, the air is so thick and cloudy that we can never see them. Our scientists didn't realize that the other stars were out there until they had learned to build a craft that could fly up above the clouds and give them a view of space. That's why we all enjoy walking around this beautiful desert at night. We can't do that where we come from.

"After you saw the stars at night, surely you didn't think you were alone in space?" she asked playfully.

Once again I had to laugh at myself for having been out thought. "Yes, but it was very silly of me," I said. "Do you have nice summers like this where you come from?"

"Yes," she said, "However, we do not have fall or winter like you have here. We also do not have any birds or animals that fly. That's why we all laughed so hard when you thought we looked like giant white seagulls.

"We don't have any insects that fly either. Things such as bees and wasps terrify us a greatly. If a bee stings us, we can't just brush it off as you did two weeks ago. We have to go to the hospital immediately before we collapse."

"Are there many planets like the Earth out in space?" I asked.

"Yes," she responded. "There are quiet a few. However, humans are the only people that we have seen who live so closely with their animals. For example, you feel comfortable milking cows, riding horses, and playing with dogs. Every one of those animals could kill you, but you naturally use your intelligence to determine how each of those animals is thinking. Then you naturally take control of them. Only humans do that. On most planets, once people become intelligent, they don't want to have anything to do with the animals that are much less intelligent then they are, so they kill them off.

"Also, humans will eat almost anything. On all of the other planets, the intelligent people will only eat plants. We, for example, only eat plants."

We laughed together. Then she said, "Well, we have to leave now, Charlie. The children are becoming tired and they need their rest."

We said good night to each other. I returned to my weather shack to finish my computations. They gathered into the horse formation and floated off quickly up the road towards Range Four. I stayed late that morning and watched them from a distance before I headed in for breakfast. After they reached Range Four, they headed up the valley towards the northwest, obviously heading towards the bunker that Wayne had pointed out to me.

A few uneventful days passed and the night of the full moon came. One more day passed. During those days my breakfast appetite increased a little, but my ability to sing off-key remained about the same.

The next morning, 3:00 a.m. came soon enough. The drive out to Range Three was another beautiful experience in the warm, moonlit nighttime desert. As usual, I was singing to myself as I headed out through the sagebrush on the Range Three road. As I left base, I noticed that all of the range power wagons were parked in their normal places inside the fenced area of the motor pool.

A quick stop in the generator shack to start the diesel, a few minutes to open my weather shack, a couple minutes to get my radio turned on good and loud, no muss, no fuss. I was in business. As usual, prior to filling my balloon, I walked and sang my way out to unlock and level my theodolite. As I reached for the padlock, something seemed out of place. The padlock felt like it was hanging in a different position than when I had locked it the day before.

Shrugging off the feeling, I unlocked the lock and removed the heavy metal cover in a single smooth motion. I removed the inner watertight plastic cover and took stock of the situation. The theodolite was still in perfect condition, but it wasn't pointing towards the east as I had left it the day before. Instead, it was pointing towards the northwest, towards the arroyo that Wayne had identified. I stood quietly studying my equipment. It took a few minutes for the implications to sink in.

At first I suspected my range maintenance friends. I supposed they were the cause of this. I was annoyed thinking they hadn't respected my equipment. Then, remembering how tired the Range Rats usually were at night, I decided that the Teacher and her friends must have been using my theodolite during the night. However, she and the children had much more fun looking through the theodolite while I was taking my balloon measurements. After giving the matter careful thought, I decided that this must be the work of a new group of white children.

When I looked through the theodolite to see what it was focused on, I couldn't see anything at night. When I returned the theodolite to the same settings after daybreak, I still couldn't see anything but sagebrush and sand.

When the 2:00 p.m. run was finished and I had phoned the winds in to Desert Center, I slowly walked back out to my theodolite to lock it up. There was still nothing but desert and sky to be seen anywhere. I decided to begin a new habit. First I locked up the theodolite as usual. Then, back inside my weather shack, I took my just completed weather reporting form and made a small letter 'X' in the upper left hand corner. Next to it, as lightly as I was able to, I recorded the azimuth, elevation, and magnification readings for the theodolite when it had been opened up that morning. Then I stored the weather form in its normal place, locked my weather shack, shut down the diesel, and drove back into base, singing loudly as I did so.

The next morning began normal enough. It was the usual beautiful drive for the entire 22 miles out to Range Three. I left fifteen minutes early so I would have some extra time. I was healthy as a horse, well-rested, happy, singing, and intensely curious about the state of my theodolite. I started up the diesel as normal, opened up my weather shack, turned on the lights and radio. Then, flashlight and clipboard in hand, I walked slowly out to my theodolite. As I unlocked the padlock, I mentally noted that it hung backwards from the way I had left it the day before. Appearing not to notice, I removed the metal cover with a smooth motion, along with its protective plastic bag. Just as the day before, someone had been playing with my theodolite. This time, however, it was pointed towards Mount Stockton that lay some 70 miles to the northeast. The theodolite was focused in on a place just below the upper tree line. Other than a forest of trees, along with a few rocks, nothing in particular could actually be seen through the theodolite. I quickly committed the readings to memory and carried on with my work in a normal manner. Returning to my weather shack, once again I recorded the theodolite readings by writing them lightly in pencil on the back of my weather form.

I continued this habit of recording my theodolite readings whenever I opened up my theodolite for the next two weeks. At first my theodolite was out of position only when I first opened it up for the 4:30 a.m. run in the early morning. Then, some days my theodolite would be out of position when I came back from breakfast or lunch. Many times, it would be pointed to one or the other of those two places, the desert arroyo from the mountains to the northwest, or to the upper tree line on Mount Stockton to the northeast. Occasionally it would be pointed to anyone of three other places in the desert north of me. On one morning, it was pointed towards the star Arcturas.

Then, just as suddenly as they had begun, whoever was using my theodolite stopped doing so. I noted that the last morning my theodolite had been moved was just one day before the new moon. Now, morning after morning I would find my theodolite in its shut down position, exactly the way I had left it the night before. Naturally, the entire episode made me curious. However, since it wasn't actually a problem for me, I did not wish to ask the Teacher about it on those occasional nights when she and the children came to play.

One hot afternoon, while I was killing time until the last run of the day, I decided to try a new approach. I took one of my spare clipboards and 10 empty forms. I left the top 5 forms blank. Then, on each one of the bottom 5 empty forms, I carefully copied a different complete balloon report. I included the release times, the azimuth and elevation readings, everything. I chose all of these runs from the same day. I picked a day with ordinary light desert winds. Using large letters, I labeled the bottom 5 "Calculation Training Sheets", and made them appear to be part of my training materials. Then, on the back of each one of these, in very light pencil, I wrote the 5 sets of azimuth and elevation readings for those 5 special points out in the desert and mountains to the north of me. This allowed me preserve those five settings even if I took part of my annual leave and another team of observers replaced me for a few days.

Then, I began a systematical study of those five places towards which the theodolite had been pointed. I did so under a wide variety of sunlight and weather conditions. At first I couldn't make out much of anything. Everything just appeared to be desert rocks, sagebrush, and sand. Then, one windy morning as the rays of light from the early morning sun were just beginning to illuminate the desert and the mountains, I suddenly realized that all five of the places were protected playground areas for children. I was stunned by the simplicity of it all.

I knew the white children loved to play the game Hide-and-Go-Seek with their mothers, but until this morning I had always thought of the game as a game that was played up close. Suddenly I realized what had been going on. The tall white communication systems covered the entire valley. Their communications easily allowed a young mother to make the long journey down to Range Three, and use my theodolite to play Hide-and-Go-Seek with her children, while her children remained hiding on their protected playgrounds more than 70 miles away. Yet the Teacher always brought her group of children with her. The conclusion was inescapable. During those two weeks, there had been a second young white woman with a new group of children visiting the Ranges. My mind continued to the obvious conclusion. If the tall whites need a base on the Earth to repair and re-supply their craft as they cross the huge empty bubble of space in which the sun is located, then while they are here on earth, the young mothers would naturally take their children out to those protected playgrounds and let them exercise in the fresh air and sunlight. I was stunned by the simplicity of it all. The white craft from deep space obviously came and left on schedule. The young mother had arrived on the night of the full moon and left on the night of the new moon. Just like Steve had told me so many months before, there were cycles and schedules to things here in the valley. Each schedule corresponded to a different craft making the rounds to and from a different place, just like passenger airliners servicing international routes. I was absolutely stunned by the simplicity of it all.

I also realized what else it meant. It meant that somewhere up on the mountain to the northeast, very, very close to the tree covered playground, there had to be the entrance to a very large hanger.

It was mostly out of curiosity, then, that I began a regular study of that area of the mountain. For several weeks, all I could identify was the playground area and its trees. Then, one unusually cold windy morning, just as the sun was coming up, I noticed a small cloud of steam and smoke rising above the trees a short distance on the mountain above playground area. During the 4:40 a.m. balloon run, I had measured the winds aloft at the same height as the upper tree line on the mountain as averaging almost 70 mph. Of course, the trees bent and swayed as each gust of wind passed. This allowed me to see more details than I had previously been able to. I followed the cloud of steam to its base. There, hidden behind the trees in the granite of the mountain, was the entrance to a huge underground concrete hanger. Using my theodolite and the principles of trigonometry, I measured the entrance to be at least 100 feet high and at least 500 feet wide. Such a hanger would be able to hold the largest of the ocean liners, so I decided that it could hold large deep space craft as well.

That morning, as I drove in to breakfast, I thought things through. A gravity powered spacecraft, coming to earth from outside the solar system, would be very conscious of the position of the earth's moon and the direction that the earth was traveling in its orbit. A pilot of a large, hard to maneuver passenger craft would almost certainly prefer to land at sun down during the night of the full moon. At that time, the earth would be moving away from him so he would be approaching the earth by first trailing it in its orbit in much the same manner that a navy pilot lands on an aircraft carrier. He would have the full moon on his right and the sun on his left, and therefore be entering a smooth balanced gravitational field as he approached the earth to land.

On the other hand, when such a pilot wanted to take off from the earth again, of course he could wait a full month for another full moon. However, after waiting only two weeks, he could also take off easily at midnight during the night of the new moon. During such a take off, he would be taking off directly away from both the sun and the moon and heading directly out of the solar system. He could quickly accelerate to whatever speed he desired because during the night of the new moon, the moon is between the earth and the sun, so taking off at midnight, the pilot would have gravitationally smooth empty space in front of him during the take off.

As I drove in to breakfast, I noted the phase of the moon and wondered if seeing a deep space craft was really going to be that simple. It was. At sundown of the next full moon, I stayed late at my weather shack. Using my theodolite, I watched a large black double domed shaped craft wait for more than 45 minutes for all of the doors on the hanger to open. It had windows all around it. It was sleek and polished and, obviously, it was totally repairable from the inside. It was so large that it probably didn't have more than 3 feet of clearance on either side of the hanger entrance, or on its top or bottom. When the doors were open, it finally floated slowly into the hanger. Two weeks later at midnight, during the night of the full moon, I watched the hanger doors open and the same craft silently float out to the concrete tarmac out front. When it lifted off, just as I had expected, it headed straight up. It was out of sight in less than four seconds. With that rate of acceleration, I suppose that it could reach the speed of light in less time than it took the hanger doors to close again. Since the solar system is only eight or ten light hours across, I suppose that if the pilot had chosen to, he could have passed the planet Pluto before I had time to lock up and return to base.

And just as I had guessed, I could see that craft again, anytime I wanted to. All I had to do was wait for sundown on the night of the next full moon.

Favorite Pony

> … They so love to wander
> that they do not spare their feet.
> … Jeremiah 14:10

One evening the Teacher, the three children, and the two young male guards were playing on the Range Three graveled area, as I was finishing up my 4:30 a.m. morning balloon run. They were all wearing their protective fluorescent suits.

Usually, whenever they came in the evening, they wore their fluorescent suits. However, when they came in the daytime, they only wore the suits on special occasions. Usually when they came during the day, they came wearing ordinary nylon or cotton clothing and footwear. The protective suits were battery powered. The suits had to be recharged after only six or eight hours of operation, and the tall whites apparently considered the suits to be a bit of a nuisance when they wanted to enjoy being out in the warm sunshine.

This night the two guards as usual, had taken up military positions along the eastern wall of the Range Three lounge building. The Teacher was standing 50 feet or so west of me. She was enjoying herself watching her daughter play with the other two boys. After I had written down the last readings, I picked up my clipboard and pencil and told the children they could look through my theodolite now if they wanted to. Then I walked slowly over to where the Teacher stood. "Good evening Teacher," I began. "The children look happy tonight."

"Yes, Charlie," she laughed in return. "See, you never had any reason to be afraid of us. We never get in your way. We let you go anywhere you want, anytime you want."

"You're correct, as usual," I replied. "At first I was afraid because you looked so different from me."

"You have never been afraid of any of the people you meet up in Las Vegas. Those people are from many other places on the earth and they look very different from you. If you were not afraid of them, why were you afraid of us?" she teased. She loved to out think me. It came so easy to her.

I had to laugh at myself. Then I said, "You're correct as usual, Teacher. It was silly of me. I just didn't know how to act at first when you and the children came around."

Then the Teacher, laughing, replied, "We just want you to enjoy being around us when we come."

Every time I remember the Teacher, I remember her, the way she was that night.

Some weeks later, I had just completed the 12:30 p.m. early afternoon run out at Range Three. The front door and the side door of my weather shack stood open. The gentle afternoon breezes cooled my weather shack nicely. My radio was tuned to a good music station. I had just finished phoning Desert Center and was hanging up the phone when I heard some meadowlark type sounds coming from out in the sagebrush. Then I heard the Teacher speaking loudly to her daughter. She obviously intended that I should hear them. She was saying, "It is such a beautiful day. I wonder if Charlie can come out and play with us."

Laughing a little, I stepped out of my front door and replied, "Hello, Teacher. Yes, I have an hour or so to play."

Sitting out in a clearing in the sagebrush a quarter mile or so straight to the east sat the "RV" scout craft. It sat facing the south with the open door on the far side. "I was hoping that you could walk over to where we are parked and talk to the children for a few minutes, Charlie. You know that they always enjoy it."

"Yes, teacher. I am quite happy to talk to the children," I replied. The three of us, then, the Teacher, her daughter, and myself walked over to the front of the scout craft and around to the other side. The two guards had erected a small canvas awning outside, and this provided a reasonably sized shaded area for the Teacher, the three children, and I, to stand in as we talked. The Teacher, the children, and all of the guards were wearing ordinary white nylon and cotton clothing and footwear. As usual, it appeared as if the USAF had ordered their apparel directly from a department store catalog.

As requested by the Teacher, I took my truck keys out of my pocket and held them in my out stretched left hand. The three children gathered around me to my left, and slightly behind me. They stood there like a bunch of baby birds, giggling.

The Teacher asked them, "Do any of you children know what these are?"

After waiting a minute or so, while the children giggled, she continued, "Those are the keys to Airman Baker's truck. You see, children; Airman Baker does not want anyone except himself, to drive his truck. So whenever he isn't driving his truck, he keeps the keys in his pocket."

The children's giggles broke into open laughter.

Then the Teacher asked me if I had any pictures in my wallet. "Yes," I replied, and took out my wallet. I opened it up to an autographed picture of a young movie star. The movie star had handed it to me directly during one of my previous visits to the USO in Los Angeles.

"Do any of you children know whose picture this is?" asked the Teacher playfully.

"Is it a picture of airman Baker's girl friend?" asked the Teacher's daughter. Then the Teacher and all three of the children began laughing.

Then the little fat boy raised his hand and asked, "Teacher, if the American Generals brought that lady out here to the desert where we are, would airman Baker let her drive his truck?"

With that, all of the white beings broke into hysterical laughter. The children, the Teacher, and the guards were all helpless with laughter.

The laughter continued for a time. When the Teacher was finally able to compose herself, and she continued, "You see, children, I told you Airman Baker was more interesting than any of the other weather observers before him. In fact," she continued, still giggling herself, "I am going to inform the American Generals that our class has taken a vote and we've decided that Airman Baker is our favorite pony."

With that, pandemonium broke out among the white beings. The laughter continued for some time.

Every time I remember that little group of two guards, three children, and the Teacher, I remember them that way, the way they were on that sunny afternoon.

Tarmac

…But a Samaritan, as he traveled,
came to where the man was;
and when he saw him,
he took pity on him.
…Luke 10:33

Any night at the Desert Center weather station could turn out to be a quiet, lonely affair, but Sunday nights could especially leave a man counting the walls, hoping their number had changed. This rainy, lonely Sunday night in November was certainly no exception. The cold rain and drizzle had been going on for hours, drenching everything in the valley. I was surprised when the emergency phone from the tower rang. Picking it up, I answered, "Weather station, airman Baker speaking."

The tower operator on the other end seemed almost afraid to tell me why he'd phoned. "Charlie, I'm sorry to do this to you, but I had no choice."

"Do what?" I asked.

"I've had an in-flight emergency forced on me by the Palmdale air traffic controller. It's a really bad one, and I'm afraid that not even you are going to be able to handle it," he said apologetically.

"God handles everything," I shrugged, "I just handle the prayers."

"Here's one we're probably both going to need God's help on. I have a damaged F105 in-bound to Desert Center and he has to land here, right away. He'll be arriving in about ten minutes."

"I don't understand," I answered. "As you know, I've had the base closed since 4:00 p.m. this afternoon. Our east-west runway can't be used because there's a big section in the middle being resurfaced. For more than two hours now, a huge thunderstorm has been sitting over the north end of our north-south runway. I don't see why he wants to come in here. He has a much better chance of landing safely if he heads up to Las Vegas McCarren or heads up to George."

"He can't," responded the tower. "He's in desperate trouble. He was flying over near Kingman when his plane got hit with hail the size of grapefruit. It smashed his cockpit window and shattered his left arm and his left leg. His right wrist has been damaged too. He can barely fly the plane. He's groggy from the loss of blood. He's been bleeding all over the inside of his cockpit. He can't bail out in this storm. That would kill him for sure. He doesn't have enough blood left to make it to George. Las Vegas won't have him. They're covered with storms. They've already given him up for dead. They say he's too injured to be able to land his plane anywhere, and they're afraid that he would do too much damage by crashing into a civilian airliner or into a lounge.

"I had no choice, Charlie. I had to take him. He's coming here to either land or die. You'll have to bring him in somehow. Palmdale located a navy captain in an A6 who was headed for Navy Miramar at San Diego. The navy captain changed his course and came back across the Mojave Desert to help the F105 pilot make it to Desert Center, but he's going to be short on fuel when he gets here. The navy captain reports that the pilot is almost unconscious and he doesn't think the F105 pilot can make a safe landing. We're going to have to think of a way to bring both planes in, Charlie. I'm out of ideas. I just don't know what to do."

"We'll just have to show the other airfields how things are done, I suppose." I answered. Still holding the phone in my hand, I walked outside onto the tarmac. A cold steady rain was falling, and I was shivering as I walked. I studied the clouds over the runway in the distance for a minute or so. Then an idea presented itself. Speaking into the phone, I said, "The storm over the north end of the runway is too bad for the F105 to land from the north, and it's probably better for him if he lands on the north-south runway by making a straight-in approach to the south end."

"But the wind is from the south," answered the tower operator. "He'll be landing with the wind. It'll mean that he'll be landing fast and have very little control."

"I know," I answered. "But the wind isn't very strong. The down drafts from the thunderstorm mean that once he's a little way down the runway, the winds will change in his favor. I want you to re-deploy the two fire trucks that are out by the runway. I want one of them to take up a position along the far side the runway, one third of the way from the south end. I expect the winds to change there. I want the other one to take up a position in the middle, also on the far side of the runway. That's where the heavy rain begins. Both trucks should have their lights on and flashing. Have the ambulances take positions next to the fire trucks."

"Roger. Copy," responded the operator.

"Now tell the navy captain who's helping the F105, to have the F105 put down its gear as soon as the pilot can get it down. Have him shepherd the F105 straight towards the south end of the runway. Tell the navy pilot to be on the west side of the F105 as it comes in so the wind doesn't blow the two planes into each other."

"Roger. Copy," responded the tower.

"Remember, on the first pass the F105 is going to land, but the navy pilot is going to have to go around again for his landing chance.

"Tell the navy pilot to treat the first fire truck as though it marked the end of the runway. Have him bring the F105 in as low as he can and as slow as he can. Make sure the F105 pilot is below 20 feet when it reaches the first fire truck. Tell the Navy captain to have the F105 pilot locate his parachute deployment lever. As soon as the F105 reaches the first fire truck, have him deploy the parachute and cut his engine. It'll slow the plane, suddenly, and it'll drop right onto the runway in between the two fire trucks. That way the pilot can just let the airplane roll. The parachute will stop it."

"Roger. Copy," responded the operator. A short pause ensued. In the distance, I could see the fire trucks and ambulances moving to their new positions. Then the operator came back on the phone, "The planes are four minutes away now. The navy captain reports that the F105 pilot is too groggy to reply on the radio, but the captain believes he's still conscious because the gear came down as requested."

As I strained my eyes looking into the rain in the distance, the storm clouds seemed to part a little, letting the two airplanes appear through the darkness and the rain, as though flying down a valley between the clouds. The F105 pilot was obviously struggling to control the plane as it headed through the lightening and the rain. Pieces of metal around the gaping holes on its left side could be seen tearing away from its fuselage. Speaking into the phone, I said, "I see them. Do you see them too?"

"Roger," responded the tower.

As I waited anxiously, the navy captain quietly shepherded his precious cargo down over the runway. Flying alongside the wounded F105 he brought the two planes down to less than ten feet above the runway. Then as the planes reached the first fire truck, to my great relief I saw the parachute on the F105 deploy. The pilot, with his last conscious act cut the engine, dropping the F105 perfectly on to the runway. Un-noticed at the time, the navy captain had risked his life to help the F105 land. Refusing to abandon the damaged F105, he too had brought his plane down to less than 10 feet above the rocky grass area on the western side of the runway.

The F105, once it touched down, rolled part way down the runway. Then, as the pilot went unconscious, it rolled to the right and came to a gentle stop, completely blocking the runway. It happened that it was positioned directly in front of the second fire truck. This allowed the rescue crew to reach the plane and the injured pilot immediately. As it did so, the Navy Captain at last fed fuel to his engines and began regaining altitude.

I waited a few minutes. Then, speaking into the phone, I said, "How is he?"

A long pause followed, then the operator answered, "The ambulance driver reports that the pilot was unconscious and a pool of blood covered the entire floor of the cockpit when they got there. He's going to live, but it appears that they are going to have to give him more than six pints of blood to save him. He would have been dead for sure in another 30 seconds. Honestly, Charlie, nobody could have brought him in safely except you."

"Thanks for the compliment," I responded. "How much fuel does the navy captain have, and how long will it take the ground crew to clear the runway so he can land?"

A long pause ensued. Then, sounding almost desperate, the tower operator responded, "Charlie, I'm afraid I have even worse news."

"What is it?" I asked.

"The navy captain is circling overhead waiting to land, and we're not going to be able to bring him in," answered the tower operator, sounding despondent for the first time. "I thought we were going to be able to avoid crashing an airplane but there's no way we are going to be able to bring the navy captain down safely."

"I don't understand," I responded.

"The F105 is damaged so badly that it can't be moved without the use of the crane. The ground crew reports that it will be at least two hours before they can clear the runway. I was just talking to the navy captain. He is down to approximately 25 minutes of fuel. We don't physically have an open runway where he can even crash land safely. In these storms, he doesn't dare parachute out. I was just talking to the state police. He can't land on the highway out front because there are too many wires and too much traffic to clear a stretch of highway for him to crash land on. All of the other airfields are too far away. I don't know what to do, Charlie. He has to land here but I don't have any runways to work with anymore. I'm just at a loss for ideas."

I thought for a minute as I studied the storm clouds out over the field. The cold rain was steadily increasing. For the first time, I truly understood the courage of the navy captain. He had given up a quiet safe flight to Navy Miramar and had come back several hundred miles through the storms in order to save the life of a pilot he'd never before met or seen. Now, low on fuel with no place to land, he faced the same death that he had fought so hard to save the F105 pilot from. I felt God owed him a safe landing. I hoped that God felt the same way too.

Looking around me carefully, I noticed that the tarmac on which the planes parked, was blocked only by an Air Force maintenance truck. Speaking into the phone, I said, "Hang on. I'm going to put down the phone for a minute. While I'm gone, tell the navy captain that I have a safe place for him to land. Tell him to orbit over the main gate to Desert Center while I move a truck."

"Roger. Copy," responded the operator sounding surprised.

I stepped into the weather station momentarily and carefully laid the phone on the table next to my weather instruments. Then I ran quickly the few hundred feet down the tarmac to the maintenance truck. Just as I had expected, since it was a military truck the keys were in the glove compartment. Starting up the truck, I drove it back up to the weather station. I parked it on the far side of the tarmac, in the grass, with its headlights pointing down the tarmac. I left the engine running, and the headlights on bright.

Then I ran indoors and quickly turned on all of the indoor and outdoor lights around the weather station. Feeling a little like the commander of the aircraft carrier Desert Center, I picked up the phone.

"Tower," I shouted, "I'm back."

"Roger," responded the operator.

"I have a place for him to land safely," I said.

"Where is it?" asked the operator. "I can't imagine where it would be."

"I've cleared a stretch of the tarmac right up here by the weather station," I answered. "It's more than twice as wide as an aircraft carrier and it's clear for at least 10,000 feet. The winds up here by the station are only 10 miles an hour, so there won't be much turbulence. I'll talk him in, just like they do on the aircraft carriers. He'll make a safe landing, easy."

A short pause ensued. Then the operator came back on line, "He's willing to try, but he says it's been more than a year since he's landed on an aircraft carrier."

Laughing a little, I said, "That's no problem. Tell him it's just like riding a bicycle. Once you learn, you never forget."

A short pause followed. Then, the tower operator laughing, said, "He's down to fifteen minutes of fuel and he's eager to try. One thing, though, he's never been to Desert Center before. He doesn't know where the weather station is or what direction to be heading when he lands."

Studying my maps for a minute, I answered, "Tell him I'm going to bring him in right over the weather station. Tell him he should be maintaining a bearing of 187 degrees as he comes over the roof. As soon as he clears the roof he should descend gradually until his wheels touch down."

"But except for the station lights, there aren't any lights over there. Won't he be landing into a dark pit?" asked the tower.

"Yes," I responded. "The lights on the roof of the station are 18 feet above the pavement. If he brings his plane in just over those lights, he'll only have to descend another 20 feet or so until he touches down. Remember he has almost two miles of clear tarmac in front of him, so he can come down as slowly as he wishes."

A short pause followed. Then, "Roger," answered the operator. "He's willing to try it, but he can't locate the weather station. The heavy rain on his cockpit is obscuring his forward visibility. He really doesn't know where the weather station is, or where he's landing."

I thought for a minute as I carefully studied the clouds north of the field. The large thunderstorm that had sat for so long over the north end of the field was matched by an identical storm some three miles further north. The clouds between them drifted in quiet beautiful patterns, as though forming a stream in a valley with two huge trees on both sides.

Noting that I was running out of time, I spoke into the tower phone, "Here's what I want him to do. Can he locate the main gate to Desert Center?"

A short pause followed. "Roger. That he can locate," responded the tower.

"Good," I continued. "Have him come down to 100 feet above the trees so he has decent visibility. Then have him come in over the main gate to Desert Center, heading just slightly northeast. I'll be watching for him. As soon as I see him, I'll begin flashing the station lights on and off so he can locate the building. Have him continue on that heading and up in between those two thunderstorms just north of the field, until he's about 3 miles up in there. Now he doesn't have enough space there to turn around horizontally. When he's ready to turn, have him make a vertical loop. This will give him a good look at the field. I'll be flashing the station lights all of the time he's doing this. Then, when he's come back down and leveled off, right side up, of course, have him come back on the opposite heading. Tell him I have the truck out here to help mark the spot.

As he's coming back, I'll be looking for him, and talking him in. OK?"

A long pause followed. The operator responded simply, "Good luck, Charlie. Here he comes. He only has enough fuel for one of these, so don't wave him off."

Almost immediately, the navy plane appeared less than 50 feet above the desert flying past the north of the station. I was taken by surprise. By the time I began flashing the lights, he was already past. He obviously couldn't have seen me.

Undaunted, I continued to follow the plane with my eyes. It was immediately apparent that in the darkness and the rain, he wouldn't be able to see the thunderstorms either. I continued to watch his plane as it headed up into the valley between the storm clouds. As his plane flew blindly up the valley, I spoke into the phone, "Have him perform his vertical loop now."

As I watched, the little plane bravely began its vertical loop, heading straight up into the darkness. Then, flipping over and rolling, headed back down towards the desert below. My heart was in my mouth as I realized that he was performing the entire maneuver blind, trusting only in his flying skills and in my directions.

Speaking into the phone, I said, "Have him level out now, coming back on his opposite heading."

In the distance, the plane leveled off and began heading back my way. I realized that he had no idea where he was heading or where he would land. "He's at 50 feet. Have him put down his gear and come down to 30 feet," I said.

"Roger," responded the operator.

As his plane came opposite the lights on the north-south runway, realizing that he still hadn't located my station, I said, "Have him began a slow 90 degree turn to the southern heading of 187 degrees."

In the distance, the plane began turning towards me. "Slower, turn a little slower," I said into the phone.

In the distance, the plane's turn slowed slightly. "Have him look straight down," I said. "He's going to be passing right over my station at 30 feet."

Slowly but surely, the little plane closed the distance between us. As he came right over the top of the weather station, it was apparent that he still had not seen anything because of the rain on his windshield. Speaking calmly into the phone, I said, "Tell him to straighten out on the 187 degree heading. Bring the plane down slowly the last 30 feet and land."

As I watched, the Navy Captain straightened out his plane. Then, slowly and gracefully brought his plane down the last 30 feet as I guided him, landing gracefully on the tarmac. As his plane rolled slowly to a stop, he opened his canopy. Now for the first time, he could see where he was.

"Charlie," exclaimed the tower operator. "You're so good you make it look easy."

I really didn't know how to respond. I was happy the Navy Captain was alive, but I was humbled by the courage and bravery that he had shown. He had performed the entire makeshift landing blind, trusting in God that I was giving him the proper directions.

Summer's End

It was cold,
and the servants and the officials
were standing around a fire
they had made to keep warm.
. . . John 18:18

The cool days and cold nights of late fall arrived. Wearing their new autumn foliage, the desert valleys and their surrounding majestic mountains took on a beauty that my four hand painted pictures could hardly dare dream of. Once a layer of snow was lightly dusted across the tops of the surrounding mountains, my beautiful desert valleys seemed transformed into a totally different world.

One cool sunny and windy afternoon out at Range Three, my friend Wayne drove up alone in a power wagon and parked outside. He had a mild case of the flu and was running a noticeable fever. Steve and the other Range Rats had been working out in the valley to the southwest repairing the Range fences. It was brutal work, especially for a man with the flu. Good friends all of them, they had sent Wayne up to my heated weather shack to rest and recover indoors. I had my oil heater going. My shack was warm and comfortable. I left the front door open for ventilation. I gave Wayne my best chair next to the stove and shared some of my cold medicine, water, and a candy bar with him.

His mother had danced with a lot of sailors. He had never been certain who his father was until he and I had reasoned it out together one day last summer. On his next trip home, he went to meet his father and shook hands with him. The two had subsequently become quite close. Now, the two of us shared a common bond of trust.

After he got warmed up and the cold medicine began to take effect, we began chatting about our military experiences.

"When did you first see the white people?" I asked Wayne.

"One warm day in the spring when I first got here four years ago. I was sick that day. I had stayed on base to bring the noon chow out to the rest of the Range Rats. I had my power wagon parked on the road to that spring in that valley west of here. I was sitting on a big rock down by the spring, next to the bushes and trees, when Range Four Harry came up over the hill and began speaking to me. I couldn't run away because he was between the power wagon and me. I was too terrified to move at the time, anyway. Harry told me about the chalk white people, the women and children, and wanted to make certain that I understood the rules for the spring area. Basically, I was never to harm any of them or I would be killed.

"In the weeks that followed, whenever Steve, Doug, and I were working over in the valleys west of here, we would have our noon meal brought out to us. We would meet the chow hall truck at those springs and enjoy ourselves. The tall white women and children would come out and play where we were. They were so much like us that I forgot that they really aren't human. There were always three children, a little girl and two little boys, a fat one and a thin one.

"One day, the thin little boy wanted to see what was in my bag lunch. He opened the brown bag and was looking inside. Without thinking, I shouted at him the way I might have shouted at a human little boy in the same circumstances. This frightened him and he went running over to his mother. His mother became instantly outraged. She took out this short white pencil like device and damn near killed me. I was absolutely helpless against her. She had me down on my hands and knees begging for my life. She was screaming, 'Do you think we are fools? Do you think we can not protect ourselves? Do you think we do not love our children?'

"She hurt me Charlie, with that white pencil of hers. She hurt me real bad, deep down in my stomach. I was two or three weeks healing up. She would have killed me, but Harry came over after a few minutes and said that since the little boy hadn't been harmed, the American Generals probably wouldn't understand if I died."

"You sure were lucky to survive," I sympathized with Wayne.

"You're right there, Charlie," replied Wayne. "Ever since that day, Steve, Doug, and I have been so damn terrified of ever upsetting those tall whites that there just aren't words to explain it. You can't imagine how glad we're going to be to get out of the Air Force and just go back home."

"I can certainly understand how you feel, Wayne," I said.

"Tell me Charlie," Wayne asked. "Besides these tall whites, do think there's any other kinds of aliens coming here to visit Earth? There must be more inhabited planets out there in our galaxy."

"I don't know," I replied. "If there are, I certainly don't want to ever meet them. Meeting aliens for the first time is just too terrifying. Just like you, Steve, and Doug, I'm going to be perfectly happy finishing my enlistment in the US Air Force, hanging up my uniform, and just going home. I'm not going chasing after UFOs or anything. I have always loved having a private life, and I'm going to just love going back to one.

"One thing I have always wondered about though, is whether or not there are already aliens who look just like us, living here among us. After all, whenever a medical doctor or a dentist treats someone who looks just a little bit different than ordinary, they never ask if that person is actually human. They always just suppose that person is a human with an unusual genetic pattern. I'll bet an alien with webbed toes and only 24 teeth could walk into any University medical center in America and receive any medical treatment he desired, no questions asked. All he would need is medical insurance and a good story about how he grew up in Scandinavia and loved winter.

"Consider that flu you have, for example. Viruses and germs have been around here on earth ever since life began. Every time a large meteor has struck the Earth, it has blown many tons of germs, viruses, dead animals, and other living material off the Earth, and completely out of the solar system. The explosion that killed the dinosaurs, for example, probably sprayed living germs, plants, and dead dinosaurs all over every planet in the solar system and all over every planet revolving around stars as far away as fifty light years. In just a short time geologically speaking, such as 50,000 years, that material, dead mice, dandelions, everything, could easily have been falling on planets revolving around stars such as Bernard's star, Tau Ceti, and Arcturas.

"The reverse could also be true. Meteors striking planets on which life had already evolved could easily have sprayed the same type of material all over the earth and the other planets of our solar system.

"Consider, the shrimp, the germs, and the sagebrush that live in the dry lakebed up at Range Four. They can be completely sun dried and come back to life after five years. All it takes is a good rain and warm weather. Those things will grow anywhere they are blown to."

"Or carried to," Wayne reminded me. "One warm fall day two years ago, Steve and I saw a group of those tall whites out there in those mountains collecting plant seeds. They seemed awfully happy at the time."

"You don't say!" I exclaimed.

"Yes," laughed Wayne, teasing me, "I didn't say. By the way, Charlie, your little speech got me to thinking. I've always been meaning to ask, you are human aren't you? I mean, you're always so willing to come out here alone."

He was obviously feeling better now, and the two of us enjoyed a good laugh. "Yes, Wayne," I responded. "Every time you think of me, remember that I have always claimed to be human."

Then, Wayne got up from his chair and hugged me. He walked back to his power wagon and went back to work on the Range fence. Steve, Doug, and Wayne, we had all become friends forever. Every time I remember them, I remember them the way they were that day.

The nights continued to become successively colder. Mornings at Range Three become lonelier and lonelier. The chalk white beings had bodies built only to take the heat of the hot summer days. As winter approached, seeing them out in the open now became a rare occurrence.

One moonless Monday morning in late fall with the temperature at 48 degrees Fahrenheit, I was just completing my last balloon reading. The three children and two guards floated slowly out from behind the Range Three lounge and approached me slowly. They were obviously very cold and probably a little sick. Even though the suits that they wore allowed them to float, and certainly kept their bodies warm, they were wearing only open helmets. Consequently, they still had to breathe the cold air.

I suppose those same suits could probably have been fitted with a different style of helmet and breathing equipment so the tall whites could use them out in the empty vastness of space. I suppose those same suits with proper helmets could have been used on the moon or on mars, floating from crater to crater. Tonight, however, the cold air that they were breathing was simply too much for them. I stepped back a few fee from my theodolite as they approached, and waited for them to look through it. We trusted each other. Silently they assembled into a small group in front of the theodolite on my left. Each of them was obviously having trouble controlling their suits. One of the guards helped each child in turn up to the eyepiece for their last look through it. Then, still in total silence, they walked, not floated, back to the east side of the lounge building. They formed up in a line next to the wall, enjoying what little protection from the cold wind that it provided. Then I saw the scout craft come up over the ridge that lay a mile of so to the northwest. It came in as close to the northwest corner of the lounge as it was able to, and set down. The door on the side opened. The two guards and the three children stood looking at me for a couple of minutes or so. They obviously wanted me to see them one last time before they left. Then they formed up into a line with one guard in front and one in back, and headed off toward the scout craft.

The next morning it was even colder. I measured the air temperature at only 42 degrees Fahrenheit. As I was finishing my balloon reading I saw only the little fat boy and one guard come floating out from behind the lounge towards me. They were still wearing their open helmets and they both appeared to be extremely weak. With great difficulty, the little fat boy finally made it to where I was. He floated in front of me at eye level for a minute or so, as if to say, "Good bye, Charlie." Then, he and the guard both began floating over to the bunker road and began heading east towards the ammunition bunker. The little fat boy hardly made it a quarter mile before he set down on the paved road. The guard, shaky himself, picked the boy up and stood waiting for the scout craft to come pick them up. While I watched, the scout craft rose up from the hidden depression in the desert east of me and floated slowly over to where the guard with the boy stood waiting. It sat down slowly on the bunker road and opened the door. Then the guard and the little fat boy walked on. The door closed, the craft took off, and headed slowly up the valley toward the mountain base to the north.

Winter had come to the Ranges.

About the Author

Charles James Hall is a physicist and an Information Technology professional. In Millennial Hospitality and Millennial Hospitality II, he tells in entertaining novel form about how we might interact with aliens. This novel was inspired by his experiences as a weather observer in the USAF during the mid 1960's.

Made in the USA
Lexington, KY
07 April 2011